BOOKS BY PAUL WEST

FICTION

LORD BYRON'S DOCTOR

THE PLACE IN FLOWERS WHERE POLLEN RESTS

THE UNIVERSE, AND OTHER FICTIONS

RAT MAN OF PARIS

THE VERY RICH HOURS OF COUNT VON STAUFFENBERG

GALA

CALIBAN'S FILIBUSTER

COLONEL MINT

BELA LUGOSI'S WHITE CHRISTMAS

I'M EXPECTING TO LIVE QUITE SOON

ALLEY JAGGERS

TENEMENT OF CLAY

NONFICTION

SHEER FICTION

OUT OF MY DEPTHS

WORDS FOR A DEAF DAUGHTER

I, SAID THE SPARROW

THE SNOW LEOPARD

THE WINE OF ABSURDITY

BYRON AND THE SPOILER'S ART

LORD
BYRON'S
DOCTOR

PAUL WEST

DOUBLEDAY

NEW YORK   LONDON   TORONTO   SYDNEY   AUCKLAND

LORD BYRON'S DOCTOR

A NOVEL

PUBLISHED BY DOUBLEDAY

a division of Bantam Doubleday Dell Publishing Group, Inc.
666 Fifth Avenue, New York, New York 10103

DOUBLEDAY and the portrayal of an anchor with a dolphin
are trademarks of Doubleday, a division of
Bantam Doubleday Dell Publishing Group, Inc.

Library of Congress Cataloging-in-Publication Data
West, Paul, 1930–
   Lord Byron's doctor : a novel / by Paul West. —1st ed.
     p. cm.
   1. Polidori, John William, 1795–1821, in fiction, drama, poetry, etc. 2.
Byron, George Gordon Byron, Baron, 1788–1824, in fiction, drama, poetry,
etc. 3. Shelley, Mary Wollstonecraft, 1797–1851, in fiction, drama, poetry, etc.
4. Shelley, Percy Bysshe, 1792–1822, in fiction, drama, poetry, etc. I. Title.
PR6073.E766L67   1989
813'.54—dc20   89-7735
                                                CIP

ISBN 0-385-26129-2

Designed by Bonni Leon

September 1989

FIRST EDITION
BG

Europe was uncommonly cold in the summer of 1816. German wells froze solid in May, and in August snow fell near London. An enormous plume of gas and ash from the eruption of Tambora, an Indonesian volcano, was cruising the world; it had been the largest eruption in recorded history, and directly and indirectly it changed many lives irrevocably.

PART ONE

To leap always the same height, to receive the same number of blows at a sparring match, to gain the same number of notches at cricket, to fence, to dance, to ride,—all pall; for when a certain degree of excellence has been gained, the boundary becomes visible, and nothing more remaining to be attained, the ambitious mind droops. Mathematics and positive abstract science, require years of constant uninterrupted study and application before there is even a possibility of going beyond a Newton or a La Place by one thousandth part of their knowledge, and before an individual gains a name like theirs, centuries must elapse, while thousands of martyrs perish in the study, after spending their lives in merely suggesting hints.

—Preface to *Ximenes,*
The Wreath,
and Other Poems,
J. W. Polidori

Polly, he called me, from the first, as if I had had no life at all until then and was to have no other thenceforth. He never actually said Pretty Polly, but it was in his eye, all right, and I suppose I was a bit of a parrot when _____ around him, aping his this or that or pretending that I, like he, could fall upon a chambermaid in some foreign town like a thunderbolt, after having borne the horn to do it with all the way from London, by stagecoach, packet, coach again. That kind of rocking motion always egged him on, making his juices run, his fancy fly. He rocked himself into a lust. He was never what I would call sentimental. Who would sentimentalize a laxative? he said. People were there for the plucking.

I had always gone in awe of *titolati*, doctor that I was. Who ever went in awe of a doctor? But there I was, taken on to minister to that failing body, I the unknown with the most famous rake in England. We would talk and talk, and I would receive my second education. I was supposed, he said, to keep him thin, choose his dishes with an eye to that; but I knew how self-willed he was and how much of a whoremaster his stomach was, not just for wenches but viands too, and poor Polly would come rattling along behind, cautioning him in vain as he troughed and tupped, prating the while about what he called the concubine of snow, to plunge into which would purify him.

In Ostend, that once, he roared at the very sight of this porcine-looking drab, as if he had seen none such in all his days, then fell to wrenching off her millinery with his hands and teeth until a goodly amount of flesh began to show, and yet she did not run away. To prime her (he called it making them "wet up"), he administered her a hard dunt in the belly, at which she squawked and fell, but he was upon her straightaway, with his parts released and streaming what looked like brine, as if they had been soaking in some bucket before the onslaught and salvo. Large they were, in-

deed, and sproutier than a handful of old potatoes. He seemed to
will the prepuce back without touching it, and then he was upon
her, pounding while she wailed, battering for the way in, but he
turned his head at one point and smiled at me with wolfish tenderness. On he shoved, cuffing the girl hard about the face and breast,
then slapping her thighs and buttocks as if to provoke in her convul-
sions so fierce he might not need to move at all to sate himself. It
was soon over. The girl cooed at him and spat into his face. He did
not seem to notice as he reeled to the far end of the chamber,
cupping his parts in his hands and moaning as if injured. How often
I came to know that moan of his as he appealed to me, as a doctor,
to examine his parts and tell him what ailed him, why they hurt so
much afterwards, and the one testis always tried to slink back into
the body cavity. In truth, my lord was squeamish and nesh.

Or was he acting a part because he knew I had agreed to keep a
diary of his doings? Perhaps he thought I had agreed to keep a
record of his part's doings only, so often did he unleash it and set it
wobbling in my sight in all its leprous brown, swelling and shrink-
ing like something in a swamp fog. His fondness for his own sex had
not escaped me, of course (to think so were tantamount to missing
the mountainous quality of an Everest), so I held back, I shrank
from inspecting too closely, as from inhaling too deep that odd
aroma of his lower body: mothballs and cowshed admixed with a
soupçon of leather. My disability in all this was that I, capable of
being unmoved by the sick and the dying, as by the dead, had
naught but soft and tender feelings about the opposite sex, believing
they should not be ill used, shoved, buffeted, until they asked to be.
He would have none of this, but held to rough handling as the ideal
introit, thus abolishing maidenly modesty with a blunderbuss.

Anyway, as this slut in Ostend kept roaring what sounded like
wake, wake (it was a harsher word), he kept his silence except for a
Scottish-sounding rolled *r* as if he kept readying himself to utter a
word beginning thus, but never let it all the way out. He seemed to
be a doing a Highland purr.

The sight and smell of all these parts bounding and rollicking should surely have incited me to lusts of my own, to be gratified by the hand-gallop (he urged me), but they did not. Instead, I thought of embalming fluids and how cut off, how marooned, even such parts as his would one day be: worn to death, limp as silk, and quite without memory.

"Work it," he told me, "always work it, Polly, and naught will go amiss. The same with our brain. Even when there is nothing to think, work the brain. Fret it to an indecent fever. Never leave anything alone, my dear."

Then I would tell him my views about the place of tenderness in lust, and he would guffaw as if I were a milkmaid.

"These," he would say, exposing himself, "have seen wars, plagues, agues, trenches, vats, tunnels, chimneys, spinneys, copses, nests, foghorns, sumps, and the crystalline ice-shelf of Lady Byron, our reverend lady of acute angles. With not a tender word spoken even in jest. There was never time, there was never need. Save that for after or never, my bully."

All I ever did was shake my head, hoping he would put his private luggage away and not go on airing it like some puppy whelped from within his trews. Only once had I given in to his entreaties to shew him mine, and forthwith he had knelt into the posture of the bibbing postulant, his tongue at the ready, curled to sample. I jumped back, he shuffled forward on his knees, whole acres of finery dragging behind him as he moved, and then I hit the wall, cannoned off it into his very jaws—which were wondrous cool, that first time anyway—and began, I must say, to experience the onset of the exordium of the preamble to the—whatever it was. He was all teeth, but I had no time to protest, for here was this slut of only two hours earlier, this Ostend baggage, setting up a howl that I had felled the lord and was doing him an injury. Well, that cooled all for a while, until the two of them began again.

Add together all the hours I did of looking away while he swyved, and you have a goodly sum. I was that troublesome figment, the healthy prude, with all the passions and appetites due a young man of Latin blood, even to the extent of sometimes wondering, in the orbit of my lord, which sex I wished I truly were; but I was tender yet, unused, unschooled: not a virgin, yet my mind was full of curtseys and bows. After a while I established that, where he needed to bite and bleed, I was delicate in the part of me that did two things: beheld the dead and the sick, and doted on my mistress of the moment. This last pairing is odd, or so I thought. The gentle side of me was cold, which meant that I was tender with the dead and cold with the beloved. It was the side of me that never roared or longed to sink a fang. This side he lacked altogether, being something of a life-swallower, a devourer, eager for chastening only after the act, when he was tired and *triste*. As a poet he was a spewer, filling his margins with seed, pumping his stanzas up with an artificial fervour; yet he had done passing well with such frottings. I do believe he yearned with every atom of his thunderstruck being to seize the aforesaid concubine of snow and make her come into heat —so much so that, in the act of cooling his ardour, he set her on fire from within and consumed her quite. He talked often of this contrary fancy, and I half thought he meant his wife that was, whose zone was frozen solid half the year.

It was the year 1816. My life began then, and all else. My lord had had an enormous bottle-green coach made for him, complete with *lit de repos,* plate chest, library, and a tiny brothel-like dining space with every kind of eating apparatus. In this schooner of the land he proposed to reach Switzerland and the Shelleys, who would soon be there, and then they would all go on together to other haunts of idyll suitable for poets. It was important to go nowhere unsuitable. The further south or east he went, the further would he be from Anne, his wife. I was only twenty and so should be forgiven those bouts of mine, in which merely being with him, the Scotch unicorn of England, sent my head into a thrilling dither, and all I could think was: I am watching *him* ply his parts, I am watching *him* write, I am watching *him* travel, I am watching *him* (on request) make water, and whole intimate epics more. In the beginning I was possessed, and he knew it, although he did not seem to mind. He minded only later, perhaps because I was too good, too keen, an audience for him, too young. *Tout court,* I was his doctor, son of an Italian who lived in London and had done *The Castle of Otranto* into Italian. I was one of *them* already, it seemed. Then I had been the youngest man ever to receive a medical degree from the University of Edinburgh. I was a demonic apothecary born, with five hundred guineas from the publisher to take notes on my lord's daily doings and undoings. Indeed, should Lord B., by any chance, fall sick in a Gothick castle in Italy and require a Scottish-minded surgeon, I was the very lad to set him right, get his spirits bubbling again, his juices back to flow. I would not need to be told or asked. I was to be so close to him, a soul in parallel, that the twinned ache in my own frame would tell me where the ache was in his. And I was to keep calm, even among the wildest of their antics, the most audacious of their sallies; I was not to be the copycat, oh no, or to presume to equality. I was to be serenely and deferentially *by,* just in case, a doctor hired against the brunt of fate: with them, not of them, but eligible.

Yet how often can one be invited in before assuming some kind of permanent entrée? You cannot treat someone as an equal and then swat him back into the waiting room, the place where doctors gasp, their hands still red and greasy from rummaging about amidst the tripes of colicky milords, who have blood where their bile should be, and bile where their sperm should be, and itinerant sperm feeding into their brains. *Put it right, Polly,* I would hear, and Polly *would,* marvelling at Lord B.'s inflatable paunch right out of the Arabian Nights, past which he could not see down to the thing that fired him and took him beneath dog-sprayed bridges in the depths of night, there to kill the stone-ache or the itch with no matter whom or what.

I began as a calm individual, not given to sudden uproars, but being close to milord set the appetitive side of my nature running. I wanted, at least in my mind, what I had never wanted before, or so much as thought about. I began to feel overwound, close to a cry or a roar, as if until 1816 life had never been intense or impetuous. Just to be close to him had an almost electrical effect, as the rays or heaves of his mighty temperament made themselves felt across the space between us. When was he ever calm or, in his heart of hearts, at ease? It must have been never; he was everlastingly in pursuit, raging, denouncing, letting fly, putting somebody or other in his place, flinging a piece of his mind across the room as some poor simpleton tried to voice an idea contrary to his own. They say this is often the way with cripples, just as much with them as with lords. Had I had a club-foot myself, might I have been just as churlish? Perhaps so. I think it enraged him to see me, whole of limb, prancing about among his friends, and this was no doubt why he began those rumours about my uncurable clumsiness: "Our Polly has the falling sickness. Mayhap his feathers do not carry him too well." Taunts abounded whenever I slipped or wobbled on the dampest or the most uneven terrain. "Our Polly is so happy he need not look where he is going. True, true. He goeth ever to the ground beneath him." This was Byronic wit laced with vitriol. It had all the charm of the paralytic reviling one of the able-bodied waltzing by.

There was that early tiff, for instance, unless it were squabble, row. It could not be said that things deteriorated early on; they had not even had a chance to be wholesome before he was trying out his sallies on me. By May we had only gone as far as Cologne (where he was to strike some Byronic poses at the Rhine, half Rhine Maiden, half Newfoundland dog), and I was holding forth to him about the verities (to them, he and I were no strangers), maintaining that a day or two in the dissecting room with a cadaver is worth a year of reading poetry, at least as far as insight into human mortality is concerned, and he exploded, at which I told him, "Pray, milord, what is there, excepting poetry, that I cannot do better than you?" It was partly in jest, of course, a mock-humble way of deferring to him; I knew full well he had never dissected a cadaver or been in any such place, still less entertained his quivering mind with the principles and tenets of surgery. He seemed calm, but his face was pale, his lips were manoeuvring, barely under control. I had cut him to the quick with my merry question. How without defences he seemed! "Three things," he answered. "First, I can hit with a pistol the keyhole of that door. Secondly, I can swim across that river to yonder point. And thirdly, I can give you a damned good thrashing." It was as if I had challenged him to a contest in aquatic marksmanship, with the loser to stand passive while the other beat him senseless. "My lord," I told him, with calm lips while his twirled and flitted about, "I might just as readily remove your eyelid from your eye without spoiling vision in the slightest. I might just as easily let your blood from your body without wasting a drop. And, as to thrashing someone, I could surely endure such handling from you without blinking an eye. A composure such as mine might well endure it without a tear." I could have poisoned him that very day. I could have knackered him while he slept with a knife so sharp he would have awakened as a eunuch before he knew what was afoot. I could have cut me a lady's gulf into his belly in a trice. I told him none of this, though, lest he think he had successfully provoked me into boasting. He stalked off with a boldly averted gaze while I, more in sadness than affront, remained behind, my hands hanging close to my knees as if to reassure the body so recently threatened with a thrashing.

Milord was in a pet, to be sure.

I, however, was in a state of mind more akin to fraternal sympathy. Byron was vexed. Let him be vexed, then. He had a right, wifeless as he was, deformed to boot, and a virtual exile. He had burned his bridges and the river too. Whatever he said or did provided me with things to set down, lest that notebook wither for want of a spicy tale or two. Lord Byron's doctor would be faithful to his other chore of spy.

Yet, of course, those barbs lingered and festered, poisoning the flesh that would otherwise have adored him. So: he would shoot the

keyhole of the door. Nothing is more vain, more like the sly peacock, than the boasting marksman, who might surely be conjured
into shooting himself with high accuracy. It was not that. Nor was it
his prating talk about the river. Who is a bigger fool, who cuts a
sorrier figure, than the vainglorious merman: not enough man to
love and too much fish to fry? What had sunk deep into me was his
talk of giving me a thrashing, as if I were the baby Byron and he the
nurse May Gray, taws in hand. *(I* knew who had so meddled with
that little testis, forcing it up and away into the nest it had only
lately descended from. Betimes a doctor knows things without ever
being told. I knew how raw and forceful she had been, half squeezing his manhood and his man's gruel from him before he had even
begun to sigh and sweat for another sex.) Who was he to venture
thrashing me? What was his cause? He was heavier, that was all, but
he had the smaller hands of us two, and I do believe *I* could have
thrashed *him* and held him down to do it. I could hear milord's
frenzy as he writhed under the shocks I gave him, first about the
mouth and eyes, then the nose, the belly, the groin; I would smite
him hardest there, that being the chief seat of his offence, I believing
his ill humours came from lust denied. Which was amazing since he
had *so much* of it, and yet ever wanted more, lusting after lust itself
in some wild metaphysical pasture of the mind. Ay, I would tap him
in the tupshop and see how he would like a thrashing there with fist
or cudgel. I could treat him as some Arabs treated their own, first
cutting the lines with a scalpel or a razor, and then tugging sharply
down on the entire scalp of mons pubis until it came free of the
flesh, and then I'd peel the organ itself, leaving milord so raw he
would solicit codfish for their oil. He was fair to me so long as we
were in England, but the instant we left its shores he was spoiling
for me at all hours, as if the very image of a young Italian Scotsman
violated his notion of decent humanity. Faith, he winced and
sneered, scowled and smarted, until the only notion you had of him
was that of a scalded dog denied his kennel. Were he to try me, I
would acquit myself with competence, I being none of your street
brawler, but enough of a ruffian to give him pause. Let him biff me,

I would slam him back with interest aforethought. Never let it be said that a Polidori shrank from fisticuffs. I'd touch my hat and flatten him, which is what Edinburgh might do to ladlass Cambridge any day of the week. Box his ears, then wipe his face with them. Done.

To settle my mood, I would think of the mornings as I sat writing verses in just about any east-facing room I could obtain. And then the sun would warm me as it rose, and our twin orisons would interact in an ovation of warmth and light (I writing to the rhythms of the universe), at least until milord burst in to scoff and scold. I do declare he wanted to *be me*.

PART TWO

The universal belief is, that a person sucked by a vampyre becomes a vampyre himself, and sucks in his turn.

—*The Vampyre: A Tale,*
J. W. Polidori

In the very beginning he called me "Doctor Dori," which I did not mind. There was a modicum of dignity to the appellation, even when, only a few days before we set sail from Dover, he was ridiculing one of my three tragedies after Hobhouse had read parts of it aloud in that pompous, squeaky way of his. In any event, he (Lord B.) was full of that very day having lain flat on the grave of the poet Charles Churchill, after which he gave the sexton a crown to turf it. What interested milord was not the writings of Doctor Dori but what the sexton said in answer to the question, "Why do so many come to see this particular tomb?" Why should he care? "I cannot tell," said the sexton. "I had not the burying of him." And of course our lord's mind was on the impending sea journey, after which he designed to go to Bruges, Antwerp, Ghent, Brussels, and so forth. We had with us good enough fellows named Fletcher and Rushton, and the Swiss guide Berger, of whose names he made no sport at all. Here was our poet, our "romantic" poet, who had already published two cantos of his *Childe Harold,* befogged by a minor poet's grave, fussing about the contrary winds at Dover, almost being vomited upon by a fellow passenger, and repeating as if to engrave it on his brain, "Tell Hobhouse not to forget the cundums and two new pistol brushes." I, the doctor, had no more on my mind than the mortality of our passengers, one of them in most extreme particular.

The voyage was simple, but I kept resailing it. The land journey was laborious, but I kept travelling it again and again. Such was the novelty. At Piccadilly Terrace he was in a tremendous fidget to be gone, at long last saying, "This is kind, very kind. Tomorrow I quit." That was April the twenty-third. Next day we went off to Dover, intending to sail that day, but the winds were wrong and we spent the night at the Ship Inn, departing the next morning right after breakfast. All up promptly save milord, who lingered even as the captain was protesting that he could not wait. Lord B. and

Hobhouse took a turn on the quay together, having one of their murmuring talks in which they paused and walked, then walked again, limiting their talk to neither the one nor the other. He was aboard soon after nine, showing a long morose face as the packet began to slide away and Hobhouse gave a final wave like a coup de grâce. Such love there seemed between them. We arrived at Ostend toward midnight, some said almost a dozen hours earlier than expected. That was when the chambermaid appeared, et cetera. We left Ostend at three o'clock on the twenty-sixth, aimed at Bruges. It was the fabulous beginning of the most enthralling journey in my life, spiced a little by milord's never having paid Baxter the coachmaker the five hundred pounds owing for his Napoleonic coach. I was half in love with the journey's perfection, with my own idea of it perfected. It would never happen again. We would hunt the Golden Fleece and bask on it for ever.

One day I spoke of death to him, in the blithe way that only the very young can do, thinking themselves immune. "Isn't it strange," I asked him, "how, compared to the immensity and permanence of death, the smallest things loom large, being full of life? As when someone scratches his ear lobe, say, or blows his nose, or promises himself to blow his nose in ten minutes, being too lazy to do it now. That laziness seems full of life, milord."

"Who gives a fig for living?" he said, without even pausing. "Death is a nothing. We know all about dying, but death—is not an alternative to anything. We Byrons are a short-lived nation, on both sides of the family. They say that longevity is a matter of heredity, and I accept that notion. You might say, my dear doctor, that Lord Byron is already near the end of his rope. I don't give a damn for death, but I do dread its sting. I am not among those who dote deliciously on pain—not my own, at least."

Then he went on to inform me, as if one thought led to the other, that his main bodily concern, after the gratification of his member, was to keep thin. He grew easily to fourteen stone, he said, and got the weight off by eating only biscuits and soda-water, which had always given him the devil's own gas, and then a poor repast of

cold things: potatoes, rice, fish, and some greens, all soaked in vinegar. "I gobble," he said, "like some famished dog." With this mess
he took a glass or two of Rhenish, mostly sour. "I have no palate,
my dear," he said. "All things taste alike." In this way, he claimed,
he kept his mind clear, his eyes as well, but I had my doubts,
knowing this would be an effective way to procure a fainting fit. He
who consumes his own fat will lose his muscle too, and the sense of
balance. He had little idea, when speaking to me thus, that the
mention of death and starvation touched on thoughts of my own,
harbored in my head since my first cadaver. If there were no life
after death, in some heaven, say, then could there be a life after death
on earth? Could the defunctus be brought back? Not, as some had
said, by rubbing a paste of ordure and semen into the eyes, ears, and
nose (a wan and feeble remedy in view of all the great stoppages the
flesh is prey to), but by focussing the mind, say, or even a bolt of
lightning? I had never spoken to milord of such matters, sensing that
he would soon enough speak of them to me, he seeming so ready a
talker, always ably informed at the drop of a subject, as if he could
prophesy the impromptu thoughts of others.

Yet some things enraged him beyond all measure, as when
someone would tell him how well he was looking, this when he was
more than a little heavy. "Am I a hog," he said, "being fattened up
for Hogmanay? Mark my words, gentlemen, I will go down to
eleven stone or I will shoot myself. Any heavier than that, and I
cannot bear to stand. All I eat turns into tallow laid thick against my
ribs. It is infernal to be thus. There are days when I am fit to ask our
Polly here to take his knife and slice away the better part of me and
feed the blubber to the poor."

He had proposed no such thing, even in jest, but I could see
him, if not thinner, then at least deader, and then brought back to
life by some magical process I had not yet discovered, even if he did
come back to us with a permanent twitch, a slur in the speech, a
member that had no rise in it. Looking at him, in my lyrical-forensic

way, I saw the corpse he would soon be, then the Byron brought
back to life, followed by the next corpse he would have, and then
the next revival of him. Each resuscitation would wither him a
little, make his color worse, make his breathing noisy (a quinsy that
came and went with, each time, a croak like that of a bigger dog
being throttled), and make him more and more forgetful, so that he
would sometimes think he had been alive in the seventeenth century.

In a reasonable universe, I told him, that has so many draughts
for death, should there not be the same number of draughts giving
life? If only we could find them nested in the lesser celandine, the
slug's armpit, the fox's brush. "You make too much sense of it," he
scoffed. "I think of your universe as accidental, as with pregnancy.
Best fix on the things we have at hand, not go longing after conjectural boons. After all, my dear Polly, are you not a doctor? When I
need the cure, I want a simple humdrum one, not one of your fancy
ones only a few pounds of angel dust this side of a miracle. Lance
the boil, scald the cut. I had not imagined that surgery at Edinburgh
was quite so finical. The devil save me from cleverdick sawboneses."

I kept silent but my mind roamed on, wondering if one day I
would dandle that brain in my hand or be charged with sundry
intimate amputations: the member, the cullions, the club-foot, the
heart itself. I was not after medical curiosities but, rather, after evi-
dences of magic. I wanted to eye the pathways through which genius had flowed or shot. Coursed was the word, cursed the prospect.
I was a very young doctor with a hankering for what *he* liked to call
cold obstruction, meaning what stands in the way of our continuing
to live and awaits us at the other end. Heaven, I thought, was like
Ampleforth, my old school, where you died a little every day, and
we were taught by all those devout old Catholic dominies that the
end of life is death. Such is life's aim, its fruition. I half believed it,
sensing even in my early years of school that, once you accepted
death, the rest of life was one sustained lying-back, head against the
antimacassar for ever. No need to try. There were those who believed in God and those who *loved* him. Well, I was among those
who, without actually believing in him, loved some of the bodily

processes by means of which he levelled us, then took us off. Hence my surgical bent, my passion for what I had several times in milord's hearing (the Scottish one, not the celestial) called "the magic of morbidity," at which he laughed aloud, slapped me on the back, and said, "Dearest Polly, there is a phrasemaker in you somewhere, like a stinking nanny in the midst of a handful of rotten apricots. Out it shall, and then we'll have it to trial for its offence. Like that damned Coleridge, who read his 'Kubla Khan' to me one morning in Piccadilly and then fell to such a perusal of my face that I felt downright embarrassed. He motioned with his hands in midair as if caressing a model of my physiognomy, dimples and all. Then he said this thing to me: '*Is*-ness, my lord, is all. The glue. The gum arabic.' Imagine that. I parodied him a thousand times, just as from the Germans and God knew who else he stole half the phrases I wanted to steal from him. Oh yes, Polly-Polly, we will try you and have you hung. By the toes or the tongue, 'tis up to you. We poets are very jealous of the image of our own death. We want it as we ourselves devise."

Hearing all, as Murray knew I would, I should have been writing more of it down for my diary, to earn my five hundred guineas. I should have been less fascinated by his presence, by his gleaming and arrogant effrontery; but I gaped away, very much the junior, in truth having too good (and bad) a time to be the correct amanuensis, and indeed having my nature changed by so many close passages with him, never mind what my own mind conjured up in his presence. How swayed I was, how smitten, like Judas Iscariot playing bezique with God. I noted down landscapes and townscapes, but the hot lava of his chit-chat swam away from me. I was in part his darling, one of the many, of course; but I was also his pest, his fool, his jackanapes, so much so that he did not want what of me was good to be good at all. Only he and his cronies could be young or mad or cockahoop; dear old Polly was a commodity like bread or breakfast, to be sampled and then left on the plate to dry.

Could he read my mind? Did he know that, more often than I

cared to confess, my memory lingered on the way children ran over the turf of tombs or graves, heedless and unwitting? Again and again Thomas à Becket's tomb soared out of Canterbury Cathedral towards me, neither lofty nor awe-inspiring, but comfortably beautiful—what an ideal final housing, never mind who you had been. And the very coast of Dover, far behind us, came at me again and again. Not that I was homesick for all that barren chalk; the image was all bound up with her who had commanded me, upon my leaving England, to think of her, she in India, whom I sometime called my Arrow, to whom I should have winged a way both straight and fast. Truth told, then, Miss Eliza Arrow was the dour cliffs, as commanded, and I wondered why I had never given myself over to that passion, not writing letters about the possibility of its coming into being but taking passage to India instead, there at least to tear her bodice from her with my teeth, over her token protest. I was too young for such a long entanglement, yet too inexperienced to ape milord, falling upon this chambermaid or that in his pantherine fashion. Too, my Arrow was a relative, and I had always felt the deed of kind best done with strangers, at least not cousins on close branches of the family tree. What I needed was an Italian girl, of satin skin and houri eyes, as Byron said.

Well, they were all around us, like the phosphorescence on the foam when we sailed over. The *jeunes femmes* of Ostend wore elaborate headdresses, and they clattered about in wooden shoes, blinking and shy, approachable no doubt and capable of being persuaded into service, but not Italian. I somehow wanted to celebrate my return to the land of my father by smothering my desires in Italian satin. Why not? There, in Ostend, they spoke no French and precious little German (they laughed at my German). Every bookseller's window was full of blatantly sexual works, as if to incite the browser into some brothel of the mind. And there I was, actually turning the pages of one while holding another, the one about a girl with a donkey, the other about nuns doing unspeakable things to a friar. Up a small ladder, not standing straight, I almost fell but recovered, except that the donkey book fell on the head of a young wench who served in the shop. In my confusion I, who had been peering at her polished-looking green eyes, bought both tomes to cover it, but in so doing expended all the initiative I had for that day. I should have set both books down and made my overture, in terms none too delicate. I imagined how milord would have conducted this turn of events. He would have upended her in the shop, and she would have given him both books in recompense for service rendered.

Where did the bungler in me come from? Who was the I that went outside to sulk, saying that the smell of fresh paint in the room had given me an awful headache, as in Ostend? Or I would say that the tea was perfumed and it was setting my nerves on edge. A surgeon should have had surer hands, a less wavering eye. There was always something operatic in what I did, the result doubtless of mixed blood. Part of me wanted to be stable, even stern, whereas the rest of me was all emotion and wanted to paint the world with it. I was excitable always. Standing on the very soil where the siege of Ostend had taken place in the early sixteen hundreds, I felt myself shuddering with rage and sadness. Some forty thousand souls had perished here, feeding the fowls and manuring the soil, all for money. I stood there, getting exercised, all for naught. Milord would have spewed forth a poem about it had he been there. Out they always came, like a snake's questing tongue. Each poem seemed ready-made, and I suspected that he had within him poems stored like baker's loaves, requiring only the insertions of a proper name or two to become the very poem *d'occasion*. He had this gift for impromptu generality, as if nothing were new to him and he was an old soul who had experienced everything already and, perhaps with his lady wife's assistance, factorized it. He knew the algebra of misadventure, back to front. So all he needed, truly, was to travel across landscapes, borders, dropping off a poem now and then as the occasion seemed to fit one he had already baked. It was no doubt odd on my part to harbour such feelings about my idol, but his feet of clay walked into his poetry, and I always felt that anyone who ridiculed the work of others as much as he was bound to have something wrong with him. So professional a contempt for the world, as for its letters, argued surely a certain shallowness of mind.

Off to Bruges we went, with four horses, the postilion an ogre of the whip, forever smacking it about as if to get himself noticed in hell. Boots to the hips. Leather hat with a quaker brim, haloed with black ribbon. Coat of blue and red. A face like Satan, his lips jutting out so far they seemed to have been tugged after being weighted vertically with a huge stone. He could have kissed any one of the horses and not been overlapped at the lip. Our luggage went on without us in a calèche. Bruges was all fretwork, washed and neat, the women therein fetching, yet of a stolid-looking gentleness. Milord said the only way, when a given woman was not pretty enough to be looked at close, was to add one to her and thus distract the esthetic sense from the one with the other. During the casuistical appraisal of their charms, he said, one might arrive at a passable heatedness. Was this one more bovine than the other was sullen? Or was the other more porcine than this one was wooden? Such considerations, he claimed, added spice to the otherwise humdrum chase and conquest. In my diary, mind on the five hundred guineas, I wrote *Flemish face has no divinity—a sparkling eye in a full round,* which was faithful enough, I thought, to what surrounded us. Women cut from butter would have been as well. None of them was a match for the roof-fretted streets of Bruges itself as the twilight brought its blush to bear. In Ostend the men had lounged in the sun, lazy and indifferent; here they promenaded through short avenues of trees. I saw a boy with a handful of sand, letting it drift downward, and milord observed that we had been given a warning about our tenure on this earth, as we saw farther on, where a brass band of labourers played brisk and sundry marches, the one fellow puffing into a huge trombone, clearly not long for this world, from his yellowed aspect, yet blowing his consumptive breath abroad for all to try.

Always an arrangement to make, something to be mended. I

had begun to watch the diarist in me, noting this or that for the spendthrift Mr. Murray, trying to provoke milord into a bon mot, trying to provoke him altogether. The Polly who wrote things down was a more attentive soul than the Polly who, wherever he is now, writes or intones this. That Polly was buyable, not the dreamer or the romantic. That Polly was more or less obedient, whereas this one is a later version of the Polly who, all through the Low Countries, fretted about the ugliness or plainness of the women, for all the world as if life were nothing but a series of trysts: collisions between intended souls, divinely matched bodies, compatible infatuates.

I have not, I wrote, *seen a pretty woman since I left Ostend,* whereas milord had already helped himself to half a dozen, not so much as if he were making love as ploughing the local fields, where the literal plough slid through as if through water, the soil being light as sand. It was no surprise, to me or to him, when I fell, stimulated no doubt by the apparition along a canal walk called La Copeure of a pretty woman, but fat and sixtyish. For a while I dawdled with thoughts of roaming about among her petticoats, inhaling the mothballs and the aroma of rotten apples. They all used potpourri. No less a tupmaster than Lord Byron, I yearned for pleasantries, evasions, ways of becoming ever more indirect. So, coming back along the canal, I tourized off to the Roi d'Espagne, to a coffeehouse type of thing full of card tables and women of a certain stamp. It was hard to choose, I the fanatic of chance confronted with both gaming and women at my disposal. They did not whore through the streets but foregathered there, legs crossed casually over their diseases. Indeed, what a game of chance that was, as milord kept saying. "Plunge in, and devil take the hindmost," as he said. "Box the pox." I was a doctor, though, and I knew the ravages that might follow. Instead of contracting with one of these rather glum, recipient wenches, I instead felt about among them, during which they were quite passive. And, milord not being with me, I felt free to evolve my own style of palping and frotting them, pretending I had no language at all. They let me feel them deeply, bite them on the back of the neck, and plant kisses on their cheeks.

One hussy stuck out her tongue, something like a horizontal capstan, and, bidden, I shoved my own tongue against it, feeling the tingle in all my parts and places. I was primed, to be sure, and I agreed with milord that the member has no name, nor the trench it stuffs. Nor, indeed, any of those other especially sensitive components of us. It was like having venery in a Dutch master, watching myself in one of the many mirrors set up throughout the room, with, in the background, dicing and carding and billiards. Coffee and lemonade, dispensed by a woman at the end of the room, whetted more than our throats. Urged to it by one wench, determined that she would not let me away without having performed at least one service, I allowed myself to flood full measure into my trews, this for the merest handful of coin, at which she tut-tutted (or whatever the local equivalent be), as if this had been a false start and I was forthwith to begin again. I was an Onan by courtesy of deus ex machina. Something like.

Milord, already mentioned in the *Ghent Gazette* as being on the premises, at once whiffed me out, telling me, "You smell of the rankest spillage, Polly. Was it a sheep or a pig?" I could tell how foul a humour he was in, but even that failed to keep him from coming close, setting his hands on my shoulders, and inhaling deeply, nodding, humming, as if vetting a prize specimen for an exhibit. "Do go on with your tragedy. Cajetan: What a suggestive name. We will never again make fun. Just keep the juices on the move, my dear Polly; for, stagnant, they develop barbs and devour our essence from within. Keep the gland trembling, wondering if it can ever keep up with you. Always out with it and set the machine making you some fresh supplies." I marvelled at his candour, and his deceit. He would never have mentioned my tragedy if I had not reeked of what I spilled on the Roi d'Espagne.

"It is that impersonal, my lord?" I said to him.

"It matters not."

"No tincture of the unique soul." I felt game, for once having done something of his.

"Only with unique souls," he said. "The rest you have to treat as if you were the coalman, heaving bags of it from his car to the cellar. Heave ho. Spend, spend. It is all a matter of exercise, damn it. They never know they want it until you have given it to them— except for some bold and uppity few, whose sweat smells mannish."

Humbled, I nodded, remembering how the whores wore gigantic gold earrings, ponderous wooden shoes, and an overall smock something like a Scottish bed-gown. Spunk, I realized, smelled of bat-infested caves: ammonia, or the good old salt of Ammon. It was this smell that came off the Sixth Lord Byron, as the *Ghent Gazette* dutifully called him, and as I too sometimes did when at my most inward. As if he were some distant tropical island and I, and all others, were mariners sighting him as a vertebrate lump along the horizon, far off yet wafting its aroma out to sea to puzzle and dismay. Inspecting him as from time to time I had to for the Neapolitan bone-ache and such, I marvelled at how little he washed himself off, persuaded as I was milord was a fanatic of the swift cathartic plunge into whomsoever, to be followed by a swift and thorough cleansing of all traces, as if the deed of kind were indeed too close to that other place. One of our quickmasters, he should have been an ablution slave, but he was not, and indeed, at his grossest, he would make all manner of ribald jests about the aroma of cheese and fish emanating from the trousers of any true man. "Reek of the roaring boy," he said on one occasion. "Stink of the stud," he said on another. I was more fastidious than he, but then I knew more about morbidity than he, and I practised it more. Why, the very *lit de repos* in the coach hummed of him, and I declared (to myself) that if we were to bottle it we would outsell even his poems. The day would come, I knew, when I would have the chance to convert him to a cleaner way. As it was, my gorge rose at what he inflicted upon those he rampaged, as if determined to keep part of himself an irrevocable fungus. Cundums he had, but often (he boasted) neglected to don, wanting, as he put it, the frank union of flesh, as if disease were some sort of moral ordeal. Yet I did not disgust myself enough, reeking for once of what often enough reeked on him, and I was convinced I was beginning to ape him in all ways even as I loathed his very style.

And so to Antwerp (I too had read the classics of our native tongue), its cherry-tree furniture, its cafés where playing dominoes was the very thing, and its Americans, milling about in the streets with that strange unself-conscious abandon of theirs, as if they had all been let out of a punitive schoolroom and were determined to make a hubbub. That hubbub was guaranteed them by their so-called constitution, which legislated (or appeared to) so many things a gentleman took for granted. The women were better-looking, a feast for the roaming eye, although more for the soul than the loins. I had begun, I thought, to demand some depravity in the objects of my lust, some degree of fatness or noxiousness, all because—I told myself—lust and beauty did not mix. It was possible, or so milord told me, to find a woman both beautiful and sensual, whose beauty fanned the horn to an almost unendurable degree, but he had encountered this marvel only twice or three times in his entire career of lusting. It was so rare that a wise man did not hope for it, for he would forever be trying to discern the signs of it and so sap his pleasure. Hags and whores, of either sex, enlivened him no end, whereas real beauties brought out in him something Promethean, as if the headmaster were watching.

Antwerp cathedral was being looted, the locals said; it was the French, carting off altars and defacing columns. It was not as if they had nothing at home to look at, but some mercenary craving of theirs. Lord B. was visibly tiring of the tour, as of this region's art. "I am weary of churches and pictures," he burst out. "If we have to have daubers, then I will take Vandyke over Rubens a hundred times over. But who am I to say? I tell you, Polly, it is more important to know nature intimately than all this painterly folderol. I had rather know, plumb to the depths, the mind of a murderer, and be with him second for second during his execution. This I *need* to know. Indeed, I need to know the human animal in all its sorts and conditions, writhing and yelping. I have taken up from a bench a yataghan, or Turkish dagger, and unsheathed it, wondering how it would feel to use it, taking life from some poor innocent or from some enormous dastard. How would *that* feel? Is that not one of the primacies in life, the keen edge of annihilation?"

Rather than answer or debate, I made some kind of blustering noise which he took for assent, and on he went, caught up in yet another maelstrom of ideas. The train of his thought darted all over the place as if he were being tugged at, as if something in him kept on exploding.

"The other side of which is, as I happened to find out, giving a life back. The governor of Constantinople had had some unfortunate girl sewn up in a sack, in which she was to be tossed into the sea. They do it all the time, having a rather limited and perfunctory view of women. On seeing the procession, I inquired what was afoot and at once intervened, drawing my pistol and telling the chief escort that he must desist, and forthwith return to the governor's house, or I would blow his brains out. After untold bribery and threats we managed to have the wretched girl pardoned on condition that she left the city. I had her despatched to a convent, thence to Thebes, all the while lamenting how many others there had been unsaved. Polly, one must always act. One must alter the thread of life from day to day. Your connoisseurs are all a pack of thieves. You might trust me in any church or cathedral; I care not a fig for such things. But give me a girl in a sack, a murderer on the scaffold, and I with a pistol or an opera glass, and I am ready to plunge into the thick of life. For that is where it is, not in the twinklings on the periphery."

He had worked himself into a perspiration during this, clearly reliving one episode or the other, but with blatant relish. It was an exploit, whereas peering at the delectable white sheet in a Rubens crucifixion was not. I could see that. I could even see, never mind how dimly, how one could come to dote on endless action, or, if not that, then on one or two main feats, in the course of accomplishing which you had lived more intensely than at any other time. It was what he called having a "boisterous nail" within the skull.

Anyone less impressionable than I would have agreed and passed on to other business, preferably that of the alert European traveller. I was too taken with his ideas, however, and my mind was tangling with his. So this was what made him who he was, this opportunistic voracity that cared less about taste and culture than about the raw entity squirming with life in the teeth of death. He dealt in extremes, sometimes ordinary folk in the grip of dreadful powers, sometimes heroes standing vast at the horizon. He wanted to push against life, against those living it, and in this sense was not a consumer, an observer, a follower. In short, he was milord. He rated it more important to know fisticuffs than French, for instance. Some said he rejoiced in throwing his weight about, which was true, but he also adored causes—the put-upon, the downtrodden, the betrayed —and you had to admire the flame-hot social zeal he did things with.

If anything, he was too many men in one, capable in one spoken sentence of cruel phrases about his deformed foot, a guess at the mind of a lifelong criminal, a joke about his having begun a novel of an epistolary nature (its first letter one from a certain Darrell to G.Y.), intimations of illicit intercourse with his half-sister or an Eton chum, and the various ways of pronouncing his name. He would even, at the flash of a cake or a splash of rain, begin to discuss, ever so learnedly, John Locke's theory about an innate notion of the Deity. It was hard as I scrutinized him, either his member (as he required me, as if I were some kind of animal tamer or trainer responsible for the beast's well-being) or his afflicted foot (which he very often reviled to its face, as it were, talking down the length of his leg to it while airing it this way and that on the hinge of his ankle). It was hard to keep a sufficient sense of who I myself was, as distinct from his rapt confidant, his devoted sawbones. I was certainly the witness of his acutest infirmities, his most bilious moods, his most skull-crushing headaches, and I many a time wondered if there was nothing *moderate* about him. Mild on the outside, he was forever cooking beneath, prey to some doctrine of his own that, if you were to live at all the life of a poet, you should inhale life deeply and vent it fully. He believed in swallowing things whole and afterwards discharging them, at which time, either time, he was no one at all, no person, no lord. This done, he turned into himself again, or one of his familiar selves. I sometimes fancied he thought of himself as a lightning rod, or then as a net, a python, a bag for the Bosphorus (like that poor girl he rescued). The impression he gave me was of one who would burst, there was so much going on inside him; he had to lower the pressure of the steam. But what he did not know was that his Polly had a similar head of steam. I simply lacked his gift for getting things from the inside to the outside. I felt every bit as intensely as he, was capable of being just as demonstrative and extreme, yet I held back, as a mere twenty-year-old would, waiting for extreme events—some radiant invasion of my being by the god-head—to force me into things. All the same, the more I lived along-side him, sharing his woes and tantrums, the more I began to learn how to live with that same fierce impetus, lacking his spoiled foot, his ambiguous passions, but every inch a crescent disciple.

We quarrelled little but discussed much.

We both knew about the flesh and its rampages, and we often communed silently in its presence.

We yearned to be in Italy together, although for no doubt different reasons; Hollanders and Belgians put him off, whereas I would be going home, to the basking land of my ancestors. Italy: *Ee-tal-eeya*. Did not my very name mean golden-headed or golden fowl?

I even, as I set things down, began to lard into my entries the self-interrupting dashes he himself spoke: *more pollards—more apparent misery—more villas, some pretty* (I wrote)—*more clipped hedges— more like England—fine, large, town-like villages.* So much for Ant-werp. We made off to Malines, or would have—carriage broke down again. Would Polly-woddle please have it repaired once again? Polly-woddle, no one seemed to remember, was the doctor, not a carriage-hand but minister to the body human. I did as asked, although with lessening grace.

May 1 found us in Brussels, nothing as good as Antwerp, Bruges, or Ghent but padded with lush green lawns. We read our *Morning Chronicles* at the Hôtel d'Angleterre. The town was swarming with soldiers, swarming with the English as well, and of these the women stood out: pleasantly fresh-complexioned and none too stout. Oddly enough, they saved their French-style clothes for London and in Brussels went abroad vested in unmitigated Anglomania. It was like being at home, except that the bookshops had on show all manner of gross and disgusting tomes. I wondered if the English dames came over to look at these but saved face by dressing *de Londres*. By and large, with milord in agreement, the Belgians presented a sorry spectacle: short, unkempt, and greasy, close relatives of the gargoyles who in their public fountains belched streams of water with a vomiting hop as if copying the drunkards in the streets. Oh, for Italy! I said, and went off to the theatre by voiture. Filth everywhere. Seven violins were our orchestra. It was one of your French farces Belgianized, which is to say puffed up with marsh-gas disguised as the French of honking pigs. Ideal for moving phlegm. Behind-stage was an uproar. Terror wherever one looked. There had been so many hisses.

The police entered before the riot began, ordering the actors to quit the stage while I was doing my best to urge two absolute goddesses to spend more of their time in my company—flanking me, as it were—but all they would do was tell me again and again how the audience regularly pelted them with rotten eggs. As I left, alone, people were demanding their money back. A mob had formed, shoving the police this way and that. At length I took refuge in one of the more tasteful booksellers' shops, musing on my two goddesses, one of whom had reeked of lavender, the other of roses, and I thought how comforting it would have been, *somewhere,* to have inhaled them for hours, making our spittle travel to earn its keep. Milord would have known better how to do it. He would have bundled them severely inside a butter churn or aboard an old barge, heedless of the rats running across the backs of his ankles. He would have been tasting their damp softies in no time, working them from a murmur to a dedicated stertorousness and thence to a bemusedly quiescent whimper. Oh, he knew, but all he had told me, when I asked, was "Take hold, dear Polly, and be the terrier." I asked again, only to hear him say, with an almost wheezing guffaw, "Cundums for cuntdom, my dear. All else shall naked be, not to mention the yearning for dark-brown urning."

I had some idea of this, although no old Harrovian, and I knew he had tearful encounters in the boots cupboard in mind, to which he had become accustomed, he said. The sexes were all one to him, the main thing being to *spend* and thus clear the mind for matters more important: the next canto, the new play. Clearly he saw the deed of kind as a laxative, senna pods for the soul. What puzzled me was this: having purged, he then cleared his head for precisely that which clogged him up again. It would surely have been wise to purge and then give up poetry for ever. This suggestion vexed him in the extreme. From the midst of a spontaneous towering temper he instructed me that "Those who can choose to give it up do not have it in the first place. It possesses them. As like for a pussycat to give up chess as a true poet to eschew his muse. Or some unthinking polly parrot."

"Nay, my lord," I said.

"Enough," he snapped. *"Satis est."*

"As you wish, sire. I meant no harm."

"But you did much, enforcing a choler on me just when I was self-soothed. Have done, Polly. Seize the wenches and do with them as you will. Most will accept a feeling hand."

Once again I had the dismal feeling that, instead of going with Byron to see Europe, I had gone to Europe to see Byron. I had, but without intending to be so close, so much under the influence. I felt as if the neat pack of my personality were coming apart, some cards falling to the ground, others getting irretrievably shuffled. I had never wanted, I supposed, to be close enough to discern the potential for bloat in his jaw—three or four extra pounds set it into motion—or to notice how fast his hair became greasy and therefore sat lower and lower on the capacious crown, making him seem bonier beneath the chestnut curls. Some days he limped not at all, others without pause, as if recollecting a role learned by heart. He almost had too much personality to be any one human being. He came at you swiftly, from a series of different angles, and each thought whirled from the center of a different mental commotion, uttered not merely as a contribution to some ongoing intercourse but there to sum up an hour's agonizing, a morning's upset. Something torrential in him afflicted me, ridding me of peace and quiet, agitating my own agitation until it no longer had much relevance to me but had become a dramatic disturbance evocative of mankind in the round. Oh, how he affected me! And, the farther we went, the more churches and towns and pictures we peered at, the more rocked out of my settled self I felt.

Listening to him with mercenary care, I noticed how often he used such words as "twisted," "stunted," and "blighted" and their kindred, and how much notice he gave to misshapen trees, fruit, and furniture. He was ever on the prowl for what lightning had struck, or the ague, the pox, or a fit. It was well known of him, as I eventually gathered, but in the beginning unknown to me. "Something is afoot," he liked to say, burying in the exclamation his pique and hard-won stoicism. There had been a time when he expected his foot to right itself, through some mediation of magic, but that was long ago, and his arrogance of profile said it all for later years: up jutted the whole face, the lip curled ever so little, and the breathing halted. The eyes narrowed at this point as well, as if he were pretending to turn himself to stone from within. And then, across his entire countenance, there passed a ravishing symphony of vulnerable-seeming despisals addressed not so much to humanity as to the very foundry of Creation. His face was getting its own back. Or *his*. I marvelled at so many facial expressions no painter had a hope of capturing. They shifted and changed like cloud formations on a windy day, the while his thoughts blew hither and thither. Keeping up with him emotionally was out of the question. You guessed at his mind, at the thought's neighbourhood, but by then he was two thoughts further ahead and several changes of mien. Byron-watching, nonetheless, was a way of life. Scores had succumbed to its lure, losing themselves in adulatory measurement as if his face were a prize sow or a foal.

Here he was, then, on May 2, in Brussels, and here was I, putting a good face on things, telling my sister Fanny how pleased I was to be with him, just about on an equal footing with a suite of rooms shared between us. He had not shown any passion, I lied to her, although a series of mishaps with the coach (three) had put him into the prelude of a paddy, whereas they almost drove Polidori over the brink. *Some time you will either see,* I told her, *my Journal in writing or print—Murray having offered me 500 guineas for it through Lord Byron. L.B. is going to give me the manuscript, when done printing, of his new cantos of "Childe Harold."* Had I known how another sister, Charlotte, would cut her version, rending out what she considered indiscreet, I would have handed the thing to L.B. himself to take its chances with the Hobhouses of this world. I was to set down the truth, warts and all: the stews, the drabs, the lusting after his own kind, the voluptuous addiction to whatever lay beneath a robe.

Before Waterloo, he and some hearty worthy named Gordon got going about their schooldays and there was much prattle about nurses, lancets, bleeding, water-gruel, and the so-called brochan, which this worthy had preferred to bread and butter. He had fourteen years ago lent L.B. a pony on which to ride in Hyde Park. And he had been in love with a Miss Mary Duff. To myself I declared that, if the next revelations were to be earth-shaking as these, the Lord Almighty would vacate the heavenly throne and come down to join in the sport of the massive memories. Then they got on to obesity (at which the Lord A. would surely have taken *voiture* back to heaven), and L.B. confessed to having only too natural a tendency to put it on. He kept referring to me, this Gordon, as "your *compagnon de voyage,*" which irked me. He might as well have said Dr.

Polidori or just doctor. These Scots, I knew them well: when gushing, at their slimiest; when not gushing, as rough as hedgehogs.

Then we were moving through the gloomy forest of Soignes, milord having a fit of the taciturns, and next we got out at the monuments, where milord stared about him a full five minutes without uttering a word, then said, as to an audience of several hundred, "I am not disappointed"—as if the whole thing had been staged for him only—"I have seen the plains of Marathon, and these are as fine. Can you tell me where Picton fell? because I have heard that my friend Howard was killed at his side, and nearly at the same moment." Gordon pointed to some hundred and fifty yards away. When we arrived, L.B. sighed and said, "Howard was my relation and dear friend; but we quarrelled, and I was in the wrong: we were, however, reconciled, at which I now rejoice." He saw not Waterloo but the scene of a quarrel, not the other deaths but a rift healed with a precious kinsman. Mostly he mused, little taken by Gordon's account of how the troops had been stationed on the field of battle, whereas the desperate defence of the château of Hougoumont caught his imagination and he melted somewhat. Myself, I was still musing on three bulldogs I had seen pulling uphill an enormous load, a goat fastened to a child's car, and the frock coats I had bought but had not worn. I too could be caught up in trifles, like the buttons and books pressed on us by the boys of Waterloo, a scene neither desolate nor romantic, but gently undulating: few hedges, fewer trees. I did point out to him white splashes of plaster where the houses had been repaired after the cannonade. In the garden, only 25 English killed; in this one field, 1,500. I wondered about the grapeshot: that which struck a man would vanish for ever, but that which missed would career on for some distance and then drop to the grass, there to be found in later years. Yet we had come upon none such. Here the short-kilted Scots, whether fed on bread and butter or brochan we knew not, had fought to the death, neither yielding nor whining, and this impressed me more than it did milord. Where Colonel Howard had lain buried, under three trees, had been ploughed over, the body long since having been taken to England. But, oh, what a recent war it was; we were in war's hot wake.

We saw the untouched chapel that had served as a hospital, where the fire had burned away the toes of a crucifix. We saw the gate and the sward where some thousand corpses had lain, and the very same gardener who with his dog had been detained by General Maitland at Hougoumont. Then we saw the red-tiled house which, rebuilt, was Buonaparte's final headquarters. Milord became increasingly gloomy, as one of high station being affected by one of high station in the act of being toppled, or something such: the kind of thing that rarely afflicts common or garden doctors. I could see from the twitching of his face what lordly emotions were at war within him, that he wished with all his heart he might simplify his life by engaging in some such encounter and not go away burdened with trappings—cuirasses, helms, swords—of departed warriors. We bought eagles and cockades to add to our collection of battle stuff. As we left the field he began to chant some wild Albanian song, which I relished in silence, knowing I had seen milord at his most covetous, full of thwarted noble yearning, wanting to be killed and remembered for it, not for poetry but for epic bloodiness. I had always thought that the romance of bloody deeds would die a sudden death if the romancer or the dreamer had assisted, only once, a surgeon in the practice of his calling. There was no romance in blood. Blood was cheap.

With Saint-Trond behind us, thank goodness, we beheld yet again the lower orders, miserable in benighted perfection. Not only did they have dunghills in front of their hovels, but ditches of black foetid water as well, across which they set elementary bridges. We saw them swaying as they walked over, with every step pressing the boards deeper into the ooze as if doomed to some subterranean Stygian rendezvous within the next year or two. Never had we vented so many *ughs*. After three bouts of passport nonsense (they visiting us three times), we saw Liège from the steep hill above it:

cots and villas, towers and domes, within a patchwork of minutely divided fields. As the cottages got better, the road got worse, full of pits and runnels negotiated better by urchins yelling *"Donnez-nous quelque chose, Monsieur le chef de bataillon"* and *"Monsieur le général, un sou"* than by our ramshackle, expensive, foundering coach. Fresh horses came to hand, and Lord B. and I argued the toss between stopping there and going on to Aix-la-Chapelle. Off we went, as into a mirage of pious hope, to such a knocking and a jolting as I had never known. Lord B. roundly accused me of giving bad advice, even as we hammered onward. His mood improved with the road, yet not before I had had yet another chance to peer into the vault of his personality, where storms and lightning came up with marine suddenness, and nothing temperamental was done by halves. On we stove, axle-deep in rainwater; but, shone upon by the sun before reaching Aix-la-Chapelle at half past twelve, our moods mended. I had always given my best advice, even when I knew that we would dislocate our bones by pressing forward. I wanted Italy, even Switzerland, rather than these barbaric workshop towns, like something nameless between a Valhalla of chimney-sweeps and a sump of slop-lovers. I knew that, even though he wanted to stop, once stopped he would begin to seethe and fidget. His body, perhaps not all of it, needed motion, as if to lull him, or stir him up into something like intellectual readiness. For a born leader, he could be remarkably passive, more a responder than a decider. Once I had taken the initiative, he blasted me for taking it; but he would blast me for doing nothing too. It was hard to please him; after a few days I had decided no longer to attempt it, instead imagining myself a true doctor applying myself to the malady of his journey, compressing it here, drawing it out (even bleeding it) there.

In truth, I think he wanted to settle down somewhere and get on with a sustained piece of writing; and, if not that, then with some piece of energetic protracted tomfoolery. It was burden enough being his itinerant doctor, forced to eye his deformed foot several times a week to see if the journey were affecting it amiss (I saw something gnarled, distended, although polished like an old root that had sat by the fire, acquiring a patina of soot and black lead). Or his member, whose welfare interested him extremely. Were the cullions being compressed too much, absorbing too much heat, too much jarring? Behind the hood of the prepuce, was there too much foreign matter? Always I told him to bathe it until he could stand the feel of the thing no longer. As for the foot, bathing helped, of course, but I told him to massage it, stroke it, whenever he could; and he got various serving maids to do this for him, sometimes urging them to extend their ministrations from the foot to the loins, bathing or coaxing, I was never quite sure, and I often noticed, like some heathen peepshow done by candlelight, milord lying back as one dying, being lathered and larruped in the one motion by a team of sluts whose behinds he held in sundry pincer grips of his own devising. There was the occasional giggle or intemperate squeak, followed by the final uproar as he spent. I thanked my Maker he did not have a deformed member too, though he kept asking me about the effect upon it of a heavy stone pendant, as in Africa, and upon him of certain drugs which, lethal if improperly administered, could prolong the delight of engorgement, detumescence, and spending, if only taken at the correct time. "When, Polly, when?" I heard that litany from dawn to dusk. He was eager to manoeuvre his humanity into an extreme stance. *What would happen if?* was his motto. In this he was a serious, chronic, natural historian, though reckless to an uncommon degree. He yearned for infection though he dreaded it, as he yearned for death, etc. He was one of your leapers, jumping into a pack of wolves, so to speak, to see if their conjoint furs warmed him. As I construed my mission, my assignment, I was to furnish him all help without killing him off. I think he knew that my natural bent was less to keep the ailing alive than to find matters of the liveliest interest in cadavers; I was a natural pathologist and, as such, fascinated by his dominant figures of speech, from the deformed's being miraculously transformed (and vice versa: angels into Calibans) to the concubine of snow, the package for the Bosphorus, and verse as the supreme laxative. I was on tour with a self-defiling snowman suffocating in an oven full of gingerbread men swelling and bulging as the heat grew high. Or not. Such formulations enabled me to vent the spleen I always felt at being *an employee,* not a proper gentleman companion of professional standing. He mocked me, of course, but I vengefully metamorphosed him as well, milording him to his face: awe tinged with love and hate. How I would have enjoyed having him in some greenhouse atop an Alp, cutting him open with nursery deftness, and connecting up his blood vessels in a wrong way that nonetheless worked. He would wolf his food through his rear, vent it from his mouth, make water through his nose, and have a heart beating in his grossly magnified foot. Nor would this be to travesty what he wanted, for there was something Satanic in him that wanted to go beyond the decreed, the permitted, until the matrix screamed and exploded. Little though he knew it, we were tamperers together, as like to have severed heads for company in our boudoirs as to have mothers, and to have paramours with ill-assorted breasts arrayed round their chests like moons round a planet. All in the interests of being different, not as God intended—though as milord often argued, after the drabs had emptied him out and rubbed his parts to numbness, "If God gave us the capacity, then God must have wanted all that the capacity could do."

Except, I would say, for the things made available only to test our will in denying ourselves all of them.

"No, Polly," he would say, "God is positive. Universes make themselves not by hanging back. Their essence is to bulge forth and carry all else with them." In those or similar words he lofted his theology in the dead of night, soothed into an apostasy that belonged in Dante.

"Well," I liked to say, "I would cheerfully be the first man out of whom a flower was growing—a hibiscus, say, or a begonia. Or who shared his lungs with an acceptable feline."

"Or a snake," he said, grinning twitchily.

"Drinking the blood of others."

"Padding through the fogs at midnight," he said, "in the loneliest reaches of London, as a unicorn emitting a poisonous gas."

We often warmed to our theme thus but always ran up against the problem of how to get started: which potions to drink, which lotions to apply, all of it to be done in an almost holy eagerness, not so much the wilfulness of the naughty boy grown up as the young Prometheus asking why his brother Epimetheus was backward. Boiling acids, reeking tars, filled our small-hours dialogues as we envisioned monsters of palpable ingenuity, Faustian presumers who knew that, in going too far, they were warping the usual ideas of life and death. In those talks we were no longer lord and liegeman but Don Quixote and Sancho Panza, Mephisto and Faust, each of us both of them turn and turn about, and I would lull him to sleep with fierce tales of what I would do to his veins and his brain once he set the scalpel in my hand. He whispered, "Dearest Polly, cut away."

Then how did I soothe *myself*, apart from fondling my memories of Miss Arrow? I did it by imagining milord and I were en route to some preternatural laboratory run by club-footed geniuses, awaiting our arrival—and our very special skills—before getting to work. Flowers with voices would grow from out of the sludge— nay, the very dunghills we had seen in Saint-Trond and Liège—and we would be transforming just such towns into gleaming metropolises where each family had a doctor unique to it. Our only fuel would be the aimed energy of Lord Byron's brain, which lifted spoons and unearthed coal from the bowels of our planet. "Here's to you, Tom Brown," he carolled through the day, no longer the petulant *maudit* but someone between witch-doctor and savant, as open to suggestion as closed to bigotry. We boiled over with love and brilliance. We read each other's minds without writing anything down. And we reinvented the idea of Belgium, modifying it until it was a little Eden with sprouts.

As often as not, however, just before dozing off after these beautiful sallies, I thought of the two surgical boots he had had enforced upon him, for his right foot, for all the world as if he were a Chinese baby girl, and saw the withered ankle like a root of celery, and fell asleep, if I could, genuinely wanting him made right before Italy.

   Without thinking much about the gesture, I paid my compliments to the cathedral in Aix-la-Chapelle, crammed with believers hearing mass: they every bit as automatic as I. When I asked a boy in my broken German to guide me to the *baths,* I ended up at a quite different emporium, in company of my own sex and so lascivious that I fell quite speechless, knowing what they wanted and offered. Lord B. would have rejoiced in this place. They would have made him an honorary member, I told myself in feeble jest. I wondered what his unmentionable crime had been with Lady Byron, the act that split them asunder and sent him abroad. I thought I knew but had never dared ask him, among several things I needed to speak to him about. I had always meant to ask him about my being both prudish and lecherous: how, perhaps, to bury the former in the latter, because being prudish held me back and I wanted to go forward, into blame and perdition, just like milord, paddling about all day and night in self-destructive ecstasy. Talk was that he had buggered her when he was drunk, or forced himself into her mouth while she was talking (when he was drunk or sober), but I myself wondered if it had not been something else, something I might call Latin or German, done with an apparatus or a tongue. Perhaps he had done something with fire, a blazing wand of exquisite carving. It was clear that he had done it alone, but not clear with what mechanical aids, etc. One might spend a lifetime guessing, and Lord B. would not go near the matter, perhaps hardly able to credit what he had been carried away sufficiently to do. All I knew was that, whatever it was, it was bound to be among the familiar range of his crimes: nothing new, nothing he had not done before, with half-sister, whore, or boy. The question was why he had thought it necessary to marry in order to attempt it again when all the brothels in the world remained open, as did the legs of ladies of the night. I

wished he would school me in such depravities, lest I waste my
homecoming in Italy.

His retort was always hearty, jocular. Urging me to "make it
up for myself, as lust list," he contended that he who needed to do it
knew how and what. It was no good skulking around roués such as
himself to pick up hints; the devil chose his own and guided them.
So: had the devil guided me to the Turkish baths? Had that been my
true destiny working itself out, offering itself up? If so, I had taken
no advantage, having felt not in the least tempted. One felt a minor
flicker in the member, of course, at the mention or evocation of
almost *any* kind of buttocks, but that was far from enough to effect a
conversion. No, I was destined for another sex than my own: for the
red lamp shining forth from within a pair of red knickers enclosing
a bisected tuft. Surely milord would relish that as some kind of
piratical standard to fly in all weathers. Surely his travelling companion might emulate as well as decipher him? Only that March,
John Cam Hobhouse was supposed to have set down his famous
blacklist, writing down every vice and sin, crime and horror, a
human being was capable of. He had then confronted Lady Byron
with it, asking her to name which one of those things, if any, Lord
B. had done to her, and she had said it was none of them but had
refused to specify further. How worldly was Hobhouse, though?
Had he based his list on milord's poems or on his life? Surely Lord
B. should have drawn up the index of condemned sins himself; it
might have proved a vital document in the education of the world.
After all, it had been said that Hobhouse, instead of writing the
word "sodomy," had put a dash. Now, how competent was somebody that delicate to plumb the depths of a sexual scandal? Only a
moral desperado would have done it well, or a true man of the
world such as I had hopes of myself becoming. Perhaps milord no
longer remembered, or thought he did not. Or Lady B. and her
solicitors did not know the word for the depravity that had taken
place and did not like to spell it out, hoping for the blessed relief of
concinnity from someone else. I could have been useful, I thought,
gauche as I was, for I had the courage to probe the core of awful-

ness. Young I may have been in the ways of the world, but as a physician I was accustomed to probing the dark heart of nature, and it was nature, after all, that encompassed everything done under the sun, even the diseases and death inflicted upon us gratuitously by the Lord of hosts. I would have set Lady Byron behind some comforting sheet, had her strip bare the zone of trespass, and then have her point, touching her here and there, as befitting, with a little neutral mirror. It would have taken fifteen minutes at most. "To me, Lady Byron," I would have said, "all apertures are as one—as to the rest of my calling. We are not prudes. We do not judge. In this we are kin to carpenters and joiners." It should have been done. The conversation could have taken place. It still might, I thought, or—almost any up-to-date worldly doctor would serve. She would not have to be told, unless she asked, that the anus develops as a slight invagination of the epiblast a short way in front of the posterior end of the hind-gut, and perhaps she would wince at so bald a formulation, preferring (milord) the rougher-and-readier language of everyday obscenity or that of enraptured lovers. What use to talk to her (since Lord B. did not) of the vestibule of the vagina, or of the slight eminence of the clitoris—Greek for "twig," your ladyship—since this was hardly the area of complaint, it being the fit orifice according to tradition, whereas with the mouth it depended upon what was put into it, not upon the mouth per se (a not necessarily holy chamber since, presumably, he had taught her how to French).

On I droned, setting matters right as best I could behind the screen, helping Lady Byron feel more at ease with what I fondly thought of (already) as "her places," could I but roam through them and among them with all the assiduity and good temper of one out on a nature walk. Another question, not one too easy to put, was crucial: Had he in fact used his body or something extruded from it? Not to be too polite about it, had he given her a golden rain cloud or a brown peg? I almost compiled a little table of horrors, exhausting the permutations, but found they came readily to mind; there were so few, and the important categories were four: (1) organ, (2) product, (3) implement, (4) another person. I dismissed number 4 without much thought as, clearly, there had only been the two of them in Byron's hell. Why could she not have told? Could she, even now, be persuaded to set the matter right and so (just perhaps) deprive him of a shocking reputation based more upon vagueness than anything precise? Could the travelling companion not become the bedroom Sancho Panza as well? I presumed, of course, but with the best of motives, wishing to learn from him; and learn from him without knowing him I could not. Here was a man who had, if one read the evidence aright, invented something new: a sexual variation so dastardly that even someone as depraved as he was supposed to be would not dare name it—say the name or invent one for it. I wondered, despite thoughts of Miss Arrow in India, what kind of prudery-shop the world was coming to, if language failed us in extremis. Was this the variant ever to be known as Number 666, as if there could ever have been 665 others? Or was it doomed to be done by hand signals or interrupted rising pillars of smoke, as in North America? Had we moved, in one step, from the crime that dared not say its name to the crime that did not know its etymology? As a doctor, I was aghast, since my profession had done well in con-cocting Greek and Latin names with which to blur *hoi polloi* of all shapes and states. Down with decorum. Up with *lingua medica*. Let Lady Byron form a club of women who had been similarly abused, and let them parade with a big banner down Piccadilly, proclaiming the hurt. If Lord B. wanted to go on being notorious, let him hold nothing back at all. The black angel diving, flap-flap, into the abyss should know naught of peccadilloes.

"I had been wondering, my lord," I began, "if your travelling companion and physician might be of even further use to you."

"Nay, Polly," said he, "what with carriages breaking down and the almost total lack of decent roads, I fear you are exercised enough. Pray rest, and drink in the Rhine."

"In quite another matter, my lord, than those at present beset-ting us, but nonetheless of great moment."

"*Childe Harold?* No, you cannot mean that."

He peered at me, waiting, willing.

"In the matter of Lady Byron, sire."

"In the matter of Lady Byron? *You*, Polly?"

"In the matter of the thing unmentionable—"

"Polidori, I know you jest. Kindly desist; I am not in the mood. There has been too much pain."

"I was wondering if I might help in the matter of ascribing a name to the dread offence."

"Oh," he said. "And your natural tact, having quite expired, you choose to bring up that. You do not choose or try to interfere with something private; you choose something that has no bearing on the heart of anyone who matters—really, this is too much." His voice was ice and broken glass. "If Polidori wants a ball shot through his skull, let him talk on, let him meddle even further. I command you, doctor, cease."

His choler shocked me. After all, were we not drinking friends? Fellow swyvers? I had put the matter politely enough, every bit as politely as your Hobhouse and Company, so what was the rub? I was a mere slip of a lad, twenty only, yet nonetheless a *doctor*. Surely the greenness of the one mellowed the impersonal sagacity of the other. Lord B. was in no mood to listen, but perhaps he had all the same divined a shred of my good intent, as when I offered to lend him Casti's salty *nouvelle* (which he poo-hooed). I would have to come back to the matter on another occasion, possibly with medical text in hand: an anatomy, to substantiate my serious aspiration. Where the lawyers had failed, physick might prevail, though I dared not tell him this, he who glowered now at the Rhine as if it had all issued in a torrent from his nether body. Perhaps all milord had done was bellow at her, only *threatening* half a dozen of his pet abominations, and she had quailed at this assault from the coarse and bumbling world of men, where a penny upright was all that mattered, to be rubbed into submission by a drab in a lane. At that instant I longed for London, for the cries of its violet- and lavender-sellers, for the sound of hooves on cropped turf in some park or other. The further into foreign parts we went, the more foreign to himself milord became. I let him be. We saw our first vines. The Rhine was a valley of sweet waters.

We had never seen so many crucifixes, of stone or wood, as if the whole world—Cologne as far as Bonn—were being crucified bit by bit. An innkeeper made us fill in his book each night with name, profession, and age, as if through some devilish alchemy all three had changed in a few hours. I could tell that milord, vexed by this, had some kind of retaliation in mind, but in the end he did nothing after some mighty brooding. All this put us in the mood for ruined Drachenfels, once a storied castle, close to which was a monument commemorating the place where one noble brother had slaughtered another. Gradually the landscape was becoming softer, more southern, thank goodness. It pleased me to think that Lord B. had been charged much the same sum for his thundering, lumbering, fake Napoleonic coach, green of darkest oak leaves, as Murray had offered me to keep my journal. Where were his wild Albanian songs now? He was sulking on the verge of paradise (surely not at my civil offer of intimate help). All about us spread the geometry of cultivation: hedgeless beds rather than fields; women at work therein; oxen and horses ploughing; the peasants jolly-faced and working with a will on the swollen river's flank. Aurelius, Theodoric, Napoleon came this way. In particular, the last of these was everywhere; they had not forgotten him.

Only yesterday, as one of our postilions blew a horn, twin rainbows appeared, as if summoned up by sorcerer's apprentice, one of them up close atop the trees and shot through with greens from the leaves. It was as if we had lumbered over into paradise. Lord B. wrote to his sister about this or something else. Family secrets. *Half* secrets, anyway. I drew a squiggly map of our journey, I having some skill with a pencil, but the coach's motion jumbled it, so I tossed it out into the breeze, knowing it would soon help some traveller to get from Aix to Ghent. We saw the place where printing was supposedly invented, but the French, who had much to answer for, had pulled down the house; then the cathedral, roof pierced by bombs during the last siege of Mayence. We beheld beheaded reliefs and one German marshal gravely jutting his head forth from beneath his tombstone: "I am here," he said, and we wondered if he wanted to be hauled out entire or pushed back into fame and peace. It was here that things began to go truly wrong, in all ways. Mayence to Mannheim, for all its loveliness, jarred my serenity and his. We crossed the river on a bridge of boats, and then a fever struck, rendering me unable to write, unable to observe, unable to make sense of anything, as if a sulphurous, acid, narcotic damp had eaten into my brain, and I saw bridges where there were none, and Lord B. where only a fly buzzed.

Only a little recovered, I set off (May 15), among ample alleys of Lombardy poplars and horse-chestnuts, with crisp, rather Scotch villages. I call them *Scotch* because only to a non-Scot is the word offensive and does the other word, *Scottish,* occur. To Carlsruhe I clattered through a grove of Scotch firs, only to enter the (non-Scotch) inn reeling and perspiring, jelly in the knees and needles in the eyes. Heal thyself, I said aloud in bed, and dosed myself with ipecac, *Cephaelis ipecacuanha,* with 15 grains of opium. There followed vertigo, headache, and a tendency to syncope, none of these helped by magnesia and lemon acid. I cheered but felt worse, in some phase of my dementia imagining I saw a long shelf with my life's works (books) all arranged with titles in alphabetical order, but I could see only the first letters of these titles. Someone had dusted the gilt tops of the pages. The books looked as if they had never been opened. The shelf was a shrine. Only peasants would bow at it.

So why then did I force myself to go out touring with Lord B.? In and about the town, the glare of all the white stucco made my eyes burn and the headache worse. I took some stewed apples (local delicacy approaching fetish) with more magnesia and lemon acid, to no effect. I lay down without sleeping, then got up after two hours of it. I was on the point of going out again, to escape somehow from myself, when Lord B., observing that I had in hand a plated candlestick, took it from me and gave me a brass one instead. After a few steps more, I fainted, crashed to the stone, which noise brought the servants to me in a hurry. Now I took four pills and witnessed Lord B. once again exchanging candlesticks, this time making the servant take brass for plate. Again I went to bed, trying to persuade myself that Lord B. had wanted me, on each occasion, to have the candlestick with the longer candle in it. Surely he had no intention of insulting me. What he had in mind was an invalid's needing a candle that would burn night-long. And light him into the next world if need be.

More medicine gave me slicing pains in the abdomen. I vomited. Then I slept, waking weak. When at length I made to leave my chamber, there at the door stood Sir C. Hunter, full of my almost dying. I invited him in without more ado, apologizing for the fug of a sickroom and assuring him that the windows had been open an hour. He was a bosom friend of the Grand Duke. Lord B. entered, and they carried on a conversation for which I had not the strength, the upshot of which was that Sir C. sent us a few hours later the *Guide du voyageur en les pays de l'Europe,* begging in return some of milord's poems. I went out again and stared at gilt-thick columns, Corinthian and regular as fir trees.

Darkness attuning itself (or so it seemed), we moved on from dirty Moudon to Lausanne, having seen the castle in which————defended himself against the French, though to us it looked so fragile. The Swiss castles, with their conical roofs and lack of battlements, take us less than the German ones. Below us, the lake was at first a cloud and we felt like spiders walking serenely above their dewy webs, sure of a soft catch if we were to heel over sideways. In Lausanne I refused a collection of bad books offered me at four louis (it was never any use patronizing foreign booksellers at random). Besides, who wanted to read as we moved on to such classic ground as Staël, Voltaire, and Rousseau had trod, not to mention Buonaparte, Necker, and the rest? Genthoud, Ferney, and Coppet were all close to the road. The lake itself looked narrow, but Mont Blanc in the distance, sixty miles off, looked ethereal, a dream dreamed by Lord B., whose smile might have graduated into a leer. He knew where he was now. It was all lordly enough for him. This was what he had come for, all this way, Mahomet to the mountain. "Lake Leman," he said. "Its face woos me and undoes me quite."

On May 25 we entered M. Dejean's Hôtel d'Angleterre on the outskirts of Geneva (this was Sécheron), and Lord B., in a magnificently hyperbolical mood, entered his age in the register as 100, causing the uppity innkeeper to send him a letter of query only half an hour later, he intent on treating his centenarian aright. It was worthy of a novel. *It begins again*, I wrote, *to be the land of the vine.* And the women, ugly up to the Pays de Vaud, were improving greatly, as if the word had sped ahead of us, and the world here, no matter how small, knew that we expected nothing but the best. M. Dejean made Lord B. change his age to the correct one, twenty-eight, but not before certain persons had seen it and been delighted. Compared to his twenty-eight, my own twenty was hardly an age at all, more a declaration of an unknown pupa.

Next day the *voituriers* were trying to gouge us for further drink-money, so we took a calèche, or rather ordered it, but happened to enter the garden, where we caught sight of a boat and took it out onto Leman Lake, where we rowed and dreamed, it was so smooth. When we came to the ferry, a waiter, *désolé*, told us it was taken for *un monsieur Anglais*—Monsieur Shelley. Or was it Southey? Lord B. grumbled in his Scottish way, not a word separate from the others. I rejoiced: I had *ridden* with him on the field of Waterloo, had *walked* with him to see Churchill's tomb, and now I had *rowed* with him too. Then we *bathed,* and I added another word. "Milord," I whispered to myself, and it sounded right. Lord Polidori.

PART THREE

And with him, one of form almost divine

Came running as a spouse into thy arms,

Wrapt in such splendour, eyes unpurified

Could not the brightness bear—I bowing fell.

—Ximenes, IV. iv.,

J. W. Polidori

At times, the existence and powers of the Deity were canvassed,—at times, the reality of beings intermediate between God and man; their qualities, and the facts related concerning them, came under consideration. Other evenings heard discussions upon the nature of virtue, whether it really were definite and felt, as is beauty, in every breast, or whether it were not merely an object of policy and self-convenience.

—Ernestus Berchtold,

J. W. Polidori

Of a sudden, we were almost two centuries earlier, visiting the house that once belonged to Dr. John Diodati, the Genevese Professor of Theology visited there in 1639 by John Milton. Lord B. had had the brainstorm that he would like to live there, not so much for Milton's shade (though this mattered to him on some heroic plane) as for its lovely view, although the house was somewhat narrow and not entirely square—"squishy" was the word I used. The asking price was five-and-twenty louis per month, its common name the Villa Belle Rive, but Lord B. was already calling it the Villa Diodati, whereas I was all for dubbing it the Villa Milton). After we returned, Pictet, a local bigwig, arrived to call on Lord B., but Lord B. said he was "not at home," being somewhat out of sorts about the villa, which he had been hoping to take that very day. Next day we took a boat for 3 francs the day and rowed to Sécheron, where we breakfasted, took a carriage to the banker's, and changed money. Byron to Pictet: poetic justice, Pictet being not at home. I had the vision of two men, neither particularly eager to see the other, putting on the guise day after day of being not at home, *for years.* How nobility dissembled, knowing what it did not need. As it was, my own temper worsened from all this to-ing and fro-ing to no purpose and gentlemen being out to one another ad infinitum. Off to Diodati we went again, by boat, only to be told we might not have it since it was already promised to an English family. Not for three years, they told Lord B, who exploded into an allusive tirade, explaining to me how not only Milton had wandered along this romantic shore but also Thomas Gray, who had informed the world that the Alps could shock an atheist into new belief, and Hazlitt the critic and essayist, who mocked Gray for this, and then Rousseau, Gibbon, Voltaire, and Mme. de Staël. I had heard all these names before. Milord wanted to join the host, having already fixed on one little room for his bedchamber, which got the morning sun.

From that verandah, he said, running as it did along three sides of
the villa, one might see Lake Geneva from a thousand angles. It had
to be. What was an English family compared to this? I truly
thought, for a moment, that the agent had meant the august English
family of Milton, Gray, etc., returning as opportunistic and sentimental ghosts, but I knew I was dreaming. Let it be said that George
Gordon Noel, Lord Byron, prevailed, as he intended to. Back and
forth by boat we went, Polidori in a humor with teeth by now, and
then it was as if the angel of providence had intervened. "Look, by
gad," Lord B. said. "I do declare." We had run into Mary Wollstonecraft Godwin, her sister Claire Clairmont, and Percy Shelley.
In a flash they were all over one another, none of them giving the
faintest heed to a mere physician, who made no bones about it, got
into the boat, shoved off, and lay along its bottom, letting chance
sail me to the middle of the lake, where I remained, put in my place,
dawdling and cursing aloud. With no warning I had been deposed
to number four or five in milord's roster of interests, now truly
made back into a Polly-woddle or worse. I had just witnessed the
outward semblance of noblesse prevailing in that Lord B. got his
precious villa almost as soon as becoming infatuated with it, and
now he had become newly infatuated with some new but old people
of his. Indeed, from what the Shelley person said, *he* had come here
to Geneva *expecting* to meet Lord B. for the first time. How shy they
seemed in each other's presence. How forward was the Clairmont
woman, who had arrived two weeks ago with the Shelleys, cooing
to Lord B., "I wish you had not grown so old, though I thought
you must have been *two* hundred, from the length of time you
took." "Bah, these coaches," Lord B. muttered. "Drunken postilions." "I have just written you a little letter," she told him, "in
welcome, wishing you sweet sleep and saying how happy I am."
This was Lord B.'s London mistress, very much a woman on his
track, as anyone could see. I would have taken no small pleasure in
doing a little impromptu careless surgery on all four of them, in
their sleep or not, joining up their tripes and organs to make a real
four-part creature: double Siamese. We now had three extra persons

for me to be serf to. It was too much to bear. I sensed that, months later, if someone would think of Polidori again and ask, the locals would say, Oh, they had not wished to interrupt so jolly a conversation, but the boat with its load of non-Burgundian bones had floated to shore weeks ago. The good doctor had been found dead with, open across his face to hide it from the sun or the rain, a copy of *Childe Harold*. How neatly they combined: each had his inamorata with him now. The Shelleys were out at Cologny up above the harbor, in the Villa Montalègre, and now Lord B. and his London passion would be in a villa of *their* own, several hundred yards higher up. Had this been a plan? It must have been at least half planned. All I had was a letter from a Dr. de Roche inviting me to breakfast on the morrow; not a word of invitation, to me, from the author of *Queen Mab* and other effronteries, the bashful, consumptive one, twenty-six years old, he too severed from a wife, stuck to a brace of dames, one of them wholly or in part Lord B.'s plaything.

I had his age wrong; he was twenty-three, not that it made any difference to what I readily perceived as his monopolizing presence, he wishing to impress Lord B., milord wishing to impress him. All those dreadful battles and their dead had fallen away from memory, to yield to this circling dance of two bantam cocks as they planned excursions on the lake and into the mountains, and long sojourns round the fireplace, as well as, I did not doubt for a moment, crisscross trespasses into one another's beds. Gone was my boyish hope of having Lord B. squire me into one of the local red-lamp shops, to show me how; local in any locality. He had even jested about getting me work in such a place, since he himself was in such rude health (he was not), inspecting the ladies of the midnight, ridding them of worms and sores, poxes and gruels. Perhaps I should make myself fall ill or attempt some form of violence upon my body, sleepwalk, have bad dreams, go from one to the other of them, screaming or twitching with a fit. Fawn on them I could, having been schooled in such behavior by Lord B., but they were so wrapped up in one another that even a fawner, bending his knee, oiling his smile, would need several trumpets to get started. Instead I

got me, from Lord B., fifteen pounds towards the price of a watch, a
repeater with minute-hand. Bought off by time.

I supposed it was his way of ensuring that I would never be
late when I was supposed to serve them or otherwise oblige: even,
on some ethereal occasion, make up a fivesome. It was his way of
winding me up. With me, from London, I had brought various
things no one knew about, including my tureen of leeches, for the
usual purpose, but also—a trophy from Ampleforth of a day when I
had removed three batsmen in three balls—a cricket ball, made special within, battered yet rollable still. This I proposed to release
toward them, along the floor, whenever I wanted attention or (more
likely) when I refused to come, having been summoned with some
such uncouth cry as "Come, Polly," "Polly, come hither," or "Pol-
Pol, *please.*" All they would get would be the hollow clonk of the
ball as it toured towards them, tapping the skirting board, knocking
a final melody from the fire-irons, where it at last came to rest. If
they picked it up they would smell the scythed grass of yesteryear,
perhaps even the sweet-sick aroma of cow flop, the bowler's sweat
long since having evaporated. Polly had not always been one easy to
summon, send away, ignore, make fun of. Now, of course, I was
much more on my own than when actually figuring as Lord B.'s
travelling companion. I was the extra one, the one without a someone of his own, never mind how faintly Lord B. had fulfilled that
role for me. Now he had become a personable mirage, no more than
that; hence his horological bribe.

I must have got it wrong about the villa because we had to go
off and look at the house of Mme. Necker, going at 100 a half-year;
but that was only milord's caution prompting him, should the Villa
Diodati be struck by lightning, say. On May 28 I breakfasted in
Geneva with Dr. de Roche: keen mind, steady listener, an even
steadier listener to himself, the essence of good sense. He told me
that, on their marches, armies gave themselves a fever—being
smothered in animal filth, living irregularly—of the most malignant
typhoid kind. "They have epidemics," he said. "What about armies
of poets on the march?" I asked him. "Do they too generate malig-

nant fevers? If so, of what type?" He had no idea, quite missing my ungentlemanly point. "A whole column of it," he said, "spread from Moscow to Metz, and it caused here in Geneva the only almost epidemic typhus for ages." He took a developed interest in the fever I had recently had, telling me it was a military fever. Indeed, he talked about it, how to quell it and avoid it, all the way home to see Lord B., with whom he wanted to talk politics, making most of all one case: that it was in the interests of Europe not to have too many free-roving Frenchmen, which struck me as trying to banish the squirrel from the animal kingdom. He was talking about policed borders, I supposed, and immigration barricrs: an old Swiss obsession.

By letter, Mme. Necker had told the hotelmaster that she must ask 100 napoleons for three months. Pictet had also written, inviting Lord B. "and any friend" to go with him at eight to Mme. Einard. We decided to go, but first of all (so much for my assumptions about the Villa Diodati) went to inspect some other houses, all found wanting, and Lord B. beginning to foam at the mouth a bit. On our return, Mr. Percy Shelley came and invited us to join him for dinner, but we debated about a previous commitment and agreed to dine with him on the morrow. Walking with him awhile, we stepped into his boat to sample it, even though the wind was blustery and made little waves. We saw Hentsch the banker, who said to Lord B., "Sire, when I spoke with you yesterday, I had no idea that I was addressing one of the most famous lords in all England." Milord smiled. The foam fell away from his mouth. "It has been said," he answered, "that Buonaparte when praying actually said aloud, 'I am addressing one of the most famous deities in all heaven.'" An impromptu riposte, it sounded like sarcastic parody, but Hentsch took it in good part, roared politely, and Lord B.'s ample smile seemed generously to withdraw it.

Chez Mme. Einard, we trod into a room of eight men and two ladies. They announced and showed Lord B. but made no mention of Polly, his Polidori, *as if* (I set it down in my journal for Murray to read) *I were a star in the halo of the moon*, invisible, and again my feeble role was to appreciate and savor others higher-born, wondering if I would ever join some rabble and do my best to have them beheaded one after the other with dirty old women knitting close to the spillage. I could see whence this other, almost-military fever came: not the typhoid kind but the kind that guillotined. As Lord B. essayed a couple of words of his bad French and gave up, forcing M. Einard into bad Italian, I spoke a little with a Signor Rossi, who had joined Murat at Bologna; a decent, upright sort, admirer of Dante, not of Ariosto so much, he held forth about manliness in language, as distinct from effeminate prancing, and then he confided to me, with some little disappointment in his eye, that the women of Geneva were "amazingly chaste even in their thoughts." I had rather been hoping otherwise, I told him, and he laughed, asking if I were in pursuit of "the local Venus Pandemos," who had no thoughts at all save of venery and money. "Only in the most manly, professional way," I told him. "I like to keep abreast of the incurable," which set him cough-laughing over Mme. Einard's teacups. We took sugar with our fingers, then viewed some of Mme. Einard's historical pieces done in *acquerella:* rather good, really, but a little too fussy, too Franco-exquisite for the taste of a crude, unnoticed physician. We had to leave before ten or have the gates shut against us, but not before Rossi had given me an address where researches of a lower order might be undertaken for a fee. On the way home, Lord B. told me an old joke about the sugar: how some upstart hostess had questioned the use of tongs and had been told that the gentlemen in even the finest company were never too scrupulous about washing their hands after handling themselves in the lavatory, so at her next tea party she placed tongs in the jakes to turn them fastidious. Lord B. roared at this, he the teller, while I, I nodded hospitably as at all his many manly lines. I would very much have enjoyed having my name said aloud to the assembled gentry, as if I were at least a fox, a maggot, or even a well-qualified physician. I knew from that day on that, if I were ever to come down with some fatal disease, with only weeks to live, I would first of all go about cutting throats or dispensing poison. To all who had treated me amiss, and could be reached, I would say my lethal adieu, beginning perhaps with Mr. Shelley.

Or not. He did at least introduce me to Mary Wollstonecraft Godwin; I was *presented*. He called her "Mrs. Shelley," and I wondered how giving she might be in bed—not quite so hot, I reckoned, as Lord B.'s Claire, who seemed an importunate, forward woman, easily navigated but not so easily sent packing. She had glue in her.

"Doctor Polidori," he said, "having no biography of his own, has been chosen to write mine. Yours next, my dear." Mary, however, for all her demented looks—a strong wind seemed always blowing through her mind, her features—was only nineteen, a few months my junior, and therefore an object of some gentleness on my part. She and I might have been sister and brother, and she felt interested enough in me to speak to me of her Scotch girlhood on what she called "the blank and dreary northern shores of the Tay, near Dundee," as she recollected them, taking pains, however, to say that in her younger years those shores had been the landscape of her mental freedom, where she conversed with the creatures she imagined. "I was not confined to my own identity," she said, "and I was not really as interested in myself as in the beings I invented. I was fancy's child, truly." This was better than not being introduced; she was talking about herself in a wholly unaffected fashion, not for effect or in gaseous bombast. She would be twenty in August, and I was not to know how much alone she would be as Lord B. and his parasite Shelley went off on this or that excursion: the sun and the wind off touring together in hopes of building a storm.

We talked of literature, she and I, of romances and the Gothick, I telling her of the Polidori formula for converting romance into Gothick. "Instead of *house*," I told her, "write *castle*. For *bower* put *cavern*, for *sigh* write *groan*, and so forth. Father becomes giant, fan becomes bloodstained dagger, telling glances become assassins, an old retainer becomes a fearsome monk, compliments and sentiments turn into skulls and skeletons, any attorney or usurer turns into a gliding ghost, and all marriages into midnight murders. Redingotes become suits of armor, haughty lords become demons from desolate moorlands, and young doctors become insane scientific experimenters, bringing corpses back to life." She chortled quickly, little knowing I had culled these ideas, some of them, from a satirical poem of the age, whose footnotes explained how to transmute a novel into a romance. All I had done was to reverse the order, but clearly the shift made me more interesting, and no one had heard of the poem anyway. Polidori was giving it a new lease of life. Perhaps things were looking up, what with our Scotch connexion and divers matters of intellectual interest that we shared and might, no doubt, pursue on other occasions. Indeed, without being attracted to her in the fleshly way, I found her something ethereally apposite for me, a mind-goddess, for I had always sought to worship where I ended up, alas, like Lord B., tupping or thinking loathsome vulgarities. She was a mind, a soul, to awe me and convert me to purer ways, although Shelley was no doubt corrupting her fast.

Hey-ho, then, I lived in a more populous world, although perhaps not for long, obliged on the one hand to put up with milord's caustic references to a former doctor of his, Dr. Romanelli, privileged on the other to regale Mary with the sports of my mind and memory. Lord B. now spoke not so much to me as past me, with Shelley on the other side, so all the things he might have addressed to me grazed my face only on their way to Percy Bysshe, whom I privately named Percy Bitch. It was like being the personage who in one of Shakespeare's plays impersonates a wall, in which there happens to be a chink for lovers to talk through, the chink being two fingers parted.

Chez Mme. Einard, an encore, in the course of which I looked at her picture of a cave in the Jura where in winter there was no ice, in summer an abundance of it. How Byronic. No one was announced or introduced. We might have been glaciers. You spoke with whomever it pleased you to, and when. Which was better, I wondered, a world in which no one knew you because you yourself were never introduced, or a world in which no one knew you because no one else was introduced? We talked with a certain anonymous civility, charmed by the novelty. For once, Lord B. was a man of the people, the man next door.

Gradually a new style of life established itself, I taking tea with Lord B., Shelley, and the two women, the menu usually science on toast. Lord B. and S. went on about politics the whole time, unless about the spiteful poet Samuel Rogers, whom B. ridiculed ("how horridly he carves turbot"). It had been Rogers who asked Lord B. to fight a duel for him against some Ward who had insulted him in print. In the end he and Rogers meditated a journey up to Cumberland together. "How do you mean to travel?" said Rogers to him. "Oh, with four horses," Lord B. answered, and Rogers went forthwith to company and slandered him, saying, "It is strange to hear a man talking of four horses who seals his letters with a tallow candle." Such bloodsuckers abounded in the literary world in which they moved, and that was perhaps why they all lived on a knife's edge, ever alert for the next insult, whereas if they had even for a day lived the life of Polidori-in-the-corner, they might have sobered up, been glad to be addressed at all, never mind how insultingly.

On the lake once, while rowing (*I* did the work), I struck Lord B. on the kneepan, rather violently since it was my wont to work hard at such chores, and he, without a word, turned his face away to hide the pain in it. Lord B. was a stoic if nothing else. After the pain abated (I had gone on rowing, with Lord B. well out of the way), he at last spoke to me, as if I were Samuel Rogers, the reviled villain of another piece.

"Be so kind, Polidori, another time, to take more care, for you hurt me very much."

Without thinking, for my mind was on the rowing and I had already converted sorrow for what I had done into anger that he not only made me row but failed to keep clear when I did, I said, "I am glad of it." It would teach him a lesson, I thought, that he would remember. It had been a way of introducing Lord B. to my world.

"I am glad," I went on, "to see you can suffer pain." In other words, I was not dealing with a god after all.

Visibly calming and suppressing himself, Lord B. took deep breaths, then said in a tone of vinegar, "Let me advise you, Polidori, when you, another time, hurt anyone, not to express your satisfaction. People don't like to be told that those who give them pain are glad of it, and they cannot always command their anger. Indeed, it was with some difficulty that I refrained from throwing you into the water; but for Mrs. Shelley's presence, I should probably have done some such rash thing." It was the schoolmarm tone that irked me most. I had spoken in heat and exertion. When you are rowing several people, you do not have the beef or the breath to polish your utterances, as anyone conversant with the rowing classes would have known. You say what you have gusto for. Such tiffs should appear in my journal, I thought, but not my intimate responses, since the journal was to be about Lord B., not about myself. Yet that would, literally, be only half the battle. Later, I asked him to show me the hurt knee, but he refused, saying something about lordly knees' not bending. And besides, not long after this incident, he had cheered up sufficiently to sing an Albanian folk song. *"Bo, bo, bo, bo, bo, bo"* (six bo's, I remembered), *"Naciarura, popuso, / Naciarura na civin / Ha pen derini ti hin."* It was like Waterloo all over again. What he sang meant, roughly, "Lo, lo, I come, I come; be thou silent. I come, I run; open the door that I may enter." I always rejoiced when Lord B. consoled himself by calling on some nation's intellectual high points. Perhaps the song improved. He had told me of one in which the singer wonders why Albanian men had such lovely buckskins whereas their womenfolk had nothing under their little yellow boots and slippers "but a well-turned and sometimes very white ankle." In one song he had found an echo of Socrates, who himself had allowed his arm to touch one of his *hypokolpioi,* Critobulus or Cleobulus, and felt a shooting pain in his arm for days afterwards. The moral, Lord B. said, was never to touch downwards—socially, that was, or intellectually. In that event I had touched upwards, a Promethean inferior, and I wondered who should feel the pain. Lord

B. did, obviously, so both Socrates and the Albanian bard were vindicated. I had broken a genetic law, *bo, bo, bo*. Bo-hoo for poor Polly, the wild man of Lake Leman. A wind getting up almost drove us against the piles, but Polidori's muscle worked again, and all was saved. It was not everyone who had a surgeon for a skivvy, and it were better, I thought, that he should hire someone else for these duties, reserving his Polly for lively banter with the Shelleys about idealism and other fripperies. If our heads were to swim with gilded rhetoric and ghoulish galvanical thoughts, then someone else should row. And so, eventually, it turned out, with Lord B.'s acquisition of Maurice, both vain and handsome, the pet of all the Lake Leman English, a Byronist born, calling Lord B. "milor." But that was later, after milord had settled down more. In any case, he had Berger, the Swiss he had brought with him from London; the point about Lord B. was that he needed retainers, and he had them, whereas Polidori was both travelling companion, professional expert, and odd-job socialite as well. Not a role so much as a bouquet. If he managed to take the Diodati instead of the villa being touted by Mme. Necker, widow of the old Minister of Finance, he would need all kinds of help both to move him and to minister to the grounds. Polidori was something that did not exist: a doctor to their minds, their moods, their hubris sacs.

Breakfasting and dining with the Shelleys reminded me how much I admired *Queen Mab;* he was a swift, infatuating talker, full of mystical insinuations that drew us away from everyday entanglement and released us into unworldly dimensions, unsuspected untrodden ways. Lord B. was sure of certain things, such as evil and matter, whereas Shelley contended that the whole of Creation was spirit to which, in his inimitable and excitable way, he wanted to add some almost mathematical abstract idea of love and beauty. He meant spirit pervaded, as it was not in the suave formulations of Bishop Berkeley (to whom he alluded), by some lovable aloofness capable of being read as a mental substitute for God. Alas, I was always asking him to be more precise, as a physician should when grappling with a poet and a metaphysician, so much so that Mary would ask me to desist, saying, "No, let Shelley speak" and "Don't spoil his flow." It was as if I never belonged in their conversations, being as they thought an amateur writer even if a professional doctor. Shelley I found soothing, rather like chamber music, although I never ended up agreeing with him. He got so worked up, so inflamed, that you had to distrust what he said since it set out to overbalance the minds of his listeners.

"Yes, what *is* it, Polidori?" Lord B. would say as I asked my innocent questions. "Must we forever have a costermonger among us, crying the price of his cabbages when we are involved with the mighty infinitudes of Man and God? Peace, Polly. Let us ponder." How many times he had to say that, I had no idea; after once, I would leave the table and go outside to contemplate the lake or the Alps, wishing with all my heart I had been born with the divine right to snub those who, although awkward in their conjectural formulations or their abrupt, earthy questions, were nonetheless sincere: children of an uncouth god. I was not, however, and was not going to be. I was one who tagged along, for whatever reason, while the intellectual House of Atreus vexed itself further with questions to which there could never be answers but only shimmering, homesick hypotheses. Polidori winced every dinnertime, whereas breakfast was less sedate and I sometimes got away with what seemed to them my one and only question: "Do you not, then, think I have some legitimate hope of becoming an author?" They stared and giggled, then said their patronizing yesses. I should have gone outside and injured myself, leaping from a height or skidding into the pitch-black lake, just to get them to register me on the plane of humanity heartbroken.

What saddened me even more was that Mary, in some ways my ally and sympathizer, never took my part when Shelley was present, seeming not to realize that Shelley was a lustrous and somewhat histrionic windbag, Lord B. a pawnbroker of others' motives, and yet gullible as only hard-boiled androgynes can be, whereas I

was one whose response to things dictated how I saw them. I muti-
lated the world according to how I felt about it, as other doctors
have. It was one thing to know the ills the stomach was prey to, but
another to *feel* about those ills. Shelley felt about the universe, never
anything less, Byron about the Rialto and the Alps and the lake,
whereas I felt about the *corpus humanum,* the necessity of having a
perishable and morbid body: the fleshly hull for the spirit's sail. My
life I had consecrated to the well-being of the bones and meat, the
viscera and skin, as noble a destiny as a man could have, but these
three, among whom Miss Clairmont was the quietest although possibly not the least dangerous, floated through the empyrean like well-
bred feathers.

When I had a chance to talk more intimately with Shelley,
when he had me on my own, he filled me up with tales of his
upbringing and childhood. He had gone through intense misery,
thinking he was dying. He had married a girl merely to let her
inherit his money. Then he got better and could reclaim nothing. He
paid Godwin's debts and then seduced his daughter. He begat a child.
At fourteen he published a novel for thirty pounds. His second work
earned him a hundred. He always drank tea, always would, he said.
Something farouche and foxlike came out of him and circled round
him. Then Lord B., to whom I recounted much of this, feeling for
once the centre of narratorial attention, poo-hooed it all, saying,
"He is romancing you, Polly. Remember the novelist in him. He
sees you as easy meat. His novel *Zastrozzi* came out when he was
seventeen or eighteen. For *St. Irvyne* he got nothing like a hundred.
That was for something called *A Poetical Essay on the Existing State
of Things*—a most Shelleyan title, if I may say so. Published for the
benefit of the Irish agitator Finnerty. It did indeed earn some hundred pounds, so he told me. Take what he says with a plateful of
salt, dear fellow. He does not live, mentally speaking, among ordinary mortals. To him dyspepsia is a god moving through. Death is
icing on the cake of life. A burning coal to him is an ingot from the
poetic mind. He is polite to God and pious towards women."

Shelley, it was clear to me, was yet another sample of rich

lunacy. Betrothed as a boy to a cousin, he ended up being left by another for his atheism. He lent a friend, Godwin, some two thousand pounds, who would not come near him later, when Shelley was starving. His father had tried to consign him to a madhouse when he was just a boy at Eton, and only strenuous efforts by a Dr. Lind, the Eton physicist, rescued him from an unthinkable fate. I thought of dry little Shelley among the mouthing and raving maniacs, but then decided he must have frightened them to death anyway. When, in Mary's presence, he spoke of her father, Godwin, he suppressed his name, but it was clear who took his two thousand and then snubbed him. "The bleeding cut," he called it, meaning someone who had bled him dry, then cut him dead. What Shelley had done to Godwin was apply his antimatrimonial theories to Godwin's own daughter, and that had not sat too well with the philosopher. The Shelleys were scandalous to begin with, he having deserted his wife and run off with Mary to this very Switzerland, on their return from which the full brunt of censure had descended upon them. I felt a certain antagonistic sympathy for the pair, but also that they required too much attention, he especially, full of his unregenerate naughtiness. Ideas excited him. Then he lived on the excitement and forgot the true impact of the idea. That was Shelley, with whom Lord B. was becoming increasingly enchanted; indeed, he had begun to change milord's thinking on several issues, making him more mystical and less sceptical, so much so that I missed Byron the war-dog of old, the born suspicioner, the no-nonsense rake.

In the great world of Geneva they were at last mending the roads, having for the first time in years come up with the money. A young girl of eighteen died suddenly, prey no doubt to some fever roaming through, perhaps the one Dr. de Roche had mentioned. One was always awaiting the next inexplicable disaster: life was short, we were all young, and inevitably one of us would fall first, be the first to taste the universe's full dose of disenchantment. I was feeling more wanted, at least professionally. One day, June second, I breakfasted with Shelley, in my usual mood of twinned elation and resentment, then read some Tasso with Mary, who was a born reader, and then took their infant son, William, for a vaccination, a service I could not myself perform, not having the vaccine. This beloved child was not yet half a year old, so that vaccinating him was almost like abusing an idea still in the mind of God. In return I got a gold chain and a seal from the one I sometimes disdainfully referred to as "an Englishman," especially in letters home. I never told my family that I had encountered and was virtually living en famille with the mad atheist Shelley, sent down from Oxford for his religious beliefs—or his lack of them. I could feel my life settling down: to be sure, not exactly as I would have wished it, but I discerned the beginning of a social milieu in which I might fit, as only an impressionable twenty-year-old can, green and fumbling, no nearer to social standing than to equanimity with God. I was learning to spread myself out, going one day in search of Rossi, another, Roche, glad to be rid of Byron and Shelley for a time, letting my overtaxed mind whirl away while watching lads and lasses of the village dance to tabor and drum, doing waltzes and cotillons, as if nothing in Switzerland were serious. While milord busied himself with matters of *moving in,* setting up house, linen and plate, I explored the environs and the city proper, one day actually presenting myself at the address given me by Rossi, being welcomed in, offered a glass of wine while making my selection from among the quite unworn beauties on display, and then having a royal tup, upstairs, in the capable hands of Mlle. Saxonnex, first name Gabrielle, Gaby to me. Of rather broad and stout build, she had long pliant hands and a small mouth that opened much wider than you would think. I was quite smitten with her as she praised my manliness and then, after she had ferreted out of me that I was a physician, my intellect. I simply had to examine her, she said, but I promised to do it better next time; I would bring my bag, I said. As it was, I did pass a cursory and inflamed close look over her parts, those smeary gelatinous folds glazed by my recent effusions, and found them both wanting and wanting. Next time, I vowed, I would use a cundum borrowed from Byron if I must (how he would cackle) and bring a glass, some lemon acid, and a little opium. In almost the same breath, or gaze, I thought of the little child William and how, only recently, he had arrived by means of this same passage in Mary, and it was as if all parts of all women came together, and all children. I felt immersed in the world, and more than a little taken by my mercenary Gaby Saxonnex. All a man had to do was take a coach to Dover, cross, then travel along those appalling roads until he found a billet for his appetite in Geneva, at the age of twenty. So easy to do. How few did it. I felt all of a sudden *brought up,* but putting none of this in my journal. John Murray's interest in Polidori's loins must at least be limited.

Bad for myself, I was already fantasizing how I would become an inspector at this discreet house, ridding the ladies of this or that, advising them on matters physical and mental, making myself indispensable, but most of all to one who was already my favourite. In no time at all I would be the venereal match of both Lord B. and Percy Bitch. I could see myself inviting them to accompany me for an afternoon's sport, counselling them about the special aptitudes of this or that lady. I saw us all three in one vast bed together with as many women of the night, a veritable Laocoön of lust. After all, my duties already included the appraisal of Lord B.'s member, so I might well extend them to include Shelley and the women, all with the correct degree of impersonal affinity. This would be my private and illustrious practice even as I widened my clientele to include the best English families in Geneva, curbing their colds, healing their bunions, hearing their overstuffed hearts, and in general behaving quite unlike the twenty-year-old I was, of whom they would soon be saying, "Mature beyond his years, my dear, quite extraordinary at the bedside and with his hands." Polidori might have a future in Geneva yet, free to test his theories of the electric on both the living and the dead. All I needed was a *population,* none too healthy, and suitable premises in some commonplace back street.

I dined with Shelley, as often, then went off to the lake with all of them, saw their admirable house, which Mary called their cottage, and, coming back, quite surrendered my senses and my incipient mystical side to the chiaroscura of the sunset, the rosy flush on the one side, the black mass of the mountains on the other, the wreathlike mist forming on the hills, the stars emerging against that indefinable blue-grey incapable of darkening. The dome of heaven where the moon slid, spilling light upon the lake, seemed oval. We landed at ten and drank tea, as always with the Shelleys. And talked about the nature of God into the small hours—was God immanent or apart? Did God's nature change ever? Pantheism and panentheism. High-sounding words. Was madness divine? Was God a madman? Before becoming too sleepy to continue, I argued that the conditions of human life—being born unconsulted and therefore obliged to die —were such that madness was the only natural result, which meant that, *mutatis mutandis,* all humans were mad. It was only a matter of degree. There was in all of us a stoical component that varied, and the degree of madness varied with it. "A damned namby-pamby theory," Byron called it, but Shelley said he could see my point, although he wondered what part reason played in my theory. Mary nodded by candlelight, her mind on something else, more terrific perhaps, wondering what horror would assail her next, what menace from behind the sun.

On June 3, English Day, we all went to Pictet's and, on the evening of the next day, to a musical evening at Mme. Odier's, where she herself (president of this little musical society, some dozen members) read a memoir on the following theme: whether a physician should inform a lover of his beloved's state of health, or indeed anything else both secret but pertinent. I spoke myself out on this, until tea, being one of the doctors present, another being Dr. Gardner, who came along with me in the calèche. Mme. Odier had invited me to attend her soirée every Wednesday, and I once again had the feeling of belonging, so far from home (this being either Scotland or Italy), and so many years short of my maturity, whatever the fond ladies and gentlemen of my premature medical dreams said of me. In contrast, however, or perhaps because of my mounting social *réclame* (after all, no one ever said *Doctor* Byron or *Doctor*

Shelley), the two of them had waxed rather spiteful, more than usual. They laughed at me all the more for having confided in them my attachment to Gaby Saxonnex, whom I had referred to as a young lady of emiment station, a Swiss Alsatian. I had prospects, I told them, and they giggled, Lord B.—who seemed to know everything about everybody—saying "He means a percentage, Shelley." One day, Shelley and I had a race of sorts, the lake being calm, although the day was dreary and threatened rain, as that summer so many days had. The objective was to be first across. There being no judge, Shelley declared himself the winner, a claim I roundly disputed, whereupon he sneered something about "a whore's helmsman," then laughed again, accusing me of being cross-eyed from the pox, a theme that Lord B. then took up, asserting that I had "an Alsatian bitch to keep me on the leash, whom we have not met because anyone with a coin can meet her any hour of the night. Ha."

"I challenge you forthwith," I said to Shelley. "I will work upon your carcass the many feelings of this moment." How stilted it sounded, but surely it was the formal language of honour as best I could remember it, never having needed it until then. Shelley giggled, as often, and Byron broke in, saying, "Wait, Polly. Recollect if you will that though Shelley here has some scruples about duelling, *I* have none and shall be, at all times, ready to take his place. If you challenge him, you challenge me."

"My quarrel is with Shelley," I told him. "Let him stand up for himself."

"He giggles too much to stand up for anybody," Byron said. " 'Twill have to be me. Choose your weapons, Doctor."

"Fiddlesticks," I said. "Shelley or no one."

"Behold what a terror I have become." Now Lord B. began to laugh too. "Can we all settle down now? Mary and Claire will be wondering what has become of us."

I dropped the matter, saddened by the low opinion they seemed to have of me, loathing me because I wanted some kind of life for myself, a modicum of respect even if I was at the beginning of my own literary career. I remembered that awful thing Lord B.

had said to me on the Rhine when I had asked him, "After all, milord, what is there you can do that I cannot?" He varied the answer. "Why, since you force me to say, I think there are three things I can do which you cannot, Polly. I can swim across this lake —I can snuff out that lightbuoy with a pistol shot at the distance of twenty paces—and I have written a poem of which fourteen thousand copies were sold in one day." He then shot out the lightbuoy, proving his point. I challenged him to swim the lake forthwith, and he refused, and I corrected him that *The Corsair* had sold more like *ten* thousand on the day. Ever after, when his mood was foul and he had a pistol handy, he would ask me to ask him what he could do that I could not.

"Yes," I told him in a huff. "There is one thing you can do that I cannot. You can save Shelley from his defective sense of honour."

"Polidori beds down with Alsatians," Byron jeered. "Shall we to home?"

As we clambered back onto land at the other side, I overheard him saying to Shelley, "He is just the sort of person to whom, if he fell overboard, one would hold out a straw to know if the adage be true that drowning men catch at straws." I said nothing in retort, but I saved the remark for perusal later. I knew the two of them were planning a tour of the lake without me, as if they were somehow jealous of my social life, the natural vivacity I felt when someone such as Mme. Odier made me welcome. I resolved to tell Gaby that night, knowing how she would upbraid them from a distance. She did, but without the combustive empathy I expected; instead, she soothed me with her body, taking no one's part in the dispute, but telling me not to race again. "A lake is a lake," she said gamely. "Who cares which side is which?" I inhaled her perfume—attar of rose, I thought—and told myself that anyone under twenty-one (not she, by five years) should be judged not by his excesses but by his openness of heart.

This kind of ridicule had another side. I had already learned
better than to extol my Gaby's virtues, especially her physical ones,
such as the way her lips appeared to bulge and bloom, as if stung by
bees, and the exquisitely cut top of their ample rose. The point
immediately beneath the septum was a miracle of blending and con-
touring; it stood out, yet it conformed with the rest. Instead of
talking about such things, I had learned to Byronize, although it
must be said that, in secret, he longed for his half-sister Augusta and
felt on her behalf acute contortions of the spirit, having in his trappings what looked like her death mask, but it was made from the
life. This he either wore in order to look at himself in a glass or
forced against the face of the drab he used on this or that occasion.
My own theory was that, as much as a sign of his needing his
Augusta, this was a sign of his longing to possess himself physically,
wishing his yard were long enough to bend round the corner and
reach his bum.

One evening, as the glowering skies permitted a brief interlude
of sun that burst from the dark grey like a bolt from heaven, turning
a precisely limited zone of the topmost foliage into golden tracery, I
tried regaling Lord B. and Shelley with altogether more coarse accounts of my doings, larding my narrative with tavern words they
might relish, using *chair* for penis or flesh, *cordial* for semen, and
bower for vagina. This cheered them up no end: at last Polly was
talking the language of men. "Ah, what a *Mater Omnium*" I told
them, "full of cordial and sluices. I have never known the like. All
from exercise. Never has my *kit* been so erect, so taut, so wrinkled,
as when *stifling* that *clack*. No sooner goes my *rod* among her *feathers*
than I yearn to spend." I even made a fairly standard pun about
"Cony stone water," a covert allusion to Conistone Water the lake,
but then intended to say "pudendum testes semen." I felt ashamed to
be thus diminishing her to her crudest attributes, but it was the only
way into their attentions; nor did she know, and, after all, she was a
woman of the streets; it was no choir girl whose lascivious aspect I
was making public in so encoded a fashion. Lord B. and Shelley
laughed out loud, mainly, I thought, at the spectacle of their Polly

talking such filth, little realizing that Polly had other tricks up his sleeve, sometimes during the act of love imagining himself with the pepper (the clap) or with his nail being severed by some insane whore with a knife, or even leeches all over my parts, drawing from me both fluids that mattered. There were ways of making keener the journey through *vallis lucis,* less the vale of light than that of sluices.

Indeed, my Gaby, not knowing English beyond a few primal words of urging, not these, would laugh when I used them to her during business, thinking I uttered them to excite myself whereas I used them mainly to confirm to my inmost part what I was engaged in doing, as if in mesmerized surprise, as if doing some bookkeeping on the job. When, at length, I explained in a fit of postcoital exuberance, she chortled in that deep voice of hers (German, I always thought it) and made as if to memorize the words, most of all those she could best pronounce. Then I realized she was storing them up for use with other clients. I sometimes clean forgot that she had other customers, to whom, doubtless, she was just as faithless as to me, with whom she was just as expert at tweaking and tamping, as if all men were one and their respective kits were one, to which night-long she addressed herself with anchoritic zeal. The important thing, I told myself, having now embedded myself in such rough-and-ready venery, was to cultivate some mental image of unassailable purity to think of during our sessions of puddle and nail. Or even some real lady of unimpeachable virtue on whom to dote medieval fashion: not Miss Arrow, lost amidst the bazaars of India, though her long-gone image served almost as a crucifix, but some august delight who quoted poetry and thought continually of flowers.

Not Mme. Odier, but a younger incarnation: some belle, with or without *merci,* who knew her way through the salons and the soirées, whom I might parade on my arm with a debonair smile. It was time to be infatuated, as Byron with his half-sister, as Shelley with his imitation wife; and, if not with an individual, then at least with the flesh itself. Perhaps I was going to the devil without knowing it, but I was at least walking away from milord's *pronunciamento* that "Poets are for each other." Couched in my lonely bed in Di-

odati, I had heard Lord B. and his Claire at their labors: the crashing
of furniture, the rhythm of the bed, her screams and his huzzahs,
then the long silence of quiescence until a muttering broke it, and
began again to go on all the night, keeping Fletcher awake too, I
didn't doubt, accustomed as the valet was to the racket. If that was
love, I would take mine elsewhere, like someone going to the jakes.
I wanted my depravity to be private, except on the plane of vocabulary; and, down in a distant dell of my whoresome itinerary, I could
see a role in such doings for ether and opium, leeches and vitriol,
when the palate jaded and the member-kit wearied of doing. None
of this I confided to anyone, and I suddenly realized that I had
planned to make a stay in Geneva, whatever milord intended, and to
make of it some temporary home.

For the time I revelled in what I had, and this included my
quarters in Diodati, of which I drew a diagram in my journal, little
though the entry would please my employer Murray. *My rooms are
so,* I wrote:

Picture Gallery	
Bedroom	

To have things so neat pleased me somewhat. It was better than
floating from hotel to hotel and having my bones dislocated in this
carriage or that. I knew what I was coming home to, at least within
the confines of my sketch. The unpleasurable side, however, now
included pains in my loins and a languor in my bones, requiring
frequent administrations of certain substances. At Mme. Odier's we
got onto the subject of somnambulism, oddly enough the theme of
my Edinburgh thesis: *Disputatio Medica Inauguralis de Oneirodynia,*
and I wondered always, after writing it, if I too wandered at night
in search of God knew what, under the devil's impetus. The English

at Odier's had wide-open mouths and glowing eyes; one might as well, I wrote later, *make a tour of the Isle of Dogs*. The Genevois were quite different: witty and forthright, as nimble to agree as not. Besides, the English talked only among themselves, an island indeed. As I left, Odier gave me several articles he himself had translated and edited, especially those on somnambulism, hoping for my opinion.

Was I at last beginning to thrive? Only last year I had printed my treatise on somnambulism, although it had sold many fewer copies than that damned *Corsair* or indeed that Irish thing of Shelley's. (If there were somnambulists at Diodati, then both were crippled, milord from birth, and I ever since my new habit of falling, falling, down.) I was writing poems and prose, although chary of showing same to the local company. I had myself a leman (lame joke I kept to myself until this) and a long narrow room in which to read Lucian, Tasso, and divers bits of pornography. Lord B. had taken the Villa Diodati for six months, and I could see him extending the lease, although I could not see him taking the voracious Claire, Mary's half-sister, off to Italy. That lady, I predicted, would receive her marching orders long before then. My duties became more onerous, requiring me to read inventory and examine Berger's accounts, as well as keep an eye on Maurice, the new boatman, who claimed it had been Napoleon who had made him father all his children—so as to meet his demand for recruits; but he had been able to work at normal pace only, having failed to breed twins. I wrote home, then to Shelley, renewing my challenge. It was so odd to have literary and philosophical conversation with him all day but be ready to shoot him in a duel. Time and again I wrote down my challenge, and all he ever did was laugh, if he heeded me at all. It must have been his tea that made him so several-minded, quite separating the Polidori of the lake encounter from the one with whom he dined. If I sobbed from time to time in bed, under the sheets, it was not owing to that or to him; it was more a reflection of my homesickness, my still not having that which would make every second glow with light. I longed for joy; I got contentment only. That was why, sometimes, unable to sleep, I drove my hand hard against a sharp and

solid splinter that stuck out from the frame of the bed, pressing and
shoving, each night a little deeper until I bled and had to take
measures. I needed to prove to myself that I was *alive:* a Byronic
notion—to feel that he existed, even though in pain. Surely he
would have kissed the blood away, and perhaps he had during one
of his midnight excursions, stealing into my bedroom and crouching
at my hand to lap its blood while I slept, almost vampyrelike. He
was welcome. He was just as likely to cross the room in the half-
light and embrace the anatomical figure I carried with me, upon
which all the muscles and blood vessels stood forth in hideous yellow and maroon colours, the whole seeming to have been flayed.
Alas for him, it had no orifices, nor indeed any viscera, but gleamed
there like some gargoyle imp, tempting the viewer to take it seriously and advance towards it, hand or tongue outstretched.

Had anyone been looking hard (or caring), they would have
witnessed the debut of the social Polidori: Polidori *coming out.* On
June twelfth, for example, it being a Wednesday, I rode to town,
entered a subscription in my name at the circulating library, and in
the evening attended Mme. Odier's, alas finding no one of surpassing
interest. As we waited, Mlle. Odier played for us the "Ranz des
Vaches," *plaintive and warlike,* as I wrote later. Perhaps it had an
effect because people began arriving soon after, as if she had summoned them forth from within their cheeses and cuckoo clocks. I
still had chance to confab with Dr. Odier about priapism, not that
he or I suffered from it, but we knew of one or two who did. The
pain of it we agreed on, but not on the potions to prescribe. Dances
began during our talk, waltzes and cotillions, French and English
country-dances. For the first time I shook my feet to a French measure, and very pleasurably. I was young enough to dance, old
enough to notice how the English, no doubt affected by a summer
so English, stayed put, just frowning. I met Mrs. Slaney, who invited me for the next night. You asked to dance without having first
been introduced, and the girls simply refused the men they disliked
the look of. This went on until midnight. I went and slept at the
Balance. Rode home the next day, then into town again, to the ball

at Mrs. Slaney's, musing to myself that my Gaby must wonder what had become of me, especially after my paying her with the watch Lord B. had bought me, then the gold chain and seal from Shelley. I danced endlessly, with agile formality (I hoped), then played at chess to cool down. Outside, lightning and thunder had arrived, and I got wet, then doubly wet after getting lost, on my way to the Balance on foot. The police proved to be my final guides: helpful, drenched, and very Swiss. Next day I rode home and then, to vary things, rode almost all day, then dined with Rossi, my arbiter of venery, whose company I thrived in. On the fifteenth I rose late (Byronic habit), began some letters, then walked down to Shelley's, came home for dinner, after which it rained hard. What a summer! Lord B. and I were standing on his balcony when we espied Mary trotting gamely up the slope to Diodati, and Lord B. said, in his roughest man-of-the-world tone, "Now, Polly, you who wish to be a fine lady's gallant, jump down—it is not far—and offer her your arm. What if she were to slip?" I was eager, of course, and leaped down; I would gladly have escorted Scotch Mary up the Calvary of life and gone to the cross for her on certain days; but, as I landed, having ill-judged the site of my arrival, I slipped on the wet ground and sprained my left ankle, to her genuine dismay. Her knight-at-arms was down. To cheer me, they all talked of my play and set its value at naught, Lord B. in particular reading passages aloud with an exaggerated Cockney accent that made havoc of my most solemn dignities. He was paying me back again. One thing he could do (not *I*) was hurt me.

The house became a hospital, my foot went up on a pillow on a sofa, and Polidori's social life began to endure a cramp. Lord B. was so solicitous that I said what I later on regretted: "Well, I did not know you had so much feeling." Not the best of remarks. Not even, I supposed, an average remark, but, in view of all he had said about being willing to blow my brains out on behalf of Shelley, about letting the drowning Polidori grasp for straws—all that impromptu hatred—I felt little remorse. Lord B. sometimes deserved

what he got, and he only rarely got what he deserved. What if Sir
Walter Raleigh had slipped on laying down his cape: would they
have laughed at *him?* Whatever I did, they regarded me as the
author of two plays, *Cajetan* and *Boadicea,* both of which they
thought swamp-poor fustian, and that was that. I was among the
damned for my prose and verse; and, of course, Byron was a Cambridge man and Shelley an Oxford man, and that made a difference
too. I thought, on my bed of pain, about the highfalutin arrogance
of the "men" those ancient universities produced, born to look
down their noses at everyone. Cambridge men lisped. *Cambwidge
men lithped.* Oxford men pobbled, which is to say spoke with a
pompous gobbling sound from the bottom of the mouth, so much so
that they remained incomprehensible except to one another.

Byron, I knew, had either a club-foot or a deformed leg; perhaps the oddity I had discerned in the foot was the result of walking
with a deformed leg. Lord B.'s habitual gait was more of a rapid,
sliding slither than anything, and I had noticed how quickly he
entered a room, almost at the run, as if simulating precipitate eagerness. Then he stopped himself suddenly by planting his left foot (the
better of the two, medically speaking) firmly on the floor in a silent
stamp, and remained thus for quite a while. Out of doors he had
none of the indolent lounge, both languid and effete, of the fashion-
able *flâneur,* but rather a lubricated-looking traipse, exactly what
you would expect of someone trying to walk on just the toes and
balls of his feet. From my own observation, the right foot was long
and slender, although contorted, and I thought of the story I had
heard from Shelley that, in his early youth, Lord B.'s mother had
taken him to a certain Sheldrake in London, all the way from Aber-
deen, but had taken him to the wrong one: not Sheldrake the instrument maker but Sheldrake the quack, who had rooms hard by.
When Lord B. eventually found out about the mistake, just before
setting off for his travels in Albania, he hastened to see Sheldrake the
True, allowing him to make a plaster cast of the defective foot. At
any rate, professionally speaking, I had some time ago arrived at my
own diagnosis—spastic paraplegia brought on, I suspect at birth, by

some haemorrhage on the surface of the infant's brain, the result of a delay in the onset of respiration. Part of his cerebral cortex has thus been injured, and the voluntary movement of his limbs was severely affected. He was prey to rigid spasms. Up he went on his toes, with his knees tightly pressed together. The little boy had been born in Dover, to which town his mother had hastened back from Boulogne for the confinement. Her pains began during the crossing. Lord B. was lucky not to be born at sea, in fact. Between his first few seconds of life and his thirteenth year, little was attempted and all was lost: treated by Drs. Hunter, Livingstone, Baillie, and Laurie, and the quacks Lavender and Sheldrake, Lord B. also suffered, in my view, from fits or seizures, instants when something amiss in the cortex "took" him and had its way with him.

I felt sorry for him, of course, handsome and athletic as he was, yet doomed by this flaw not so much tragic as pathetic. Clearly his moods depended on how his legs and his brain were treating him. I had looked and peered, noting irregularities and lumpishness, but the real clue to his condition was in his gait; at rest, asleep, or in repose, he seemed shapely enough about the feet and legs, although a little withered, a little overtapered, I had thought. But I had seen the boots he wore. He was neither an Apollo with the feet and legs of a satyr nor an Adonis with a cloven hoof. Indeed, he was a thwarted cricketer, as Shelley had told me. In 1805, Lord B. had played cricket for Harrow against Eton, in the annual needle match, although he had had someone to run for him after he struck the ball when batting. He had insisted on playing and had managed to override the opinions of attuned judges, even Lloyd, Head of School, who had passed around the word that Lord B. had played very badly. Harrow had lost by an innings and some runs. According to Shelley, Byron had been all the more eager to play because another player in the side, a good one, bore the name Shakespeare, and the game was to be, as usual, at Lord's cricket ground, the Mecca of cricket. In the event, Lord B. scored 7 in the first innings, and 2 in the second, although the story he spread had him making a total of 18, more than any but a certain Ipswich. Swimmer, yes, and a fair boxer, but a cricketer never, as I knew well, having myself gone to a school in Yorkshire where cricket was no laughing matter. It was their sombre, horrible religion. So it was in something less than a merely teasing mood that crippled Polly asked the only sometimes crippled Lord B. to please bring down from his bedroom the old cricket ball, with which to fidget and fool. "Once I am recovered, my lord," I told him, "we must all have a game out on the lawn. You were a cricketer of note, my lord, in your day—better than Shakespeare or Ipswich *or* Lloyd." He stared as if I had removed his liver, kidneys, and gallbladder all at once. Caught by one of the two Barnards for 7. Bowled by Carter for 2. "Cricket, I mean." He still stared. "The two of us lame ones, the two of us with the gammy legs, we could take on everyone else. Polly learned his cricket in Yorkshire, which is like learning your Catholicism in Rome."

I spun the ball from hand to hand, knowing it unscrewed into two halves; making faint plops with it, then actually threw it a short distance from one palm to the other, making a harder, stiffer sound. "Damned English game," he said. "I scored more notches than everyone save Ipswich. *I* will be one side, all of you on the other. I may need a runner. Fletcher will serve—not all of him is foreigner yet."

So there was going to be garden cricket, not croquet, at Diodati, and the locals would no doubt come to see, gawping at our play as they had gawped at our arrival, deciding it was not another version of bocce but some foreign perversion played with a dun ball by lame fatheads. Bat and stumps we would need. Berger or Fletcher would have to carve them from stock, make them smooth for ladies to handle, and we would not bowl fast or overarm. It was our childhood coming back to us in the shade of John Milton's ghost. The ball itself was a ghost, a double drinking cup filled with clay.

Ghosts we always talked about, half frightening ourselves to death with ogrish imaginings in the darkest cellars of Diodati or its cobwebbed outhouses, where rotten gates creaked and rats made their own shrill music. It was usually Shelley who started these conversations off, at his most brilliant, I thought, when he engaged the subject of whether or not man was an instrument, a means, devised by the planet or the universe to test certain hypotheses. Could man be made perfect? Another of Shelley's questions was this: Is not the universe something brought into being by certain powers to answer a question? In either case the created being was far from gratuitous (as my own thinking went), but was purposeful, intended, an instrument indeed, like a scalpel or a protractor. In each case, something else was using us, some unfathomable power which, as I saw it, because unfathomable was also beside the point; the only certain thing worth conjuring with, worth exploring, was the human being himself, his limits, if any. If life had once been created, as Shelley argued, could it not be created again? Could not the created being itself create life? Create it from something dead? This went much farther than Dr. Erasmus Darwin's legendary findings on having left a piece of vermicelli in a glass case until, through some undreamed-of means, it actually began to move through spontaneous generation. Both Lord B. and Shelley discussed the chances of piecing some creature together and infusing it with life—but where to find the vital principle, how to apply it?

"Everything must have a *beginning*," Byron said.

"Which does not," Shelley murmured, "come out of some void. It comes out of chaos, out of givens. Not *ex nihilo*. How do we proceed *ex nihilo?*"

"Or *ex Shihilo*," Lord B. said, jesting on the nickname, Shiloh, he sometimes used for Shelley. "Only gods can indulge in genuine godlike behavior. 'Let there be light' strikes me, dear Shelley, as a truly godlike feat."

"Oh, but the thrill, Byron, of one dawn finding the dread thing clambered up from the cellar where you hooked and stitched it together, come to see you with its rheum-yellow eyes, its still-seeping wounds, its terrible majestic deformities, like a dog that was not a dog, unable to speak but gratefully gibbering at your sleep-thick face, grateful for the gift of an awful life."

Byron simply said, "I have no desire ever to feel that godlike, ever." The matter dropped, but always boiled up again, especially as that summer was rainy; we talked ourselves to death indoors, at least until I forgot all such profundity in dreams of cricket, Gaby, or Miss Arrow, or the need to call Lord Byron's mistress Miss Clairmont and not Miss Godwin. One learned slowly, wondering who to whom was what, and for how long. By June 17 I was no longer laid up but even able to attend a ball at Mme. Odier's, where I met a Princess Something or Other and a Countess Potocka—Poles both—and had long confabs with them, certainly not about the vital principle of life but Genevois manners and Swiss weather, Lord B. (of course), and the Villa D. I did try to dance, but felt intense pain, and had to tell the Countess Potocka, grand-niece of the Stanislaus Augustus who had been king of Poland until 1798, what had happened. She was a ripe forty, juicy and swarthy, eager to be doing things. I think she liked me and found me responsive to something feral in her. Alas, I was *hors de combat* but able to tell her what had happened last night when the five of us talked into the small hours and beyond them into the soggy dawn, with the fire still giving off its cordial hum. "We all agreed to write a ghost story," I told her, "having been reading several volumes of them purchased locally: *Fantasmagoriana, ou"* (airing my French) *"Recueil d'Histoires d'Apparitions, de Spectres, Revenants,* done into French from the German. Crude, but powerful. It was Byron's idea, I think, but we had all been pondering some such idea before he spoke. We would not all publish together, of course, but the several stories will perhaps be related to one another in some incestuous way." She gave her high-bred, dark-eyed Polish laugh, then intimated that she too would enjoy a *nuit blanche* with us, in whatever robes we chose. She had a fancy-dress orgy in mind, I suspected. The visual impressions of that night at Diodati had remained with me as if carved into my mind's eye: each looking at the other as if seeing some unspeakable being behind the other's shoulder, and aghast at the view; then each in turn seeing the ogre behind all the others' backs, mouthing and slavering even as, too drenched in hideous imagining to turn back, we vowed to invent monsters of our own to frighten others with, until the whole race leapt into the sea to save its reason. I alone of the group, it seemed, had not begun my story, but then I had been in pain, out of sorts. I told the Countess Potocka so, but she said what better state of mind or body in which to begin something so twisted. "With pain as the midwife," she said in her high, hectic voice, "surely the baby would come out crooked." Perhaps she was right. I knew that, when my leg hurt so much I felt chills all the way up to my groin and my head ached with icy spasms, the sensations were almost the same as those I had felt when we read the ghost stories aloud. Pain and terror were first cousins at the very least, even if only related by association, like the drugs in my travelling chest of carnage: arsenic, quinine, laudanum, and digitalis, which we physicians prescribed and used, although never quite certain of their accompanying effects, even if we were certain that for every ill there was a specific in nature. So purposeful a universe we would never have dreamed of, or rather one in which the Creator went to such trouble to cancel things invented. Better never to have invented some of them in the first place, as Shelley said. Was it a perfect universe in which that kind of redundance held sway? It was as if the First Cause were making it up as He went along. Byron said that it was impossible to believe in ghosts without believing in God, but Shelley argued that one might believe in the universe without believing in any God at all, and I, the liturgical lip-server who knew naught of the Deity, I wanted to believe in ghosts without believing in anything else.

By June eighteenth, my leg was much worse; I should have left it resting instead of chasing after the Countess Potocka and the rest. On that day, pained as I was, I experienced an ecstasy quite unlooked-for when Mrs. Shelley referred to me as her "younger brother," even if she was eighteen and I twenty. Sometimes I shook with excitement when I remembered, and took stock of the fact, that she and I were so young, and Claire only seventeen. We were advanced children: very much the juniors of the ménage: a majority of minors, almost. We were doing awfully well, I thought, considering the dissolute ancientry—Byron, Shelley—we found ourselves

among, and not merely keeping pace but setting it, prompting the
two poets to push ever deeper into the recesses of abstruse cosmic
thought. Sometimes, I thought, from their sheer undeludedness,
those who were not quite adults tapped sources unavailable to their
elders, who for thinking too sharply on things lost sight of universal
relevance. For my part, I had as soon never grow up, but thrive on
in gullible incipience, at which Claire was best—she who looked the
madwoman's part with her utterly round eyes and habit of ungainly
scrambling about, whereas Mary was more stately of bearing and
had a Scotch burr in her speech that gave her an air, a tone, of
cautious, reticent profundity.

In my delight at what Mary said, I began my ghost story after
tea, letting my mind race and linger, at first addressing myself to an
image that merely "arrived," of a skull-headed woman punished for
watching through a keyhole something so unspeakable I did not go
on with it, but the first gist was a Muslim athlete on a mat being
massaged by a blue-eyed dark-haired English ingenue from India,
whereas the second was a series of copulants all addressing one another from behind, the first one only being female, of course. Having gone not very far with either of these visions, or with the skull-
headed woman, who seemed destined only for a terminus, I began
again, mentally at any rate, envisioning the departure of two friends
from England, one of them dying in Ephesus, after getting from his
companion an oath never to mention his death. Neatly, then, as I
thought at the time, I revived the dead man and had him make love
to the sister, or fiancée, of the other, this a lady who had spent some
time in Switzerland, where, alas, she had succumbed to a desire for
low life and had become a little tinged with scarlet. Gaby Picton I
first named her, then Yvonne Lehman, but those names fell away as I
began to conceive of framing my tale with a Letter to the Editor, in
which the purported author wrote from Geneva, dreaming of Rousseau and Voltaire, Bonnet and Mme. de Staël, Abelard and Héloise,
and the house built by Diodati, friend to the poet John Milton, I
alleging all this *as if it were imagined* by someone sitting in, say, his
rooms in Piccadilly. And then I brought in the famous poet Byron,

and I trod his floors with a feeling akin to that of walking into Shakespeare's dwelling at Stratford-upon-Avon. I saw into the poet's bed-chamber, on the same level as the saloon and the dining-room, and was enthralled by the account of his servant, an expatriate Swiss now brought home again, who said his master retired to bed at three, rose at two, and lingered over his toilette, never went to sleep without a brace of pistols hard by and a dagger within reach, and never touched animal food of any kind. Each day he rowed, or was rowed, upon the lake. I fancied him like a scathed pine tree, head erect in the storm, found my way down to the port where his vessel used to moor, and made conversation with the cottager who took care of it. Only once did he go into society in the town, when Pictet de Sergy took him to the house of a lady who gave soirées. All found him uncivil, notorious for inviting persons to dinner and then failing to put in an appearance, leaving behind his physician and travelling companion to make his apologies—the gentleman had gone to Chillon. Another evening, having been invited to the house of Lady Dalrymple Hamilton, he promised to attend and almost did, but upon approaching her ladyship's villa perceived the room to be full of company (a disease he shrank from), set down his friend, begging him to make appropriate excuses for him, and at once returned home to brood and pine. Such was his lofty nature, the reverse of Dryden's "He left not party, but of that was left." The report having been that his own countrymen walked out of the one door as he arrived at the other. No, *he* left *them*. Arriving at Coppet, and following the servant who announced his name, he witnessed a lady being carried out who had fainted at his very mention, although she soon returned and conversed with him, like one raised from the dead.

Then, like some phantom arising from the ashes of many a wasted ghost story, came my tour de force as I set down, mentally, the name of the Countess of Breuss, a Russian lady resident some three or four miles out of Geneva who made a great deal of society at her mansion and knew well the key to the whole riddle: Lord Byron's physician, who used to cross the lake almost every day by himself in a flat-bottomed boat and return about midnight even as dire storms flickered about the surrounding mountain summits. This gentleman knew of a ghost story that Lord Byron began once, almost as a lark proposed by him to the others in his circle at the Villa Diodati, included among them two ladies, the aforesaid lonely rowing gentleman-physician, and Mr. P. B. Shelley, after they had perused a German work entitled *Phantasmagoriana.* As his lordship recited the beginning of Mr. Coleridge's poem "Christabel," Mr. Shelley, affrighted, ran from the room screaming, only to be found by Lord Byron and his physician, standing against a mantel-piece, with ice tears of perspiration tumbling down his face. His keen imagination, under the impetus of the lines read aloud, had pictured for him the bosom of one of the ladies as having eyes instead of nipples, like heavy-lidded studs. All now decided, when order had resumed, to write a story on some such theme as the impact of a supernatural agency on receptive souls. Three of them did it, and I, as the confidant of the Countess of Breuss, claimed to have obtained the outlines of these stories from her, favouring most of all the one by Lord Byron. All three went off to the unnamed editor in question, drawing his particular attention to the *ébauches* of so great a genius, and reminding him of the universal belief that a person sucked by a vampyre becomes a vampyre himself, and sucks in his turn.

I thus appeared in my own story as more or less myself, but without surrendering ownership in acknowledging my debt to Lord B., whose story contained nothing of the dead man's revival and his later lovemaking. Thus did Polly write about Polly, but the Polly in the story was different from the Polly who wrote these words. Other thoughts came to me that day after tea, so it might be said that, in a short space, I conjured up the germs of three tales: the skull-headed woman, who went nowhere; the two friends, one of whom revived; and the story I later called *Ernestus Berchtold,* eventually published in 1819 soon after my *The Vampyre.* I was never to forget the sight of Shelley, who had refused to meet my challenge on the lake, and with whom I had some constant bickering, shrieking from the room as, in the poem, the lady unbound her breast only to reveal half her side hideous and deformed "and pale of hue." *We* saw no eyes in Mrs. Shelley's bosom, but I thought I saw Lord Byron's foot on his marriage night entering where no foot belonged.

Had I known how often, in later years, I would be called a plagiarist, I would have taken careful notes of the whole creative onset and have Mary and Shelley sign them as witnesses, for at least the squelching of rumour. Alas, no human being can plumb the thought processes of another, any more than, as Shelley himself said, we can plumb those of the orang-outang, even though that animal perfectly resembles man both in the order and number of his teeth. Even those closest are separate in pain. Sufficient to say that, under the influence of Byron and indeed prodded by him (as he prodded the other three), I came up with three separate plots for stories, none of them perhaps qualifying at the same level of distinction as Mary's *Frankenstein,* but not utterly reprehensible either. I did not belong socially or intimately; unlike Mary I never called Byron "Albé," and unlike Byron I never called Shelley "Shiloh"; I was not on nickname terms with them, nor ever would be because I was *a hired hand,* a latter-day Boswell hovering after Lord B. as Boswell, the tadpole, hovered after the whale called Dr. Johnson.

Under other auspices, I would have had with this extraordinary group of people the kind of humane relationship I had with my increasing circle of friends in Geneva. I would not have let my journal slip by the board, neither including what I was supposed to observe nor excluding things that Murray had never had in mind. I would have noted, for example, not Lord B.'s notions of a vampyre story cognate with my own about the friend revived, but what he said about something he was going to call "Darkness," in which he would depict our planet, dying in a frigid universe, with civilization in shreds, and the last unselfish act coming from a dog who guarded his master's body until his own death. I never saw the work, but I believed he had penned some lines when he spoke of it to me. It was

as much a ghost story as I ever wanted to hear, and for once I felt of
one mind with Shelley, who exclaimed to him, "What are you not
further capable of effecting?" The same Shelley had observed to
Mary, in my hearing (or overhearing), "Lord Byron is an exceed-
ingly interesting person, so is it not regrettable that he is a slave to
the vilest and most loutish prejudices and as mad as the wind?" Mr.
Facing-Both-Ways, he charged himself up with excitement. When
he felt run down, he would say something extravagant, either way,
for the sake of saying it, and then the excitement of it all would fill
his sails again and off he would go. In a word, he made his own
energy whereas Lord B. took his energy from others, enlivening
himself with how much he hated or loved them.

In this, Shelley was independent of others, Lord B. never; but
Shelley needed to have, or give, the illusion that he needed to mingle with others, whereas Lord B. tended to keep apart from people
because he needed them so much, and he did not wish to look so
needy. And what of Polidori, coming up for his twenty-first birthday in September? He needed not to be lonely, not to be a hireling, a
Boswell; he did not need to be where he could or could not see eyes
in Mary's nipples, or watch Shelley decamp shrieking with candle in
hand, or have to splash water into his face to bring him back to the
world of every day, or to give him ether, to be a man who (as he
had said) became a river to his friends (of money, he meant) and,
once, having hired a house, suffered himself to be knocked down
twice by some bully demanding that he pay more than had been
agreed. I wanted never to need the gossip of tangential personalities,
to have to suffer through the correction of rumours, one of which
went as follows: Shelley, on the contrary, had been saved from
robbers by the intervention of his landlord, a Mr. Dare, having been
struck senseless on his own doorstep in Keswick.

What I wanted, above all, was to be able to speak freely about
the joys of my own life without being subjected to man-of-the
world ridicule merely because I did not attitudinize arrogantly and
sadly in ruined castles or tear pell-mell through rat-infested cellars
with the devil behind me. Mine was the usual plaint of the young,

the not-yet-arrived, who go through the banal hoops while the rest of the world looks on and yawns. I tried to seem older than I was, but I never quite saw the need—except Lord B. seemed to find my exuberant high spirits and even my voice painful to endure. Gloom and the dumps I had postponed until after I was fifty. Out in Geneva I felt my age, and respected for it, whether with neatly groomed and coal-eyed Rossi, Dr. de Roche, looking older and frailer than his years though with young-looking teeth, and Mme. Odier, who walked with a bounce and spoke with paralyzing finesse. Mentally, with a dance and a garden cricket match in mind, I assembled the roster of my friends, those who had already treated me with dignity in a strange land, and found it not altogether wanting in quality and scope:

> Mme. Odier
> Mlle. Odier
> Rossi
> Countess Potocka
> Countess de Breuss
> Dr. de Roche
> Pictet de Sergy
> Dr. Gardner
> Hentsch.

Gaby, whom literally I could not afford, figured less among my list of friends and acquaintances than among the list of my habits, along with opium, henbane, and senna. Perhaps she was as lethal as the first two: I saw her as an exquisite and extravagant leech, a Lilith-Cleopatra who sucked my juices in exchange for what the Yorkshire folk called brass. Rossi's too, I did not doubt, and I felt ill at ease on this score, wondering how far one might share a beloved with a friend when the nexus is money. Had I been older, I might have felt differently about her; but I had been bowled over, unmanned, sent spinning, by such an avalanche of possibly quite impersonal advances, and I felt torn between love and education, never quite knowing which was which, whereas Rossi, who was older and worldlier, knew exactly how much he wanted, and truly how little. Sometimes to me she was no more than a prancing tuft, a puff of hair, not worth a soreness between me and Rossi. At other times she was perfection arrived prematurely, long before I could get it into proportion, and I was like the young surgeon who had yearned all his days (a few) to be able to remove from a body, without harm, the beating heart, that udder of calamity, and there it suddenly was, reached for and got, like a young starling in the hand, its wings eager to go, a-tremor with beat. In a word, I had been overfaced.

Perhaps because my leg kept paining me and the opium was not working well, I managed to quarrel with Rossi, for which nervous solecism I went to the Odiers' and behaved with exceptional niceness, intending an amends to myself. I was truly irritated that, at last, Lord B. and Shelley had gone off together to Vevey on their excursion round the lake: an enterprise not so much in honour of the lake as to snub Polidori, who, however, now had the two eccentric women to himself, and little William, if I cared to dote on infants. But everyone kept going into town as if neither the Villa Diodati nor the Shelleys' cottage might be endured without a poet in each, so clearly I did not count in that capacity. I apologized to Rossi, sold books to pay for a visit to Gaby (upon whose shoulder, breast, and groin I cried myself half to sleep), and called on Dr. Slaney. My leg was going to pain me for ever more, it seemed. *Walked to Mrs. Shelley,* I wrote on June 23. *Pictet, Odier, Slaney dined with me. Went down to Mrs. Shelley for the evening,* telling her how Odier had mentioned to me the cases of two gentlemen who, on taking nitrate of silver, later on developed black faces. Pictet had confirmed it. Almost out of my wits with pain, insult, and remorse, I had burst out with a rhapsody most peculiar in a physician, about the gradual intake of prussic acid, oil of amber, blowing into one's veins, and suffocation by means of charcoal—all of which belonged in some madman's litany but had come instead from a well-behaved young doctor on the brink of an orthodox career. It was clear that, should I wish to begin to practise in Geneva, I would be able to, and without confining myself to English residents either. Provided I kept my mouth in its place: I saw several of them, Odier and Pictet included, looking at me hard, then dismissing the whole affair as something they had misheard. Noble souls, they dreaded misprision more than the pox. What had Pictet been asking me? I answered in dishevelled fashion: "To bed by three, up by noon." "Gentleman's hours," he said, "not those of a doctor. I predict that you will soon be up with the birds. You are *not* Lord Byron, after all."

Mary was much more interested in my talk of drugs and suicide than in my account of how I had bridled at this. She was even taking notes as I went on, lamenting that she had never had an apothecary's training but had dwelt among those to whom abstract ideas were manna.

"God gave us them all," I said, of the chemicals.

"And they are all part," she said, "of some enormous whole in which everything is bound to be related to everything else. It would be impossible, would it not, for any one substance, mingled with another, to have no effect on it, no matter how slight?"

I told her I thought there was a law of interaction that governed everything: nothing stayed the same, the same amount.

"And what is that law?"

"Nobody knows, Mary, it has still to be plucked alive from the bosom of nature."

"With or without eyes in the bosom." A faint smile.

"Or restorative ether." Another.

"I sometimes wonder," she said with ruminative tenderness, "if Man can be complete without all the chemicals that attend him in Nature. In each of them resides a piece of his as yet undiscovered nature. Each extends him, could we but know how."

"Or kills him off," I told her, less gently. "Perhaps they would cancel one another out, or exist together in a ratio of, say, thirty percent good, the rest of the percentage dangerous. It would take centuries of experiment."

"That is what I envisage," Mary said, "but who wants to wait that long? I keep seeing a creature, found among the ice floes or the jungles, long abandoned, whom some devout scientist has pieced together, not from trees and rocks and creatures but all from human cadavers, and the sewing shows; the reverse butchery is clear. The best has joined the best. Where the animating spark comes from is less than clear, but come it must. There has to be an available animating spirit for pioneers to use."

"It would not be sunlight," I said. "But lightning, perhaps. Although I myself incline to think of some gentle, seeping chemical process that moves through all things and need not be coerced—nothing violent or even dramatic, but the even, certain seepage of the universe, pressing all to its will."

"Why, Polly!" she exclaimed. "So lyrical these days."

"Why not? I am only twenty years old. Sackcloth and ashes is for later. Seriously, Mary," I went on, "if one keeps up, the world of knowledge looms almost too large. Only twelve or thirteen years ago, *a twenty-year-old* German chemist named Sertürner managed to isolate the most important of the opium poppy's constituents: morphine. It was the first plant alkaloid ever isolated, and its discovery started off a whole brainstorm of inquiry that has changed medicine for ever. All the other alkaloids will follow."

"Alkaloids—"

"Containing mainly nitrogen, to be found in seed plants. This morphine acts on the nerve cells in the cerebrum, halting pain. That's a long way, in a sense, from all those workers in the Orient who walk backwards through the poppy fields, in a ritual some two thousand years old, making slits in the swollen capsules but never cutting through to the seeds within. A whitish liquid oozes forth and slowly turns brown. *There* is our opium. Do you think the hand of God, or of a god, can be detected in such a finding, in such a phenomenon?"

"Whyever not?" she said, excited. "I sometimes think we are a whole generation awash in opium, without our knowing it. Who has *not* taken it in some form or other? As children we have all taken Mother Bailey's Quieting Syrup—the very name inspires awe."

"*Aha,*" I said, on home ground, "and Batley's Sedative Solution, McMunn's Elixir, Dalby's Carminative, Godfrey's Cordial—which sounds indecorous—and Italo-Anglus's Lethe-Liquor."

"Indecorous?" she murmured, not knowing venereal argot. "I don't see that, but never mind. What was the last one you mentioned? All the others sound familiar, and I do distinctly recollect having seen their dribbled-upon labels on dark brown bottles placed on a high shelf in the mixings cupboard. A chemist's vision of the afterlife!"

"A poor thing, but mine own," I said. Her face creased with impatience and pain, as it sometimes did when she thought or heard something with too sharp an edge, too banal an intonation. "Italo-Anglus was the pseudonym I used for my Edinburgh dissertation. One day I will market that very cordial in Italy, for the English at least. I am *the* man on nightmares, for the moment anyway."

"May I read this learned work?" Her face smoothed out again.

She knew Latin. "Of course," I told her. "It is only some thirty-odd pages; my one copy is already lent out, though."

"Then, please, Polly," she said. "On its return."

"We were saying," I said.

"Oh, were we?" She seemed aloof, her mind on opium without quite reminding her that we had been talking about it. I paused, letting the sounds of birds trickle into the villa, thinking with some elation: I am not in England or Scotland any more; I am among the best of my time. I am talking ideas with the daughter of the famous thinker William Godwin. This woman is the mistress of the poet Shelley. This is better than treating whooping coughs in Norwich would have been, or measles in London. All of a sudden she seemed to revert to conversation, as if appeased and reanimated.

"Did you not know," she whispered, "that Lord Byron, *Albé himself,* kept by him during the gathering catastrophe of his marriage a phial of Black Drop? It was to calm him. Lady Byron or her solicitor will one day find it among the things he left behind him, and a copy of the Marquis de Sade's *Justine.* Perhaps the two are related. I do not mean Lady Byron and the opium compound, I

meant the book and the phial. Albé told us that laudanum never
stimulated him, at least in the imaginative part of his being. Sometimes it made him angry and quarrelsome, suspicious at the very
least, and rather surly. Mostly, though, he says, it did not affect him
at all. It does help Shelley's headaches."

I am the doctor, I wanted to say, but kept mum. Instead I
returned to the theme of the well-stocked universe and its sheer
"foison," to use an old-fashioned word for plenty.

"That is why I have some hope," I whispered, as if crouched in
some distant poppy field, among the whites, the lavenders, the reds,
the purples, as much in a temple of the Deity as I would have been
in any cathedral. "My God is the supreme physician."

"But not a rationalist," she said nervously. "And not one who
has taken the oath of Hippocrates, otherwise—"

"No, Mary, nowhere near that gentle, but a doctor in hiding,
say, who never comes in the open, quite, but has laid in for us a vast
store of substances to ease our way. We have to use will and energy,
but the remedies are within our grasp."

"I only wish that were suddenly so," she said with an almost
muscular sigh. "Shelley and I think about it all the time."

"It is the *sun* that moves the plants," I said. "It is not lightning.
Seepage, as I said. Some massive but gentle motion, unseeable except
through its effects. It could all be the result of some accident, but I
doubt it. What you seek is there—the *power*—but it seems so vari-
ously distributed that only the most concerted effort would pin it
down."

"I have been thinking that any living being is naturally good,"
she said, "and that ill-treatment causes all the evil we know."

"Then where must the ill-treatment come from," I said, "the
idea of it, the germ?"

We did not know, but she skipped ahead to her story, telling
me that the doctor who created her piecemeal man had failed to
make him handsome. He was, after all, a kind of Joseph's coat of
left-over pieces and lacked the smoothness and symmetry of the
naturally born. "And then," she said, with almost hysterical empha-

sis, "because he is rejected wherever he goes, he asks his maker to make him a mate."

I knew exactly what she meant, but said only, "That is the source of half the trouble in the world."

She laughed at my fraction and went on. "The savant begins, but finds the creation of such a race too horrible to contemplate. That is as far as I have gone, if even as far as that. Much of it is still in my mind and may remain there, safely."

"Then let it out," I told her. "Set it free."

"And you," she asked. "How goes your vampyre?"

"Oh," I answered, "it goes along, from one broken blood vessel to the evil power instinct in a companion, from a Kashmere butterfly to the midnight damps, from a blue eye never lit up by the levity of the mind beneath to a naked dagger, from a speck on the horizon turning into a tremendous mass to an uneducated Greek girl, from a dead grey eye to a deadly hue in a certain face. It pourtrays all the dissipations that attend a London winter, and a good deal more." I was amazed by how the tale's scribbled phrases had stayed hard and fast in my mind, although in the wrong order, as if strict sequence had melted into a wreath of phrases and impressions; but I was no utter stranger to authorship and knew how the mind had fluxions that, in appearing to lead one astray, actually conducted the mind to fresh and ravishing material. My story was only one third done, but I already had phrases and events that would populate its final third. Heaven only knew what Lord B. and Shelley were writing on their journey round the lake, but none of it could be like mine; my phrases were my own, for ever. I mentioned the work "Darkness" that Lord B. had proposed to write, although clearly he did not think of it as a ghost story (though the ghost therein was that of our very own world), and Mary at once said, "Oh, I know about it. The day was dark, as so many others, when even the birds had ceased to sing, as if intimidated by the general pall, and we had candles to eat by. Do you not remember it? Still, there have been so many such. For some reason he could not be precise as to which year it was, thinking it only 1815, which in its way afforded him a very suitable platform out of time to perform on. I think he has written it already. I think he will not change it."

"What then of his ghost story, his answer to the 'History of the Inconstant Lover' that we all heard, and the tale about the sinful founder of our race whose kiss killed his son?"

"He made a beginning," she said, "having to do with a gentleman named Augustus Darvell—I remember its having rhymed with marvel—who was the narrator's friend. He was a wealthy person, the elder of the two, who had taken the younger man under his wing—they had gone to the same schools and university. This Darvell was a man of acute feelings, which he failed to disguise, and his facial expressions would vary at shocking speed. He was prey to some cureless disquiet, as Lord Byron called it. He told me no more and, I did believe, at that time had gone no further with it. He had no title, either. I could not tell how well the story was going, nor would he tell me, instead just humming and smiling as if he knew something dangerous."

How Byronic, I thought, even if superficially akin to my own narrative. After all, how many basic plots were there for authors to employ? I did not ask about Claire's story; but, after casting about in my memories of medical school and medical lore for a suitable simile, I at last came up with something I liked: discovering Claire was on the premises was like being one of those persons who, after a doctor has examined them, express amazement that in their armpit they had soft papillae growing they had never known about, tucked in there like soft little grubs, neither serving nor obstructing but intensely secret.

When writing at last drove me to distraction, and I found myself tinkering with such phrases as "florid blood" and "monstrous rodomontade," and being neither satisfied with them nor quite revulsed, I decided to go into town to see Rossi, with whom I had only recently made up. I wish I had never gone near him on that accursed day. He was on his way to an assignation with my Gaby, whom he was in quite a fume to see and lay hands upon. "Come along, old fellow," he said. "It's all in the family, so to speak." I had no money (hideous thought) and did not wish to sit in the parlor while he did his business with her; nor did I wish to be anywhere else. By dint of truly Italian cajolery, and by ignoring the chance of my being more sensitive in this affair than I was willing to admit, he managed to enjoin me to go along with him, I thinking the whole matter would dwindle into a mere social chit-chat followed by a departure. But no: on his arrival, she greeted him first, brought him a glass of wine, then treated me as if I were some kind of supernumerary, there to be introduced. Without making any bones about it, off they went upstairs, Rossi beckoning me to follow, on his face an impersonal leer as if he were already stripped for action. Like an automaton I followed, lingering but at last on the landing, then behind them into the bedroom, where ensued a most disgusting episode that began with her taunting me to engage in multiple activity such as I had never dreamed of.

I should have gone home after challenging Rossi to a duel. That I did not indicated the depravity and dissolution into which, perhaps under the influence of Lord Byron, I had begun to sink. My Gaby romped, naked, under the eyes of Rossi, who soon had her in a carnal embrace I had fondly, madly, imagined to be mine alone; and then this way and that, such as I had always thought our own novelties, our tryst-ingenuities, all a commonplace to him. I had actually seen him pass money to her, and then her hand approach mine as she waited for me to pay too, saying that today she would spare us both the customary supplement. We were both good customers.

"Not enough," she told me. "You are short, my treasure." Shameless to the end, I let Rossi make up the count and, after a disgusted pause, watching her wriggle and arch, I moved into position on the bed, barely unclad for the event, and she swept me up into her carnal frenzy, teasing me until lust had its way with me and, like some hooligan of the soul, I went into her where Rossi had only moments before spent with a shuddering military cry, and she

was wet with him as well as with her own excitement. Visibly this
was her preferred sport. I could hardly believe the nibbling she did
of us, as if we were twins, the tweaking, the jabbing, the coaxing
back into the fray. Up went the roars as my beloved melted away
from me and became a glutinous witch. Nothing could be serious
after this; then why was she laughing, and he, as if instead of brutal-
izing a tender sacrament we had played some horrendous schoolboy
jape for which, if we were lucky, we would not be thrashed. I saw
blood on the sheets, blood on her face and mouth; voluptuously she
tapped her tongue against it, rolling her eyes for Rossi and me to
admire. Now I knew why she had not missed me when I ran short
of funds, but I knew why she denied me access to her at those times.
An old medieval expression came back to me—the buying of souls
—and I wished some force would buy my soul from me, meaning:
redeem me for being so lustful *à trois.* I was no prude, of course, but
the vision of Gaby Saxonnex *in flagrante,* as she must so often have
been, sipping blood and other fluids, was too much to bear. I was in
tears before I knew what was happening. Rossi turned his back. She
made as if to comfort me with her sullied hand, which I shoved
away. I gave a curse, knowing that a castle made of gingerbread had
just toppled into a sewer in which, behold, I had found my own
body, functioning with a will and a feral crescendo that had nothing
to do with me. I longed to have Byron and Shelley back, even if
they giggled at my discomfiture. How could I not tell them? How
could I *tell* them, though? God knew what they had been doing to
each other en route. How would milord have conducted himself
with his Augusta, finding her taste was to have one other along?
How would our Shelley have fared with his Mary tupping Polly
too?

I wanted the whole episode to unhappen, and the stink of
sulphur and pitch to go away from my hands, the sharp acrid smell
of our spunk, Rossi and I, the jammy clammy aroma of her sluices.
Now I knew why the right vocabulary had come my way, so that I
would be able to render my self-loathing in one terrible but translat-
able outburst of feather-clack puddle and pepper nail. This was the

argot de la boue, never before needed in Polly's sheltered life but now of the most urgent import. All very well for Mary and me to talk of perfectible Being when, at the merest bidding (but really because I had been obliviously infatuated) I had leapt into her breech like the coarsest *viveur,* with a friend for ballast. This was not news to relay to my adored father, after whom I had more or less named my play, changing Gaetano into *Cajetan,* or Eliza Arrow, Indian reredos for the altar of my bestiality. If I could be that bad, I reasoned, I was going to be worse. What would my Genevois friends think of me then? Yet Rossi was one of them. Were they all the same? Mincing-mouthed in society, but slavering monsters once up the stairs? What of my Gaby, not so much lost as annihilated? I knew I was being naïve. Rossi had told me so and, just perhaps, had arranged this whole thing *with her* to prove it. Proved it he had. My wound still hurt, but seared it he had. Cautery had never been ampler, nor self-hatred keener.

A less self-conscious person than I would have attacked them, while they were about it, but I had caught myself in the act of watching, in incredulous nausea. And then I had joined in, a canni-bal, fornicating plurally with my recently adored archangel, as if, unable any more to monopolize her in my mind's eye, I would have her nonetheless, gibbering to me on a midden where one of my newest and most congenial friends played Caliban. I had become a vampyre to myself, it seemed, and I heard brass voices braying, "He seized the portrait in a paroxysm of rage and trampled it under foot," and "then seizing her hands, and gazing on her with a frantic expression of countenance, he bade her swear that she would never wed this monster." It was the voice of my story, in whose preamble I had appeared in my own persona, come to save me. I stood in a dither, wet flannel face-cloth in hand, dipped in the water jug from which she and I had sometimes drunk, eager to wash her down, cleanse her both in and out; but I made not a motion as I stared at her with heartsick love and loathing, until Rossi sent for wine. I knew I had discovered how something essential to one's life can so soon become trivial, as if all that was good had gone rotten in a trice, and there remained only the getting through the rest of one's years, blighted and broken, yet determined to be precise about the pain, even if it killed me. I was a physician, after all, and nature included all that happened: even this.

Lovers, I had read somewhere, exchange saliva and inhale each other's breath: on a conscious level, that is, making a deliberate effort to do so, almost as if trying to fulfil some promise to an outside observer. This was de rigueur. Myself, I had always preferred things more artificial, so that I wanted my Gaby perfumed, not smelling like herself. All I could think of now was to smother her in perfume as if she had some dread disease and her flesh was like a big helping of Yorkshire pudding gone mouldy. Rossi behaved as if nothing had happened apart from some laxative event he had already dismissed. Gaby herself had shooed us away, to await (believe it not) her next client. So only a dolt could fail to see how things stood, and I all of a sudden felt flooded with mawkish gratitude to Rossi for putting me straight, in the most enduring, horrible fashion. I did not think he had meant to; indeed, he had not known that such a violent corrective was needed (no sane man would have felt about her as I had, idealizing and romanticizing her). But he saw, and so did I. In a trice I had joined Claire Clairmont, the woman who had come eight hundred miles or whatever to be with Byron, on whom she doted, who treated her like month-old laundry, but with whom she contrived to conjugate at regular intervals, just because she was there, and never mind all the sophistical apparatus of love refined, passion made verbal, future made final. He drank from her because she had arranged to be near him, ever full. It might come to pass that she too, like some other woman Lord B. had referred to as Thyrza, would want him to marry her, but he would go away eastward and she would kill herself, be buried in a cross row, and therefore never have a stone erected over her to her memory, her soul for ever calling him a terrible and unfeeling person.

After all my medical examinations I had at last taken a final paper in infatuate pain, recognizing for the first time that I had been found wanting; that, between my emotions and desires and what happened in the world of the flesh, there was an ancient gulf. I was not even adapted to looking. The truth would spring upon me like a tiger and I would think, Oh, what a pleasant ripple of stripes in God's firmament! It was to realists such as Rossi and Lord B. that I should turn my gaze, observing how they took what they wanted without pretty ado, yearning less to fall in love than to squirt, but not altogether ruling out the likelihood of becoming enamoured in spite of everything. Everyone had an Augusta somewhere; everyone put up with and used a Claire, simply for the sake of sanitive exercise. So why not Polidori, not special but another man? One might even learn from Byron, Rossi, et al. the rhetoric of aversion, as when in my hearing Lord B. several times told Claire that he would have her sewn up in a sack and dumped in the sea. Not a promise or a threat, but an index to her expendability, she who, after all, had only come after Byron to ape her half-sister's scandalous elopement with Shelley. Claire wanted a poet-lover of her own, and the more notorious the better; so, like all the other ninnies who beset him, she began writing letters to him followed by a literary composition. Her valley of the sluices was wide open to him, and she received him, not in Pimlico, where she lived, but in London certainly. Unwise as it had been of him to give her in his final message before leaving for Europe the clue *Poste Restante, at Geneva,* done it he had, and here she was: eager, voracious, inflamed, *with child.* And (her relevance to me) she was ignoring the truth about him, even making a fetish of such behaviour, like someone on the blackest night driving her vessel cliffwards from the centre of the storm, *convinced* that the harbour lay that way, or eager to perish and join the long roll-call of unheeded, suicidal lovers.

Now I felt close to Claire, who had told Byron her motto for marriage: *Abandon hope all ye who enter here,* her only desire some kind of generous intimacy, and the chance to become his copyist, not his copycat, with in her belly the proof of his fertile attentions. Polidori was better off than Claire; his amputation had already taken place, his good-bye said with an uncompleted snarl marred by a half kiss as the door closed from within, Gaby shoving it with unnecessary force, evicting a couple of purged schoolboys. How did one imagine people so different from what they were? How did a *physician* of all people reach such a point? How did someone with narcotics and a set of knives manage to delude himself so far, worshipping a woman without actually abandoning his covert desire to use her as an outsize doll? How? How? Soon, Byron would send Claire packing, or send himself—he was cruel and knowledgeable enough for that—and her status as a bluestocking would in no way alter his decision. He would cut her off like any woman of the streets, making sketchy provision for her but essentially ending his life with her there and then. Ah, Polidori: you should have learned more at your master's heel. What Byron would do, in all certainty, was sentimentalize the child of their union. Albé the exuberant unthinking Albanian would take over from the man of letters. It was this ruthlessness that enabled him to go off with Shelley, pointedly omitting Polidori from the party, never mind that I too knew what it was like to cherish a manuscript in a shallow drawer, adding to it daily and waiting, almost breath held, for the day when its bulk was too large for the drawer to close. Perhaps, now that I had suffered, had been wounded in the adulative part of my being, I would be meet company for the whoremasters out on Lake Leman. Then, perhaps, Berger would cease upbraiding me about overusing the horses to the point of laming one; with his lord and master gone, he needed someone to chop at, someone of lower status than Lord B., of course.

In the end, I told Mary about my misfortune, omitting many details, just saying I had had a disappointment in love, my mistress having chosen another. She had little to say other than that Shelley too had travelled this flinty road and now he was mended, whereas Lord B. in his obtuse way thrived on it, almost daring Fate to dash him down, to take the nerves in him that others had wrung and wring them again until he howled, and then he knew, she said, "he was truly alive." I exclaimed. "No," she said, "he needs to feel that he exists, even though in hell. All his life he has had this feeling of being a shadow, a ghost, not really present among us or to himself. Agony confirms him, gives him his outline and fills it in."

Shocked, I decided not pursue that line of pain; after all, I knew who *I* was and who I was going to be. I merely had to learn that the world was a place more without finesse and tenderness than I had imagined. It was not a matter of hardening or schooling the heart but of taking the pericardium in hand and stiffening it, so that the heart beat on merrily inside its carapace: an efficient engine aloof to the hazards of the soul. Let none near it, to prod or bruise. The heart was the keel that sailed invisibly on even though the rigging and the sails were blazing hard. What you did, instead, was harden your vocabulary, so that the Rossis of the world would not think you any woman's dupe.

"Did you take me there on purpose?"

Rossi blushed.

"You thought I needed to be disabused."

"Who put you on to her in the first place?"

He had a point. "It was all my fault."

"Oh, no," he said, squirming until he managed to settle his body and his demeanour more. "She is notorious for it. She adores to bring into play the finer sentiments of our sex, so as to spoil them. She likes to break things. At the same time she likes to dabble with delicate and doting states of mind. She is a businesswoman with delusions of tenderness. She likes the formulas of devotion, but she has no idea what they mean. She is like a sow who loves the sound of Sanskrit."

This was Rossi handing me my sheepskin and degree all over again. She is your clever whore, he was saying. What you need, my friend, is the common or garden version.

"On my needs," I told him, "I am no longer an authority. I thought I was beginning to gain some purchase on myself, but the doings with Miss Saxonnex have changed all that. Consider me vacant from now on."

In his effusive yet caustic way, he tried to cheer me up, reminding me that Byron and Shelley would soon be back from their excursion, and telling me that all the other women in the world were there for my scrutiny. "The best way, he said, "is to go right back to it."

"To La Saxonnex?"

"To the act, my friend. Don't brood. Go and stick it into some other trollop with the least delay."

Oh no, I told him. Was he trying to hum or teize me?

"The best thing is to heat up again what's been burned."

He rattled on in this vein for quite a while, adjuring me, cajoling, reassuring, but always from what I regarded as the point of view of the unscathed victor, the savant of sin. I would rather, I told him, go and resume my ghost story. I felt quite unmanned, as if something good in me had snapped. Instead of feeling on the brink of twenty-one, that mysterious bourne, I now felt fifteen again, a bungler, a *naïf*, a greenhorn. I told him so, and he laughed delicately. I had all the bad signs: high blood pressure, a racing heart, moisture in my palms and on my brow, an odd weakness in the knees, a frog in my throat. It was time not only to leave him but to abandon his venereal counsel: his methods were too rough, though I doubted if there had been a gentle way of bringing me to my senses. Lord B. still had his lost Augusta to grieve over, but she was noble, aloof, like him, whereas my Saxonnex had been crude and obvious—yet it was only with the likes of me that she could have been so. I was the perfect dupe, dreaming up an idyll in a barnyard where she crowed. It was no use telling Mary, either, whereas Claire, with whom I dined (and Mary) on June 24, merely nodded and said something vague about the big flesh machine that drove us all, adding something that struck me as profound. "I bargained for humiliation," she said. "If I had to choose between unhumiliated boredom and humiliated fulfilment, even for a short time, I took the latter. I had no illusions about him; I expected to be smacked and brutalized, but it is his aura that takes me to bed, to sofa, to the kitchen table, not a man. I find myself possessed by a notorious whirlwind so heedless that it cares not what it leaves behind. It is not pleasure he takes with me, but proof."

Naturally I asked of what, and she echoed Mary's theme, telling me that Byron doted on the pleasure of pain, on the pleasure of the absence of pleasure: not love but conflict. "He fights with his piece," she said. "It is not his love-member, it is his dirk." I found all this too much to credit. I felt trapped in some sentimental menagerie in which people battened upon one another without thought or care and preyed like wolves at night. I was not hectic enough for them, but by the same token I was in some ways far away from them, deep-set in the obscure chemistry of Creation, schooled in the stuffs of matter, privy to the glory-hole of pain: how it worked, how it ruined, how it surrendered to what drug. As for the mental side, I knew that too, and how to narcotize the wound, not by eating live leeches (as some had recommended) but by gentle combinations of soothing growths. I had my portmanteau of poisons right there at the foot of my bed, and it did not take me long to foster the benign dream that had nothing to do with sleep, but took me deep into chambers of luxuriant immunity, where the only people were reflections of myself, and I did not care. This was not the first time, but the first time I had had so severe a need of the poppy, like some of the best of my time, my age, aching with them to last through the long, noxious night of near-maturity. I had gone back into harbour, where all was melodious and full-orbed, where even the most sensuous vision had no erotic component, and my appetitive side—which had burst forth from the heart of my chagrin in La Saxonnex's room —was null. From now on, I would be the neutered one of the Villa Diodati, famous for room rhapsodies couched in the prose of the blood-beat and the ungrieving eye that ran and ran with another fluid. This was how I could still go out in society—to a dinner of doctors, say, got together by Rossi (generously intended to take my mind off hurtful memories) or to the Odiers', behaving there as my habitual self because defused before arrival. Such calm I came to know that my friends remarked on it, asking what wonder had so mellowly invaded my life. How could he keep it a secret? How had they never known? When would they meet the lovely who had wrought this miracle? I could have told them—even as Rossi winked and said, "The world has surprised him, in all its richness and worth"—that mental pain worked not like a knife slicing across a wrist, say, but as a rounded scoop going through the intestines slow as a worm, cutting a cylinder or sausage that seemed endless, trapped between shoulder and groin, but infinite and heavy as lead.

I told Rossi none of this, but I did several times intercept his amused, quizzical, diagnostic eye; he *knew*. And he neither approved nor disapproved, having bought me my last tart. The problem was now to open my medical practice to the full and devote myself to work, regaling the passionate side of my nature with friendship and —I was going to say *horses,* but even that solitary pleasure had suffered a sea-change, with Berger complaining as if I had flogged them to death instead of riding them to town and back in the usual way. I went to mass, but it had begun when I arrived there, so I did not enter. My leg had improved, so Mary, Claire, and I were able to wander about, the two of them mothering me, or rather Claire in her feral, rough-handed way doing it while Mary *sistered* me, as she said, as if I were one who had come home from foreign parts with some rare malaria. She was writing at regular intervals, she said, and Claire confessed to having pondered a soliloquy she might set down, while I told them I was toiling hard, but slowly, getting my men from one line to the next with heavy breaths and lamentable indirection. We thrived, we three, at a distance from one another while becoming randomly intimate, as if the two ladies were lapsed loves of mine, and we had all three learned the errors of our ways, agreeing to stay friends. If they noticed the inebriated state of their companion, they never said; and when Byron and Shelley came back, full of themselves as if they had been to the moon, the two ladies kept on with our walks while the men resumed whatever had grown between them while away. At one point, while Claire was off doing something private, Mary told me that Byron, as he and Shelley were strolling through some vineyards, had exclaimed, "Thank God,

Polidori is not here." Another blow, it shocked me little; I would have been more disturbed had he actually longed for me.

Boating round the lake had subdued Shelley, but it had enlivened Byron, who sat at dinner in the role of happy narrator; travel had thinned him down and he had a good appetite for once. They had agreed beforehand, as I knew, to stop only at the villages named in Rousseau's *La Nouvelle Héloïse,* which was just about as literary as a boat-trip could get. "Ah, Polly-dolly," said Lord B., "what you missed. We truly felt alive."

"Well, I would have gone," I said, "had I been asked."

"Did we not ask?"

"If so, I heard nothing about it."

"*Next* time, then," Shelley murmured.

"Thank God Polidori is not here," I said with as blank a face as I could muster. They all burst out laughing; my rebuke had turned out to be a joke.

"Thank God," Byron added, "Polidori is not here now." More laughter. I made as if to leave the table. Byron held me back, urging me to stay and hear him out.

"Meanwhile," said Claire, "the women wait and worry. May one assume you will be here from now on, or with whom will the next schoolboy escapade be?" He froze her with his Byron-basilisk look and went on with his account of their row, which began with generous helpings of mountain honey at Meillerie, after which they ran into a squall, quite violent, and Byron told how he had stripped off his clothes and stood ready to save them both, Shelley being the nonswimmer.

"It would have been very classical to have gone to the bottom there," Byron said, "but none too agreeable."

"Oh, I don't know," Shelley said dreamily. "There would have been few better places to drown."

"There he sat," Byron said, "with his arms folded, quite ready to go down while the wind heaved us this way and that. It was quite rough."

"He strips for the weather," Claire said sharply, "but not for me."

"For shame," Byron said. "How would you like to be sewn naked into a sack and dropped off in the middle of the lake?"

"Then you would drown two," she said, nibbling veal.

"Let me go on," he said. "After that, we managed to get into Saint-Gingolph up at the far end of the lake, not far from Chillon, where we examined the castle and the dungeons, the torture chambers. I did some scribbling, on the wing, as it were, and so did Shelley. We were busy the whole way."

"And," said Shelley, "he scribbled his name on a wall—no, a pillar. I piggybacked him up high for it. Only the tallest visitors will be able to decipher it." I saw the pair of them, the one mounted on the other like a jockey, and began to snigger: two of our most famous poets were playing hunchback games in an old prison, where the unfortunate had been chained below the water-level and left to rot, their tissues slowly turning white and morbid. Only Byron and Shelley would have romped in such a place and then written solemn lines about the experience. I would have enjoyed slamming the cell door on the pair of them, Shelley especially, and letting the lake lap at them while they starved.

"Then we sailed to Clarens," Byron said.

"Where we thought of you," Shelley added swiftly, with a nod to me.

"Then to Ouchy, serving Lausanne," Byron said with his mouth full, his forehead glistening with sweat. "That was where Gibbon finished his *Decline and Fall,* and the anniversary of the very day, so we stood and thought about him in the old summerhouse there, and then gathered up rose leaves and acacia to send to Murray."

"And, wherever we went," Shelley said with the air of a celebrant released, "I filled him up with good old Wordsworthian pantheism."

"Wordworth physic to the point of nausea," Byron said without resentment. " 'To me / High mountains are a feeling, but the hum / Of human cities torture. . . .' Like that."

"And I," I said, determined to join in the conversation instead of riding along behind it like a fare-paying passenger, "fell into and out of love—more deeply into it, then out of it like someone being evicted from hell." The predictable male laughter followed: roars and guffaws, nothing gentle or polite.

"He interrupts like our Mme. de Stale, as I call her when she has to release some wind. Why, she farts the whole world into submission." Byron seemed proud of his sally, which effaced me quite, rubbing his hands and changing his facial expression at great speed. "Next time I see her I must tell her about our Polly-dolly, if I can get a word in against the tympany from beneath."

I began again. "Far be it from me to wax critical of minds so noble, or travellers so worldly, but I do think you could just once or twice a month take Polidori seriously. Be less hard of heart when, like everyone else, he bares his soul and speaks candidly as a friend among friends." This hit Byron like a thunderbolt; I had heard of brows darkening, but I had never seen one do it until now. I thought he was going to have a fit and lie foaming on the rug, veal trapped in his writhing trunk.

"*Me?*" he bellowed. "You have the gall to call *me* cold-hearted, *me* insensible?" His lips trembled and his eyes rolled as if he dared not focus. "As well might you say that glass is not brittle which has been cast down a precipice and lies dashed to pieces at the foot. Sir, you have another in mind. It was not Byron. And"—changing his tone abruptly to that of the inquiring agent—"what is all this about mistreatment of the horses? Berger says—"

"A lie," I snapped. "All lies. Berger is a Swiss liar."

"I see," Byron said. "We were still on the lake."

"If they are that mistreated," I flashed, "then butcher them and have them cooked." It was an unworthy shot, but my back was up. I had merely tried to join in and had started a row.

"Polly," Byron began, "this saddens me."

"It should," I said. "Whenever Polidori has an emotion you must all have felt, you mock him, but you never mock yourselves. You take yourselves with overweening seriousness, such as I have never seen." That was too much, imposing for its moderation, at least in my manner of saying it. Something had now struck home.

"Hush," Mary said at her most shy. "Stop."

"Madame de Staël is Old Mother Stale," Claire was musing. "I like that. Is she much fun?"

"Enormous fun," Byron said, glad of a new tack. "She talks and shines, shines and talks. Our lady of Coppet is the most insatiably talkative mind of our age."

I retreated, feeling myself doomed, cursing the laudanum that sometimes so freed my mouth I said anything that came into it and hang the consequences. This Byron was not the one with whom I had been accustomed to read, like two blessed souls from Dante, side by side and rapt by the images, the cadences, as if we might be frozen or turned to salt in that dual posture. We had read Lady Caroline Lamb's *Glenarvon* together, he pointing out the passages that were true, and the others that were not, as if tutoring me in his biography, I the one newly appointed to write his life. In the end I blamed Shelley for the whole affair. It was Shelley who turned him against me, I being not ethereal enough, or too close to Mary, who must have spoken kindly of me even before the pair of them went on the lake. It was Shelley who asked me—not about the gold chain and seal I got from him for seeing to his child's vaccination (that would have been too bold)—but about the watch that Byron had given me money towards. I deigned not to answer, feeling not obliged to sport the thing, even if I had actually still had it. One day, if Lord B. were not too particular where his supplementary lusts led him, he would find someone in Gaby Saxonnex's company showing it off, or she herself. Or she would hand it to Rossi as a last thrust of her knife. And then, no doubt, Rossi would hand it back to me, with a warning: "I found this in a whore's clack, sir, and had your head been loose I might have found *that* too in her posterior. Do please be wise."

I wished I could be a better diarist, or even one at all, couching things vividly, omitting nothing of Lord B.'s hectic expatriate life, which I called the pageant of the bleeding heart. Oh, to have said less about Polidori and his gaucheness; oh, to have had less gaucherie to set down! I heard parodies of how other diarists would do it: to bed at 3, up at 3; to bed at 4, up at 1; to bed at 2, up at 1. And so on. Claire was copying his poem on Chillon. He would finish "Darkness" later on. Shelley was tinkering with the "Hymn to Intellectual Beauty." Mary was beginning to accomplish huge-looking sections of her horror novel. And Polidori was polishing the opening sentence of his own vampyre tale: "It happened that in the midst of the dissipations attendant upon a London winter, there appeared at the various parties of the leaders of the *ton* a nobleman, more remarkable for his singularities, than his rank." *Commentary:* too many syllables to begin with, although this might help to tease the reader and prolong the initiating agony; too many *of*s; commas in the wrong places in the wrong combinations—should be one after the third word. I was better at the dash than at commas. But I liked the fastidious amplitude of the opening, and I left it alone, much preferring the second sentence as less nervous, less stage-struck: "He gazed upon the mirth around him, as if he could not participate therein." It was a more perfunctory sentence altogether.

Dash it, I told myself. Write it and stop fussing about its tassels. Make it bold and forthright. Lord B., I gathered from Mary, had written a page or two of his own vampyre story, but had become deflected into poetry, as was proper. I had vampyrism to myself, for the time being at least. I was still meeting people, and I almost cheered up: it was as if their lives had been incomplete until I arrived: the Marchese Saporiti; Mr. Saladin, of Vaugeron; then the Countess of Breuss, whom I'd *had.* Rossi had sent me a note suggesting that, if I were to broaden my acquaintance among the Genevan English, whose increasing presence was raising rents in and around Geneva, I might not only pursue a profitable career among them, medically speaking, but also work something to my advantage with those families bereaved. In short, I might help in seeing to the shipping home of the dead. The idea had merit, and I promised to discuss it further with him. For now, for the nonce, an author I would be, appeasing the scald of love with Arabian dreams, pipe-dreams all of them, as I developed the lingering thought that life was entitled to be a work of bravado, when one considered the enormous amount of stillness that followed it, all the irremediable non-moving-ness of the body and its parts. Perhaps I had postmortems on the brain, having recently done two; the inertness and apparent serenity of the cadavers made me wonder, Had they screamed or wept enough, had they spent enough, had they had their fill of toast and lamb chops, ox tongue and sherry trifle? All had stopped, but surely they had comported themselves in life as if they were already partly dead, the stress having been on decorum and poise. Why, I wondered, did we harp on the deathly during life? The dead seemed not to harp on livingness during death. It was like what I did after the postmortem was over: I set a rose in the cavity of each chest, thinking the gesture apt, but the official in charge of the morgue let out a great song and dance, yelping sacrilege and blue bloody murder. I had profaned the unprofanable. I vowed always to set a rose in there, and never mind the caveats of officials. I was trying to develop a funereal tact as well as a practice, and flowers were as firm a way to say good-bye, sorry, as anything else. Again and again I thought of Mary's yearning to put the spark of life back into the defunct. But find it where? Not among the dead, certainly.

Diary was misbehaving again, as almost always; it was neither fish, flesh, nor fowl. Nor was it the kind of thing one might have read aloud (like, say, *Glenarvon*) at the Villa Diodati during a peaceful fireside chit-chat when we were all somewhat indolently receptive in the pleasant fug while the dreadful summer splashed and banged outside. Had my pages been to the point, discharging my commission to a T, I might have been able to secure for myself a certain narcissistic indulgence as I crooned the doings of Lord B. to his insatiable self, never setting a word wrong, never seeing him at a

disadvantage. It was almost a writer's club, but Claire and I remained underprivileged citizens within it. Her stillborn soliloquy
and my *Vampyre* would have to look elsewhere for attention, as
would her child. The pudgy knuckles of our bulging Romeo would
thump my jaw before he listened to anything more of mine. I was
also troubled that, being unwise as Rossi said, I had trafficked with
La Saxonnex unclad in cundum, something Rossi never risked, and
now I did believe she had clapped me, which was like (for me)
having a Virgin Mary made of mouldy blue cheese. Remedy I had,
of course, but it would take time, and I was still trying to unravel
the dreadful skein of love and lust, friend and whore, generosity and
greed, that had come writhing out of that affair. Admittedly, so far,
I was not like Lord B. and Shelley, fathering bastards all over the
place, but I was hosting germs, physician that I was, and I had no
idea of the women's condition, as Lord B. and Shelley would not
allow me near Claire and Mary for any such purpose, though Byron
had once exclaimed that even Polidori was capable of doing an
abortion, a simple one, on request, at which Claire had squirmed and
wept. Better an abortion, though, than his threat: if the child was
female, he would deflower her, like an old witch-doctor.

Milord, however, feeling hale after his tour of the lake, requested that I examine him top to toe, omitting nothing, so I confirmed my findings regarding his legs, heard his heart going much
too fast, rales and squeaks, got him to admit the ringing in his ears,
and felt something massy in or near his kidneys. With more art I
would have learned more, but I knew enough already (I the addict
whoremaster with the clap) to tell him to stop drinking and to sleep
more. He told me, not I thought for the first time, that to lose even
an hour's sleep drove him demented and cast him into appalling
depressions, in which all became lugubrious and sour. As before, I
wished I had been able to examine Lady Byron with the same zeal,
and I told him this again, just to see how his blood pressure responded, and I felt cannonades in the jugular, saw his colour worsen,
and discerned an extra degree of perspiration under his jaw. He was
getting plump again; he and Shelley had empty-stomached their way

through Jean-Jacques-Rousseau-land. I wanted to bleed him, but he raved at the suggestion and I withdrew it; he could never stand to be bled. He complained of a muscle in his belly's front, that it twitched and seemed to drag after he had eaten, but I could establish nothing in this regard. When I mentioned laudanum and suggested he try it for his fits of sleepless agitation, he cried, "Lord Byron does not take Lord Anum—how do you like that for a joke, Doctor?" He had hoped for a better account of his health and was affronted when I handed him a caustic for an inflamed wart on his face.

He hated Switzerland, he hated France. He told Mary that he and she would publish their ghost stories together. Maurice, his boatman, told him that if they had stayed out five minutes more on the night of June 13, when B. stripped naked, their boat would have been wrecked. Such a night voyage was dangerous, Maurice had told him, but Lord B. answered him by stripping off his voluminous *robe de chambre* and handing it to him. He had not even stockings on. One day Byron arrived with two pistols and 300 napoleons, commanding Maurice to row to Chillon, where he had two torches lighted in a dungeon and wrote for two hours and a half. Leaving, he told Maurice to tip the gendarme a napoleon. *"De trop, milor,"* said the boatman. "Give it to him nonetheless," Byron said, "and tell him that the donor is Lord Byron." On another occasion, Byron brought his breakfast to the boat—cold duck and wine—eating scarcely anything but drinking all the wine, and then began to toss the food into the water, upon which Maurice demurred, only to be told that he too should refrain from food for the sake of the fishes. All very well, said Maurice, "but his lordship forgot one little circumstance. He had no appetite; I had."

I talked with anyone who would respond, digging out of Claire the tale of the day she began to copy *Childe Harold,* Part III. "Am I not a terrible person?" he said, and she answered in the negative, when he unlocked a cabinet and laid several of his sister Augusta's letters on the table. Claire saw that much of each was cast in the form of cyphers incomprehensible except to Byron and his sister. When he put them away he accused her of stealing one to embarrass him with, only to find it again when he re-counted. "Yes," she said, "he intends to make her the mother of my child, and me the aunt. Fiddlesticks. He stares me in the face in that insolent way of his and tells me he is very tired and wishes I would go." According to Shelley, who rarely spoke with me except to pass on something malicious, he once said, "She is not in love with me, Shiloh, she is just amusing herself with me." He adored having inferiors, to whom he was unflaggingly kind, but he dreaded his equals and superiors and sought to wound them. I wish I had heard the Duc de Broglie denounce him as dull, given to fatiguing paradoxes and impious jests, guilty of a crude liberalism. "In all," he said, "as soon as one's curiosity was satisfied, B.'s society was no longer attractive, and no one saw him arrive with pleasure." When he reviled the Genevois, Mme. de Staël's second husband asked him point-blank why he stayed among them, and Bonstetten, who had known Thomas Gray at Cambridge, observed that "an only half-honest little demon lightens through his sarcasm." I wished I had been able to speak with all who met him. Then I might have done a creditable job. I was in the role of someone reporting a god but denied contact with the angels. He did not so much exist in his own right as in the gossip of all those around him, who made an Olympian peepshow of him. He was a man in pain, as was I, but our pain was no bond between us.

On July 2, soaked through with brandy and opium, afflicted with a monstrous sense of having accomplished nothing either as physician, writer, biographer, socialite, rake, friend, lover, traveller, Englishman, or boor, and hardly able to sleep, breathe, eat, drink, or defaecate, I stopped keeping the journal, so that the endless rain could have me and wash me away, onward to Italy or home to London. *Their* lives went on, but mine began to wither. I was not even twenty-one.

On the bed, as often, I felt myself obeying some inexorable law
of weight; I sank, I sprawled, I floated in a void that was only the
mattress beneath me, and I felt my body forgiving me for being so
inert, so massy. My own aroma came up to meet me, a kind of
buttery-smelling aniseed. I had been reprieved, after so much gadding about, so many longings and lustings, all of them vain. Sleep
was all, easing me and renewing me as I lay there, with, all along the
inside length of me, cool healings part liquid, part breath. I knew I
was at last doing something right, that my body approved of, even
though I knew that drug-taking was an insult to the flesh's peace.
One day it would be over, this dizzy interim; for now I would let it
have its way. I had surrendered, for the time being, and was asking
naught. Each minute I sank deeper into a dimension that I knew was
not there, but the sense of doing so was all that mattered. I rolled
and wheeled, neither myself nor the man I wished to be, not so
much in a stupor as *outside* one, as if the stupor were some vast
helpful cloud I slowly invigilated, declining to enter. Shame was my
food, abasement my drink; I breathed rebuke and dreamed of amia-
ble, silken valleys in which, at my most active, I lolled, knowing I
had a supply that would hold me for two months, if only I could
steady my use of it. The trick was to soothe myself into discreet
economy.

How long, I wondered at first, could I go on with nothing in
my head, my brain a comfortable pulp, my nervous system a spider's
web long abandoned by its maker? When would the world break in
to haunt me afresh, and how? In whose image would hell reappear?
Increasing the dose would be no help, as I had discovered while a
student at Edinburgh, the hub of medicine in those days, when
Scotch gentry wandered into the anatomy hall and eyed the cadavers
being discussed, as if the lecture were some entertainment put on for
jaded souls. Paupers never got there alive. We never had a rich
cadaver, I was told; it was very much the well-to-do and the brilliant skinning and dismantling the bodies of the unfortunate; medicine had a downward social slant, and the implication was almost
that this happened only to the poor. Only the poor died; only the

poor were carved about, to reappear anonymous in abstract draw-
ings done with accuracy that never faltered. Among the cadavers
some wag occasionally placed one of those specially made wax mod-
els of a human with its front cut open and the contents tumbling
out. It was hard to tell the real thing from the fake, what with the
heavy cigar smoke against the stench and the habit we had of avert-
ing our eyes whenever not actually working. Then someone would
cut into the tinted wax and a guffaw would hover over the tables
until we got back to work and someone took the waxwork out, into
less serious regions.

    One moment I was in the House of the Surgeon at Pompeii,
fondling instruments that had more in common with pincers and
nutcrackers than with the ones I myself used; sets of compasses for
crude and heavy-handed giants were what they seemed to me, and I
thought I heard the shrieks of those they used them upon. The next
moment I was an Arabian physician, demanding that pus be allowed
to form in some poor devil's wound but refusing to touch the
genital areas of a female patient. For guidance, in a swoon, I looked
to the constellations Draco and Ursa Major. Then, in a flurry, while
I itched and flushed on my mattress in the Villa Diodati, I was
working on Lord B.'s leg, smothering it in Lemnian clay and honey-
based unguents, adjusting it into a wooden frame more often used as
a sling for a wounded arm, then tying to his calf a bezoar stone
taken from the stomach of a goat. "Hurt it, Polly," he kept saying,
"only make it well"; but I no sooner tried to manipulate the limb
than I was in the midst of another operation upon him, except that I
was an Arabian woman working on his loins, which were hermaph-
roditic: a member grew from within thick lips, and I was trimming
them both with a spoon-shaped knife.

    He, he said, had fathered the Shelleys' child, Shelley had fa-
thered Claire's; Claire was in love with me, Shelley was in love with
him, and he himself was in love with a woman so far away his
letters took longer than the average human life to reach her. "It was
not well planned, Polly." He sighed. "Oh, for more people with
fewer relationships among them. Oh, for more lonely outcasts." On

I worked, telling myself always to make the patient feel he will be cured, even when you are not certain, thus helping the curative efforts of Nature. "Keep off the leg for one whole year," I heard myself telling him, "and all should be well." I could believe in anything, just as, when preparing to go to Edinburgh University, I knew, I just knew, that I wanted to belong to it, wear whatever they would make me wear; and every coign of the building, every stone, was my church. Lord B. was looking relievedly at the array of surgical saws I had not used, flat on their sides, like cockatoos at rest, with looped, serrated feathers rising from their heads.

"Make him bleed," said Claire, but it was too late.

"Tell Albé," Mary said, "I am his ever. And Shelley's." He already knew. "I long to galvanize a stillborn child."

"Tell my lord," said Fletcher, his valet, talking in his usual brogue, "I will be sure to mind all 'e says, excepting now and then a bit of licence certingly." Lord B. knew all of Fletcher's tricks.

"Now *there* is one customer," cackled Gaby Saxonnex, "who has not come my way since he arrived. Advise milord that he is welcome; until *he* beds them, women have only been making do." I had heard it before.

The trance got thick. Faces I could no longer identify, nor voices. As still as a cadaver, I was among the raw materials of life, first to be opened up and cut apart, then redone with fresh organs, and I until recently in the pink. Then Shelley lifted a handle and hot rays of light soared through me, animating even the marrow in my new-made bones. Up I got, trembling, then with a lumbering, hardly human walk began to pick up the threads of my life, doctoring once more, but with awkward, careless force, damaging everyone I laid hands on, putting an arm back where a leg had been, and vice versa, failing to sew up the places I had opened, so that when the patients stood up their innards fell out of them and down. In no time at all, a mad crew was after me, demanding blood, which they got after chaining me to some kind of mast and then building a deep fire about me. I bubbled and melted away, remembered only as the monster who had screamed and thus proved himself a mammal after all.

As the trance faded and thinned, I heard the voice of Fletcher: " 'E's got a narsty flush on 'im, my lord; 'e's not long for it, if you arx me, and 'e a doctor." Lord B. picked me up, almost fell, then lifted me from the bed and set me down on the cold stone of the empty fireplace, where Fletcher mopped me down with what he said was fresh well-water, but which I misheard as *fresh well-wisher,* such being my condition. "Where's 'is medicine-cabinet, my lord? Where is the cabinet of Doctor Polidori?"

Byron found it.

" 'E 'as took the hopium again," Fletcher said. "This room is a den of it, but I see no pipe."

"Hush," Byron said to him. "The man is coming round."

"An 'arsh corner if you arx me." Fletcher would never be said. His gift was for didactic embellishment.

"No, not wine," Lord B. said. "He has stimulants enough for a whole navy. Not wine, but this." He planted a kiss on my brow, then on my lips, and stood ceremoniously back, leaning on Shelley as if he had given his all. In turn they all kissed me, the waning and mocked Polidori, who had soared out and away from the condition that disgraced him.

"Not that I have not been displeased," Lord B. was saying, headmaster-like, "but I can see we have neglected you." That was his mood just then, but it had taken much to wring it out of him, he who had not wanted to give a fig; a Polidori had to die, almost, before compassion came his way from the eagles on so high a crag. Only Claire's kiss had impetuous warmth in it, as if she knew how, among our group, we were the sufferers, the ones done-to, the play-things of their lordlyships (if such a word there were). And she, dark vixen that she was, she kissed for two; it was almost as if, through her and her child, the future cared about me after all. But Byron thought it was his kiss that fetched me back.

I loved having that audience to awaken to: Lord B.'s high forehead with its curls in retreat, his heavy-lidded sensualist's eyes, the curlicued mouth; Claire the gypsy, looking about fifteen because of pregnancy's slight chubbiness; Mary, a female dominie, her face revealing a mind that had looked into itself once too often and had been shocked by what it found—such outlandish austerities; and Shelley, the importunate boy with the aloof, unfocussed eyes, not to mention Fletcher, his face all seamed leather, his eyes purging small white seeds of something or other, his mouth slowly manoeuvring as the words formed in his mind. Any audience would have been welcome, as proof of survival, but this quintet was capital; it was all emotion, concern; for once they were thinking about someone else, not as a collector's piece or as a chunk of the usable population but as someone they cared about. Lord B., who was feeling things keenly, or was putting on a truly convincing front, handed me my cricket ball, knowing it was something I liked to fiddle with while mustering myself, deciding what to do or say. Warm from his hand, it all of a sudden occupied mine, a leather planet, and for a while I indulged the thought that they had all come to get me up to go outside on the grass, to play cricket in some unruly fashion appropriate to Switzerland, perhaps like the game I had seen on a punch bowl, the only piece of Chinese ceramic to depict the game: fleecy clouds, a cornfield of intense yellow, players on pale blue grass all grouped closely together, as never in the actual game, for the painter's convenience. The players had a windblown, stunted quality I had always admired, as if the painter had watched them through a distorting glass. My friends, however, even though they must have seemed distorted at first, as my eyes failed to settle, steadied down into themselves, full-blown and leaning over the bed towards me, upon which, evidently, I had been lying with my head over the side, dangling, and my right hand touching the floor. The bolster, nowhere to be seen, had slipped off at the other side, and my other hand had been resting on my rib cage or heart. I was a painting that came alive, then sat up, took the proffered glass of water, then the neatly cut pieces of bread. Food, they thought, was the answer, and indeed it was, although my eyes and nostrils poured, I kept getting gooseflesh and muscle twitches, and I sweated profusely. Through the hot and cold flashes I took some *pasta in brodo,* incongruous as an angel munching a sausage. The ball I set down by me on the mattress, as if meaning to go out later and disport myself. I yawned and yawned, not for sleep but driven by some languor from the opiate. There seemed no air, not that the day felt close (it *had* been raining, but the skies had cleared). I leaned forward, as if the air in front of me were more available, and tried again, breathing in so hard that I heard squeaks from my nose and bronchia. The patient was showing signs of interest in coming back to life, but he was far from well and very far from weaned.

At last, with unnecessary earnests of devotion and good faith, they began to take their leave, until only Lord B. remained, half his face disconsolate, the other half stern. "You must not," he said, without finishing. "We thought we had lost—you." I assured him, as a medical man, that I always carefully calculated what I did with my own supplies. He had watched executions, he told me, enough to teach him how "dreadfully soon things become indifferent. Or *one* does."

"It was a *congé,*" I told him fancily. "I took a holiday from you all."

"You played truant, you mean." His face glowed, then wanned. He had flushed; he looked awful.

"How long? It can't have been long."

"Three days," he said. "Messages have come from Geneva. The oppidans are concerned. Polly, my dear, you are a hit with the bourgeois. Life has opened up for you. No more London, no more Yorkshire pud. Here you shall stay. I have a mind to let them have you."

"Nay, milord," I answered, "my presence among them shall be as fleeting as life itself. I must on, to Italy, land of my father. I have a journey, sir, shortly to go; my master calls me, I cannot say no. Ah, I had it wrong."

"Quoting *King Lear.*" He laughed. "You must be recovering.

Doctor Polidori, how is our Polly today, then? Shall he to cricket with the local barbarians or back to sleep?"

To sleep, clutching the ball, I thought, but said not a word; I was too interested in this apparition, in which Lord B.'s bonhomie fought something much curter, as if he had something else he had to say but had no idea how to start. He helped me to the privy and watched me make water, as an aristocrat might, whereas a doctor would never so presume.

"You have the build of a whoremaster, Polly. It must have waxed thus from steady use." Dumbfounded, I could find no answers beyond, "It serves, milord. I sometimes wish it far enough, however."

"Oh, to set it out at midnight like the cat, to have its own encounters without the proximate shame of an attached mind. Polly, we yearn for the stars. We end up clapped."

Had he seen? No, nor had he felt the tingle, the mild strangury of dysuria. How many times had he been caught with it?

He had lost count, he said; then he quoted Boswell to the effect that he was a poor man who had never been wounded in front. "I," he said jovially, feeling the buttons on his shirt, "always go to the Colonel for protective armoury."

Cundum, he meant. Sheep's gut. He was a wiser man than I, then, but then I had no John Cam Hobhouse looking after me, seeing me off at Dover with a chest of essentials or having one shipped after I had gone. I imagined my father's face as it would be if I sent post-haste for cundums to be sent Poste Restante, Geneva. I had always thought that the nation of doctors should have come up with something superior, that such trials of intimate venery should not be left to the military; but we had done little, prudish with life, prurient with disease and death. Lord B. sent his cantos home, rhyming *canto* with *portmanteau,* and the supplies of sheep-gut came discreetly back. What if Murray were to pay me in similar kind for the journal he clearly was not going to get? In loathing, say. "I asked you, Mister Polidori, for a candid account of Lord Byron, not for all this to-and-fro about yourself. Were you even *with* him?"

"*Doctor,* sir," I'd say. "That is *my* title." It was one of the few rebukes within my power.

"To sleep, then," Lord B. said to me in the real world of drug-made stupor and disappointment funk. "It is three in the afternoon. We do not expect to see you until midnight, or breakfast."

"You have never seen me at breakfast yet," I said. "That is one communion I do not attend, unless I have to." Even as I spoke, my memory began to return: first my recollection of my most recent look at Claire, whose obstetrician I had become, not (as Byron had joked some while back) her abortionist. How compact she was in her bloat, how pearly in her nether regions—how *unused.* Where I had half expected to discover brown and faded fins, the result of Lord B.'s brutal onsets, I found only a glazed tunnel to paradise. Her hair there was finer than many women had on their heads. The aroma was sweet, although treacly and somewhat acid, as was not unusual. Her pelvis was ample enough, I thought, for her to have no trouble when she came to term. Perhaps she thought it strange to have so young a doctor peering into her, palping her belly for the healthy runt within, but she glowed with charm throughout, and I began to see what Lord B. had once seen in her beyond mere availability; Claire was ebullient and voluptuous, but her wild streak was tempered with uncreative intelligence. "I never took money from him," she told me during the last examination, "I never shall. All he ever gave me was punishment." I saw no bruises, but he no longer pummelled her or bit. He had become reconciled to her unwanted presence. How this household, I thought, runs on the seed of life. Without it, no trouble. In their passion to inflict themselves on one another, they spray seed as if there were nothing but barren land hereabouts, and so they get one another with perpetual child— children who come to unfortunate ends. Whether they were diseased or not I hardly knew, though I suspected Byron had been as badly off as I; but Claire showed no signs of infection—no discharge, the cervix not reddened or friable—and I was heartily glad. It felt eerie, the wounded doctor viewing the unwanted, unwed mother-to-be, but it was a healthier sight than that of Rossi romping with my late beloved, whose goal was pelf. How wholesome Claire was down there, whereas Lord B., when I examined him on command, seemed flaccid in the extreme, although large, and he had darkened in some areas. The entire kit lacked tone, I thought, and the lips of the meatus looked red and swollen.

"You have it, milord," I told him. "Shall I proceed?"

"Of course, Polly. Why else are you here?"

I did, causing him some distress, and telling him in the course of it that I too had been wounded there.

"Then we have both been bitched," he said. "There must have been a first to have it, who did not contract it from anyone else. They say it had its start in the pyramids, when the undertakers took to coupling with corpses."

"The germ," I told him, "did not invent itself. God made it, in His wisdom to teach us a lesson."

"God had no business clapping us," he said. "It has always seemed to me gratuitous, tossed in, out of malice. May I dress?" I told him to, but could not shake from my head the image of that inordinate shank reposing on a plate, like something dead which had once been only too much alive, writhing and tottering: a battering engine upon which, even when it was in repose, the veins bulged with unnatural traffic of blood, and the cullions hung low like slingshots. Without this, I thought, half the trouble in the world would never have been. He had tupped up more melodrama than any man alive.

All this came back as my memory recovered.

Lord B. was asking something. "Who *was* the inventor, then?"

"Oh, not Cundum," I said, "it was a certain Fallopius, milord, in the sixteenth century. He who named the ova-tubes in our sisters. Fallopius of Padua." I seemed not to have full command of my lips or my impetus of speech. Things were coming out slowly and wrong. "It was a medicated linen sheath fitted over the glans, tied securely at the base with a pink ribbon. They called them overcoats then."

"I heard," he said, "they were armour against love and gossamer against disease." Now, weeks after that medical appointment, he was coaxing me to sleep without words, his hand upon my brow while he stood there, not looking down at me but looking away, through the window, at the mountain. The most notorious man in England was enacting my lullaby, as if we had never had words between us, or had not had nothing in common. Why had he not hired some all-competent thirty-year-old? Had he been afraid he might not have been able to dominate such a man? Had my being a mere twenty been my main recommendation, when all along I had thought he wanted a sample of Edinburgh's best, an authority on dream-walking? No, by George, by George Gordon, what he had wanted was a travelling companion-cum-biographer doctor who happened to be of an age comparable to that of the two women, Claire and Mary. That was it. I was there for them, to console them about the rough-and ready ways of their older menfolk. I was there to be one of the girls when Lord B. and Shelley, the two great romantics, went off on expeditions designed to produce lines about Chillon and Intellectual Beauty, as indeed I already had been. Had I been expected to attempt seduction of them both in their masters' absence? Had I failed utterly in some implicit duty that the two poets had taken for granted? Could I have managed it? Claire, yes, I thought so; she would have done it out of pique. But Mary? Mary was too sisterly for any such attempt, but we had become more and more close. And now I was poxed or clapped or both, and smothered with opium, no use to anyone save the anatomist.

"Good night, Lord Byron," I whispered in the heart of the Genevan afternoon, my eyes closed against the man who stood there still, self-engrossed, his hand still on my wet brow; only the painter was missing. Claire, Mary, and I—the children—were sailing round the lake together, visiting Rousseauistic shrines, inscribing our names on salient walls, putting up at inns where the servants were better at tidying than at cleaning, and troughing mightily on fish. Even if he and Shelley added us up, making the most of our paltry ages, we would have composed only a middle-aged epicene, in the mid-fifties. It was clear to even my waning brain that the three of us

were backdrop to the premature aging of the other two, busily
burning themselves out in the interests of great poetry, if that was
what they always wrote. *Queen Mab* was. "Darkness" would be. It
was a noble enough role, nobler than corking the sluices of Miss
Saxonnex.

When I recovered, I vowed, I would make more love to my
occupation, revering and romanticizing what Byron and Shelley
merely *used*. There was time yet to confess my joy at their presence,
bend my lips to their knuckles without quite touching, in the manner of the Swiss; but it was too late to attempt country pleasures
with them, oh, lord, yes; I was not there to give Misses Mary and
Claire a dose of what ailed me, sympathetic as they might have been.
The hand lifted from my brow. A footstep grated on stone. I was
alone again and I took a little more, to see me off.

When I awoke, after dreams that would go on unnerving me
for days, I lay there, soothed but itching and flushed, my mind again
on Mary and Claire, the latter of whom seemed within my reach, at
least for worship, to be done on my knees or in some erect, crusader-
like stance, in which the twenty-year-old addressed his junior in
fulsome language fit for a medieval poem. I knew it now, having
long suspected it: I needed to adore, to feel the chivalry in me
spurred to life. If Claire was a fallen woman, she was also an as-
cended soul, in my book at any rate, and she could be dealt with, I
was sure, in hyperbole and sugared, elaborate phrases. She had been
brutalized, so she knew the lure of pretty talk that did not bruise,
still able to regard herself as what she was: an elegant vessel already
far beyond all received notions of dignity, and her essence as I
perceived it during humid noontime was that of a mauve flamingo
arising from the dung-laden waters of some slow African river.
Byron did not love her, like her, or even tolerate her, but he was
willing to tumble upon her as if she were some Ostend chambermaid, and she, in her state of abased infatuation (at least as it had
been), was more than willing to accept his leavings, which he

squirted into her at random, uncaring and oblivious. In this, I thought, in the viscous aftermath of my opium binge, she was like Leeuwenhoek, the Delft haberdasher who devised the microscope and set spots of his own ejaculate on slides, thus discovering that what men sprayed into women was not made of homunculi. He also discovered the vehemence of public indignation in the cries of Onan levelled at him. Claire and Leeuwenhoek were doing the experiment through their own bodies, and hang the consequences, almost two hundred years apart. He found a role for women and she fulfilled it, finding that women could take something into them from men and then deprive them of it for ever. She meant no harm, but she was lovable in her recklessness, for allowing him to push her lower and lower until she had nothing left to lose except what he could never have back from her. It was almost as good as shooting Shelley on the lake—something I had longed to do since our silly race across it.

If I could only pull myself together, I thought, I might be able to set myself up as Claire's squire, her swain, and let L.B. ridicule us both. A little pageantry of excessive politeness would show itself at the dinner table, on the lawn, on the way into town, and just possibly would catch on. I was moving in smart enough society to have learned a few suave obeisances; indeed, Lord B. had resented my constant goings-out, my need for company: unfairly, as he went nowhere himself and was no company for me. Tighten up, I told myself, and tell her how like the dawn she is, how like a river is her hair. Back to my journal I would go, to make her immortal.

When I walked unsteadily into the salon the four of them were lying on the floor, drinking wine and scribbling away. It was a literary afternoon of a languorous sort. Exaggerated applause greeted me, as if I had accomplished something major, rather than desisting from opium. Byron was working on "Darkness," he said, Shelley on his "Hymn," and Mary on her story of horror. The whole idea of a ghost story seemed to have lapsed, though I had resolved to finish mine, tempted to make a long novel of it, for something to keep me going over half a year. I knew I would not, however: a story it was meant to be, a story it was.

"Someone has stolen the sail," Byron said, as if referring to what lay beneath his hand and pen. "From the boat. They tried to take the anchors as well, but, as luck had it, I was there at the time, lying in wait since before dawn, and I fired several pistol shots at them, to scare them. They decamped, possibly wounded. Polly, you have missed all the fun. Now we cannot go anywhere at all."

"And someone tried to break into the Villa Diodati," Mary said. "But the windows were locked. They could not force them open, but the marks were there. It is as if the whole of Geneva is on the move, trying to frighten us into going."

"We guarded you while you slept," Claire said with a smudge-stained face, as if she had been weeping. "Now we are safe again."

"Yes," I said, "Polidori, king of cutpurses, famous man-at-arms, is here to defend your lives and your honour. Left to me, you will all live to be a hundred."

"I was a hundred when I arrived," Byron said. "Remember the hotel register at Sécheron."

"That was how I discovered you were here," Claire said with a wan, heedless intonation. "It seems like years ago. Everything was rather jolly then."

"And then there was this," Byron said, handing me a small packet of paper in which, clearly, some powder had been wadded up. "Magnesia, from the local apothecary. It is bad. I would like you to take it upstairs and test it." I reeled at the thought of all those stairs. It smelled quite good.

"We'll all come," Shelley said. "Oh, for a bit of real science."

Up we went, wine in hand, Lord B. shoving me from behind to speed me up, I resisting so as not to be out of puff when I arrived. First I tested with sulphuric acid as they all sighed and exclaimed, amazed by my rather simple bag of tricks, for all the world as if they were watching a Renaissance alchemist. The test specimen in the wineglass turned red rose, so the specimen was clearly bad. Downstairs again we went, though I needed my vials by me. Lord B. sent for the right local official, who came post-haste, arrogant and high-handed, refused to watch the acid test but also refused to leave. He

wanted to watch Lord B.'s ménage at play; and so, since I was the
only one of us left sober, with a splitting head I collared him about
the neck and dragged him through the doorway, in the act breaking
his spectacles. He then went and stretched himself out along a wall
for several hours, moaning and raving. Had some dark star crossed
our fates for all this to happen? Had Polidori, in his opium trance,
let loose some unbidden force of nature that would eventually engulf us all, our possessions too? No, it was bad luck. In court that
week, before five judges, I explained the events, repeated the sulphuric test to their satisfaction, pointed out that the alumina in the
magnesia might have killed Lord B., not one of your trivial personages, and ridiculed the official's plea of calumny.

"It also contained carbonate of ammonia," said one of the
judges. "It was hardly magnesia at all. Twelve florins for the broken
spectacles and costs." It was over, and I had had the refreshing
experience of demonstrating my skills in the open, so to speak. Life
had descended into some litigious phase: next thing, there was a
report of Fletcher, Rushton, Maurice, and Berger's having been rude
and insulting to the local constabulary, something I was able to
believe of the querulous Berger but not the others: Maurice was too
supple, the other two too schooled. Someone was after us, that was
plain, no doubt for the kind of cannibal market the Villa Diodati
contained: that odd mixture of stud farm and red-lamp shop, which
it indeed was. Perhaps the bouquet of spent and dried cordial that
came off B., except when he had been swimming, drove them potty,
reminding them of how much they had missed in life, how little
they were going to lose to death. Why, even Polidori had been
kissed on the brow by the same infamous lord; and, during sleep,
who knew where else? Lord B. was not above a cuddle or two,
between men, at the keyboard, when he was feeling expansive; he
liked to doodle on the notes, whatever else was happening. And I
was enough of a physician never to flinch at the unwonted touch,
not when I considered how many such touches I had given to others;
I knew the flesh, its automatic quality, and how the nerves responded heedless of who made the touch. Why, to yawn broadly

made the scrotal sac and the tip of the glans respond in kind, which meant that yawning's cousin was swyving. Indeed, it would be hard, I thought, to keep one signal in the nerves from having something to do, somewhere, with nerves in some other part of the body. Our oneness was not in question.

Was it that? Sexually, we were not what you would call interchangeable: there were many possible relationships among us that a simple permutation revealed, most of them missing—Polidori-Claire, for instance, which many might have thought likely, as in the cards; but, that aside, we were *of a mind,* as close-knit a group of abstainers as you might find, whether in Geneva or elsewhere, and much more dove-tailed than, say, Polidori and his social clique of (among the newer set) Countess Breuss, with a husband in Russia, another in Venice; Mrs. Saussure, a wax talkative figure; Massey Jr., impudent, confident, insolent, ignorant puppy; Schlegel the pompous and presumptuous *literato;* Mme. de Broglie (Mme. de Staël's daughter), that beautiful, dirty-skinned woman. And so on. We remained scattered, my Genevois friends and I, whereas at the Villa Diodati we five were a small beleaguered army, huddled together against the storm of prejudice, living the life of the questing, piratical flesh, as open with one another as seagulls. If we went to jail for crimes of intimate intercourse, we would go together, taking our babies with us, whether born in wedlock or out. Breaking the rules was the important thing, whether the bourgeoisie worried about us now or later. Much as I moved about, gliding from a soirée here to a ball there, from the Genevan Liberal Society to a discussion at Dr. Odier's, I moved in three main sets—the cantons of Genthoud, Coppet, and Geneva—whereas the Villa D. was a closed experiment, a private affinity. We suffered, I was sure, more from peepers than from burglars, and those broken windows, mauled shutters, told more of zeal than of greed.

What might they see, peering in? I had wondered. They would not see much except for Claire sometimes on her hands and knees, like a lioness padding about, her nightdress almost off, her with-held baby almost grazing the rug. Had they been subtler, these oglers, they might have considered how easy it was to catch a woman in the act of speaking, or howling or screaming, and to ride down the liquid torrent of her sound into the most secret recesses of her body. That was why I found the spectacle of women singing a voluptuous idyll. Even when Claire spoke, or cried, as when B. kicked her while she was on all fours, or when Mary (May to us) spoke shyly at length, I was engrossed by the oral cavity, the mucous tunnel of the throat, the promise of even wider lumens below. The nerves above vibrated those beneath, and these women were *open:* that was what inflamed me, so much so that a woman in the very act of speaking (no more than that) struck me as engaged in hectic sexual display. The clamorous, mobile mouth high up evoked the silent, helpless one low down, and that was enough to stiffen Polidori for an afternoon. Opium lulled me, but the drive soon came back; I was young and urgent, and my supply had been cut off. Perhaps, I reasoned, I should go back to Gaby S. on a strictly unemotional basis and think of Claire during the most violent moments, much as (if I deduced aright) Lord B. thought of his Augusta. All men, I was beginning to conclude, needed an *agape* and an *eros:* a mind-love and a body-lust.

At dinner one evening, Lord B. began to drop names, citing the eminent men he had met without being impressed, and I could not keep myself from intervening with a list of my own. The cricket match would have many more than twenty-two players now, plus two umpires. No one interrupted, it being their way to see how far Polidori would go if given enough rope. Shelley was always waiting for me to hang myself in front of his face. As it was, to abbreviate the matter, I used surnames only, fielding my acquaintances at random:

"Staël
de Broglie
Randall
Roccas
Schlegel
Brema

Dumont
Bonstetten
Bottini
Mongelas—"

"Batsmen all," Lord B. quipped. "Is that the batting order? We are surely one man short, or did Madame de Stale fart and blow him away?" They were still laughing when I resumed, with my usual sound of forbearing good nature.

"I was not counting, of course. The Saladins. Mathould. Rossi. Naple. Brelaz. Clemann. Mouskinpouskin—"

Here Lord B. burst into Scotch mirth again at the very sound of such a name and asked if I had been taking courses in pronunciation. "Did you steal sails and anchors, Polly? Did you stare in at their windows? Have you done these people any *damage* that you list them so—greengrocerly?"

"Milord, a little dignity, if you please."

"Polly, did you know that, behind your back, they call you my pimp? *Pimp.*"

He often lied thus, to get a rise out of me, and I had learned that when he did so it was akin to his kicking Claire, so I went to the end of my improvised list, amazed to have met so many. "Breuss," I resumed, "Gatelier, Toffettheim, Foncet, Saussure, Breadalbane" (guffaws, of course). I ran the last ones all together in my haste, but ended with a grateful smile: "SlaneyWhiteGalston"— a breath—"BinghamCunninghamBelgrayTillotsonTrevanion"—another breath—"MeersSimmonsLloydJablonskiDalrymple and"—as I suddenly opened up, seeing clear roadway ahead of me—*"les* Odier, Lord Kinnoul, Somers, Lord Glenorchy, Mr. Evans, Coda the songstress, Mr. Pitt, Mr. Filleul, Lord Killamarsh, Mr. Gale, Mrs. Davies, Mr. Pictet, Dr. Granquel, Dr. Gardner, Caravella, Sir John St. Aubyn, the Shelleys, and—"

Now he bellowed it, Lord B. did. "Miss Claire Clairmont, and George Gordon Byron, Sixth Lord. Tell me, Polly, have you been to *bed* with all these people, or are these the ones you pimp for?

What happened to Miss Gabrielle Saxonnex, pastmistress of diseases? This is no cricket team. These are not crickets but scuttling cockroaches, putting up with you to your face and deriding you behind your back. Polly, my dear, you have been had. These are your executioners."

"No," I told him as calmly as I could, "these are the dear people who have shielded me from the loneliness of being incessantly in your company, milord, or suddenly deprived of it, either by your absence or some sundry black mood of your most recent spawning."

"The little devil," he said, looking right at me but speaking as if I were elsewhere, "has spunk in his teeth. On, Polly. Be hanged for a sheep, my dear. On."

"Some among them happen to be my patients, as Miss Claire; as yourself, milord. I am their servant."

"Like the devil you are," he said, reddening. "What are you now, Polly? A clack-licker? A wart-fancier?"

"Don't," said May.

"Let him," Shelley said. "Let them both."

Claire looked through us all and walked out, both hands cupped against her belly.

"Clack-licker or not," I told him, boldly enough, "let us agree that even clack-lickers, when they at last venture out into society, missing perhaps the swamp noises of suction, should at least wipe their chops before presuming to kiss a lady's hand. Nor, I venture to suggest, should one reek of last Michaelmas's spending with whatever drab under whatever bridge in whatever filth-ridden section of whatever city. Ammonia does not endear one to one's friends. Nor even to fellow clack-lickers, my noble lord."

Opium or its aftermath was talking. I called it poppy courage. The more you said, the more fortitude and foolhardiness you had with which to say more, all of it gangrenous and uncivil. "Seed, milord, is not your best social lubricant."

He mumbled something about privacy and glue, but it did not

come out right, with any *éclat,* and on I went, not quite raving, yet not talking reasonably either.

"The washing of the hands should precede the laying on of hands, milord. It is elementary sanitation, milord."

"Puppy," said the accursed Shelley, who dreaded live burial.

"Hound of hell," said his May, galvanist of the stillborn.

Without a word, Lord B. left the table, pounded upstairs with his limp worsening all the way, and returned with my big tureen of leeches, all of which he dumped into the fire, even going so far as to peel the last few away from the inside of the bell jar with his hand. The fire sputtered and crackled, and I smelled the burning blood.

May seemed delighted, while Shelley stared at me as if defying me to save them. I budged not, knowing I had another supply in a closet, and those were the leeches to which I had fed opium. They clung without sucking.

"Well," said Lord B. "How was that for sanitation?"

"Splendid, milord," I said. "I love a lord to clean up after me. Good scrub-boys are hard to come by."

When he was at his most furious, Lord B. would confound you with one of his famous changes of direction, showing little of what he truly felt and masking it behind something else. You had to decipher him. Out of the room he limped (during fits of anger his limp got much worse). We could hear him rummaging about for something, cursing as he opened and slammed drawers, then doors; but eventually he returned, cackling, a small pouch one foot square in his hand. "Next time you go off to shame or otherwise degrade a ball, a soirée, Doctor Polly-wolly, take this along, send the children packing, and show them these one at a time, with all the ladies seated. This is sometimes how they do things off on the byroads of Turkey." He opened the packet but made no move to show us its contents. Being the physician, and therefore the appointed handler of dubious objects, I felt in and fished out—what? A pen-and-ink drawing so horrible to contemplate that, in a reflex motion, I shoved it back. I had seen a groin, presumably male, minus its sexual kit. I tried again, and again shoved the drawing back: a headless torso, as like to have been dreamed up in some vice-den in Constantinople (or London even) as among the back roads of Turkey. I was looking at fantasy horrors, I thought. The third was so awful, but Claire and Shelley so eager to see, that I held it out, revealing a person whose throat had been cut, which was bad enough, and whose tongue had been dragged through the gash and split in two. Claire howled and ran. May appeared to faint. Shelley felt at the front of his trews, no doubt composing some hymn to phallic beauty, and Lord B. nodded sagely, man-of-the-worldly. "Has it not a remarkably cleansing quality, Polly? Surely my physician has not gone weak at the knees? Vesalius, after all. This they call the Anatolian cravate. I once saw it done, and the procedure required much juggling and adjusting. This is what I had in mind for our thieves, Polly, those sail-stealers and anchor-robbers. It could be applied to almost anyone with a long enough tongue." I handed the packet back to him, half wondering what Rossi would do with such a thing. Perhaps indeed it was a brothel trapping. Lord B. was looking at me with a sardonic smile, part derision, part appetite; he lusted for me, I was sure. Thank God we were nowhere near the piano stool, which always set him off. He refused to accept the packet back until I had retrieved the Anatolian cravate, then insisted I mount it in my bedroom next to the crucifix. "To remind you, Polly, of what happens to those who provoke the Byrons." In the end I took the thing, but with no intention of displaying or mounting it. Claire came back, May recovered, Shelley lay back and yawned.

It had all been in a day's horrors. Was this what May's story was going to be like? Or my own? Exhausted, I climbed those stairs again and began to write my ghost story, this time moving on from the first appearance of Lord Ruthven, as I fixed to call my vampyre, to his effect on Londoners of his glaucous eyes and the leaden rays that seemed to flow from them with viscous indirectness. All wished to see him, he was so peculiar, especially those devotees of sensation who had already sated themselves during the summer and autumn preceding that winter. Lady Mercer, who doted on monsters, threw herself at him, to no purpose, and she left the field. He had a winning tongue, all said *(this* was the link with Anatolia then!), but he plied it mostly among virtuous matrons, not among the courtesans.

Then, casting about for another name, I thought of Aubrey, to be my other personage: an orphan of wealthy parents who had died young. Aubrey had a sister, of a very sheltered disposition, whereas he himself had a high, generous soul full of romantic candour. Many mothers beset him, and their daughters too, giving him a false notion of his merit and his talents. All his life he had yearned to find such a ghost as he had read about (I heard Lord B. shouting to me from downstairs; I was too engrossed to answer), but he had found none, until Lord Ruthven, with whom he would go abroad, making the journey known as the Tour, which saved young gentlemen from looking like innocents fallen from the skies. Now Aubrey noticed that the generous Lord Ruthven passed out his largesse not to the deserving and the virtuous, but to the base and vicious. On I went:

> At Brussels and other towns through which they passed, Aubrey was surprized at the apparent eagerness with which his companion sought for the centres of all fashionable vice; there he entered

—I took a little more laudanum, and some wine—

> into all the spirit of the faro table: he betted, and always gambled with success, except where the known sharper was his antagonist, and then he lost even more than he gained; but it was always with the same unchanging face.

This looming monster left behind him a trail of ruined youths and bankrupted fathers, yet without making any kind of profit himself. All he won from the innocent he lost on the next hand. I took them to Rome next, where letters from his guardians awaited him, exhorting him to return and quit this evil Ruthven, under whose influence the benign matrons of his acquaintance had all undertaken lives of vice. Now, in Rome, Lord Ruthven was romancing a young Italian woman of noble family, upon whom his intentions were bestial. I wrote:

> Aubrey retired; and, immediately writing a note, to say, that from that moment he must decline accompanying his Lordship in the remainder of their proposed tour, he ordered his servant to seek other apartments.

Aubrey I now propelled towards Greece, and Athens in particular, where, under the same roof as he, there lived a being so exquisite,

> so beautiful and delicate, that she might have formed the model for a painter, wishing to pourtray on canvass the promised hope of the faithful in Mahomet's paradise, save that her eyes spoke too much mind.

She had the sleepy, luxurious look, I thought to say, of an animal suited but to the taste of an epicure. This was Ianthe, the Kashmere butterfly of my tale, the gazelle who told him stories while, Polidori-like, he sketched the ruins. One tale she told him was of the living vampyre, elsewhere known as Vroucolocha, Vardoulacha, Verdulak, Broucoloka, and Goul, making his blood run cold with images of young girls fed to the monster. "Mock them not, dear Aubrey. All who refuse to believe in the vampyre are vouchsafed a dreadful proof." "Then," he asked, "how do they look, these monsters?" Her description fitted Lord Ruthven exactly, against whom he yearned to protect that frank, infantile, uneducated young Greek girl of an almost fairy form. Something dreadful was hovering over them, even though he believed no more in vampyres than before.

One day, obliged to journey forth on an expedition, he had to pass through a wood, which they told him all Greeks avoided after darkness had fallen. Ianthe begged him to wait until daylight, for dusk was near. He scoffed and said there were no vampyres, in that wood or anywhere else, being a young man of exalted bravery.

Then I wrote a small part that pleased me much, more for its horrendous implication than for what it shewed:

> He did not perceive that day-light would soon end, and that in the horizon there was one of those specks which, in the warmer climates, so rapidly gather into a tremendous mass.

I scratched out Ianthe's begging so as to have him not perceive, etc., and rode him out into that sudden sunset.

That was all. The rest of my tale lingered on my own horizon like the tremendous mass of which I had written. At least what I had done thus far was no longer a mere speck, and in the amphitheater of my mind's ear I called out to May, "I have got my man up, May, if only on horseback." Opium or good intentions would accomplish the rest. I was one of *them* again, the writing family I took my sustenance from, and no end delighted by the way certain personages in my story or its accoutrements—La Breuss, La Dalrymple Hamilton, Pictet and Bonstetten, Lord B., Shelley, and even myself—came from daily life in Geneva or Diodati. To be on both sides of the fence while doing famously on either was an alarming pleasure, evocative of the strange hinterlands we lived in, thinking our lives a dream, wishing our fictions lives. As far as I was concerned, this was the literary life lived to the hilt, even if I was to walk with a slight limp for ever after or have recourse to the poppy at the merest incident. Polidori was graduating from the status of hanger-on, permanent appendix, to that of fellow-artist, accomplice toiler in the same vineyard. Had I had the energy, I would have executed there in my room (where Lord B.'s grisly Anatolian cravate did *not* hang next the crucifix) a neat little jig, just to celebrate my membership. I did a horizontal version, anyway, determined to read aloud to them my recent writings as soon as confidence had sprung anew. And that meant a bigger dose of what soothed me. Was I, I wondered, taking that much? Was I taking more, even, than most children did when they had the croup, and a spoonful or two of some vaunted elixir came their way, to soothe at bedtime? Laudanum-takers all, we were a nation, a society, made one by narcotics, and never a thought was spared as to how much went down our different throats. At Diodati, however, I was the only one taking anything, apart from Lord B. and Shelley with their drink. To them all, the air of our planet was intoxicant enough, it seemed: they breathed in, and their brains coursed with preternatural zest.

I had not liked, however, the way Lord B. looked at me or seemed to threaten with his ghoulish displays. I had opened my mouth to his disadvantage, thus exemplifying the worm that turns, and he would not forgive. I had already told him that, among my travels among the *ton* of Geneva, I had been acquainted with certain opportunities that had arisen in the Brazils. The Danish consul himself had advised me, if I cared, to take a developed interest as soon as possible if indeed I meant to quit Switzerland. I saw myself tending helpless savages along the Amazon or routing plagues deep in the jungle. Lord B.'s response had been only that the savages of Geneva at least spoke French or English. What need to stir when, visibly, the world lay at my feet? That was his sarcasm, of course. Little did I know that he was already formulating a letter he would later on send to John Murray, his publisher, indicating that I was about to return to England (untrue), with a view to taking passage for the Brazils (I did not go). I understood my calling well, he thought and said, and had no want of general talent; my faults were the faults of pardonable vanity and youth. But my remaining with him was out of the question. He had enough to do to manage his own scrapes, which were legion; and, as precepts without examples were not the most gracious of homilies, he had been thinking that it would be better to give me my *congé*, although he knew no great harm of me, and some certain good. How coy of him. I was clever and accomplished, he wrote, knew my profession, by all accounts, well, and was honourable in my dealings. Not in the least malevolent, he said. I wondered about that. May had told me that Shelley had heard him out on this matter, and his mind was made up. Polidori was to go, and never mind the fact that I had disrupted my entire professional life to accompany him thus far on a wild goose chase; I might, instead, have accompanied Miss Arrow to India or stayed in England, there to reap a lucrative living in the treatment of sleepwalkers. Here I had run into sleepwalkers of a different stamp: not mere somnambulists, but the living dead in all of their heads, meaning the ghosts they had left behind—abandoned wives and children, dead wives and dead children, discarded mistresses and undone sisters: the wreckage of their genius, if genius it were. In truth, I had been ministering to a flock of cuckoos, and my only reputable practice had been in Geneva itself, among the English and the Genevois, whose living and dead had become my medical parish. All I needed to do with Lord B., then, was to decide the matter before he did. In my heart I had decided already, but was far from ready to move on, having formed too many sundry links. Besides, my patients depended on me.

Little did I know then, although Claire had dropped certain succulent phrases of it in my vicinity, that his true opinion was less mild, and that he had already been airing it among them. The sole companion of his journey to Geneva had been a young physician who needed to make his way in the world, having seen precious little of it; he was therefore desirous of seeing much society, more than Lord B. had the appetite for. Polidori was altogether too gregarious. Lord B. had presented him to those gentlemen of Geneva for whom he had letters of introduction, and, having thus set him up —seen him in a situation sufficient to make his own way—had more or less left him to it. Lord B. had been at some pains to explain even to those who knew it best that in Geneva he had retired altogether from society except for one English family—the one in the Villa Diodati. His truest sentiments, however, had knives in them, and he had already had several outbursts, in one of which, said Claire (who warned me that he intended to be "rid of us both in the near future, both the mother and the doctor"), he had expressed himself as never more disgusted with any human production than with THE ETERNAL NONSENSE AND TRACASSERIES AND EMPTINESS AND ILL-HUMOUR AND

VANITY OF THAT YOUNG PERSON, even if he did have some talent, was a man of honour, and showed certain dispositions of amendment in which he had been aided by a little subsequent experience. He might turn out well yet, he said. At this, Claire faltered and began to cry, knowing that he had already determined her own fate: she was to turn out badly.

"Then we should depart together," I said, reckless and very much twenty years of age. "I will deliver the baby for you."

Now she sobbed. "It is already settled. I leave with the Shelleys. He lacks for fresh bed-partners. He cannot, he says, abide the reproductive aspect of the universe, what he calls the inordinate toll exacted by the nursery upon the loins of man."

"Even so," I said. "Plans may be changed. To Italy, then. I am a doctor, the very thing. Have no fear."

If we were to be thrown out, orphaned, discharged—whatever the appropriate phrase was—we would go with all colours flying in the tradition of the Navy. We would not plead or grovel; we would square our shoulders and stalk away, more offending than offended, with the whole of three cantons grieving behind us. Things ended. Death erupted in the midst of life. None of this was new to me, but to Claire it was a sea-storm of humiliation: to be sent packing for having loved and conceived. Neither of us had done that well, in the intimate part of our being, in Geneva, but she had had by far the worse outcome, being both fruitful and contemned. I offered to plead her case, not to mention her belly, with Lord B., with whom of late I had developed a way of talking. I would be straight and strict, needing no peepshow of horrors to make *my* point. From him I would exact something in writing that provided for her and her bairn for the next twenty years, so that he might be torn several ways before being pulled quite apart, as in the olden days with teams of horses pulling a man's living flesh into several different fields all at the same time: George into one, Gordon into another. No, it would not be that neat. I would enlist the aid of Lady Byron and Miss Caroline Lamb, both of whom had scores to settle with him.

Indeed, these women, I thought, should band together into an anti-Byron league and cut him down.

"I have been hearing things," I told him. "It seems you mean to dispense with my services, medical and other."

"By the way, Polly," he said aloofly, "what became of the watch I gave you? Did time swallow it up?"

"I gave it to a lady of no mean renown, milord, for fleshly services rendered."

This impressed him no end, and I could see him hover, wondering if I might be a useful fellow after all. But he shook himself and returned to his ungiven answer, saying, "Oh, but there is no need, Polly. The household is to be broken up forthwith. The Shelleys are taking Claire back to England, and I am setting out for Italy."

"I have nothing against Italy. My father—"

"No, Polly, I fear it is graver than that. You are too sociable for me," he said, seeming to wince and making an ample gesture that included the whole of Genevan society, from Madame de Staël to the lowliest whore. "What I need, if anyone, dear Polly, is someone less *busy.*"

"This is because I fell in love," I said, showing him my best sulk, jutting lower lip and all; I said it to see what he would do.

"And out, methinks. Polly, your lord desires to be alone: Shelleyless, Claireless, Pollyless. You must understand the pressures upon me from England."

"If such are the pressures," I said, sincerely from the bowels of my Hippocratic oath, "then the very person you shall need by you is the physician. Milord, you are in no condition to go gallivanting off without some guide. Who will inspect you? Your heart, your lungs, your kit, your foot."

"With luck," he said, producing his most self-loathing leer but contriving to infuse his expression with an almost unbearable tenderness, "my kit will drop off, and so will my foot. I will soon be

swyving with my elbow, Polly, and walking on my knees." I mentioned the clap, which he had not yet rid himself of; indeed, it had
seemed worse on my last inspection, and I had noticed pallid warts
on the scrotum, which I had treated with vinegar, with the result
that he came out smelling like a well-dunked salad.

"You do not seem altogether certain about the banishing of
Doctor Polidori," I said. "Is he *that* bad?"

"For your own good, my dear," he said gently. "Had I had
you round longer—no, were I to have you around me longer, I
would in all likelihood wish you to be more than my doctor, and
that would not be professional. Imagine the spectacle of two old
buggers sharing the Villa Diodati, and all the local peeping toms
coming to watch us thread each other." I was not shocked: I remembered the piano stool and the upstairs kiss that had roved, roamed,
from my brow to my cheek to my mouth while I feigned sleep. He
knew whereof he spoke, of course; never had a man thrilled more to
have a genital examination, painful as it sometimes was. He rejoiced
in the handling, often rising to the occasion and letting out a tremendous Albanian war-whoop.

"Milord," I would say, "this only makes my job more difficult.
Pretend there is ice on your belly. Brrr."

"But think of the pleasure you afford me, Polly, for once not
to be twirling my own meat or having some hussy do it for me."
While examining him, I should untruss myself, he said, just in case
"inspiration struck," but I never did. And now I never would.

"Well, milord," I said, coming back to the issue, "do I go or
not? I would be more than willing to join you in your Italian
journey. I do not hate the Swiss as you do, but I am more than
willing. It is my *alma mater,* after all."

"Byron," he said loftily, but without the faintest pique, "needs
to be by himself. I was fifty years old when I was born. Polly, how
old am I really? Am I *young?*"

"But, milord, all the more reason—"

"Nay, Polly: two old puts in their dressing-gowns being gog-
gled at by all and sundry." He meant him and me, but I was only

twenty; he was twenty-eight. Then I realized he was being prophetic, as always, never content with the present but always delving
into the life to come, using it against the tedium of today. He was
not going to budge, I could see that. He had thought too much on
it, even if he was wrong. Polidori was going to be banished for
being too tempting. Now *there* was a story for Mr. Murray.

"Would you go with them to England?"

Italy was my destination, I told him, and had been all my life. I
could meet him there, perhaps, and resume my employment, for the
sake of the diary only if his health were no longer an issue. He
neither yea-ed nor nayed this, saying only, "I propose, if it be agreeable to you, seventy pounds, 50 for the three months, and 20 for the
voyage." He did not say "50" and "20" (one cannot), but "fifty" and
"twenty." It seemed little enough to me, but I was not in a carping
mood. "Let us agree on it now," he said, with a voice of brooding
sadness, "and then the parting may be swift. We will not be haggling
with tears in our eyes, our hands on each other's bottoms."

"My lord," I said. "If it must be."

"Ay, Polidori," he said, and then I knew he meant it. In his
usual fashion, he was determined to break things up, as if renewal
inevitably followed dissolution. He enjoyed the breaking, really,
afraid as he was of wholes that bound him and to which he might
have to remain obliged. He was always the leaver, the enforcer of
good-byes, behaving like something in a Shelley poem, at the behest
of the wind.

Even I was too stable for him, and *I* was not pregnant with his
baby (whereas, according to later events, he was to think I had been
pregnant with his story, which in the outcome was a stillborn thing).
Looking into cabinets for missing leeches, I came upon it in the
Diodati and thought it a paltry thing, full of bald and vacant conversation that led nowhere, and, apart from some fine rolling phrases
at the beginning, non-Polidorian. He had written finely about himself, it seemed to me, referring to a certain "power of giving to one
passion the appearance of another," and evoking himself too in saying of his Augustus Darvell that he suffered from "an inquietude at

times nearly approaching to alienation of mind." One reference to Smyrna we had in common, but Smyrna was only Smyrna, whereas *his* narrator had buried Darvell by the fifth page, in a shallow grave in a Turkish cemetery. And that was it. It did not chime or ring for him and he abandoned it; the notebook I had unearthed from a cabinet had clearly been shoved in there in such a way as to suggest heedlessness, and the application to the manuscript of what I would call ultimate dislike. It could never have been Polidori's, nor my vampyre tale his, whatever people alleged. Now, if only I had written "Darkness," but I did not, nor could I have. Back into the drawer among likenesses of young Harrovians he had loved I pushed the story, knowing my own was my own and the better tale.

Clearly, I had not influenced Lord B., not in a literary fashion, anyway. Nor had he influenced me, though May had, and in a non-literary way so had Claire. We had all been playing mental incest. But who knew what had or had not criss-crossed our conjoint minds during those haunted evenings at the Diodati, with Milton's ghost presiding and our nerves unstrung by shrieking Shelley, woman-beating Byron, weeping Claire. It was odd, but I was in two minds: thinking of the group as all of us, but also thinking of it as two or three within it—I and the two ladies, perhaps, or on the good days Byron and I, at one with each other, chips off the same block. There may not have been electricity from the skies, not such as would raise the dead for us in some convenient demonstration, but there had surely been the electricity of our heads. I could almost predict the years in which I would dine out on how May and I came to write our vampyre stories, Byron his "Darkness," and Shelley his "Hymn." What Claire wrote was in her belly, a story in itself, which only she could tell. Ill-assorted, often at odds, and physically involved with one another in all sorts of outlandish, unconsummated ways, we were a family; but how different it might have been if Polidori had not been the only one without his woman, the lone wolf, the Vroucolocha of the set.

In spite of all the partings to come, I suddenly found myself yearning for the life of the hospital: for the rapt step of the dresser accompanying the surgeon on rounds with the plaster-box (badge of his humble office) in his hands; the bandages, the bleeding, the groans of patients half stupefied with rum. At the same time, I began to think of how to dress while aiming towards Italy, and I fancied I would dress Byronic, in the guise of the poet, turning down my collar, sporting a thin black ribbon round my bare neck, and, just perhaps, growing a set of Byronic moustaches. Not that I wished to be taken for Lord B., but I wished to seem more like the man who was writing *The Vampyre,* or who may have *written* it before he took his leave. New ideas began to fly into my mind like swallows. I wrote at speed, creating the shrieks of a woman in a hovel as Aubrey approached through the appalling forest, "one almost unbroken sound," and I thought about another story, perhaps, which would be nothing more than a sustained report of someone shrieking, perhaps in some hospital. In the hovel he found a woman, no longer screaming, but a corse with an open vein that ran. His mind took refuge in sheer vacancy even as a fever struck and Lord Ruthven arrived to nurse him, kind while he was ill, cruel again when he began to recover. Then the pair of them set out to travel once again, only to run into bandits, who shot Lord Ruthven in the shoulder, the wound infecting his entire being so profoundly that he asked Aubrey not to breathe a word of his death for a year and a day. When Aubrey woke, the next day, the robbers had taken Lord Ruthven to the top of a neighbouring mount, there to expose his body to the first cold ray of the moon. Determined to give the body a proper burial, Aubrey went up, but found nothing, and so set off for Smyrna, and Otranto or Naples. In Rome he inquired after the Italian lady to whom Lord Ruthven had once been so close, but she had gone. A breeze from Calais soon wafted him home, and, bit by bit, he began to forget the horrors of his tour, safe in the mansion of his fathers, in the embraces of his sister, now grown up, although as yet unpresented to the world. At the next drawing-room, she would come out.

But why had he sworn not to reveal Lord Ruthven's death? I wondered if his having sworn thus, and his wondering about that act, might not send the reader or the listener too abruptly to a conclusion: that Ruthven was going to appear again. A subtler story than mine would have kept them all waiting, both readers and listeners and the persons in the narrative, but in vain. Lord Ruthven would never reappear, but in my story he would have to; I could see nothing else for it.

Already I was planning. I did not wish to leave my story unfinished, nor did I wish to take it with me. It would be best, I thought, to leave it with the Countess of Breuss, perhaps to impress her (after all, she appeared in its preamble). I had told her already about Lord B.'s tale of Augustus Darvell and his worldlier friend, but she had expressed surprise: "Can anything be made of such a theme? Ghosts and revenants? I suppose so, but I might not wish to read the result." She was a sophisticated woman who had acted in plays at the Hermitage under Catherine, but who had moved into the large world, handling its things and people as if playing chess. Unable to secure a divorce, she left Russia, went to Venice for a week, stayed six years, married, bought villas in the Venetian husband's name, and left. With her she had only, by way of family, Mme. Gatelier, ever eager for me to prescribe medicaments for her (she was on the fringe of addiction, bless her), and her almoner, a person from Brescia. They all loved summer-houses, had a mania for them, and porticoes and baths. She adored little artificial islands, roadside summer-houses of Moorish design. She laughed when others went in for calumny, and she loved to write little farces in which, without a care, we all took part. She was not Lord B.'s type of person at all. She responded to the side of me that craved gaiety, getting me to act (in two pieces already: *Le Pacha de Suresne* and *Les Ricochets,* at both of which there was an immense number of spectators). I had even pondered the notion of adapting my vampyre to the stage; I would have adored Lord B. to play Lord R., but that was out of the question. I could only hope that the beautiful Miss Galston, although not of the Countess B.'s social set, might somehow be imported to play Miss Aubrey, the sister. Certainly it was no role for Polidori, though I had impersonated the sex in a charade on the canton of Genthoud.

Lovely world, that, whereas at the Villa Diodati I had work. Half offering, I found myself demanded of. Would I please examine medically the ladies before they departed? Shelley had declined, saying the universe was good to him, although my own practiced eye told me he was prey to neurotic fits and to jactitation. Thus, with my secret passion for the *vallis lucis,* I was at last able to peel open his May, shining my miner's lamp into her golden tunnel with barely suppressed exclamations of delight. I knew enough of her writing by now to think I had actually peered into the abyss of Victor Frankenstein, and all by way of duty. She was in perfect condition, although her muscles had not returned to normal after the birth of little William. I prescribed exercises, which I was certain Shelley would not let her attempt. The little chap was in excellent fettle, chirpy as a robin and strong to boot; he had no cough, no sniffle, and no tummy trouble. He had survived inoculation well. May, however, sat too much, toiling on her story, and I told her so, urging her to do plunges and twists for those muscles whenever she could; perhaps, even, to swim a little—not paddle or dip.

"In London?" She laughed. "What are you trying to save me for, Polly?" Had she intercepted some glance of doom? After all, here was a woman whose mother had died soon after giving birth to her. Only weeks later, on Mary's return to England, her half-sister was to kill herself, as was Shelley's first wife, Harriet. Three years later, little William was to die too, and Shelley himself, drowned, three years after that. Looking back, one might be excused for blaming oneself. None of the signs were there. Medicine, I lamented, was not prophecy, except when it was prognosis. Yet who knew how to prognosticate the mind of man? This was August, her birthday month, and all seemed well.

Polidori was practising again, and not on strangers either; although, out in the big world of Geneva, almost no one was a stranger to me by then. How, then, could I bear to leave? Only by

——

promising myself that I would return, and pick up my practice once again, after silken Italy Yet, although the idea of going to Italy pleased me a great deal, that of *going* at all pleased me little. Staying put would have suited me more, even though in Geneva I had had a couple of setbacks: La Saxonnex and Lord B.'s rebuff. A civilized man, I thought, should be able to work out exactly what such troubles have done to him. Well, they had not made me decamp, they had brought me out of myself in one sense, but the former had sent me back to drugs and to those ill-considered flirtations with suicide I had entertained ever since seeing my first cadaver and admiring its peacefulness, its rent serenity. I was far from the intact person I would have liked to be; buoyant as I was, I was also a drowner by nature, rather like Shelley, whereas Lord B. was a born survivor, a fighter. He survived, though, by killing off those about him, so much so that, even in extremis, he would have looked the picture of vitality since there were so many dead, battered, bleeding, hopeless, doomed people in his retinue. How *he* felt mattered most to him, which of course was why I was going to be sent packing at the very moment at which I could have introduced him to more personages in Geneva than he had introduced me to at the outset. Ah, that was it: *la grande foule* was mine, not to his taste at all, whereas, if I had made the acquaintance of some unknown desolate crags, he would have been delighted, up there in the thinner air with the sun laying his face. How little I had understood my Byron I thought; he was the sort of man who, without going away, became the perpetual stranger in his own home. He wished to be a force, I thought: a star, a peak, a wind, untrammelled by intercourse. If he was not the last man in the world, as in the poem he was writing, he was the last man *of his kind,* and he knew it, as like to have a thousand imitators (Polidori included) as to die unique: deformed, misanthropic, pretty. It would be no trivial good-bye when it came; I would have to rehearse for it, careful to put no word wrong, no gesture, but at the same time leave a tender lasting impression of myself for him to gnash his teeth over, bursting into tears when they

——

asked him about me: "When will Polidori return? Where is our good doctor now?" What would I ever be to him again?

Preparing to examine Claire, as he had requested (which I would have done in any event out of care and liking), I wondered if Lord B. had the faintest inkling of how lovely she was, how her beauty was a beauty still in bud, and never mind what harsh treatment she had sustained from him. I knew her better than he did, at least mentally, and found her wildness full of charm. She was, or had been, full of fizzing youthfulness, part of the Shelley ménage to begin with and therefore doomed to fall; going along with her half-sister when she eloped with Shelley had, as it were, certificated Claire as a public ne'er-do-well. If her sister could have an affair with a famous poet, so could she, and she did. Falling, Lord B. met her in the act of falling too. Each had a vanity to smooth, and the other smoothed it, with disastrous consequences.

"Mid-January," I said to Claire, who seemed to be writhing at the very thought. "A next-year child, by a week or two."

"He will give it to his sister to bring up," she said. "As soon as it is born, I will be its aunt, no more."

"Piffle," I told her, exposing her tummy, on which I saw what seemed long black birthmarks: leeches, in fact. She was smothered in them, out of some desire for self-abasement, certainly not in any hope of treating herself for the nothing that ailed her. Here was the solution to the mystery of my missing leeches (my opiated reserves). In an odd way, perhaps because they were every bit as dark as she, they belonged on her, but we soon had them off, back in their jar, and she seemed to cheer up. She had wanted the rather crude kindness of anyone's picking them off her; hoping to have Byron do it, she had to make do with me. She had been hoping, she said, to entice him to bed and then to shock him with her naked appearance, Byron having a horror of both leeches and blood-letting. "One could become accustomed to them," she said, "as travelling companions."

"Call them Polidoris if you want," I told her, "but do not do it again. Not even to upset Lord Byron. I have nothing against theatrical grease paint, Claire, but leeches are a little *too* theatrical. I have had them on me—all medical students have—but I wish we had something else. It may be natural, and it is said that France imports forty million leeches a year, but I find it unscientific. I am always crying for the moon—I have always wanted a tranquillizing chair, with restraints and a box that straps about the head of the patient, but what can one do? My hope is to live long enough to see medicine come of age and leave quackery far behind. Paris, if not Edinburgh, might be a good place to pursue such a goal. As to you, you are in spanking good condition. Do you sleep?"

She wandered the villa at night, she said, looking for she knew not what. Always hoping for a somnambulist, I asked her if she did it in her sleep, but she thought not—she was really looking for Lord B. and she sometimes found him, shirtless with sword in hand, ready to impale burglars, or (she claimed) at Polidori's door, eavesdropping on all those drugged and deathly dreams. Nightmares had plagued her even as a child, she said.

"He dotes on you," she said.

"He is sending me away. I am to be dispatched."

"Only because his bosom friend Hobhouse will arrive any day. And Matthew Gregory Lewis too. Dear Polly, we are novelties no more. He will soon find himself another seventeen-year-old victim." Her voice faded away.

"You went after *him,* Claire—I would say that you got your money's worth." What I really wanted to do, now that her leeches were off, was lie full length on her naked body, just to see how it felt. Claire never seemed to know or care if she was naked or not. Without more ado I did it, fully clad, taking care not to press down on the baby.

"Why, Polly," she said, "how tender."

"I have my human side," I said, "and my lustful one too"—fumbling myself loose, the cundum into place.

"Well, then," she murmured at her most provocative—gipsy, tigress, courtesan— "are you waiting for Lord Byron to show you how? It will needs be quick. Let us." We did, making perfunctory but thundering love we both had been saving up. I wet the baby's head, I supposed, and lay there, reminiscing about my days as a medical student, then telling her about the high life in Geneva: the counts and countesses, the divorced people, the eminents, the plodding English wives, the young and ailing husband of Mme. de Staël, twenty-two to her forty-five or so. She said she wished she could have taken part in just such a life, and I marvelled: it was the first time I had heard anyone envy me any aspect of my *modus vivendi*, unlikely and impromptu kaleidoscope of horrors that it was. Did she even know that, once a month or so, I actually took a little too much opium, to see how closeness to death would feel? I pretended I did it for medical reasons, so as to empathize with dying patients; but the real reason was my fondness for what was rotten; I sniffed at the fungus of the mind, I licked the verdigris of the soul.

"You did it just like him," she said, bridling.

"I can hardly have been *watching.*"

"You never know, Polly. You creep about, I know."

"*Doctor Polidori* does. He is a student of human nature."

"Here," she said, seeming to hum and sigh at the same time, as if to express what a tut-tut would have said better, "not so human as animal. Well. It is so."

I agreed, fondling her naked belly, feeling the bairn, then kissing her navel, my eyes closed above the outsize orange of it. Then I got up, gasping from my various efforts, crossed the room, and teased the cundum off my dwindled nail, left, walked along the cavernous hall, and entered my own room, there to play Leeuwenhoek with my microscope. Claire had followed, so we two peered together at the surviving tiddlers: the best peepshow in the world. "Oh, Byron," she said, not using the vocative, but intending the expression as one might use "Oh, God." She saw the root of her trouble, the harbingers of bliss, twirling and shuddering to get at her again.

"I wore it not for these, against *them,*" I said.

"I beg your pardon, Polly."

"Oh, *I,* not you."

"You are infected."

I confessed. "So is he, Lord B. Too many are."

"Our *doctor,*" she said with authoritative disgust, and I felt like one sent out by night to undermine the race until the hospitals were bigger than the cities; rather than the dispenser of guaiac and mercury (this in often fatally enormous doses), I felt like one who sucked on buboes. I had done it wrong again, feeling, perhaps rightly, that there were occasions on which even an honest admission was a gaffe. I had erred in assuming, without even thinking about it, that one so abused as Claire had been was not one to fret about disease, not in one of comparable age. She had never seen a cundum before or had one used upon her, which told me about Lord B. She risked more from him than from me, but it was me she found fault with, thinking my finesse less civil than his unclad, unmastered importunity. Why had she, upon examination, shown disease-free? Superstitiously I thought the baby and its acids had protected her, and I told her this, at which she smiled. And her smile, when she gave it, was of an indefatigable delicacy as if, deep within her being, there was another person whose only duty was to tend that smile. She smiled at all the overlooked tenderness in the world, most of all at the image of emotions never vouchsafed her, who had courage in the extreme and tended therefore to be treated or regarded roughly, as if she were a man with a man's fortitude. In fact she was sensitive and zealous, attentive and loyal, going to waste in Lord B.'s harem. It was wonderful that she would soon be severed from him, as all people were who approached the climactic point of serious business, Lord B. having no patience with the serious enterprises of others. There we were at one end of the leech-shaped lake, and it was as if summer were ending in winter, with all our deep emotions awry, Polidori having neither ended nor begun, though we all (saving Claire, perhaps) had scribbled. *Had* she? I asked in the gentlest fashion, inquiring about her soliloquy.

"It is done," she said with a baleful stare. "Why do you ask?"

I was doing my own story, I explained, and May hers. Byron had quit his when only a few pages in, and Shelley was not interested. We would never see it, she said, or she would be stoned in

Piccadilly Circus. It was about a special type of vampyre who preyed on women during their monthlies, who lived in a dog kennel in Smyrna, and regurgitated the blood for an infant vampyre known as Degorgonogre, who lacked eyes and, according to the rules of the menstrual bloodsuckers, had to be put to death when it reached the age of seven. Until then it had to be fed and nurtured, kept clean, and taught to speak, but that was all.

I gasped at the audacity of this, asking if the soliloquy was that of the baby vampyre, but she said no, *Soliloquy* was the name of its disease, medically known as Degorgonogre's Soliloquy. Was she making fun of Polidori? It seemed not. I was the only person to have taken an interest in *her* story, she said; the others had assumed she was too backward to write anything such, but she was, after all, William Godwin's stepdaughter. Typical utterances of this (rather precocious) vampyrette were: "Are you satisfied?" "Be kind and good to me, dearest." "You might be dead." "I know what you will say." "I cannot pardon." "I have unloosed myself from the trammels of custom and opinion." "I have loved." "My dreadful fear is that you will quite forget me."

These utterances, as she said them, quite brought me to tears, for I recognized who was speaking through the mouth of the blind baby. I had unloosed in her something she had held in tight, but our encounter on the bed, and then at the microscope, she so fertile and I so arid, looking at my wasted progeny, had joined us in expendability, and we, who did not matter, now had that in common, in the open.

I had fallen in love with her voice, that mellow mutter from below, or rather with her way of using it, as if she were making up her phrases at the very last moment, and therefore speaking without intention, almost muddled, near to babble, yet managing to direct her speech at the listener with such haphazard charm that one held one's breath, unable to look away or not to listen, such was the magic of her wandering elocution. She spoke as if she had no idea who she was, and the phrases were making themselves physical in spite of her. Not that any of these came from Byron, Shelley, or

Mary, least of all from Polidori, who would have been easiest to parody for his overuse of medical terms. And, oddly enough, as she spoke, she seemed to get younger, so that she would begin a sentence as the young woman she was, but end it as someone only months old, the final lisp or sigh, or lip-smack sounding so newly born that one held out one's hand to cradle the proffered baby bottom. All her *t*'s and *d*'s ended in *z*. There was about her, in all her raving darkness, something so pulpy, so untouched, that it was a miracle Lord B. had not destroyed her utterly, cleft her beyond repair. Yet suited him she had, without whining, and leave him she would, suffering as she had implied from the disease known as Degorgonogre's Soliloquy, for which there was no known cure save death.

When she leaned over to the bedside table and reached into the little cupboard, I thought she was in need of the chamber pot, but she brought out a notebook bound in white vellum and handed it to me with her finger marking the place. Surely this was her soliloquy? It was nothing of the kind, but one recipe among others, this one for Ague, reading, as I recalled it:

> *1 Oz. of best red Bark*
> *1 Nutmeg grated*
> *1 Table spoonful of beaten blk pepper*
> *Coarse sugar*
> *To be mixed with Syrup of Poppies into an Electuary. A large Tea Spoonful to be tkn as soon as the Fit is quite off. Half the quantity for a Child.*

"Doctor Claire." She laughed.

"I thought it was your story," I began.

"My book of bits and pieces," she explained, if explanation it were. "I still have several others to fill up before I begin using it. I jot things down in it from time to time, but I'm keeping most of the pages for the final version, if I ever finish it." I saw her, long after we were all dust, an old lady with white curls, sitting in her boudoir somewhere, with her albums and diaries beside her: white vellum;

brown hide; oblong pocket book bound in red roan with its clasp broken and the pencil sheath torn away, even some quires of loose leaves partly browned and curled by fire, and wondering, in her turn, who would be the next reader of such private book-keeping, with its benign miscellany of recipes, addresses, phrases *(Nondum amabam* inscribed by Shelley), sketches of trees, asides ("I have nothing to do but fry in the sun for your amusement"), notes about black silk stocking ("blk slk stkngs"), ivy leaves, and shoes, even a "Thaumatrope," from Papyro plastics, modelled from paper.

"No," she was saying, "it is in another book altogether, with red marbled paper. I would not dream of showing it to anyone yet. Perhaps I should distribute it among several different notebooks, so as to confuse nosey-parkers. I shall probably burn it." I pleaded to see it, but she said she knew the best of it by heart anyway, and she again and again recited certain phrases to me in her best voice. How could I resist? Claire, whom we had all underestimated as if she were some Polidora, was just possibly the ablest of us all: certainly the most prompt, the most efficient—a born diarist, I thought. *La belle dame* who shuffled albums in which she had always had other people write to her, so that, just perhaps, she had adroitly manoeuvred Byron and Shelley and others into penning words of dialogue for her in spaces left blank. Cozened into eternity.

Life, being a process rather than a university, teaches us in untidy ways, schooling us (if that be not too neat a term) in its heedless monotony. If we are not to have this person, then we may have that, as if life insisted on quantity and even quality, but without being specific as to whose. We get a modicum of this, a modicum of that. The principal thing, I taught myself, was to regard yourself as a piece of raw material to be worked on in various ways. You had to stand back and watch the phenomenon of yourself develop, all the while remembering that the essence of being alive was to be constantly at one's own disposal: surgeon and hedonist to oneself, rhetorician and dancing-master. One could not be everything, but one might, in any given sphere, become competent enough to observe the act of self-tuition. If it was not to be Gaby Saxonnex or Eliza Arrow, for example, it might well be Claire Clairmont, although under wholly different auspices. This, I thought, was why Lord B. seemed such a scattered man, a man not of parts but of particles, for ever dodging and ducking until the next dramatic stance, but never long enough in the stance to develop it as a life-style.

"You were always getting in the way," Claire was telling me, "when I wanted to get close to *him*. I was quite jealous of you, as if you had designs of your own on him."

"Oh, never," I said. "Which is not to say that he might not have had designs on me. I think he did, rather."

That was wholly different, she said; that kind of behavior was peculiar to men and had nothing to do with love in the main. It was what they did when they could do nothing else. I found this remark insulting, but, in view of our recent congress, I did not argue, I let her ramble on, usurping what I had always taken to be the male privilege: *post-coitum garrulus*. Unless I had it wrong and the tradition should read *dormiens*. I did neither, nor was in the habit of such, preferring on those occasions (I caught myself ungallantly beginning to count them up) to lie back and muse, an activity which the physician in me explained as some primitive need to keep the seed-bearer close to the female so as to have a second chance at impregnation. A true savage is what I felt, lying there, obeying the dictates of the racial memory.

"To him," she was saying, "appetite needs to be renewed, which cannot happen with the same partner, so he is always hunting someone new, who by his standards might just as well be someone who is also hunting someone new. Promiscuity seeks promiscuity. I never felt like that; I was quite obsessed, and I have paid the penalty. I need very much, now, to become un-obsessed. Polly, be my exorcist."

"From Switzerland, from Italy?" Geography numbed me.

When they had first arrived—or, rather, when we had first

arrived where they already were—in my eagerness to get things right I had called Mary Mrs. Shelley and Claire Miss Godwin. Now, after a period of thinking how silly I had been to do so, I now began to see how correct I had been all along, in both instances. Mary was very much the wife, and Claire was very much her own woman— neither daughter nor half-sister; indeed, her father had been Swiss, she said, so she was in a sense at home.

"Then why go?" I could see her on my arm, tart and tubby.

"I need the Shelleys. I belong with them, certainly for the confinement. Later, we must see. Where will you be?" She moved her head as if scanning an ocean.

"Europe," I said vaguely, having no plans other than to visit Italy. I was also thinking how, in one sense, my father would be glad; he had always opposed my appointment to Byron's retinue, predicting some disaster from it, and he would be glad to have me in Italy. On the other hand, I was now out of steady employ, or close to being so, and that would upset him, tolerant as he was of authorial vagaries. "Italy," I added. "Always Italy. They will never get me out of it, once I am installed."

"And who will be *your* biographer en route?" Her right hand wrote in mid-air, an aerial subscript.

How sardonic she could be. "Polidori himself," I said. "The position is vacant." Again I heard that mottled, vagrant, childlike laugh: shall I say the aural equivalent of an exquisitely unused throat and mouth, as soft as lily petals, as mucous as her lower slit. I could see that I was beginning to become quite the connoisseur of ladies' parts, knowing at long last that ladies wanted what I wanted and that the sexes did not differ as to venery: they just wanted the same event from the point of view of having wholly different equipment. They too knew distension, the stone-ache, the clogged-clotted prelude to spending. Why we were not more candid about these things, I did not know; the physician in me wanted all in the open, like the Countess of Breuss, who once upon a time said, in a moment of acute and somewhat demented merriment, *"Avant de me coucher avec les jeunes hommes, je me couche avec eux, pour les débarrasser."* What her two husbands made of this habit, I knew not, but it seemed to me enlightened, like having the chimney swept before lighting the fire. What better lady beside whose knee to complete my story before I left Geneva, with my notebook resting in her lap, and, rising from behind it, the scented aroma of readiness as, no doubt against her better judgment, she waxed wet and syrupy for me? Oh, the glands, Oh, God.

As for Claire's own tale, I would never have believed her— that she had written it down—if there had not been within it the name Degorgonogre, which I sensed had to be an anagram, and it was. GEORGE GORDON was the source. People did not improvise such things orally; indeed, their appeal was to the reading eye, so the manuscript must be somewhere in the Cologny house. She refused to say, however, and I let the matter drop after telling her I thought her tale had an originality that Byron's lacked, but that mine aspired to. "Were we not all going to publish together?" Only she had remembered this. The notion had died a natural death when Shelley backed out, not in the least interested in another novel, and Byron packed it in. Now we had a trio, I thought, a trio of tiros, and the world would blaze with our fame. Claire would no longer be a cast-off mistress, Mary would be no longer just Mrs. Shelley, and I would no longer be the former physician and biographer. If only we could stay together, remain in contact through the written word, having the Hobhouses of this world lug our bundles of letters for us through the gates of this or that city, across whatever stretch of water. That was how Lord B. did it, with those he remained in touch with: a method laborious and slow; but, short of the carrier pigeon, what could be done? We had no runners with split sticks.

Then, with a glass of wine in hand, after equipping me with a cognac from my own stock, Claire began to berate herself for never being herself, in a manner decorous yet incisive, almost as if she were quoting an adversary, a jealous and derisive rival. "Who am I after all? I had him write to me as Madame Clairville, Post Restante— Clairville because he said he liked the name Clare, an old infatuation at Harrow—but not *mont* because of a certain very ugly woman.

You can see how obliging I was from the outset. I was a fool. 'I chuse to be married,' I told him, 'because I am so'—meaning I was already with his child before he came to Geneva—'and madames have their full liberty abroad.' I said then that, were I to float past his window drowned, he would only say, '*Ah, voilà.*' Never mind. My real name was Mary Jane, but I had been calling myself Clara, which became Claire. Who am I now? All I know is that I am not Lady Byron, but Byron's lady, and there is a world of difference in between, mostly made up of paper." Did she mean his works? Or lawyer-stuff?

"Nothing worse than his being Albé," I said, "no doubt from his Albanian cult—*Albaneser*—"

"Not a bit of it," she answered. "It comes from his initials: L.B. Thus Albé, to be spoken with a grave or acute accent, or without an accent at all. The word suggests dawn."

"I hate nicknames," I said. "Mine most of all."

"They shrink us," Claire said. "I hate them too. But what I hate most is the way I fawned on him from the first, like the time he wrote in the hotel register at Monsieur Dejean's that he was a hundred years old, and I sent him a note saying I was sorry he was grown so old, but that I suspected he was *two* hundred from the slowness of his journey. I asked him to meet me on the top floor, but without asking a servant to show him up, lest they take him to Shelley. Then, walking in the hotel garden, I went to great lengths to bump into him just when he stepped out of his boat onto the gravel."

"I know, I was there," I said. I had been cursing.

"I did not see you, but then I only had eyes—"

"Full length on the bottom of the boat, feeling out of things." Not one of Polidori's better days: a *cafard*.

"He never hurried up to see me," she said, warming to her pursuit, "or anyone else. I had called the Shelleys my *Otaheite philosophers,* and this had put him off right away. All I wanted to do was sit on a stool at his feet and tease him about his Scotch accent. Later on, and I am sorry for this, I told him, 'For heaven's sake, Albé, please send Doctor Polly to write a dictionary or to his lady love, in which case she can be his pillow and he will go to sleep on her.' It was late at night and I did not wish you to see me coming to be with him. I realized later that he was using you as an obstacle, to keep me away." I could not believe this, but who cared now?

"Examination over," I declared in my most formal tones, and she giggled, asking, "Do you always examine your patients so thoroughly, Doctor Polidori? Do they ever complain about your ardour? Or do you only examine thus those who have covered themselves with leeches first?"

"Only in Geneva," I said. "I only plough where Lord Byron has first sown. Did you know that he suffers from bouts of dizziness, and deafness too? His hair is thinning out and going grey, and I did find some teeth had loosened. He is tearing his body to pieces, did he but know it. Without a doctor, will he do worse? With one, he has not done too well. Cigars and brandy will undermine him fast, especially in a body he refuses to nourish. That thin slice of bread for breakfast, with tea. The light vegetable dinner, with seltzer water, tinged with vin de Grave. And then, in the evening, a cup of green tea, no sugar, no milk. Why is he not light-headed all the time? Not just in bouts. How in the world can he, with a woman, rise to the occasion?"

"Here, dear Polly," she said, "the only woman he has trafficked with is I." And *never* La Saxonnex?

"No excursions to the *grisettes,* or the red lamp?"

"None: he is most palpably unsociable. I just adore the Geneva Byron. He behaves. In Italy it will be a different matter. I have already reconciled myself to an enormous outburst of profligacy." She pretended to sob and fume.

Then it was done. They were gone. No more Claire, no more May. No more chance to duel with Shelley or, in the dead of night, thick with opium, shoot him out on the lake during a moonlight sail. The gone leave energetic ghosts, to whom we talk, with whom we sleep, and whose leeches (in some cases) we go on removing and removing. Not only were there tears and hugs; there was anger too, on Claire's part, and Lord B.'s as well, for she poured out her devotion to him, in full view of coachmen and servants, making him hold her belly and listen for the little Byron within. It almost looked to me part of a charade at the Countess of Breuss's, with strangers playing the roles. It would end, I thought, and then we could go back to our dishevelled lives, Lord B. and I strolling down through the vineyard to see the three of them in Cologny, the three of them puffing uphill to see us for dinner. Of course, we had never had our cricket match. We would never be able to use such arcane phrases as "imparting spin to the ball" or "stonewalling even the full tosses." Now I knew what the guillotine could do to you. My head was full of sentences that began "They had no sooner gone from sight than—" and never ended, as if metaphysically sapped. All I had was Byron now, and the dismaying sense that I too had overstayed my welcome, now transferred to Hobhouse, just arrived before that grand departure on August the twenty-ninth.

What, I asked myself, is a good-bye? More than the traditional small death, it is a succumbing almost sacrificial, winding up the nerves into a useless mass, reducing us to the status of mere apologetic statues. It hurts, of course, but it also links us anew to those beasts of the field that we outlive: the ox, the badger, the mayfly. Unless it is a relief, I said, then it is also a relief, making only dumbshow sense of my thought; I meant that even to say good-bye to a loved one was a relief from the hard labour of happiness, which we rejoice in only when we have forgotten oblivion. Happiness is the blur we crave, but we are all the time blowing it up to blot out the horizon, wishing the inevitable will never happen, and some-times, if we are skillful, blotting out God, ramming happiness down God's throat to choke off the future, the fell design locked into our flesh and bones, our lymph and our blood. I said my good-byes before, during, and after, not so much good-byes to them as to myself, to that part of my life inextricably enmeshed with Claire and May, which I dearly wished to place in its box, back on the cotton wool, unused and unplanned for, perpetually virgin: a life like unborn cloud. One wanted to weep blood, to cough up fragments of bone. Had I told Claire often enough how much I admired her story, whether it was oral or written? Had I told May how momentous her tale of Victor Frankenstein was going to be? Had I ever said, enough, how inspiring it had been to be with them, even as they contemplated the ruins of their little young lives and looked forward to the next disaster? On that promontory within Diodati, we had worked miniature wonders within one another, candidly wanting life to be different, aching to piece its sundered elements together again under the impress of fire or love; and no amount of holy fuss would change our eagerness to be at one with the universe in its dark, devious workings. We too wanted to be part of that process, whatever it was, and whose.

Now we too were a Frankenstein monster, far-flung, incapable of being brought back together, and I thought that May saw this at the last as her face gazed, crumbled, then sealed and froze as the coach rattled away from Cologny, a place I would not dare to revisit lest my heart's beat falter and cease. If Diodati had been our grand salon (with a grand salon to itself, on the central corridor, on the right, past the dining room), then Cologny was our sweet bower of bliss, where we took tea and kept our boat. Only the heartbreak of this, the first parting, would fortify me for the other, with Byron; having had the hardness of heart to get through the one, I would be hard enough to manage the other, for in my truculent way I had revered him, even the clay of which his feet were made. Defenceless for medical examination, he had been the most vulnerable of men, wounded indeed in several places already, showing his hurt that I or others might heal it, and ready with a smile when there was nothing to be done: the dizziness, the deafness, the falling hair, would not end, any more than the foot would come right or the faint residuals of the clap ever quite leave his system. And what was amiss with his brain, causing the foot, would never heal either. If only we had all been born later, I thought, echoing a familiar yearning of men throughout the ages, when steady amelioration would have per-

fected medicine itself, making it, if not an art, then something unan-
imously intact.

No more rough-and-ready.

No more rum.

But proper titrations.

Some heed of the mind as a suffering entity.

And clean knives.

I did not know how Lord B. could bear to leave the Villa
Diodati, whose lake view on three sides was surely the loveliest
prospect of his life, or mine. He himself doted on it, writing there
on the balcony, upon which, supposedly, the staring boobies with
viewing glasses watched him from the very Hôtel d'Angleterre
where we had stayed and he had briefly been 100 years old. On that
same balcony robes and flounces had dried; so went the story put
about by such as Lord Glenbervie the scandalmonger, who thought
Mary the wife of one Shelley who kept the Mount coffeehouse.
Even the scandals and lies endeared themselves to us, living there in
that square block of grey stone, entered by the tree-screened court
on the side that did not face the lake. We had three Dante-like levels:
Diodati; the other house, down through the vineyard; and the little
boat harbour. At three in the afternoon on the tenth of June we left
Dejean's hotel and as an entourage moved ceremonially in. Then
Byron and Shelley, for twenty-five louis, bought the boat, with its
keel that held it upright during all but the worst of the lake squalls.
It may have been too peaceful for Lord B., too chaste, as Claire had
surmised, but surely, I thought, it had been more of a world for him
to think in than felling the chambermaid at Ostend *(that* kind of life)
or that other one, in Cologne, whose red cheeks and white teeth so
inflamed him that he seized her in his habitual manner, and the host
of the hotel, not seeing clearly, thought milord had nailed his wife,
until she appeared from within another room, and Lord B.'s local
vallis lucis went about her business, ruffled and even pinker-cheeked.
He needed constancy; he lacked an evenness without which we none
of us felt sane.

For months I tried to puzzle out what had happened to me at the Villa Diodati. Under Byron's wing, and so bound to make some kind of conquest among the sex, I had fallen into and out of love, or desire; but had I fallen out of love with myself merely because Gaby Saxonnex had proved unworthy? Had I ever loved myself? Before coming to Geneva I *had,* in a damp infatuation based on my success as a medical student; I had told myself that, after being bullied at Ampleforth as a foreign-looking boy (wop or dago, the hostile ones said), I had matured into a not-too-tall Italian-looking young man of rather melancholy aspect, and not as outgoing as I should have been. Far from being the actor type, I was attractive enough to win a few glances, and I carried myself with a certain pride. In Geneva, however, although I went gadding about a great deal, I had sunk deep inside myself, perhaps because every situation both with and without him set me in competition with Lord B., with whom nobody might compete and retain his stability. The ironic truth was that I had become a sociable introvert, and the more I saw of *le ton* the more I became a creature behind a façade, whereas, left to my own devices away from the shadow of Lord B., I might have come out normally and flowered into an almost prepossessing young man-about-the-lake. Being with him so much, and indeed sometimes almost of him, had overfaced me, strained my resources, put me into the wrong league, and that was why I had listened so avidly to Rossi's brothel stories, why I had homed to the red lamp like a copycat moth (mixing my metaphors along the way), and finally gone to opium to remove the anxiety, the shudders, the high-strung fidgets that threatened to disassemble me from ankle to neck.

Hence my leap to Claire, whom in other circumstances I would have found too prosaic, insufficiently devoted to things of the mind, too reckless even in small things. Any port in a storm, but if she were my heart's refuge, then she was also a ruin that Byron had knocked about a bit, and I suddenly saw myself doing myself in all over again: solving something Byron had caused by resorting to someone Byron had used. It sounded cheap. I should have looked again into Genevan society and put my fate into the pale, pastry-making palms of some English rose, all decorum and self-denial, having all the attributes of a nurse without gracing a hospital (as the rumour about English lasses went). I realized that there were many, many shadings of pain I had never guessed at; that, in order to have what I fondly referred to in my mind as a life of the heart, one had to take risks all the time and sometimes try to emerge shining from the most loathsome mire. It was no use paddling about in the gutter, hoping for a miracle. And it was no use having my soul cool its heels with the Platonic. In between, as the Rossis knew (even *they,* not to mention the Byrons), there was the whole putrid swamp of compromised emotions, amidst which one could not just wear a label—*viveur,* innocent, idealist, flirt, *honnête homme*—but had to bounce from setback to setback, from triumph to triumph, setback to triumph, triumph to setback, as if this were one's chosen style and one knew what one was doing. Craving something from one another, but unable to settle for just that, the men and women in this middle zone of capricious longing lived from emotion to emotion, using one emotion's energy to annul another's. I had discovered, perhaps too early, the mixed quality of life, its discordant spate, and I was far from ready, a tiro among roués, thinking the language of sexual conquest or sexual affinity was French, whereas in fact it was one of gasps, whispers, and cries.

Well, Claire was gone, and with her something raw and elemental I had needed to study; *she* had not lost her mind, but she had maltreated it, and it had paid her back, turning her into a parrot's echo of herself, uttering the same phrases of dedication to Lord Byron as she began with. Claire had made herself into a wind-up toy of the eighteenth century. Anyone might wind her up, and she would quack only the same call, seeing all men in one Byron, Byron in all men, which in a way was a relief: you could use her without being yourself—you could be Pepys, Lavoisier, or Napoleon, and she would treat you just the same, having been swyved into routine. It was not Polidori she lay with. I heard again a conversation we might have had, which was more real to me than the words we actually exchanged.

"Who am I to you?"

"An Arabian," she said in that bright, lenient voice.

"How do you know?"

"Because I am flying."

"Where to?"

"Never ask that," she said. "I am your magic carpet."

"I am your doctor," I told her. "I certify that you are well. Your child too." At my most pompous, I thought.

"Yet you, you are infected."

"We physicians are not saints." My most trite.

It made no sense to her. A long silence followed. Then she said the one word, "motherhood," and I realized she was away into a private dimension where men, as the seed-bearers, were not welcome, since women did the growing, the nurturing, in comparison with which men were simpleminded watering-cans, generic and crude.

Yet I wondered: If my life had gone wrong, taken a wrong turning, was that not what I had wanted? In the days of my innocence with Gaby Saxonnex, when I thought I had the monopoly of her highly tuned body in its elastics and silks and bits of blood-hot white rubber, even as I began I wanted it to be over; I wanted the carnal delights of the next fifteen minutes to be over in a second. I wanted the pleasing aftereffect more than I wanted the rush of cordial; I wanted to bypass her body, even if I would have to pay double for the non-privilege. It was hard to work it out, this wanting her both ways. If she had died during our pleasure, I would not have grieved; indeed, brooding back on our few weeks together, I found myself more upset than I would have been if told she was dead. Clearly, I wanted her on my own terms, which was why I wholly overlooked hers, and how lewd and mercantile they were. It was as if I had wanted my cundum not to have come from the innards of a sheep, cleansed and stretched and oiled, but from the cottage industry of heaven. How many men had been that gullible? I went from mistake to mistake, and becoming something carnal for Lord B. would have been yet another mistake; I saw myself at eighty, preening myself on all the mistakes I had *not* made, not having lived, unlike Lord B., Claire, Mary, Shelley, Rossi, the Countess of Breuss, and the rest. I needed to do something extreme to myself, in hopes of growing up.

With departure in mind, and a host of other things such as fame, money, opium, prussic acid, and self-defilement, off I went to the Countess of Breuss, who had cajoled me into finishing my story at her lap. Indeed, this was what I did, heaving my long body close to her from a sitting position, opening my notebook against her flank, then stationing it on top of her thigh and writing away, determined to do it as slowly as I could, even while her stomach rumbled and her breath grew heavy. Not once did she interrupt although, on looking up to stare into the middle distance, I several times intercepted her look, one of mellow exasperation. So I read aloud to her as I wrote, and this pleased her, although she chided me for making her wait as inspiration struck or failed. But I did not read it all, having perhaps taken from her certain visible aspects I gave over to Miss Aubrey, whose "blue eye was never lit up by the levity of the mind beneath" and whose melancholy charm suggested more her awareness of some brighter realm than it did mere misfortune. I knew not what I took and did not take from her, other than the sheathed pulp of her presence amidst the mingled aromas of lavender, camphor, and eau de Cologne. What an aromatic muse she was! I giggled internally to think of Lord B. crouched thus at the flank of Mme. de Stale, holding his breath.

Then, in a rush, the dénouement wrote itself, or so it seemed, and Lord Ruthven appeared again, murmuring "Remember your oath." Frantic, Aubrey thought of killing the monster with his own hands, but Lord Ruthven had already transcended death. So Aubrey shut himself away, eating nothing, then began to wander the streets unkempt, "as often exposed to the noon-day sun as to the mid-night damps." I relished the balance of that line. Then, to try to save his friends, he went back into society, shuddering and stuttering; his guardians once more intervened, hiring a physician to watch over him. "Darling," I said to the Countess, "they have just hired a physician to take care of him; he lives confined to his chamber." She nodded, smiled, and patted my cheek; I was a good boy, obviously. On I wrote, making him emaciated, lacklustre of eye until he became glassy-eyed (a variation), and having him continually warn his sister of Ruthven's true nature. Yet when she asked him why she should avoid one whose constant attentions flattered her, all he would say was, "True! true!" He kept his oath, while waiting for its period to expire, and his guardians thought they discerned an access of better cheer in him as the year wore on.

Upon the last day of the year (the year came back to life like a vampyre itself), they were talking in his room of his sister's marriage, only the next day, to the Earl of Marsden, whom Aubrey thought a dashing young noble he had met, and he rejoiced. But then he saw her locket, in which Marsden's image sat, and Marsden was none other than Ruthven, which put him into a frenzy, trampling it under foot.

"And then what?" said my muse, trifling with the lobe of my ear. "I have been a patient writing table, Poli, so tell me now." Speedily, lest I lose the rhythm of the final crescendo, I told her the gist, then, even as I wrote it down in many more words, gave her the ending like a crust.

"He helps Aubrey to recover, but with nothing good in mind. He gains an important embassy abroad. Aubrey writes to his sister, begging her not to marry Ruthven, but his physician fails to pass the letter on. At the wedding, Aubrey tries to halt the proceeding, but Ruthven hurries him out of the room, and he suffers a ruptured blood vessel, an aneurysm. His sister knows none of this. She marries the fiend and leaves London with him. As the oath expires, Aubrey at last tells his guardians what Ruthven is, all of the story thus far; but it is too late. It ends like this: 'Lord Ruthven had disappeared, and Aubrey's sister had glutted the thirst of a VAMPYRE!' "

Chortling, she asked why Aubrey stuck to his oath for so long, and I said, "He was a gentleman. A gentleman would. In any case,

Ruthven told him something dreadful would happen to his sister if he didn't keep mum."

"*Keep mum?* There are too many gentlemen these days."

"Seal his lips on it." Every now and then the Countess was very Russian, especially when confronted with English slang. It was Ampleforth English, spoken nowhere else.

"I think he loved his sister excessively," she said, and rang for tea. "It is a very Byronic story, if you do not mind my saying so. Does not your lord have a sister in England to whom he is— passionately—attached?"

This she already knew. I had told her, gossipping.

"And you too?" I too had three sisters: Frances, who was Fanny; Maria Margaret, known as Mary; and Charlotte Lydia, who was to become one of my most prudish readers.

"You say it as if you mean she has typhus." Sometimes the Countess could be brusque; she had found my story melodramatic, whereas I thought I had done a satisfactory job of toning it down. What had she meant by Byronic? Could she possibly know about "Darkness," my favourite poem-in-progress? Or did she mean empty and attitudinizing? I did not ask. Would she have said something of his was Polidorian? I wondered how long you had to live, and slave, before you became an epithet in the pampered mouth of a Russian countess with two husbands. On this red-letter day I had finished my story at her knee, and here she was being categorical. "More Shelleyan, I think," I said. "More like *Mary,* not P.B."

She had a way, an endearing way, of pretending that our tête- à-têtes were public affairs full of people, and she would say, "Please, Poli"—pronouncing it *polee,* she said, not to echo Byron, whom she had not met, but because I was "polite, polished"—"do not go straight home. Linger awhile and be close." It was odd to be thus invited, as I so often was, to detach myself from the crowd of myself and begin a tête-à-tête already an hour or two old. It was pleasure nonetheless, and she even went through the charade of wagering with me as to whether or not I would accept her invitation; it was her way of demonstrating that her allure never failed and, as such, was less a wager than a metaphor for self-satisfaction. At first it was hard for me to assimilate the fact that a lady so high-toned had physical needs and drives like the rest of us, but I remembered the two husbands and then forgot them in the onslaught of her avid, slight plumpness. The cundum she took for granted, like something one wore to a dinner or a recital. There was a married feeling about our liaison, and it had pleased me to betray her with Gaby Saxonnex, then to have the delicious feeling afterwards that, come what may, I was free of all entanglement. She did all with a faint, frothy good humour, as it were depriving the sexual act of its mystery, its forbidden and primitive aspect; it was, after all, as our use of idioms revealed, another mode of conversation, which was another mode of intercourse—indeed, in our day, the only one.

She was bold, not least because I had told her that I was somewhat shy, and shy people, I said, already had one foot in the grave, having hung back from life, having not gone headlong into it. They were more easily subdued by the destroyer of delights. This was not to say that I lacked confidence, but that I did not like to manifest it in unworthy pursuits; I had the confidence to be diffident, as she saw.

"Another name for vanity," she said, "but never mind. You are forward enough for me. I always like to have to pluck a beau fresh from the box, so to speak, teasing him out bit by bit. These Swiss are so damned prosaic. They need a few more Russians on the premises, and many fewer English." It was she who encouraged my literary pretensions and told me to do something every day in my notebook, just to keep in trim. "Don't be spasmodic," she said, "like Lord Byron."

"Oh," I explained, "he works like dammee when he starts, scrawling all kinds of alternative phrases in the margins at enormous speed, and coming back to them later on. He pours it out. He works very hard when he works at all." She passed this by, returning the conversation to me and my ways. I was to heed the Latin blood within me, she said, let it melt the English reserve, at least in matters literary. I told her nothing of my drugs, speaking of them only as a physician might, when I romanced on about having better stethoscopes and more powerful microscopes. In some ways, our medicine could not be bettered, I told her: why, we could even defibrillate a skidding heart with a Ramsden type electrostatic generator such as Luigi Galvani had given us. Who could surpass Cheselden, who took out bladder stones in less than one minute? Who could ever improve on Desault's bandage for fractured clavicle? None of this would be real to her until she was carried screaming or inert to the nearest hospital for her first dose of theriac, say, Hoffmann's anodyne of opium, Fowler's solution of arsenic, or indeed William Withering's miraculous *Digitalis purpurea*. To her it was all an abstract science, as it always was until people beheld the saws and lancing pins, the bleeding-knives and the dove-shaped sucking-bottle used for feeding patients flat on their backs (it was of heavy pot, carefully painted with feathers in pink and yellow; the patient sucked through the beak; the nurse filled it up through a wide hole in the top of the back). Not until the tube went into the belly to siphon out the fluid did the dropsical patient understand how physical we were. Not until he felt the actual cancer on and in his scrotum did the chimneysweep fathom the true nature of soot. If only, in my vampyre story, Aubrey, who died of an aneurysm, when one of his arteries outpouched, had had the services of John Hunter, whose special operation had saved hundreds already, he would have survived to save his sister—but I shrank from becoming too technical, and besides his function in the story was to quit the scene. Like it or not, as I told the Countess, I was part-custodian of a mystery, an incomplete and evolving one to be sure, but graced with a tincture of the godlike, which perhaps accounted for my reticence: I had an appalling power within my hands, and a licence to practise. The world was at my mercy.

"So you would do us harm?" She blanched, aghast at what she had cozened into her boudoir.

Everyone, I answered, should have one of those wax cadavers cut right open, just to get the human wonder in perspective. Glistening, crammed viscera were the basis of our lives, our best ideas, and we should never forget this, never be lost in some exalted rhapsody about the dominance of mind. "We are chemistry, madam," I said, with some pride of ownership. "Much of us is slop."

"Then we *are* mere bags of *merde*," she said, "as the old abbot, Odon of Cluny, once said. Actually, he was speaking of women only, with prejudice, as a monk would."

"All of us," I said, my mind faltering away to the big heaps of detritus piled up in pits to one side of the Villa Diodati, where the *merde* met the ashes and, later on, thoroughly mixed and weathered, served another useful purpose, becoming a kind of gravel for use on paths. *Cendure* I had heard it called. The great Goethe himself had once said that, although we had learned to build palaces and castles, we still spent an untold amount of our lives on getting rid of our accumulated wastes. Whole planets passed through the tripes of this planet's population, century after century. The sheer bulk of the waste appalled me, although, to be logical, it took up less room than the consumed foodstuffs had in nature: the big, luxuriant leaves, the radiant apple tree, the woolly lamb. Humans compressed the planet's bounty and then gave it back, but in a useless and offensive form— even doctors, hardened to odours, thought so. Having told her some of this, to her heaving fascination, I ceased, knowing how far I could go: not very far, before she became flippant and dismissed the whole thing as a Swiss obsession.

"Clean," she would say. "I prefer polite and witty, like you." She was often so generous, and with her body too. I found her useful rather than intoxicating, rather as Byron had found Mme. de Staël. I still needed my *amours de la nuit*, my gutter *congé*, from time to time, my young lunges. She understood this and accepted whatever I offered, which in a young man approaching twenty-one was physically a great deal of energy and homage. I would allow her to be maternal and then go one stage beyond, gently opening her legs to air the isthmus, as it were, and then I had that exquisite sense of breaking the rules, of shattering the idols of the tribe as, ever patient with her, having been schooled by her in what to do, I elicited from her, as if she were the most patient of patients, first a few approving murmurs, then sobs, yells, roars, as her Slavic nervous system reached a peak. I adored her at such times, amazed by her capacity for enlightened surrender, her total disregard of my own needs until she had completed her crescendo. Only then did she take me in hand and coax me to mine, murmuring, "Doctor, doctor, Polee, Polee," as if these were forbidden words for some entity unthinkable.

We were allies and physical collaborators, then, each anxious for the sensual part to be over with so that we might resume our chits and chats in the aftermath of a taboo tenderly broken; I never called her anything maternal, though, but "countess" or "cuntess," at which she laughed.

How, after such a time spent, was she able to go forward with her evening's plans, hosting a performance of *C'est le Même*, with a girl from Lausanne doing the lady with great skill? Like Napoleon, the Countess kept different problems in different drawers, closing and opening as the mood or need took her. Once a drawer closed, what was in it did not exist. Once a drawer opened, there existed nothing else. I envied her this gift for the closing of the mind, and I rather resented it too; I wanted her to have a bad evening and not go lauding the costumes, lamenting the fact that there was not a role for me (I who had played the part of Flicflac so well in *Le Pacha de Suresne*, in which she played Mme. Dorsan). They knew I was leaving, but the news was hardly the catastrophe of the evening, dear as they were to me, and I to them. I felt like the man who, after giving up his employment, has time on his hands and thus discovers the true nature of existence: exactly what life gives to us without saying when the vast, unoccupied tract of days will end. With no distractions, such as work and friends, one sees the offering in all its nakedness as if one were a wren or a fox, cognizant only of dusk and dawn, certain rhythms of living, and the quality of the air. I could sense in my bones how it was going to be without Lord B., the Shelleys, Claire, the Countess de Breuss, and all the friends of my three cantons; without the Villa Diodati, and Cologny, and the familiar servants, Fletcher, Rushton, and even Berger, and Maurice the boatman, and on and on. I had lived in a small but constantly swelling encampment here, unaware of my good fortune until now, and having not the faintest idea how to say good-bye, to whom to say it first. My twenty-first birthday had vanished into the rumble of time; I did not miss it, but I was going to miss the sight of Lord B. writing a hundred verses in a morning, out on the balcony in the gloom, testy and rapt, strewing penmarks all over the pages of his notebook. There were some places, I just knew, in which human beings ought to stay, having at last arrived in them and by accident found a haven. Had I had the means, I would have stayed on in Diodati alone, in order to maintain the lovely life I had sleepwalked into. That would have been half the battle; I would not have lacked for visitors, I would have been out every evening, more than ever, and perhaps addressed myself seriously to the art of writing, like milord. I might have filled a shelf. As it was, Lord B.'s narrow bedroom would soon be empty, and so would mine. Either room seemed a premature coffin, I thought: odd when the other rooms were so big. I gave the Countess my writings and kissed her in full view of them all. There was nothing to say.

Returning in the gig of a friend, Lloyd of good Welsh blood, his former name Ap Griffith, I lamented Berger's influence over Lord B. I was no longer to have a horse. We brushed against another horse and the carter flung his whip at me, striking me on the back; I jumped down, and then six of them came at me, except that they could not reach me, I being between a hedge and a wheel. When Lloyd jumped down on seeing this, three of them took after him while one of the others untied from his wagon something to beat me with even as I fended off the one with the whip, who managed to graze my face. I jumped back, then forward, putting my fist with full force into *his* face, and he retreated, hand to his nose. Next came a fusillade of stones, which we advanced into and grappled with them. Along came an English carriage, to which we called, the while flailing about with the six; some of those who tried to divide us got blows too. What an odd, violent good-bye to Geneva, hardly my image of the place, but there were ruffians everywhere, the amazing thing being how few we had encountered. Swindlers we met by the dozen, but easily sent them packing.

My heart began to go in slow motion, but everything around me sped by. Mme. de Staël gave me three letters, as if I were Mercury; the physician in me was. Countess of Breuss, with whom I had been in lukewarm love, had cried in her guarded, mature fashion, telling me that we would soon meet again. She knew it. The fight with the carter and his bullies had done me good, relieving me of an extra energy I had not known what to do with. Nothing in my head connected meaningfully with anything else. I was adrift again, as I had been before Sir Henry Halford had recommended me to Lord B. I had no energy for the journey, for all the strangers to come, the unfamiliar meals at the wrong times, and the Byronless vistas, the empty beds, and, indeed, the increased consumption of opium that I knew was to be my lot. Such a diary as I had kept was of no use to Murray, and now my opportunity was over, botched and wasted. All I had to look forward to was the publication, in *The Pamphleteer,* of my essay on the Punishment of Death. What a lugubrious young man to be wandering alone among the Alps, wishing myself fifty years old so that I would not have to keep trying for something I could never define and did not want! I had touched fame and been found wanting. I had dallied with true greatness and insulted it. I had been taken into august company and failed to recognize it. In a word, I had been too young and green to be let out. At six in the morning of the sixteenth September, Lord B. saw me off from Cologny, having walked me down, and gave me back my cricket ball.

PART FOUR

It appeared that this German was much distinguished amongst his countrymen for his talents,—that he was generally esteemed a hater of all the vanities of the world, but that he passed many hours at his toilette; that he was deemed broken-hearted from having been crossed in love; but that he was incapable of feeling that passion, being wrapt in selfishness, that made him sacrifice every thing around him to the whim of the moment: that he was deemed irresistible, and that no woman upon whom he fixed his eye could withstand the fascination of his tongue, but that he never dared to tempt any woman, who was not of the most abandoned character. . . . Things, of which, even at the moment of action he was ashamed, were often done by him in the view of proving himself capable of excelling even in vice.

—*Ernestus Berchtold,*
J. W. Polidori

Will on him subtle poisons pour
That all his future prospects sour—
For he who drags his poison's weight,
Diseas'd and rotten while to wait,
He's doom'd.
—*Chatterton to His Sister,*
J. W. Polidori

I was an ant on a map again, my mind less impressed by the scenes I floundered among than haunted by sundry things at random: how, early in August, Byron and Shelley went into town together to buy a telescope for ———— his birthday present (Polidori not invited, even though I pored over a microscope); Mary's hair, a burnished mousey, if anything a little too fine, yet capable of making a cowl round her face and throat, on her shoulders setting and moving like a train—how electrical it was; and the book Claire told me she had once intended to write, to be called *The Ideot,* about the improvement of the mental faculty, but with no plot or series of events. It was the world I had to leave behind me, but my mind would not behave as I breakfasted at Doraine, dined at Thouson, tried to go to sleep at Saint-Gingoux, went to the Chillon earlier visited by Byron and Shelley as a twosome, saw Bonivard's prison, from which one Frenchman had escaped, actually getting through a window and boarding a boat. I saw the instruments of torture, including a pulley used, I supposed, for squassation. It was in Chillon that I discovered how I felt about death, surrounded there by the implements of undoing and nagged at by the lugubrious exaltation that B. and S. must have felt in there; indeed, they went there to indulge a certain kind of fulsome emotion in which they had a professional interest. I did not want death to play any part in my life. Death, I reasoned, played so large a role, so permanent a one, that to admit it into the puny span of one's life was almost like wishful thinking. If death was so dominant, and I had no evidence to the contrary, it needed no helping hand. Did the mayfly spend its day worrying about sunset? Doctor that I was, I never shared Byron's and Shelley's passion for attitudinized morbidity; I was more prosaic than they, I supposed, actually much more accustomed to dealing with death and the dead. Death was not the grandest of tropes; Byron said it was not even an alternative to anything. Death was the blank we might not question, could not stare down. I kept up my diary, careful to banish all such thoughts as these from its ticking, prattling pages, but more for company than for anything else. I must write to my father, I told myself repeatedly. I must take better care of my feet; heaven help the pilgrim with chilblains or corns.

Having entered a chalet and ordered whey, I was unable to make my diary entries for the noise they made about my ordering something they fed to pigs, and they would not be paid. The noise abating (they finally let me pay), I was able to pen some sentiments on the landscape: high up, the water seemed merely *an inlet of sky*. I then could write no more for a natural well-spring of tears unmanning me quite. I had not intended to be here, alone for having been found *de trop*, having no one to travel with and only fatigue as my anodyne, not when I had been used to Diodati and Cologny, to the three cantons of friends. In my misery I would ask the unlikeliest of people to dance with me, but they could see the crackbrain in my face, the ponderous misery of it all, and they knew I wanted to dance not out of ebullience but out of desperation. Not the Swiss.

No drugs. Too tired to bother with them.

Some merriment at Château-d'Ox, where a fair was going on, but thereafter not a soul, in torment or otherwise. If one loved chalets, torrents, pines, chalets, torrents, pines, ad infinitum, it was all very well. There was a shred of hope at Gessenay, where French gave way to German; but, at this watershed of patois, all I wanted to do was turn round and go back, apologizing to the Countess for leaving them all, begging a loan so as to take the Diodati for myself.

But no: places with such names as Bottingen and Wyssenbach and Erlenbach, Lauterbach and Meiningen, whose vowels were fractured ice, urged me ever onward. The people had a stolid generosity as I got nearer to Thun and all that God-given scenery in a great valley. Beauty, I found, at least of the countryside, does nothing to rid one of melancholy, especially the kind that intensifies when one is alone and therefore feeling out of sorts with the surrounding glory. Had I landed in some Low Countries slum I would have cheered the instant my foot landed on the mud in front of the dunghill in front of the front door. One looked for broken angels, rotting in the gutters, demoted for having failed to speak German. I could feel my face settling into that dour visual growl I had not known since Ampleforth, but known it well I had there, too much of a foreigner for those well-bred boys for whom life ended at the Channel.

Rising at six, from a sleep so transparent it felt like a night full of activity, I addressed myself to letters, most of all one to my father, keeping up appearances:

> *We have parted, finding that our tempers did not agree. He proposed it, and it was settled. There was no immediate cause, but a continued series of slight quarrels. I believe the fault, if any, has been on my part; I am not accustomed to have a master, and therefore my conduct was not free and easy. I found on settling accounts that I had 70 napoleons; I therefore determined to walk over Italy, and (seeing the medical establishments) see if there proves a good opportunity to settle myself, so that I hope I am still off your hands for nine months: perhaps Lady Westmorland, who is at Rome, is desirous of having an English physician for longer, I having a letter for her from Mme. de Staël.*

Already so stiff by the twentieth of September, four days into the odyssey, I wrote to my father about Italy, my trunks, the Alps, Thun, Mont Blanc, the Jungfrau, Grindelwald and Grimsel, the Simplon and Milan. To the Polidoris of Milan I was Giovanni, and even that cheered me as a glimpse of some new, refreshed identity came to me, in which I would not be Lord Byron's former anything. I was in good health and spirits, I lied to him, and I asked to be remembered to my mother and to Mary, Fanny, and Charlotte. How odd to be mixing the names of my loved ones with those of the highest mountains, as if there were no difference between them. I aimed, over the long view, at my uncle, Luigi Polidori of Pisa ("Zio"), and Vaccà the surgeon there. There I was, a physician among the Alps, with not a single sick soul to minister to, and it seemed I was that most sterile being, doctor to the mountains, in newly bought shoes and stockings, aching to find a bookseller's shop.

"I am always surprised," said the man who attended me at the post office, "that so many come to see what we ignore and have never seen. Perhaps the English ignore their own country's beauties in the same way."

"Sir," I told him, "I have just come from spending some months in the company of the noble Lord Byron, whom none in our country ignore. I was Mahomet. Now I have come to the real mountains after hobnobbing with the lions."

He did not fathom a word of this, but I was almost out of practice with speaking; it was such a relief. I prattled on like a man rescued after two weeks in the middle of the ocean, and then, in the midst of my reprieve, noticed with what glee he petted the dog that had come out of nowhere to follow and adopt me in those barren places: a mongrel phantom out of solitude by rage. It would leave me just as fast, I thought. Dogs, although common in those parts, never came near him, he said; he thought it must be the way I smelled to them. "What is his name?" When I improvised one right there and then, and told him it, he took his hand away and stared hard at me, finding me odder still. *"Ambulance?"* he said. He did not know that it meant *walking* as well as something medical, then confessed he suddenly saw what a good idea it was, up here, among the St. Bernards. Had I changed the dog's name for Switzerland? Up here, they did not like to see Englishmen without their dogs; without them, they seemed more incomplete than men of other nations.

"I am very much with him," I said. "He has been poorly of late and, I fear, ate something that poisoned him. He has defiled many a patch of decent mountain with his vomit." Along he bounded, bounding slowly, eager not to miss glaciers, torrents, and precipices, and lovely luxuriant fields like green handkerchiefs. One minute the lake was hundreds of feet beneath me, and the next it was close to my feet. Guided by two children, as lost, I took to forming in my mind's eye, since I could hardly talk to them in their native patois, little hymnal-boards of the day's doings, in this way able to savor the utter, craggy foreignness of the names, which, as usual, I spell in my own way, so gaining power over the landscape:

Nilterfingen
Oberhofen
Rottingen
Morlangen
Neuchaus
Unterseen
Two Englishmen.

The little cascade of seven or eight fountains I had seen while lost was much livelier than I, trying to impress the two Englishmen with tales of Lord Byron (Life with Him) and the feeble exploits of a dog called Ambulance. They had not heard of Lord B. and they did not care for dogs. They must have upset the custodian of the post office. I showed them the cricket ball, at which they came briefly to life, held it, caressed it, then started a silly throwing contest across the dining room without inviting me to join in, so I reclaimed it, wiped it on a napkin, smeared it with butter, then polished it dry. It almost reflected the three of us, but it had never been shiny. They were going to Grindelwald. Had I been there already? All places sounded alike in this thorn-thicket language. No, I had not, so I agreed to go with them in a char-à-banc which they referred to as a Shah-Rah.

The foot I had hurt when leaping off the balcony to aid Mary Shelley on the slope at Diodati was getting worse. So I took my familiar painkiller and got much relief, although at some cost of diurnal consciousness, seeing the bridge at Interlachen, and the famous view between two lordly crags, as through a mist. I met a *maréchal* who had been in Vienna and Bohemia and had seen the available world, sampling places a day at a time. He belonged nowhere except among those mountains: a wanderer, a grasshopper, a geographical agnostic. Off we went on horses after breakfast, through Zweihitschirne (which I could hardly say) to Lauterbrunnen, making me coin and save up for my journal the phrase *pine-clad craggy valleys*. Thence to the Staubach falls, nine hundred feet high, the water turning to vapour before it landed. I noted how opium garbled the sense of space and time: I had come from far out among the stars in order to behold the Jungfrau like this, and the whole technique of looking felt like something new-learned, easily forgotten and lost; and my journey to this point had occupied hundreds of years, during which I was only a little boy, trotting and nose-blowing. There was nothing frightening in this, but it made me feel a member of a race different from my companion, who lunched with me, hardly noticing me for the backdrop, at which he glared as if it would soon go away.

How fitting the names were, designed to evoke sinew and ice-ribs, glaciers and sheer overhangs: nothing of the giving, nothing soft and fertile, nothing peopled, except by some breed of insulated monster—Mary's creature, say, who needed this kind of emptiness and massiness to bounce his temper off. After Zweilütschinen we went to the Grindelwald, the Saxe-Gotha all before us, and the Eiger and the Wetterhorn—names like that, both chilling and bony. It was a relief to find, almost like a God-given contrast one might have prayed for, a couple of girls who gave us cherries and spoke so freely with us that I thought, They too have had no one to talk to for weeks; they have been wandering about up here in hopes of company. How odd, I thought, that the land does not resist you; without inviting you in, or on, it awaits your pleasure, heedless, mindless, the left-over portion from some big ruction (a Yorkshire word) at the beginning of time. Ice. Slate. Slab. Granite. Peak. Glacier. Alp. Listen to those words, I told myself. How welcoming are *they?* And crag. Compare with, say, field, meadow, brook, stream, rill, river, rivulet. Dreaming? I was. The qualities of both worlds came from my mind now I was out of pain, even though my ankle refused to function; it felt as if shreds of bone were trapped in the joint, impeding and grating.

Much talk of mules followed, price 18 francs a day, and I wondered what the life of a mule was like. A lively, gay party arrived about eight, badgering their guides and yodelling like souls evicted from hell. When I dined, at seven, there was more talk of mules, and I thought, If he had only been bigger, Ambulance himself would have been my mount, with a barrel of brandy strapped under his chin. Had I ridden him when I was a little chap? How could I have? I was hundreds of years older than he, older even than the Byron who had set his age at a hundred when arriving at Dejean's hotel. Visions of amputation had begun, and I saw Ambulance scampering among the peaks with my foot in his jaws. Surely I had not willed this ill upon my own body, just to be like Lord B.? Those who live with those who limp, I had heard, will limp themselves, out of magical sympathy. Hoping for a cheaper mule, I went to bed. Rising, I found them no cheaper, and my foot unbearable, even with opium, enough to intensify all the colours around me, turning them into a pouring kaleidoscope. Nonetheless, with no hopes of a medal, I trudged off with Captain Rice to Interlaken, managed to get into a boat rowed by a boy and two men. Brienz. Calne. The Griesbach cascade. Words only. If pain could be this severe, then, I thought, somewhere God had written a law against jumping off balconies. The others in the party went up to see the cascade, but not I, left to keep an old woman company, an old woman who talked all the time like a copper wind-up bird from the previous century *(Avis prolixissima)*. I desired the daughter, who went up, only to find herself being pursued by one of the men accompanying her.

It was here that, as I sat there with my boot off and the old woman tapped my injured ankle with unmanicured fingers, as if to drive some evil genie out, a carriage arrived some distance away, disgorging an array of gentry all talking loudly like the people who had arrived at the inn with guides, but in an English that carried far and one that I could understand. I scarcely looked, too busy with taking a few more drops of laudanum, then (as a physician, of course) giving one or two to the old crone, to quieten her. Whenever I looked up, I saw something quite artificial: a stage-set church marooned in millions of acres of rock and ice, with only the actors or singers omitted. Dun green pastures which were truly there filled with cows and huts as if someone had lowered them into place for yet another play, to demonstrate to the mountain people what life was like elsewhere on the planet. I awaited the arrival of a dining table, an electrostatic generator, and a rocking horse. Could this be Switzerland, or a land I had imagined and wanted to quit?

Then my hands began to quake, my face to become moist, my mind to race giddily, for the person limping toward me with almost a smile on his face, his stick upheld in greeting, was none other than Lord Byron himself, the author of all my travels, the creator of my loneliness, the sponsor of my homesickness, the cause of much. My dog recognized him too and bounded toward him to be patted and massaged. "Ambulance," I said to remind him of yet another forgotten friend.

"I thought his name was Legion," he said without so much as a smile, determined to be witty even among the Alps, even at a dog's expense.

"Milord," I said. "Yourself again. It has felt like weeks."

"Polly," he answered. "May God forgive you for saying your good-byes to none save me. Geneva will never forgive you. What a dreadful day of parting that was. I soon get attached to people, as you know." The rest of them, Hobhouse included, came up and saluted me cordially. There was going to be no fuss, I could tell that.

"I would rather be here, among this positively unreal barrenness," he said, "than at that dreadful summer festival, or carnival of the fatuous, given by Hentsch and Saladin at Mon Repos in July. Six hundred English, all talking like chaffinches. How are you, Polly? Who is this aged lady?"

"None of mine, milord. My taste is somewhat flightier: her daughter, now up the mountain however, but worth waiting for on the descent—"

"Any clack in a storm, hey, Polly?"

"*Provided,*" I said. "How do you fare with what ailed you, my lord?"

"Middling," he answered. "I have not clacked since Claire; I have felt rather quiet in that zone. What did you give me to quieten me down so?"

"The truth, milord. Rest merry. Do nothing for the germ. Give the mercury a chance to work."

The old woman's young daughter, nay, granddaughter, appeared, bubbling over with good-natured refusal as some army gentleman in mufti pressed his pointless suit. Milord bowed, swept his
cloak, reached for her hand to kiss, but she passed him by to begin
babbling in German to the old woman. Like one turned to salt, Lord
B. waited for her to attend to him, but she went on ignoring him,
clearly not in the mood that day for attentions of any kind. Perhaps
she saw him as he had seen Claire; but this BDSM (Belle Dame Sans
Merci) was golden-haired, a Teutonic hoyden. Rough-haired Claire,
with her chubby cheeks and restricted, narrow mouth, her face a
study in imminent boredom, would have had something to say, even
if only a quotation from one of her favourite works: *King Richard
III* or *The Corsair,* the work of milord's that she grew up on in
Skinner Street, where, on execution days, the *canaille* roistered by on
their way to Newgate, sucking on ices and ginger-pop from the
barrows of Italian sellers.

"So the Villa Diodati is emptied of us," Byron said. "Never
have I rejoiced in a view more."

"Or in such company."

"Ah, the *company,* Polly."

"For my part, my lord," I told him, "I had as soon be back
there, among us all, as peering at these gloomy peaks. This is the
worst of Switzerland. I long for the vines that grow high and make
a shelter to sit under, whereas the grapes of France hug the earth.
Oh, for Italy!"

"Down there," he said, pointing south-east. "Better than all
this mountain stuff, these vast masses of the Deity."

"Agreed on that, my lord. Pray let it be soon that I shall have
the advantage of serving you again, even as my capacities increase
and my experience grows longer." It was as gracious as I could be.
Perhaps it was all right to get it in before he made some careless
imputation of villainy to the world at large, implying that nothing
was worth doing, not even a gorgeous, exalted thing. Hobhouse, as
was his role, would be intervening any moment, never one to let his
own primacy go to waste, never mind how game the other's conver-

sation might be or how welcome his long-postponed presence. Perhaps he would enlist his Polly again, to do for him in Italy, in a different set of moods, with all that ice behind him, Claire off his hands, the pang of exile beginning to soften. I would volunteer, I told myself, could I but find the idiom, not exactly saying I was sorry for this or that caprice, but in general lamenting the untoward lack of perfection. B. and S., I now called them mentally: Byron and Shelley, or Brandy and Soda; my heart was less on my sleeve, but Shelley was gone. There was hope of a reconciliation, of my accompanying him more, of our talking more about books and ideas. Instead, however, I began to prattle on about the Geneva I missed, the pageant of my stillborn popularity.

"La Toffettheim," I said to him. "Now there was a nice unpretentious lady, pleasant and affectionate. You never—no. Son full of liberty talk. Once I did a pantaloon-dance that I refused to do at the Saladins', and they felt it a personal refusal. The Saladins were always rather coy about the Countess of Breuss, my friend and literary adviser. The daughter, of course, had misconstrued my attention to her, thinking me in love when I was merely being polite and, as it was then, knew only her. There was a young Mr. Massey after Mme. Mathilde, who made up for wit with noise, and slaps on the back, shifting most of your food forward. Oh, how vivid they still are, like ghosts at a roll-call in paradise. Auguste, a neat simple fool, a born buttock sniffer. Alexis, oh yes, bovine *mari complaisant* to Mathilde. Massey Sr., lively fencer and dancer. Massey Jr., dyspeptic puppy, insolent and ignorant. Then there was Mme. Saussure, a garrulous waxwork. Mlle. Jacquet: half in love with that one, milord, or her eight thousand a year. Her face was the remedy, sir, and her epiglottis, whereas it was wholehearted adoration with Mme. Brelaz, a Portuguese, who reciprocated despite opposition from her daughter. Her daughters very possessive. I must have been in love with five or six. There were so many, of fastidious gentility."

"Polly," he said with his lewdest scowl, "I had heard it was more a matter of the red-lamp district, and the encounter a multiple one with an Italian gentleman, a whoremastering professor from

Bologna. Were you not clapped thus, turned into a shambles when you had expected an encounter between just you and her, her *vallis lucis* all clean and powdered for you?" As long as I had known him, Brandy had not been able to keep his mouth shut about anything tender, and there he was regaling Hobhouse and the rest right on top of my intemperate reminiscence of the Geneva *ton*. I had not even got to Clemann and Auguste, Miss Harriet and Marianne, about whom, all four, he would have loved to hear—what he was missing for being such a misanthrope and recluse.

"You heard about that, milord."

"It was all over Geneva, how you had pawned your all to pay your way into her. No one sympathizes more than I, Polly; the sex blinds us with its insistences and its need for proof. You came out of it passing well." Little did he know it was not Gaby I missed, but the sense of being a moon to his planet, not deferring or obliging but being needed, being the one to whom he turned in the full spate of the dismals. When a friend happens to be a doctor, certain barriers never even go up, because your friend knows you will never be censorious, having seen the best and the worst, no stranger to what I fancied to call "deinosis" (from my Edinburgh treatise on night-mares), meaning to see things in their very worst aspect—or, even likelier, the disease of doing so without pause. So my profession, inured to deinosis, offered him a friendship trimmed of customary curbs. If a Byron is a man of the world, a doctor is several, able to see in all his friends the cadaver they will one day achieve, the puling baby they were born as, and so on. I nothing held back, aiming to meet him more than halfway, but I did not think he saw me coming. Soda got in Brandy's way, so to speak, and their physician ended up a mere supernumerary, fondling his laudanum, doting on Mary and Claire.

There we stood, no more than casually eyed by Hobhouse and the rest, as if on some promontory of the known world, the lord and his hireling. It could have been an ancient saga. The air was benign but the view was cold, and I thought of all the eyes and minds that had fastened on his frame, his very name, marvelling at his this or that, wondering what led him to do such things, to behave openly in so bad a fashion that he set the whole world trembling, for they too wanted to behave just as badly. When eyes had pressed on someone so much, surely they left an imprint or a vibration. His skin, his hair; his lips were not like the lips of other mortals but had the hum of cynosure: harmless to the touch but extraordinary to the eye. That woman had fainted—Lady Elizabeth Hervey—but had come back to talk to him with renewed animation as if she had been dipped into a Leyden jar and emerged quivering. These were the hands that had done the unmentionable but feasible things. These were the lips that had failed to obey. That was the hair they wanted to crop a lock from. Not only was he a thing, a creature, of mystery; he was also one of overexplanation, of renown plus renown. And, in a weird way, he seemed to have come out of Mary Shelley's head: the ghoul, patched together from a thousand misdemeanours, failed lives, wasted loves, atrophied parts. He was a scarecrow of rumours that incited folk to come nearer and nearer, not to flee like birds. An unholy magnetism drew them on to sin and deviltry, against their will perhaps. Would I, the latest victim, say, ever have gone lusting after Gaby Saxonnex if I had not been joined with him over a spell of several months, from April to August or September? Under his influence, I might have lusted after anyone—Claire or Mary. I did. And who next, then? It was not a matter of hoping to outdo him but of reciprocating in kind. If you were a mere twenty, a world-famous reprobate of twenty-eight was a venerable past master.

Was I in awe of him? By the time I had languished in the Alps, I was like someone who has wandered along in the dark through countrysides of extraordinary appeal, feeling his way through stiles and along bridges, but unaware of the constant magnificence, or of the dangers lurking. As a sleepwalker I had lived at the Villa Diodati, as used to seeing Lord B. in the long hallway that bisected the villa as to seeing Ambulance chasing tiny Italian birds in the bushes. Then the dream ended, and I came away imbued with something just a touch lordly; I did not, in the beginning, wish to mingle with folk unlike himself, who were unknown, but as time went on I

craved human companionship of almost any sort. Most of all, I
wanted him to turn round and go back, or take me onward with
him to Italy, even if only as his doctor, of whom he had undeniable
need. I need not be his companion; indeed, to be his physician
sounded more imposing than merely being his companion, which
Hobhouse was. There was only one doctor. My skills were going to
waste. I could not even heal my own wretched foot. It was time for
Byron to call on his Paracelsus, telling Fletcher, "Without Polly,
there is no going right. There is no healing." Or he would say to
Rushton, "Fetch my Polly to me now, my blood feels brackish and I
am liverish. Call for leeches." No, he would never call for leeches;
we would have an agreement about *them* and about bleeding. Perhaps he had already run out of mercury? I asked. No, he had not
even been applying it, which was a good way of staying alive—
mercury was dangerous. Had he been drinking sufficient milk, then
(Polidori's nostrum for pressure of the blood, unproven, but as good
an educated guess as many others)? No, he drank no milk, it was an
infant's drink. So his blood pressure would be high. Would he care?
My bag—

Not a bit of it, but his hand held my arm, at first as if to detain
it from lifting the invisible bag, but then as if plugging me in to
some supply. Did I feel the current leaping between us? The face
peered at by a million faces peered at mine, close up, and I marvelled
at the soft, transparent texture of his skin, after so much abuse; his
face, though plump, was very young. And then I recalled something
more scientific—that the faces of the overweight always looked
young because that slight stretch over the extra flesh ironed all the
creases out. Even dieting, he remained a little stout. It was not like
being close to any human being at all; I was doing something commonplace with a legend, a role I had come to love, as when with
him at the pianoforte, even though he could not play, or having him
give me a good-night pat and a kiss when I had been ill. Now I was
discussing my foot, and he nodded, recalling my jump from the
balcony to aid Mary. "It proves," he said, "that those who wish to
become gentlemen should not leap at every opportunity, never mind

what *anyone* says. You were precipitate, Polly." I was Precipitate Polly, well enough, as like to hold that sobriquet for weeks.

"Are we agreed, then?" I asked.

"On what, Polly?"

"That I rejoin you, for your health's sake."

"I do not give a fig for my health, Polly. *You* know."

"You should, my lord." I felt giddy. Why did he hover?

"Polly, the die was cast. We went through all the pain of severing. Must we do it again?"

"But the joy of reunion, my lord? At the pianoforte. On the balcony. In the boat. Let us go to Chillon together."

"Polly," he whispered, rather crudely, I thought, "the Villa Diodati is no longer ours."

"Oh, to Cologny, then," I said, envisioning Shelley's house.

He said nothing but gestured grandly at the Alps. This was the present, he said. "Byegones are byegones, let them ever more be so. Byegones are not epigones."

That shook me. As soon as he waxed witty, you knew the serious conversation was over and he had begun to play. Except that the play on this occasion had a knife's edge concealed in it. I was being shed. He made as if to walk away. The old woman had just slapped the young woman's face, and I looked hard at them: the young woman's bulging blue eyes, the overdeveloped septum, the rather coarse mouth, thicker rather than wide, and saw the physiognomy of subordination. It had happened before. Lord B. made as if to intervene, then clapped his hands, laughed, and said they should be moving on. It was as if Caesar or Alexander had decided to move his army onwards. He was not going to talk to me again, and I could feel my presence beginning to fade from his view, his awareness; I had been met, dealt with none too gently, and must now resume my own miserable substitute for a life. I waved at him, five yards distant. I saluted him, six yards away, bringing my hand down. I clapped him, ten yards away by now. He halted, bowed, and made a strange flowing motion with his hand, right from his midriff horizontally towards me as if unfurling a length of silk from a cummerbund, but it was his heart, his core, that he was extending towards me: *the idea of Switzerland,* perhaps, which I was to cherish. Was he really going or was this a charade? It was, for the old woman and her now weeping daughter. He had not shot the old woman or bagged her for the Bosphorus; but I had seen him waver on the edge of interfering, and another anecdote had almost taken root. Now his extended hand rolled back as if withering and coiling up. Even that was over now. His back turned, his head he flung back, his *friends* gathered around him again as if at a signal, no doubt to laugh at Polidori's latest gaffe. "Thank God Polidori is not here." Was that an Alpine echo? Were they saying it? No, it would be more like, "Thank God Polidori stays behind." He had not even said where he was going. Then I lost all shame, forgot my medical degree and my own dignity as a writer, and cried out as loudly as I could, *"Albé! Where to, Albé?"* Without turning he shouted "Mílan," with the accent on the first syllable, and limped out of sight.

Would that forlorn cry, evoking the word for dawn, become the new call of the Alps? It was a cry asking him to come back and collect a lesser mortal, restoring him to his rightful place of subservience. Would it haunt him, he being profoundly capable of being haunted? Or would it prefigure the last of Polidori, the end of an interloper? How could he not reverse his course, telling his retainers to wait while he plunged back, being rather portly, and seized my hand, embraced me with both arms, exclaiming, "Why, Polly, it was only a jape. I was coming to get you all the time. We knew you would wait." Until Lord B., I had hoped for very little, socially, but after joining him I had come to *expect* things, and the anguish of knowing them already over was more than I could bear. Was it not to be? Would I never again have the chance to see eyes in nipples, as the high-voiced Shelley had? Or have Lord B. tuck me in during an opium fit brought on by a sprained ankle? Or clash with Shelley on the lake and have Byron offer to duel me on his behalf? I had been living high, as if born to it, as if there would never be a different mode of living for me as long as I lasted. And now I knew I would never be able to adjust. Going to the high society of the three cantons had been one thing, wonderful and invigorating, but the core of pleasure had been going home to Lord Byron's villa, even if only to be snubbed. It was an illustrious home to have, with my own bedroom down the corridor from his: equals at a distance.

I should have been the indefatigable reporter, setting down his every syllable, going without food or breath to capture the asides of a living legend. Instead, I had lived as if entitled to live thus, born to it, not on approval or remand, and that hubris had piqued him. I should have been provoking his wit, not his ire, urging him out into society instead of antagonizing him into his shell. Now I knew how I should have behaved, I wanted to have a second chance, little heeding the fact that he had moved on; he was not the same as the man who had lived in Diodati, and I was no longer the mooncalf who had moved in with him, leeches, opium, notebooks, and all. I was now the author of *The Vampyre,* due to have a far from igno-minious fate, and he was the author of "The Prisoner of Chillon," "Darkness" (in part, anyway), and a new canto of *Childe Harold.* Life, whose purpose remained ever obscure, had drawn us a little nearer to its distant horizon-point, at which we would all meet in eloquent glory. I had wept since quitting him, and mostly for that reason; had he wept on losing me? I wondered. Was he too proud to ask? Had I not, today, given him enough of an opportunity to get me back? Could it actually be that, without intending me any ill-will, he did not wish his Polly back after all? Who could replace me? None that he had as yet, and certainly not Hobhouse, the stalk-ing-horse of banality, the cup-bearer of cynicism, through whom Claire had seen in a flash. Were I to run after him, post-haste, how could he spurn me? But I was unfit even to walk, and he was already out of sight. Had he flinched at my quasi-Byronic costume, not so much copied from him as inspired by him? Had I transgressed, in the tropic of clothing? Had he heard about *The Vampyre* and smelled plagiarism, not having finished his own story? I could not think he would care about a fragment of prose when he was turning out works of poetic genius almost daily. No, that was not it. Perhaps Polidori no longer interested him. Perhaps I never had, except as a body on the premises. He had thought me perfect, perhaps, too good to be true, and suddenly he felt about me as if some friend had gone to a disorderly house and brought home news that such-and-such a woman, say his Augusta, had been taking money there for favours. He had seen Polidori for the whore he was, if a whore he was: say, a medical whore, a social one, a whore for cricket and opium-soaked scribbling. There was no accounting for his behaviour; the answer was medical, and he had overindulged, he had debauched himself into a state of chronic petulance: unsoothed, unloving, unbelieved.

And when he had looked at my face had it not affected him in some poignant way? Had he not remembered how my right eye looked away, high and transcendentally? This was my Alpine eye. The other followed it, but with a critical tightening of the lid, as if to expel moisture, and the crease of that repeated motion was there, an index to quizzicality. Surely that left eye, the weaker, should have made him feel a heartstring tighten. It would have been hard for him, as for so many young women in whom I had had virtually no serious interest, to forget the thickness of my eyebrows or the horizontal ridge (said to be of intelligence) just above them. Even shaven I seemed to have a moustache of shade among the boyish, volatile physiognomy handed down to me. My high colour was Irish, I supposed; I had heard it said; I stood out well against the snows, and my mouth: I had heard that it was pliable, perhaps too much so. *His* face I knew like a well-thumbed text, so why was there so little reciprocity? Did not older faces heed younger ones? Did nothing of my aspect haunt him, I who had nursed him and applied to him the most intimate endeavours? Was I too much like him to be visible? In seeing me, did he see only himself magically made younger and less morbid: fresher-faced, thicker of hair, pulpier of mouth? I consoled myself that he remembered my soul, my mind, and that nothing could dislodge me from his inmost core.

In a trice I had begged a ride to the brink of the overland so as to catch sight of the English gentlemen leaving. On we rattled, the driver applying his whip, and there we were on the lip, not a hundred yards from the party of them, descending to their carriages

in a curious shuffle, not so much walk as meander. They were in no
hurry to get away, once out of sight at any rate. Out I clambered
and made ready to call, my voice somehow unfit, with too much
mucus, my throat feeling narrow, even as they inched downward
and away. At last I called. He did not hear. I called again, a whole
stream of *"Albé"*s from baritone to falsetto, enough to wake the
dead. He stopped, turned, saw me with my arms held high like one
waiting to be lifted up and transported, and deliberately shook his
head. I had expected at least a "Polly, Mílan," but got nothing at all.
I saw him speak to Hobhouse, who turned and stared at me as if I
were a newborn leper. On they went, and I had not the heart to
shout again; I left him to the echoes (one faint *Albé* just dying away
behind me, of all places) and the natives, knowing that, if we were
to meet in Milan, I would do the finding, not he. Tears in my eyes
again made me wince at my own shamelessness. Why did I need him
so much? Once upon a time I had never needed him at all, and now
he was a drug in contrast with whom opium was bang-up ginger-
pop, as the signs said on the Italian sellers' barrows in Skinner Street.

   Up at four on September 23, with a sobbing heart, I decided I
could stand no more company of the wrong kind (not of my own
choosing) and went to say good-bye to the man and his two boys.
Off at five-thirty, along the Aar, for some reason determined to keep
on with my diary, perhaps for my father to read. At Meyringen I
breakfasted with two Germans, one of whom chatted all through. I
bought a pole to ease my walking through the exquisite vale of
Nach-im-Grunden, where I rested and thought I would remain,
being *de trop* elsewhere; but some old compulsion to go on won out;
the king of Nach-im-Grunden would have to be someone else. Then
I was riding on a causeway of rough granite blocks, designed by the
devil for men and mules only. The landscape became more and more
savage: less and less greenery, not grass but moss, and then only rock.
No trees, but shrubs. It was a landscape befitting my mood, with the
river's bed carved deep and narrow, forever turning and braceletted

with high single-arched bridges. The snow there was so hard that huge boulders falling had failed to break its crust. I decided I could live there, in a hut made of boulders, drinking the shockingly cold water until my heart gave out. There were only two houses between Guttannen and the hospital, an old stone building, ugly and drab, where the poor lodged for nothing.

Slugabed for solid rain, I at last set off across the Grimsel, a dismal mountain with much snow, a mile above the Four-Canton Lake. Down to Obergesteln, with my soul full of loathing for Lord B. the perfidious, my ankle full of needles, and breakfasted at ten o'clock. All the rest of the way I marched through solid rain to Mörel, where I dried with vigorous towelling, and ate dinner in bed like a naughty child sent to his room (lucky to have his dinner sent up). I was weary of the upper air and the cold, the wet, in it. Next morning my foot was swollen too big for me to walk, so I crouched double and aspirated the joint using a small copper tube, sucking out the blood and lymph and utterly careful not to imbibe it. I then took breakfast with two students from the Brig Jesuit College who had been on vacation out beyond Constance with only two *écus neufs* to spend. It cost them ten batsches a year to study at the college; I handed the modest-seeming one six francs, but he asked for more, the rascal. The Jesuits had been back only two years. At Brig I too became a student, using Latin to converse with the curate, a fine old gentleman of some sixty years.

"*Hodie,*" I told him, "*non possum ambulare multum.*"

"*Ambulare in cubo,*" he said in his concise way. "*Dormi.*"

"Aha," I told him, "*in cubo, quia non dormio, non possum dormire cum dolore, penso pensa obscena, vel manstupri vel prostitutarum osculorum.*"

He was not shocked but told me to set my mind on something cool and clean such as a mountain peak, preferably with a cross on top of it.

"Yes," I answered, "*sed penso non semper cunnorum, sed foraminum simplicorum, quaqua.*"

"*Poverus puer,*" he said, as if he heard this kind of thing every

day and not thrown from the mental depths of a young doctor in a
rage against his former employer who was *hermaphroditus atque
satyrus.*

"*Nunquam fessus?*" he inquired about Lord B.

No, I told him.

"*Ut juvenis Syphilus,*" he told me, "*in horto Salmacis, ac in fontis.
Eus non hinnus est?*"

No, Lord B. was not a hinny, I told him, amazed that a doctor's Latin could stand up to a priest's, our concerns being rather
different. He asked if I were a Catholic and I told him an intermit-
tent one.

"*Sacramentum smegmae,*" he said, astonishingly. "*Suaviter in
modo. Scelus sexualis caeditur.*"

Ampleforth was a long way behind me, but I was getting his
drift; stuck up here in the mountains, he liked to give his mouth an
occasional orgy, and I thought how much Lord B. would enjoy him,
his *joci,* his *metaphorae.*

"*Numquam stuprum fac canibus,*" he said, but it sounded wrong,
and I needed no warning that I must not approach Ambulance with
lust in mind.

I asked him if he knew about opium, and he said yes, he
suffered from rheumatism up here.

"*Jus papaveri inspissatus,*" he said rightly, and asked for some. In
no time he was in the clouds, cooing and burbling, his surplice up
about his thighs, and his knees exposed, which was where the pain
used to be. I was doctoring again, thank goodness, and corrupting
Switzerland as I went, If only Lord B. had come in at that moment,
to hear us talking poppy-Latin while the curate massaged his knees.

"*Papaver pappa,*" I said, cross-punning. He got it and smiled in
his mounting delirium, every bit the poppy pope I had called him.
In German he told me about the killings up there, when the Valai-
sians resisted against the French in '93. Only in Unterwalden had
they done the same, and then it was the peasants doing it. The
French stuck their prisoners like sheep. They had strangled an old
man of eighty, whom they found eating, setting his meat and bottles

carefully by him again to make it look as if he had had a stroke. In 1813 it had happened all over again, with the French this time trying to get in from Italy, through the Simplon. The villagers with the help of some Austrians took them prisoners. Five thousand French died here at the hands of some two thousand Swiss, their women included. One maid seeing a cannon as yet unfired took a rope-end to it and fired it, killing thirty French, which sounded enormous. They slaughtered her with swords. Some from Schwyz had to cut their way through their own countrymen, who had chosen the other side, both coming and going. He went out, leaving me with images too harsh to bear, too heroic for a mere doctor whom his erstwhile employer had once again snubbed, in the callous-casual fashion Byron and his sister were famous for. In came the curate, talking German, with an account of the Simplon, for my information; I read for an hour and a half, memorizing, then left the book behind, having also brought my journal up to date, not for John Murray but for my father. I called it diary or journal, but it was really becoming a scrapbook with numbered days. He brought me prunes, *"prunae succulentae,"* he said, and we left together as he had his church halfway along my route. We never talked in Latin again, as if having shared something shameful that nonetheless had to be aired.

Next day he came and inquired after my foot, blessed it, then offered to show me the bridge over the Massa where a big battle had taken place. In his church there was a miraculous figure found in the Rhône, a blue radiance coming off it and sometimes (he said) skeins of curving light. "I will see you in heaven, again, I hope," he said in English, and I stumbled away as best I could to Brig along the magnificent Simplon road, all caverns and ridges, wide enough for four carriages, going all the way up to the new Hospice (a place meet for Lord B.) and then going down. Along it I found houses of refuge, so-called, which had a room with a bed where one might rest in bad weather, and some folk lived in these, allowed to sell food to people passing through. They also, in the time of avalanches, escorted travellers from house to house in an unbreaking chain of conduction or conductedness. In the old hospital I got dinner in the

cell of one of the monks—bread, wine, cold meat, and nuts, not too
bad, but the monk seemed altogether *ennuyé* about something; his
words slumped out. "We are St. Augustines," he muttered, "not St.
Bernardites. That St. Bernard, he was a mere reformer. We have
been here since only 1810. We are new, in an old castle." They paid
twenty pounds a year for it. The Simplon was French. I had walked
twenty-six miles in an opium trance, and my foot was numb.

All the same, eager to get to Italy, I moved on at a shuffle,
leaning on my pole until my hands blistered, and walked into a
cobweb of granite galleries, then into a boy, whom I addressed in
faltering German. *"Non capisco,"* he said. I could have hugged him,
or anyone. Arrived at Iselle, I was a cripple when the carriages
departing late from Brig overtook me. I got a room whose floor was
thick with grease, which I rubbed into my soles, for questionable
easement, and took several grains therewith. "Alp" meant snow-
capped peak, so close to "Albé."

It is useless to describe the picturesque, or even to get up early
in order to go and look at it. That was my mood on September 27,
when, too stuporous and weary as well as pained by my foot, I lay
abed until one in the afternoon, one lump of my brain nonetheless
exultant that I was in the Italian part. It was almost as good as being
in Italy, but breakfast was an appalling sludge, and my next trek was
arduous and dramatically slow as I heaved my way towards Domo
d'Ossola. A cart overtook me. I could not resist the invitation, got
in, and lay upon the wood and hay, ready to blubber like a child.
Everything looked greener, no longer having that starched, tonic
look of the Alps, which as long as I lived I would associate with yet
another Byronic snub. If it was *the* landscape for histrionics, for
unbridled exaltation and fetching stances, it was also the landscape of
pain and loneliness and drudgery, whereas coming down from the
mountain was more suited to my state of mind, my temper; the
women wore blue and white with red stripes here and there, the men
looked acute, quicker-eyed—more Italian, I told myself as I lay

there, bumping about like a load. The gendarme who asked for my passport at once asked me to be his doctor, requesting care for his toothache. More laudanum, I thought; is the supply endless? No: be careful. That evening I snoozed by a rustling log fire, as much at ease as I had ever been since leaving Geneva. It was still possible, then, to be Polidori without feeling anguished, but not, it seemed, to have a foot that did not pain me. I worked it hard, however, hoping to summon it back to duty through sheer insistence. Ambulance curbed his trot to match.

Off at six through vine country I trudged, loving the white villas, one of them having on its flank named images of Democritus and Diogenes. I asked a woman what it was all about, and she answered, "È roba antica." That was all. It was an old affair, she did not bother about it; why should I? No one lived in it, and for a weak moment I yearned to own it, to make it my permanent Diodati, vast as it looked, run-down as it was sure to be. My guests would arrive over the Alps. The list of them was ready, Countess of Breuss first. Then I woke up, limped on to Vella and Vagagna, observing at least one good-looking Italian girl. Six miles in five hours, with nothing coming up behind me: no car, no horse, no ox. My feet were fast becoming blocks of suet. Then, at last, into Ornavasco; this was a land whose places I could say, and got more than a little pleasure from rolling along my tongue. I finally contracted for a ride to Fariolo on the morrow and took a meatless dinner, gnawing on pears and peaches, grapes and nectarines.

Gravellino to Fariolo to Laveno, I said, offering four when the carter asked ten. He took it. I was soon being rowed towards all those *Isole*—Madre, Pescatori, and Bella, on which last I toured the palace. It was a collection of grottoes with rock floors, rustic and *al fresco:* another castle for my imagination to be king in, to winnow the hatred from my system until I was a good-natured physician all over again, at least by the time I was fifty. I had meant to go for Lugano and Como, realms of evocative magic, but someone told me I might go all the way by water to Milan, so I turned round towards

Belgirate, where I troughed on *caffè al latte,* grapes and figs, longing for some meat to get me through my exertions. The very thought of going by water soothed my foot; I imagined it over the side of the boat, trailed in the element it loved, cleaving a track just as soon healed behind us, leaving no trace but actually touching every inch between there and Milan. It was the painless form of odyssey; how resist it? Yet I toured on in my relentless way, to Arona, with its enormous statue of San Carlo Borromeo. At the inn I was taken for a servant, so disreputable and scruffy I had become. Two soldiers with swords came with questions about my passport.

I left at six in a huge barge full of the English (a floating Geneva, indeed), on the Tessino and then a canal, on whose banks I slept one night, my head murmuring with distant sounds but a hearty sleep all the same, and then we got into Milan by a superb gate with a triumphal arch. I soon had rooms, forty lire the month, but had to go off in quest of my trunks, on which I had to pay. It was an hour or two before I realized I was home in Italy at last: no bells ringing to greet me, but Milan being its usual self, as I discovered after some meat (a great corrective to the lagging brain). Two hours before the evening began, I strolled to the theatre of La Scala, entered, and at once felt dwarfed by the immense emptiness of it, more imposing than any Alp. I tested the echoes, pretending to sing a vowel or two, but I was no baritone, no tenor, just a good voice for hailing a carriage. I watched *La Testa di Bronzo,* a comic ballet— perhaps the most magnificent thing I ever saw. I just wished I had had my Genevan friends with me to savor it.

After breakfasting on grapes, bread and butter, wine, and figs, I wrote off to Lord B., this a difficult task for one who felt as I did. I urged, I pleaded, I cajoled, at great length asking about his health, and Claire, the Shelleys, though it was doubtful if he had news. It was vital, I thought, to prove to him that calling him "Albé" to his face, as I never had done before, had been a slip in the frantic exertion of the moment. I apologized, saying how hard it was not to celebrate a man of parts with all names:

———

So you see, my lord, it is more a matter of our remaining conversant with each other, lest pleasant memories pall. I ask nothing for myself save your discretion. Should you ever in this land of my father need doctor, amanuensis, secretary, a second Hobhouse, please summon me from whatever quarter I am in, whatever deathbed I am at.

*As for the sex, who plague us all the time, I wonder if they go about their ordinary business aware of having that pleat neatly folded, contained, beneath them wherever they go, neatly tucked away as it were against a rainy day. As we with our kit. They—what would the word be?—*retract *it all, whereas a man's dangles free, in the way. What would it be like to have nothing there but a slash—all that clear-field openness between one's legs, except for certain lascivious occasions—*foramen pudendum repletum, *so to say, for the time being, after which the sense of void must be excruciating, most of all with the valley sluices working full tilt after the nail in the chair has left its cordiality in full view, and Mater Omnium no longer has a yard to play in, though it may have left a little pepper in the puddle. Clack on, I say. One must always find out more before stifling the affair quite. I must confess I have a taste for feathers and would relish your animadversions on this concern, my lord. I am in sore need of groping a concern or two, and wonder if you would care to accompany me on a small expedition for some good old Irish stews in which to feel our ways to heaven, my diffidence escorting your command.*

Mercurous chloride, if I may be so bold, sire. Too much will bring on the toothache, the tooth-rot, and debilitating nervousness; even an ulcerated throat. Above all, my lord, it is to be believed that the gon. is not an early stage of the syph., but they are two separate tigers in different cages: a little for the first, little more for the latter, as prescribed by Sawrey, Philips Wilson, Fergusson, and only this year Bedingfield: A Compendium of Medical Practice.

In the Alps, after our delightful Encounter with each other, I ran into a curate whose general temper and mouth were even obscener than our worldly Regency clergy. He cunnused and smegmaed his way through an entire conversation up there among the ice, as if seeking to melt things with the ferocity of his tongue in those cheeks.

More than our meeting, the anticipation of it regales my Soul, tho' not enough to blind me into forgoing it.

Your physician ever—

———

I signed without even looking, so as to make the scrawl more flamboyant (not part of my nature); it was. Poste Restante would find him, soon no doubt to be renamed Post Byronte; the gossip was all of him, the post would be all for him too.

I soon began to feel Genevois all over again, dressing up for the first time in ages, going off to see people—Marchese Lapone (who happened to be away) and Monsignor di Brema, who was not at home. Outings nonetheless, converted into bookseller browsings. I wanted Philips Wilson's treatise of 1805: *Observations on the Use and Abuse of Mercury, and on Precautions Necessary in its Employment.* How they stared when, after some fumbling, I got the title half translated. They stared again, severely, when I mentioned Fergusson's *Observations on the Venereal Disease in Portugal,* no doubt thinking I was working up to *Venereal Disease in the Vatican.* Hopeless, of course. The slight mercurial action was best for both, I reasoned, since an excess overpowered the body's good forces at the wrong time; so I would have treated even the s. like the g., to begin with. Moderation, I counselled myself, or half the world's teeth will go black and fall out. Drapery was going up for Friday, the Emperor's birthday. Returned home, I sorted my papers, pondered the new novel, on the Oedipan theme, then went for a walk on the Corso, thence to the Teatro Rè to see *Il Sogno di Ariosto,* in which Fortune, Merit, Orgoglio (Pride), and Disinganno (Disillusion) had much to say onstage, personified with all-conquering volume. A small theatre, it reminded me of the Haymarket, making me a bit homesick. I went to all these places alone, I who had been such a gadabout in Geneva.

Next day, October third, I rose late, at eight, and went off with great enthusiasm to a circulating library. My foot was mending. I took out the works of Andreini, to read especially his *Adamo,* a poem Milton had had in mind when writing his *Paradise Lost,* translated by my father. It was a way of keeping in touch with my father, although circuitous. Attended the Teatro Rè again, to see an English play in which they bowed and scraped and kissed hands more than they would in a century in England. It was the Italian

version of English refinement. I noticed in the audience several German officers in English uniforms. The whole world dressed up to
conquer. The time sped by. Brema, in at last, gave me two kisses. He
was on the point of learning English, with which he asked my help.
He did not need the language, I told him; if the play was any guide,
all he needed in England was a pair of resilient lips. I was the only
one watching, I thought: everyone else was playing cards or gossipping, all in small exclusive circles. Milanese society had introverted
itself since God knew when, but not the medical one: Caravella
dined with me, introduced me to his brother, who said the physician
at Florence was dead and promised to escort me to the hospital with
a view to my being taken on. Promising. Took an ice and went off
to La Scala, where I sat in Brema's lodge, with Monti, *his* brother,
the famed poet acclaimed as the successor to Dante. He was sixty-
two, not exactly a patriot but capable of being swayed by a whole
series of political winds, or whims, from revolution to antirevolu-
tion. Unassuming, modest, he made me welcome, and it was refreshing to meet another poet, especially one who did not say, of women,
all one had to do was give them a looking-glass and a few sugar
plums. Taking me aside, he asked about Lord B. and his plans in
Milan; I did not tell him that Lord B. had discharged me, but that he
had liberated me from duties so that I might devote myself to writing, for which it was thought I had some knack. "Be careful here,"
he said. "We have two Austrian governors, Swarrow and Bubna,
one for civil, the other for military matters. If you have ever wished
to study hubris, watch."

At first I thought he was referring to the romance-writer Henri
Beyle, best known as de Stendhal, but he meant the two governors.
It was Stendhal who had caught my eye, he the author of some book
called *Letters written from Vienna about Haydn, followed by a Life of
Mozart, etc.* I wondered why he did not make his title the body of
his book, or append a Byronic menagerie to it to give it some true
bulk. I toyed with the idea of doing a *Letters written from Milan about
Byron, followed by a Life of Shelley, etc.,* but began to yawn at the
thought. Would I call myself de Dori? I had not, like de Stendhal,

been a romantic hussar, adored a dethroned emperor, or lived in France (a country he loathed as much as Byron did), but I might pass muster, I thought. Oh, that the Countess of Breuss were by, to advise me! Oddly, these thoughts served to distract me from the habit of keeping my journal in a regular way. I wished to live a life that could not be tabulated or documented. I would make an occasional entry, I thought, but only as the mood took me. Duty wearied me, and my life began to become what it had been in Geneva: a list of those I saw, from Monsignor di Brema, who took me under his wing and sometimes into his armpit, Monti, Beyle, Monti's son-in-law, to Lord Cowper, Lord Jersey, and the rest.

My medical technique was improving. A flesh tag, or an acrochordon, in my armpit had been bothering me for weeks, having become infected, so I etherized the zone and then, as if playing some invisible musical instrument, raised my left arm high, felt for the offender, snipped it off with scissors, and then educated myself for hours by slicing it as thin as I could, then looking at it in my microscope: exquisite purple mottle in there, only recently a fleck of me, yet utterly unrecognizable as mine or anyone else's, as would be true of one's liver, one's heart, one's bladder. These parts had their quirks, to be sure, but reflected naught of our identities—something I wanted to discuss with Mary Shelley, whose passion for remnants equalled mine. Yet the complex figure that I cut would be different, *was,* without this bit of flesh my heart had only an hour before been nourishing in good faith. Could this tag have been grown on another, in another armpit? Only with a sufficient charge of electricity, I thought, more than any Ramsden generator could provide. Might the vital principle be in blood, then, available by boiling it up until only a red sediment remained?

I told Brema some of this, in between times correcting his English while he commented on my Italian translation of *Count Orlando.* Each night we met at his box in the theatre of La Scala, and I soon became, as it were, his son, reading (and weeping at) his tragedies, *Ina* most of all, and at last being able to talk to someone about Eliza Arrow, Gaby Saxonnex, and Claire, all of which revela-

tion he took in good, mellow part, reassuring me that a man had not
lived until he had venerated some young maiden, then a whore,
followed by a woman of the world. It was a familiar pattern, he
said; Crystal, Dung, and Cheese, he called these phases or intervals.
But then I told him something of the Lord Byron episode, and he
said he was going to give a dinner for Lord B. and he would make a
point, during it, of showing in what high regard he held me, not to
make milord jealous but to manifest the truth and to show what a
decent young man I must be (even if I told indecent jokes about
curates). He too, once, had idolized a young woman, who was so
deep in his affections that, when she died, his mind burst asunder; she
was a young woman of enormous accomplishments and beauty, of
noble birth. "I have made a profession of weeping ever since," he
said, at which I broke down, confessing all, whereupon he hugged
me and, to distract me, told me about *Ida,* the novel he intended to
write about the Milan revolution. I offered to translate it for him,
wishing I could be as he, eating only once daily and studying hard
all day until the hour of the theatre, except for those whole days he
devoted to visitors, showing them with outright patience what he
himself had seen a thousand times. He especially fancied English-
women, their rosy cheeks and delicate skin, admitting that he relished most of all their smell—lavender, he said, or lilac. Each time I
left him, only for a day, I felt the tears forming in my eyes; he was
the only person to have taken me as I was, without blame.

And what a lovely dinner he gave for Lord B., a dinner bubbling and joyous, with everyone on his best behaviour, and the table
full of my friends—Monti, Finch, two Bremas, Borsieri, Guasco
(the translator of Sophocles), Negri (author of *Francesca da Rimini),*
Hobhouse, and of course Lord B., at my side, taciturn at first but,
once drawn out, slyly saying to me, "That letter of yours, Polly.
Why, I am not old enough to read such filth. I never knew you had
it in you. Methinks our Polly has gone up in the world, from man's
gutter to God's. Be a little less obliging, my dear, and offer a little

less *cunnus,* if you do not mind. One endears oneself to men by
being allusive to what they think they have in common, not by
brandishing nails and clacks, puddles and sluices. Were I in need—
no, I am not, but I would, were I. Oh, yes. I would be Lear and you
would be my pranking fool. There is, however, one small favour I
beg to ask of you—later."

He addressed them loudly, and they all held their peace.

"Why, our Polly here," he purred, "talked ballocks *in Latin*
with an old curate high up in the Alps. I think we should swear him
to silence this night. To Coventry goes Polly." They then talked of
literature, Castlereagh, Burghersh, and such things, enlisting me in
their wildest laughter as if I *had* said something. After dinner, coffee
right away and then the theatre, all toffed up: lords and commoners.
He wanted me for something at last, but what?

Brema's box was our cockpit, where fat, greasy, and lascivious
Beyle held forth; where the short, tubby, quick-eyed Monti fired
himself up about politics, about which he knew little, just as, in
order to translate *The Iliad,* he got his friends to write the literal
translation word for word under the Greek, of which he knew not a
syllable; where, indeed, Lord Byron winked at me when one of the
Italians became carried away, then halted short, muttering something
about his pension.

"These fellows," Byron whispered to me, "live in terror of
being cut off. They are always plucking up the courage to publish a
Life of Galileo. Now, Polly, what of Lady Westmorland?" He asked
because Lady Jersey, her daughter, had promised to enquire of her
mother if she would employ me as her physician; but she said, Lady
W., that my having been with Lord B. was a great impediment as
she did not approve of him, he having referred to her as a "madwoman." All the same, I managed to attend her once or twice,
counselling her in a general way, none of which I reported to Lord
B., on her instructions. She was arrogant and witty, brilliant but
dictatorial, and one had to be careful as to what one said.

Far better was my link with Locatelli, physician of the hospital,
a decent, unimposturing physician, with whom I saw one case of

hysteria and another, of pemphigus, which I myself called the Bra-zilian Disease—in this case, bullae not prominent, the whole resem-bling dermatitis with tiny vesicles on show, epidermis easily de-tached. All we could prescribe was generous talcum powder on skin and sheets, Locatelli trying silver nitrate, but I doubtful about it. Some had treated it with gold, I had heard, but we both felt helpless, babbling to each other of calomel and ice. On the other hand, he said, my armpit was doing well. What a clever one-armed surgeon I had become. "And blind too," I said. "And lucky too," he added. "Only when right-handed," I told him.

Subvented by a generous loan from Lloyd, who gave me half of the sum his bankers were holding for him, I soon built up a regular day: rising, going to the hospital, breakfasting, coming home, tidying, dining, and then at seven the theatre, to which I had become, like all Milanese, addicted. One other spectacle, to which Lord B. conducted me, was the chapel of Saint Borromeo, lavishly jewelled. The corpse was dry and grimy, the skull black. They also had a nail of the cross of Christ. I saw the Brera library and the Ambrosian, which had the Virgil with Petrarch's marginal notes, some pieces of Plautus and Terence. But would Lord B. accompany me to my rooms? Never. "I have almost three hundred books now," I told him, having squandered my all on the printed sheet. "I will be happy to lend them out." No, he wanted to tell me about Swarrow when the Emperor had gone to the theatre. Some poor fool had kept his hat on, daring or oblivious, down there in the pit. In went Swarrow, with all his orders dangling and jangling, and slapped the fellow's cheeks. Big hubbub followed. "When he removed his hat," Byron said, "it was as if he had been beheaded." Such excitement apart, I had witnessed, among other stuff, *Coriolanus,* such an abomi-nable opiate that I fell asleep in spite of my pinching myself; *The Grief of Mausolea; The Death of Socrates; Montezuma;* and countless hisses and boos. I went to watch the crowd. I watched Sgricci, a protégé of Monti, doing his tragic *improvisati* in yellow boots, blue coat, and a Flemish collar. I slept through many performances.

One night, the worst, I went to Brema's box with Byron and

Hobhouse and left to stand in the pit. An officer in a great-coat came
and positioned himself right in front of me with his grenadier's hat
in place. *"Guarda a colui colla sua berretta in testa,"* I said to my
friends, saying, Look at that man, with his cap on his head. Loudly I
said it, and then I waited. He made no move, so I followed with,
"Would you do me the favour of taking off your hat, so that I may
see?", after first touching him. The touch did it. When he turned to
face me, he said, "Would you wish me to?" with an insulting smile.
"Lo vorreste?" he said, instead of the more polite *"Lo vorrebbe ella?"*
He was not being polite at all, or even civil. The civil thing to do
would have been to take the damned thing off without a fuss. *"Sì, lo
voglio,"* I told him. "I will it." I had virtually told him to do what I
wanted. He then asked me if I would care to go outside with him,
and I, thinking he meant for a duel, said "Yes, with pleasure," part of
my mind supplying the line that this was when Byron would have
stepped in for Shelley, who did not fight duels. I asked Hobhouse to
go with me, and he did. As we passed the guard-house, this freshly
minted Austrian cur said, "Go in, go in there," which I refused to
do, adding that it was not in there that I was going to go with him.
At this he cursed in German and drew his sabre with a lurid glare.
Hobhouse, however, detained his hand and kept it where it belonged, so the officer stood still, fuming and breathing hard. Then
the police came and I was delivered into their custody, put into the
guard-house, and made to hear a long recital of my offence: I had
insulted a high-ranking officer. "I am *your* equal," I told him, "and
being in the theatre I was the equal of any person present."

"Equal to me?" he retorted. "You are not equal to the last of
the Austrian soldiers in the house." Then he began to revile me in
what I assumed was Billingsgate German, in which he had clearly
been trained by his scum-spawned parents. Now the word spread
throughout the theatre that there was an affray, or trouble; Brema
and Byron came running and tried to get me out of there, but the
police were adamant, and the officer was still ranting, his face red,
his sweat copious. Brema heard the secretary of the police say to the
officer, "Don't you meddle with this. Leave it to me." Brema said he

would go and get an order for my dismission immediately, at which the officer took Lord B.'s card as bail that I would appear on the morrow to answer for my conduct. Then they let me go. All the trouble had to do with hats.

"Austrian *canaille*," said Lord B. "See how they behave in Italy. God help us if they ever get as far as Piccadilly. We were in the middle of a philosophical argument about *utility*—"

"And the poet Silvio Pellico came running to you," I said, "with the news. I can hardly believe it."

"Some twenty of us came," he said. "We all spoke at once. Your face was burning red. You were beside yourself with rage, Polly."

"And you were pale as ashes, milord."

"I was not being taken seriously. They knew who I was. All those damned women had been parading in front of us, waiting for me to pounce, or at least to ask for an introduction. I very often do the opposite of what people expect, women especially. I have my pride, my reserved side."

"Yes, my lord," I said, "and what of tomorrow?"

"You will be released. You have done nothing. Did I miss something? Did you kill somebody too? I rather wish you had, and then there would be something to get our teeth into. Yes, Polly, I wish you had. I wish somebody had. I wish *I* had. I am just the man." Then I saw: I had figured in an event of his; he had not figured in an event of mine, and he never would. Yet he still had something to beg of me; I had almost forgotten.

It was noteworthy that, as soon as Lord B. and the other *titolati* produced their credentials, which is to say wrote down their names and ranks, the officer at once forgot the insult I had offered to his fur cap and the addled pate within. A show of names and ranks (Polidori, Dr. J. W.) by ordinary mortals would have had no effect at all. The next morning I received an order to attend. Brema took me to the gate of the guard-house.

"Where do you wish your passport visaed for?" It was a change of tone, of tack, but not promising.

"Passport?" I said. "I have no intentions of going anywhere."

"You must be off in twenty-four hours for Florence," they said, laying down the law Austrian fashion.

"I cannot just *go* like that."

"You must, or something disagreeable will happen to you."

"This is disagreeable," I said. "You have no right."

Brema went off to see Bubna at once, and I to Lord B., who dispatched Hobhouse in the company of Colonel McSomething to Swarrow, to ask him to intercede. Swarrow, they told me, received them with pen in hand; he knew all about it, they said. A bagatelle. A nothing. I was still expected to go, though. Hobhouse tried to say something, but Swarrow urged him to the door: "Give my compliments to Lord Byron; I am sorry I was not at home when he called." If he had been, I surmised, all would have gone well. It was important that *i titolati* know one another socially, so that they could run the world with friendly understanding.

"But if this is all such a mere trifle," Hobhouse told them, "why take it any further?"

Swarrow: "I hope Lord Byron is well," advancing another foot towards the door so that Hobhouse and the colonel found themselves on the threshold, with nowhere to go but out, as intended; he had courtesied them off, so they left. Nothing was going to change. Brema had already been to Bubna, who received him politely, of course, and said he had already seen Colonel M. (who, whatever others did, moved about Milan at speed), who had explained the whole silly business. "All is well," he said. "The officer is not compromised. It is sufficient that Doctor Polidori should have been arrested for speaking to an officer thus."

"What do you mean?" Brema was beside himself. "I am glad that my friend will not have to leave the city."

Bubna, Brema said, just stared at him. "I will have to speak to Swarrow this evening about it."

"Doctor Polidori thought he had been *challenged*."

"Then that should teach the officer a lesson. He should make his intentions clear and use the language more. Perhaps now he and

his fellow officers will have one prejudice less. After all, I am the
military governor. Politics are not my affair." Bubna's own son, I
had heard, had himself been challenged to a duel for insulting a lady
at a public ball; after accepting the challenge, he announced that he
needed to put his affairs in order, just in case, and had not been seen
since. He had left Milan the previous Saturday. A young Italian had
had some kind of row with a Hussar officer and had challenged him
too, for which he was dragged before the police and reprimanded.
Several days later they ran into each other again at the door to a
coffee-room, and the officer said, "Do you still wish to settle this
affair?" Yes, came the answer, and in they went, whereupon the
officer and his friends struck the young Italian repeatedly, then
shoved him out to fend for himself. There was nothing he could do
except, again, challenge; challenge them all, for which, etc.

Lord B. was rather stern about the whole thing. "Polly, it
seems this officer was on guard and therefore duty-bound to keep his
hat on. To say to him *lo voglio,* as a civilian giving an order to an
officer, was an affront. He was in the right about that."

"Why," I asked him, without being in the least plaintive, "do I
always seem to be in the wrong?"

"Because, dear Polly, you have a talent for getting into scrapes.
You are a squabbler, one of the best we have. Young men of your
age often are. I do not know about doctors, but young men I know
something about. You have been here for some weeks. You have
been moving in very good society and prospering. But this was a
gaffe, unworthy of your social standing here. A more elaborate form
of address to the officer might have worked wonders, without all
this commotion. You might have said, Sir, I wonder if you would be
so kind as to consider removing your hat, provided you are permitted to do so."

"Oh," I blurted, "I could just as well have said, Sir, if I may be
permitted to address you in so crude a fashion, may I continue by
asking if I may begin to continue to ask you if you would be so
kind, if you do not mind, to consider another humble petition from
a mere civilian—"

" 'Mere civilian,' " Byron said without humour, "would have sounded provocative."

Behind all this there festered something else: Lord B.'s patrician blood had boiled when they did not know him, and then when they set his person and rank at naught. The officer had called his men, who had seized their arms forthwith as if an invasion had been announced. Then Monti had saved the day, saying, "Let us all go outside—only the titled men to remain." This left only Brema, the Marquis di Sartirana, Count Confalonieri, and Lord B. Among themselves they should have been able to sort things out, but they did not, and Lord B. smouldered.

Before I left, I had exploded ("foamed with rage," said some), declaring that one day I would return to Milan and smack the lymph out of the governor who had treated me with such scant respect. For *that,* presumably, I could reasonably have been given twenty-four hours to quit the city; but that came *after* and did not count. An additional irony was that my passport, granted by the Conte Ambrogio Cesare San Martino d'Aglia, Minister of the King of Sardinia in London, authorized me to travel in Italy, where my movements were now being dictated. It did not, however, say anything about Switzerland, where I had prospered for so long. So, one had to go yet again. I had forgotten to ask Lord B. what was the favour he was going to beg, and clearly he had forgotten too, in all the turmoil. Having lost Geneva, I now lost Milan, and would no doubt lose the next haven too, thanks to the mutual meddling of the military and the *titolati,* whom I loved but would just as soon behead once they became too self-intoxicated to be endured. I did not fancy being among the done-to in life, on the receiving end.

Somehow I managed to pack my things, sensing that I was now in disgrace; there had been a while when I was the injured party, but things had now altered radically, and *I* was to blame. They had closed ranks again. Three hundred books was too much of a load, so I would give them to Brema to save. I found a coach going to Lodi and, for the morrow, a *vetturino,* who was going to Florence, to take me up in Lodi. For a last time I went to see Brema, who had tried with Bubna again, or had meant to, catching up with him only at a meeting of the war council (how Austrian) from which no one might disturb him. The matter was closed. Once again I wept in his arms, becoming something of a Polidori cry-baby. Then I took my leave of Guasco, Hobhouse, and Lord B., far from weeping in *his* arms, but remembering to ask him about the favour. "Oh, that," he said. "It will have to be later, Polly. I am not ready. I will be in touch with you: Poste Restante, Florence? If there is anything I can do, please let me know." His guilt had begun to show. Once again his Polly was on the road to nowhere in particular; I had been so ready to defend his honour, stand his ground for him. Why, even minor matters of etiquette had become heroic, which was the Austrian influence, I supposed. It was Guasco, however, who removed the sting from that enforced departure, instructing me to call on him if I ever needed help. "The oftener I am applied to, the greater favour I deem it," he said gallantly, whereas Lord B.'s offers of help—nay, his protestations of constant fidelity— were like old gloves, gone in the fingers. Byron, I knew, liked people to like him. So he said things that would make them do it. Later they discovered he had done just that, and no more.

After too many embraces, some of them vacant and heraldic, I took my leave, eyes smarting from tears withheld. When I got into the coach, I had only five louis to my name and a heavy burden of anger and remorse, rage and grief. I was nothing if not emotion. I was like a boy expelled from school, *rusticated,* denied his friends and his social ambit for—*tout court*—sticking up for himself when the bullies arrived, as they always did. Tears spurted from my eyes like blood from a released tourniquet. The whole of my life was going to be like this, shunted from pillar to post with five louis in my pocket, whether I was in the beloved land of my father or not. Some curse had fallen on my name, my life, guaranteeing that I would never prevail beyond a certain point of refined entry, wholesome ovation, glad conviviality. I could taste the arrival of the moment

when all went sour, and Polidori the Wandering Jew was sent packing again, leaving more and more of his worldly goods behind him,
en route to another bout of sterile sightseeing, meals with strangers,
grease-thick floors, the barnyard smell of public *gabinetti,* and of
course more and more lords, people with titles, soldiers with ranks,
high-ups with palaces and a dreadful way of being calm and collected about what concerned you most. Young as I was, I felt I was
aging fast; Ambulance too, whom no one wished to tend while I
went about.

One of these days, I vowed, in my most Malvolio-like mood, I
would return to Milan at the head of an uprising and station Swarrow and the officer against a wall, there to be slapped and shot
bareheaded. I arrived at Lodi, knowing there would never be such a
rising, and wept myself to sleep, exhausted and genuinely defeated. I
would have to write to Lloyd again, asking for money; I dared not
approach my father, whose pittance as a translator was a matter of
almost holy taboo. We mentioned it once, at Christmas, in order to
show gratitude for plenty out of penury, but never again that year.

So. On. With a Prussian student, banished for slapping a Russian in the face. It seemed the whole world was standing on its
dignity and being slapped, snubbed, or exiled. Clearly the class in
power wanted to keep the dregs on the move. That night he and I
shared the same room. Such was poverty, with worse to come, unless
Lloyd sent money. Poor as I was, I went the next day to search for
books, which I had to have; one day, I promised myself, I would
build a house all of books, books I had read, and in it read all the
books I had never read. I wanted, and found, Boccaccio's *Fiammetta,*
convinced that the great minds of the past would see me through.
Towers, churches, palaces, and porticoes, all in place, perhaps for a
brief ever. My few books attracted much attention, until I told them
I was a physician and needed to refer to them all the time. I formed
the new habit, when not with the Prussian, of sitting in the dark of
churches for an hour or two, not praying but wishing devoutly for
things to improve. Came the *vetturino* with his bill, to whom I
handed a promissory note saying I would pay if the Prussian did not.

In one church I saw a coffin, brought in after dark with torches. The poor, I saw, had only turf over them while the rich groaned inaudibly under marble. I saw a cardinal's hat covering a death's head, as superfluous a piece of religiose tact as I had seen.

And so to Bologna, as one wounded, weeping at every turn of the day, whether in a theatre or not, and utterly unable to change my habits. Off across the Apennines, on the way to Florence, with the Prussian and an Italian officer. Oxen. Mist. Some passenger talking his head off about thieves, dogs, and boars. I developed a new habit, of putting my thumb over the piece of my passport that said "24 hours," out of anger and shame. I smelled, not having changed my linen since Milan. Nothing awaited me at the Poste Restante. Down to four *scudi*. Even the mental record of my days became blurred, they being more alike than not. I smoked my pipe, wrote letters (begging), knocked on doors that no one ever opened. At last I found Pontelli, old friend of Father, who fed me sausages and caviare. Going to stay with Pontelli, I gave the Prussian a missal and my desk. With a full stomach, mainly from having gone to live with Pontelli, I saw more tombs and churches, got on good terms with the Inspector of Police. Pontelli had a young housekeeper, whom he did not like me to watch; when he wished to be alone with her, he needled me into going out for a walk. Tired of him, on November 13 I set off with Ambulance and a shirt in my pocket: to Arezzo, through rain, lightning, thunder, numbing me quite, felling my dog, whom I failed to see going down. I did 45 miles in half a day, with one halt. I found my uncle's house, found them on the second storey, put on some clothes of his, ate, and slept, vaguely dreaming how Uncle Luigi had always been able to cure typhoid fever—another doctor in the family. He treated my foot, which I had cut, when I woke, brought in my cousins, Pippo and Teresa. Soon made up a daily routine of study, cards at Gori's, trying to get into the always-shut library. I got my dog back, with whom I returned to Florence, refusing Uncle Luigi's money, not having told him how things stood, with frost on the ground, foot hurt again, dog lost again, at Montesarchi. Took a carriage, unable to march, and Pontelli paid the doctor a scudo to treat my foot. Now, when he and the housekeeper wanted to be private, I went to bed, very much what up in Yorkshire they had called a "gooseberry"—an unwanted person.

Newly weary of Pontelli, I went out to sell my watch-chain, but looked in at the post office on the way and found there two letters from Lloyd, who had set off from Venice to see me but en route had lost his purse with 36 louis. He had only 20 *scudi* for me, but bushels of kindness and goodness. "While I have means," he said, "you shall never want, dear friend." I knew that such sentiments usually came from the poor. He gave me some practical advice too: "Go and cultivate the English here. Be their physician." I wanted to see Vaccà first, however, with whom my father had been lodged before leaving Italy; he had a European reputation in surgery and would surely have an idea for me. Off to Pisa I went, copying my grandfather's *Osteologia* (octave stanzas) on the way to keep myself from fretting: yet another doctor in the family, this one descended from an English mother whose maiden name, Folks, she changed to Folchi. There he was, still at the hospital, at nine; I heard an Austrian officer refer to him as the god of medicine; he was certainly the god of goodwill and hospitality, telling me to call his house my own, to come and eat there often. His friend Corsi told me I ought to be a lawyer instead, like him; and Pachiana, the wit, told me how he had once dealt with the night patrol in the streets of Pisa by answering as follows: "I am a public man, in a public street, with a public woman." He often was, a man of vast memory, also a *mezzano, cicerone, conoscitore,* dilettante, and *ruffiano*—pimp or go-between. Quite a handful of fun he was.

On December 21 I went to the Countess Mastrani's, where I had ices and heard prepared poetry and music. The people were iced too. Then to the theatre, as several times already, to watch Goldoni's *Bugiardo*. It could not be said that, confronted with the opportunity, I let the social life pass me by. On December 22, 23, and 24 I did the same. Christmas Day I walked along the Arno and on the next day, with Vaccà, went off to Leghorn, my first quest there being the sea; I

stood gazing at the waves, trying to read my future in them. I had a
lovely evening with Vaccà at the theatre, where I met Signora Bet-
tina Franciuoli—at her box the next evening too. I soon formed a
habit of going to the Casa Mastrani, gaming there with Sofia,
Biribro, Dionigi, but my mind was more on the patients I had
acquired, only to see them die, all three. They only gave me the
hopeless cases: a carcinoma, a heart attack, and a child born looking
like an old dwarf, who got older-looking the longer he lived, until
twelve or so. I was in despair, able to do nothing save console; it was
as if I had been told to mend God's evil ways with a hammer and
chisel. Not Vaccà's fault; he was doing his best to launch me, and in a
way I was being tested for fortitude (who at twenty-one has much
of that?), not ingenuity. If only, I thought, the aged boy had had the
cancer and the heart attack too; then two might have lived, and I
would have been the talk of Pisa. As it was, there were murmurs,
even at the Casa Mastrani, my watering-place, that I was in league
with body-snatchers and anatomists and would soon have to leave
for Brazil, where I intended to set up a vivisection clinic in the
jungle, doing experiments on humans and freshwater dolphins. I had
been told that, in some of the coastal towns, special shops hung up
the sexual organs of these dolphins to dry out—of enormous pro-
portions, I gathered—and I thought the story must have rebounded
upon itself; someone had envisioned me with some kind of butcher's
shop, selling parts. Yet my vision of Brazil was truly one of South
America as a whole; all the countries flowed together. Slapping at
gnats and mosquitoes, I took notes on the manatee, "the fat fish with
hands," as the river-folk called it, the power of the electric eel (how
harness *that?*), and the yellow juice they poured into twists of banana
leaf: curare, the gunpowder of the jungle. One of the child-gods
there had made love to the daughter of Curare, who had snakes,
spiders, and scorpions cached between her legs; each time he entered
her, he died, but he always revived. When she took him to her
father, he became a flea, entered the old man's mouth, and, when he
was ready to escape, tickled him and jumped clear during the sneeze.
He flew home with curare in his beak. What an exciting place for a

country doctor to go to; even a doctor from London and Edinburgh!

Yet Napoleon had landed in 1802, somewhere down there,
almost down there, and had reimposed slavery. A head was worth 44
francs. Three whites who had protested were put to death, one in an
iron cage sitting on a barbed leaf. The following year, Bonpland
caught a butterfly at seventeen thousand feet. Every one who could
afford it had a coat of arms painted on his carriage. Swathed in
ermine and purple, Napoleon would not go away; he loomed in his
crown, thinking of the enormous contractile power of Josephine's
vallis lucis. The English seized the port of Buenos Aires, but they
would suffer a tremendous defeat at the River Plate. The burning of
Judases during Holy Week ended—those Guy Fawkeses made of
rags. One miner survived by lifting a huge flat rock onto his back,
off which the bullets bounced. There, among the tooth-pullers and
witch-doctors, among the earthquakes and the colonial armies, I
wanted to go, *almost.* A certain Julien Mellet lectured on his own
travels there, last year in Paris. Why, a certain Manuel de Sarratea
had even journeyed to London, again only last year, looking for an
Englishman to take back with him to crown in Buenos Aires—not
Brazil, no, but close enough. Polidori would have gone, had he been
asked: king or doctor, it mattered not; wonderfully, perhaps both.
No, they would have preferred Lord Byron had Lord Byron
known, to be King of the River Plate. And that brought me back to
where I had been: selling parts of humans in Brazil. Ridiculous? No,
not *there,* but here. Polidori was not going to butcher anyone. It was
quite ridiculous, but those frightened of surgeons (and who was
not?) let their imaginations run riot. One would have been obliged
to save eleven hundred out of each thousand in order to keep a clean
name. I wrote to Lord B. to advise him that I had resumed practice,
assuring him of my most cordial services:

> *Milord, I hope the piles and the pox have gone. I work here with the
> illustrious Vaccà, who has been kind enough to assign me to the most intracta-
> ble cases known to him, thus freeing himself for work of greater public suasion.*

Alas, my latest three have all perished: Francis Horner; a child of Thomas Hope; and Francis North, Lord Guilford. There is little to do with cancer, heart attack, and the pathetic disease that ages children at wicked speed. Lord, here I am at the end of all my thoughts, weary from the hospital.

Here I am on prose stilts, my own, cut short from poetic ones. Life is so full here, what with the soirées of Countess Mastrani, a certain Sofia and other friends, and gaming. The English entreat me to treat them, preferring a physician to whom they can speak their own language. Please state in full any commissions you may wish executed here, and the nature of your leanings. Every dream must have a ceiling, I suppose, but Pisa caps mine quite. It is a town that misses you.

It occurred to me the other day that I had a story of Miss Clairmont, your possible intended, to relay to you. When she was a little girl, she told me, she was sometimes allowed to sit up at night; but not always. One night, Mr. S. T. Coleridge came to read from his poem the Ancient Mariner, The Rime of, *and Claire had snuggled down behind the sofa to hear. He was a short man with a bulging forehead and big eyes, and he made their hair stand on end, she said, and sent chills up and down their spines. He took them on his knee and petted them—Mary, Fanny, and Jane, as she then was—talking all the time. They did not wish him to go. All they ever wished to do in life was listen to him, but he was never invited back. A Mr. Lamb came instead and was nowhere nearly as good. I thought how like that evening was to the one in the Villa Diodati when you read the same poet's* Christabel *and I had to treat Mr. Shelley with ether and water for having seen eyes in Mary's n-----s. Such were our lives then.*

I fear I have tried your eyes with my bad writing—my pen's accursed scratches. I must end. I am being called for. I keep a little book to keep my public life straight. Otherwise. . . . No more hats. I avoid Austrians. Did you not promise me once a canto of Childe Harold, *sire? "Darkness," I must confess, would do just as well—a poem to whose completion I look forward with abandon and sympathy. Fortunate the firmament you grace, milord.*

Your affect. Pisan,
J. Polidori.

On December 31 I decided to keep my journal no more, making a New Year's resolution to that effect for 1817. It was as if a grand scheme had gone awry, with me more in the position of the beggar and the gipsy than that of the acknowledged physician and the doughty Boswell. Some strain had gone from my daily life, but also some of that wonderful sense—not ecstasy but election; I was no longer one of the elect, as I had thought myself to be in April of the year past, newly appointed to Lord B.'s entourage, with a glorious future cresting for me among golden clouds. I was a good enough doctor, whose patients happened to die in threes, but there was nothing I could do about that. I was a poor master to my dog, but Ambulance was such a dog as needed little attention; he mostly slept and, of course, walked, behind me always, which is why he got lost so often. My legs were too long for him. I had hoped to be of more use to the world. Son of a literary and medical family, I had the makings; indeed, I had been made, and the writing was becoming an adequate accompaniment to the medical flair. I had had a vision of the aristocracy, and it had undone me quite, making me wish for undoctorly things, or so I presumed. I had heard of doctors, in Edinburgh and London, who made fortunes, but my own view of our profession was that of the doctor as total altruist, Hippocratic pauper, sacrificing himself for others until someone else just like him sacrificed *him*self in the same way.

The only way, now, of walking in illustrious company would be through stories, a new one of which had insisted on coming to me in the strangest places—while being rained on in the Alps, while being arrested and marched through the immense lobby of the Milan opera, and upon regarding the dead face of the aged boy in Pisa hospital. Perhaps it came from my other story, *The Vampyre,* an echo of a sibling, with some of the same qualities and plot, but altogether more, shall I say, sharp and ingenious? At the theatre, one night, a slimy rogue of some notoriety accosts a visiting romantic poet, Lord Ruthven (or someone else, some other name), saying to him in tones befitting one of the witches in *Macbeth,* "Realize, sire, four or five hundred thousand francs; then a few friends will circulate the rumour of your death, and bestow on a log of wood the honours of a Christian burial in some snug remote spot—the island of Elba, say, or Sardinia. An authentic account of your decease goes off to England, where your ancestral estates are. Meanwhile, under the prosaic name of Smith or Wood or Ford, you may live comfortably and quietly in some such place as Lima, or Bahia. When, in the fulness of time, Mr. Smith or Mr. Wood or Mr. Ford becomes a venerable white-haired old gentleman, he may even return to Europe and purchase from some Roman or Parisian bookseller a set of *Childe Ruthven,* thirtieth edition, say, with notes and annotations. Moreover, when Mr. Smith or Mr. Wood or Mr. Ford is just about to make his exit from life, he may, if he pleases, relish one last crystalline moment, saying, 'Lord Ruthven, who for thirty years, nay more, has been numbered among the dead, even now lingers on this side of eternity—*I* am the man: my fellow-men, my countrymen, seemed to me so disgusting that I quit them in loathing.' " Lord Ruthven is so taken by the idea that he does it, infatuated by a tale. When he returns, the real Lord Ruthven, there is this evil man called M. Baal to greet him and ridicule him for having been taken in by a mere story and having wasted his life in its shadow.

It would work, I thought. I loved the idea of doubles: Lord B. signed himself like Napoleon: "N.B.," his standing for Noel Byron. Had it been 1815 and Waterloo only a year or two ago, when the whole of Spain and much of Europe was laid waste and soaked with blood? As we had found on our travels. We had been reconnoitering not Europe but the human race, and I would never recover from what I had seen, mixed in with the lethal foibles of the aristocracy up close, the sheer barbarism of the common man caught up in affairs of politics. I had seen the Austrians, and that was enough to put me off the military for ever, driving me into poetry, landscape, the company of lepers, the house of books I had envisaged, the bosom of my family. Young men making the tour were supposed to come back matured and tested, full of verve and pluck. I, if I ever went, dragging my heels home on the boat from Leghorn to London, would go home like one broken on the wheel.

Never was I happier than in the little, disused storeroom of the
Pisa hospital: mainly shelves on which to set the big jars in which sat
the various organs I culled from my own or others' former patients.
On a sunny day the light would trickle through them like so many
goldfish bowls, glinting on the viscera or extremities, so that they
spoke to me, as it were, in visible baritones and tenors. It would be
an exaggeration to think that, even as I treated the living, I hungered
for their remains to plunder, but it would be just as exaggerated to
say that I did not, with strict propriety, look forward to the one
useful contribution a doomed patient might make. There was no
distress to relatives, of course, as they never viewed the remains after
the first time, although, had they known what in-extremis strata-
gems I had attempted with my patients (using whatever drugs I had
in my possession), they might have jibbed. Many were the times a
physician with a few grains of opium in his system had dealt with a
patient similarly served—mainly to the good, since the effect was
soothing—and then it was possible, I felt, to pursue the poor
doomed person all the way into the death-throes in a feat of heroic
empathy. I had several times almost levelled myself with charcoal
and mercury, all in the interests of knowledge.

Had Mary been present, we might seriously have tried to combine the parts collected, but a designer was needed, one with a keen
aesthetic sense for the creation of a re-created creature. Nor did I
have the privacy. Jars on shelves was one thing, but an assemblage of
meat on an operating table was quite another, and Vaccà would not
have stood for it, enthusiastic as he was about any unorthodox quest
for surgical knowledge. So I communed with my specimens, from
an enormous pancreas, like one of those dolphin vulvas on sale in
Bahia, to an actual heart, stripped of its pericardium and lolling like
a puffer-fish in the liquid (the pericardium I had wrapped about a
liver for effect). After so many years of looking at exteriors I had
decided to plunge in and look at the inmost world of all of us. I
could see tubes connecting one organ to another, but nothing would
have come of it, and I had, as a student, already performed the usual
experiments with muscles and Ramsden generators; we needed a

fiercer source of power than that. I liked the Ramsden, though, with its gleaming brass, like a bedstead for a midget, and the mahogany table beneath. A Ramsden frightened no one, as those for whom it was used were usually in too much of a commotion to notice. There was one head, flayed to the muscles, in the biggest jar of all, imbuing the little room with what I had always thought *the* expression or demeanor of the already explored head: openness of rather cheerful sort, with the eyes and mouth wide to receive, especially with one or both eyes removed, and the mouth a truly inviting gulf. This was my paradise, my Alps, for which I needed neither companion nor faith. Truth told, we were a maroon fascia underneath, and I always contrived to see that hue beneath the powders and unguents of the ladies, and the flaws in the uneven bone that gave the edifice its shape. One might suffocate this creature quite easily, with charcoal dust or a puff of air or one of several acids, and I had been wondering, if one had time, which compound would take the human being off fastest of all, other chemicals just as lethal backing up the one most favoured. All the best mixtures, I thought, would end up brown, as does the mess on a painter's palette; but would they be compounds or mixtures, chemically fused or briefly juxtaposed to end a life? I had told Lord B. some of this, and he had always shown extraordinary interest, stopping short, though, of the kinds of experiments Polly did on himself, saying this was the only kind of stuff he could bear to see a woman eat. "We would soon have upon us a terrible shortage of the sex," I said, and he averred as how that might not be too bad a thing to happen, twice a week, say, when a man was trying to get on with some poems.

My trouble was that, work as I did in the hospital, I never got enough to do, and therefore depended too much on Vaccà for meals and lodging and on my father for bills drawn on Pisa. Faro (the game in which a pharaoh ruled), Quinze, or Hazard only made matters worse; I had no flair for gaming, although I had quite a gift for appreciating the excitement it created. This was merely to admit that I responded well when my blood's pressure went high, which was not a currency I could use for clothing and the theatre. Quite

often, with bloodstained hands, I got into the theatre at someone
else's expense: that new modern type, the begging pathologist. I had,
alas, already begun crating up my jars, sorting through my papers,
and treating my patients as if they were a month or two worse than
they actually were. Lord Guilford, for example, had been a real trial,
suffering from acute inflammation of the bowels, which, far advanced into degeneration, had at last taken him off. His mother had
insisted that his bowels be removed from the body and sent home to
England for his own physician to inspect. She little knew that I
already had made plans to remove my samples with me, and that his
bowels, properly enclosed, would be just one more burden for the
voyage. I no longer set flowers in the cavities I made, but before
leaving I addressed each organ in a way I deemed special, as if it
could hear. I told the heart it would one day beat again, iambic; the
bladder that it would soon be full again, a torment (but what an
ultimate blessing) to its owner; the liver that it would soon be
filtering again, saving sugars and distributing iron. What a lovely
although incomplete construction set it was to be taking towards
Dover, where the customs officers were sure to pass it by with a nod
of unschooled aversion. Doctors were a law unto themselves; I had
always believed it, and now I was practising it. Perhaps I had become dangerous, but only to myself and a few of the doomed.

The new Lord Guilford arrived to escort his predecessor, the
mother, and the widow and then insisted that I embalm the bowels,
which he wanted sent off *straight away* to England. Little did he
know he was breaking up my collection. He would pay, and that
was that. Off we went to Venice, where I had promised to see Lord
B. for the long-deferred favour he wished to beg.

"Polly, how haggard you look," he exclaimed. "Have those
leaning-tower wenches sapped your blood?" No, I had been indoors
a lot, I told him. "Ay, but beneath whom?" He handed to me with
almost superstitious reverence, as a Muslim would (if a Muslim
would have handled them at all), two miniatures of himself painted
in Venice. These would go to Murray for delivery to Mrs. Leigh, his
half-sister, a mask of whose features had been a familiar property at

the Villa Diodati. Lord B. wanted Murray to have Mr. Love the jeweller "set them in plain gold, with my arms complete, and *Painted by Prepiani—Venice, 1817,* on the back." He also asked that the English painter Holmes be asked to make a copy of each, and these were to remain with Murray until his return to England—if ever. The important thing was not to get the two pairs mixed up, and that would be Murray's responsibility. At the same time, I presumed, I was to give to Murray the diary I had begun, after heading it *Journal of a Journey through Flanders etc., from April 24, 1816, to* ———. I had now filled in the second date, *December 28, 1816,* even though it was wrong, having added two more entries, for the twenty-ninth and the thirtieth, out of well-fed exuberance. I could hardly think he was going to pay me for it, or even accept it as a gift. I asked Lord B., who said he could hardly speak for Murray, but he would put a damned good word in for me if need there were. He was much more interested in my travelling sarcophagus (I told him I had been looking for green stone), and the tale of Lord Guilford's bowels made him roar. "By the devil, Polly, you have come a long way. Here you are, with remains in jars, all neatly parcelled up, and you have just lost three patients. To lose one is misadventure. Two is carelessness. Three indicates a sublime sense of calling. So they took them out."

"I took them out, milord."

"*You* took them out," he said with operatic emphasis, "and then, on account of their discrepancies, they were sent off to England, separately from the carcass, which you have *with you.* Imagine, sir, a man going one way, his innards another, and his immortal soul a third. Was there ever such a distribution as that? One certainly has a soul, Polly; but how it came to allow itself to be enclosed in a body is more than I can imagine." I could see his incommoded leg going the same way in the long run, and so could he. "Polly," he said, "were this to have happened to me, you would surely have promised, given your oath, like the young man in your story, not to send part of me to Claire—we know which part *she* would want—and another to Lady Byron—we know which part of me she would *not* want—or indeed any part of me to Mrs. Leigh. I am tactful, I hope, in what I send to Mrs. Leigh, for she and I have suffered."

I offered to see either his wife or his half-sister, but he demurred. "Polly, I must leave you. Let us view the Manfrini Palace tomorrow. I am supposed to have seen it. I have been here all these months and have not bothered. I am for Rome next Thursday. It is my indelible purpose to go, by Ferrara." I wondered how Claire's delivery had been, but I was not to learn of Allegra's birth until I reached England; Lord B. would know when he got to Rome.

I stood there holding the miniatures, half-wishing they were for me, and then I would have been like Prince Hamlet holding the image of his father, whom he revered. Prepiani had made him Pretty Boy, with trembling scarlet lips that curled this way and that (petals, I thought), a tender lambent glance that saw through everyone and reviled none, enclosing a thinned-out neck in an ample, floppy mauve collar, and he had brought the receding hairline forward, allowing a few peccant curls to stray forward of it. The whole thing was a royal pout, done of his better side, and only the slight fleshiness of his jaw resembled Lord B. as I had just seen him. This was a life mask.

"Do you like them, Polly?" He had been watching.

"You have twins," I called. "Why did the painter not vary his point of vantage?"

"Instructions, Polly," he called. *"Instructions."*

He was gone, urging me to be punctual on the morrow. By and large, he hated going anywhere to look at anything unless it was a ship in a dry-dock. So why this? Would Prepiani have gone ahead if, instead, we had confronted him with the hypertrophied bowels of the late Lord Guilford, asking him to follow *instructions*—"a purple open shirt, a more feminine look than hitherto"? He would have fainted from the stench; but, with a clip on one's nose, one might paint a cameo of Lord B. on the dried-out surface of any given bowel. "Rops" they called innards in Yorkshire, meaning ropes, no doubt to hang ourselves with, like Lord Guilford.

Grave as the Guilford business was, I could not help musing on the irony and unluckiness of it all. Here went the fourth earl's innards, in some undetermined sense the part-source of his awful play, *The Kentish Baron,* which had actually been put on at the Haymarket in 1790 or 1791. And the next earl, who had come to escort the remains, had once published a Pindaric ode in honour of the Empress Catherine. Somewhere in that family there had been a bride so fat she had needed to be kept in ice for three days before the wedding, but I never knew which of the many Norths she had married. I longed for that ice, however, to keep my own private collection of specimens cool as I journeyed away from the scene of yet another failure. Wherever one went, there were always a score of the English eager to retail the most recent tittle-tattle, about such people as the Norths, or even to recount vivid pieces of the family's history, but only in return for gossip about Byron. I marvelled that I had accumulated so much useless information, for I made it a habit never to chatter about Lord B., never mind what he had or had not done. Denied, these gossipmongers thrust their wares upon me willy-nilly, hoping for an eventual return, from which honour always kept me back. Milord's comment summed up the Norths better that any other's. "So much ice for a swollen bride," he said, "none for the fourth earl's tripes. Tell me, Polly, is that justice or excess of tact?"

At the Manfrini Palace, his thoughts were already on Rome, more on London and Norwich; it was an absentminded reunion and tour, although an attendant swatted an aggressive bee, a big one, and I noticed that from it fell tear-shaped black shiny pellets of something—presumably honey, or just its insides. Touching one with my foot, I found it sticky beyond belief, and indeed it never came off. Lord B. was spouting his usual line about knowing nothing of painting (he was right) and hating it unless it was, as yesterday, a reproduction of something he had seen, or thought it possible to see. "Of all the arts, Polly, it is the most unnatural and artificial, and that which has imposed itself most upon the tolerance of mankind. I never yet saw the picture that came within a league of my anticipations; but I have seen mountains, seas, rivers, and all kinds of *vedute artistiche,* and two or three women at the least, that went far beyond them, not counting some horses, oh, yes, and a lion—at Veli Pasha's —in the Morea, and even a tiger at supper in Exeter 'Change." I always had the sense that he was delivering, and therefore embellishing, a speech already made, or getting one ready; yet it was his quality of being uncontainable that made him such a fine talker. He said whatever came into his head at any moment; if you wanted something broadcast, you had only to tell Lord Byron, and he would do the rest.

Our good-bye was almost curt, not for any lack of civility but because we both seemed to have a strong head of feeling not to be vented on that occasion. I promised to show Murray my play *Ximenes* and he promised to apply to his piles the pomade I had given him. If only he had looked the lord of the two miniatures, but he did not; they had both miniaturized his defects, I thought. "Be bluff with Murray, my dear," he advised me. "Let him see how travel has broadened you, and do not let him talk you down. He is a clever rascal, one of the better Barabbases, I think. He will do nothing he does not wish to do, so you are on your own." We embraced once, twice, and I smelled the macassar oil in his hair, telling myself that all the fragrance of the wide world was going away from me now, all the *joie-de-vivre* and all the celebratedness; I was to pop back into the hole I had sprung from, but irremediably changed. Would I, at this watershed, this sheer drop, get the kiss he reserved for me alone? I did. I kissed him back, and we stayed there hugging in the recoil from the kiss, our cheeks in touch, our lips, our pairs of them, isolated in the spring air.

"Albé," I murmured, and "Albé, *yes,*" he murmured back, every inch the dapper Adonis of the miniatures. It was over. He went without a backward glance, whereas I stayed rooted to the spot, marvelling at his mind, the mill-race of it, especially how he would release one thing that set off three others, and each of those three released three more, until his entire range of allusion and implication was past measuring. At last I was among the Albé-sayers; I had been received into the circle, and I could not at that moment think of anything, among the sundry obsessions of my tender years, I wanted more. Had wanted. Pluperfect. Had got it, never to be taken away. Oh, Albé, I heard the groveller in my mind's ear saying, I shall never see you in Rome, where in truth you'll need me most.

In my dim and broken way, I recognized a fact that came to me from my practice as a professional man: what I kept in fluid I was hoping, one day, to make slides from, at the least, or combine in some ultra-galvanical experiment powered by Volta's battery. There was hope. What I embalmed, however, was something I had given up on. My link with Lord B. belonged surely in the first category, but I felt it was already embalmed because the Hobhouses, the Leigh Hunts, not to mention a host of women, already had the primacy. I would be going back to what those superior chums of his called a Cockney box. I missed his impetuous nature already, his scattershot mode of affection; but my duty lay with the family of Lord Guilford, whose tripes had gone ahead of him home, to be eyed.

PART FIVE

Man can wind himself up so as to suffer death as he would the amputation of a finger. We have seen three boys, none of whom were above 18, walk with a foot so firm and countenance so little changed to death, that we asked ourselves, is this the dread of all?

—*On the Punishment of Death,*
J. W. Polidori

It would have been better for me if I had been able to go on with the Countess Breuss, indulging in a relationship none too histrionic, with its share of rumpus and fun, neither party deluded about the other in an affair both sanitive and shallow. It was Claire, however, who had attuned me to woman not so much rampaging (though she could certainly be that) as fecund, and I half fancied that, if Shelley was one putative father, then I could have been another: topping her up, as it were, long after conception had happened. Claire had told me to eat ginger and no potatoes, things like that, rooted in common sense, as if the whole man interested her; had let me catechize her about salt ("the metal Sodium," she said, "mixed with a green air called Chlorine") and soda. She even taught me the virtue of little bits of Latin erotics learned by heart, to be murmured to oneself during an otherwise tedious moment in lovemaking or when lonely yet desirous. With her girlish acumen, she seemed in tune with the delicate foppery of life's surface, but also with its churning, primitive deeps. It had been she, and none of our great Romantic minds, who spoke of getting an efficient manure by digging about in the stalks and leaves of plants, rather than tracking after beasts with a pan and bucket, a shovel, and a clothes peg for the nose. Some women, she told me, trained themselves not to smell bad odours, being able to tighten up the muscle that stops food in the mouth from going to the nose. In a word, I relearned anatomy from her in a mood both that of emergency and rapture. Nobody took her seriously—after all, she had made herself look a fool over Lord B. —but it was all in a day's work for Claire to read Tacitus, *The Edinburgh Review,* a history of England written in French by a Jew, and some pages of Landor to round things off. Under cover of being deemed a rather primitive ninny, she honed a burly mind and satisfied an almost tropical body, astounded (in the beginning) to be an almost invisible woman, so locked up in her reputation that she was

free to excel or fail to an unthinkable degree. Under cover of one
infatuation she plied many others.

It was hard for me to separate what I knew of her from what,
on that basis, I imagined about her; in my mind's eye I fulfilled her,
making her not so much into an earth goddess as a duchess of
practicality and earthy savoir faire. For marriage she gave not a fig,
more enthralled with the *petits pois* Lord B. liked for dinner, and she
would toss a pebble at it as she sauntered by. She dealt with nature in
the raw, and never so much as when she told me, in the garden at
Diodati, on a day so hot and close it brought one into a sweat even
to laugh. I had complained about the weather, and she explained that
she liked all kinds of weather, as indeed all the grades and varieties
of darkness. "All is love in the universe," she somewhat windily
began, "the silver showers of the fountain, the quiet and imperfect
tenure of the leaves, the flowery path in May, even the deep night of
heaven strewn with golden blossoms, even Albé's vinegar rages." I
think she almost lost the thread of what she wanted to say, but she
rallied bravely and drew it all together like a bunch of flowers.
"Dare one be," she said, "just one disastrous and discordant atom
amidst all these elements of harmony and love?"

"What love?" I asked.

"Not love of Man," she said. "Love of itself. The universe
loves itself. It recognizes its own excellence, its ability to extend
itself, to be more and more like itself."

I confessed I did not altogether fathom this, but I was far from
quarrelling with her; how do you quarrel, argue, bicker, with a
mystic? She lived in an earth-ecstasy I envied, as reverent of juice of
berry as of delicately situated star. She also spoke, though, about the
Deathworm that could invade one's veins, blighting and withering
—part of her blest universe, to be sure, but one she shied away from,
being most specific about its sickening crawling motion that brought
on the very dryness of heart Lord B. suffered from. Powder flowed
in him, she said, love him as she did, a disease no worse than the
wandering typhus native to the gigantic swamps along the road to
Bologna. Sometimes she wandered off, nostalgic when prophetic,

haunted by a future more precise than the past had ever been, and one of her most frequent asides was one to the effect that Lord B. had always said he would rather be an inflicter than be inflicted on. It all had to do with misery and whether you would deal it out or be on the receiving end. Being alive, she said, amounted to more than this, *much more,* but so few people wanted it to do so: they preferred a narrowed perspective, a straitened bliss. When she was very wroth, she spoke without the least pretence of logic, hoping to sway her hearer through images either caustic or exultant, as if words no longer mattered and she were either singing a tune full of notes and nothing verbal or painting in mid-air with daubs of bright colours (if this might be done).

To me she fast became a force of nature, perhaps when she first told me that "our *home* is beyond the *stars,* not beneath them. This is a vestibule," placing immense emphasis on the words "home" and "stars" and not on "beyond" or "vestibule," as one might have expected. She spoke as if her relative emphases would be recognized in heaven, even when she misspoke herself, forgot the verb or where the sentence went. The woman haunted me, a buxom ghost, a personification of all things Genevan (and even, credit the mark, Italian too). She had spoken to a portion of my being hitherto unaddressed, perhaps because it had only recently come of age; it wanted to make up for lost time, and Claire was its muse, its anchor in nature.

No wonder, then, that after I had settled in again with my parents and sisters, I began making as many trips to Bath, where she resided with the Shelleys, as to Norwich, where there had been some hope of my practising as a physician. Idiotic it may have been to ferry myself westward past Reading for love (as I construed it) and eastward past Cambridge for work, but I did it; both were much the same distance from London, and what else, I asked myself, would I have done with my life? It was not as if I had not been out in the great world, in the company of *titolati:* I was accustomed to a certain amount of fuss and commotion.

I arrived more as a doctor than as an old friend, and was received as such, at least by the Shelleys, not with suspicion or resentment but with what I must call circumspect impersonality or, if not that, frostily civil correctness. Shelley was his usual bewildering mixture of bonhomie and crossness, Mary was aloof of mind but available of manner, while Claire, after the first few "Well, now"s and "Goodness me"s, mainly for Shelleyan benefit, settled down to the idea of having two doctors coming to see her, one free (Polidori). Whenever the Shelleys went out, mainly with little "Willmouse," as they called their son, she settled back into her informal, voluptuous self. I examined her. I overreached. We took the risk and made love in the afternoon like two Italians. Nobody came back, so we did it again until we heard the door rattle and the whole house's windows (loose and ancient) rattle in concert.

"Household spies," Claire said. "Doctor!"

"Shelleys everywhere," I answered. "We are going to have to find a place of our own. Come to London. Go with me to Norwich. Let us go back to Switzerland together, for happiness' sake."

"No," she said. "Only if *he* were here would I go there." But was that the true reason? I doubted it, thinking she was just being lazy, or that she was unsure if I would be an adequate substitute for the Shelleys, just as company.

"I have more than missed you," I told her.

"You were not aiming, Polly."

"Claire the wit."

"No, Claire the survivor."

"Is it fair to you to *lodge?* How do you like being a paying guest? A pendant to Shelleys?"

She suddenly looked dark and dour. "Better than being a pendant to the Byron clan. Truly, there is something repugnant, to me, in being anywhere where I have a room of my own, only that, and having to share all the others with someone else."

I would guarantee her privacy, I told her: not exactly a lighthouse, or an anchorite's cell, but separate rooms at the very least, where she might sew or think, write her journal (she and I had both

been keeping journals at Diodati) or read. I had heard that true
lovers, or imperishably great friends, would often walk or sit side by
side without speaking for hours. I did not envision anything quite
that thoroughgoing, but I did want to dream in her presence, lay my
head on her pulpy belly and smell the future lolling there. We had
both been rejected, so we should combine our thrown-off natures
and make of ourselves a wholly wanted person, each half infatuated
with the other. She scoffed at this. "You are a child, Polly. *I* am a
child. But I am a child *with child*—it makes a difference. I do not
belong to myself any more. I never shall. Don't you see? I am
involved with all the details of another creature's being."

At that moment I wanted to remove this other creature from
her and travel with it to Lord B., to inform him that I had arrived
with his property; and the offsprung child would be swathed in
cundums, just to teach him a lesson. I could divine in myself the
seeds of a moral indignation to come. "Let us go to Italy," I said,
"and take the baby to him, offering our services, which, if he refuses,
we shall confine to ourselves. I could work in the hospital at Pisa
again to keep us afloat. Think of the weather, Claire. Think of the
food, the opera."

She shook her head, loyal Shelleyan that she was. "When I
return, if I ever do, it will be with them. I have been with them too
long to abandon them now. They are my family, Polly; you are not.
You are—blissfully incidental, my dear. You are fighting the old-
fashioned girl in me, not the sexual opportunist. I do not need a man
that much. *Men,* perhaps. I have learned that much from Lord Byron, to whom I write regularly. Imagine the temper and make-up of
a woman who, rejected and spurned even while expecting his child,
still hankers for him, for his recognition. I will never be my own
woman until I have managed to intimate to him the role of father. I
shall be his tutor, his moral tutor. Sooner or later he will come to
heel, knuckle to. If it take me a hundred years to convince him, I
will prevail. This in a way will be like making *him* pregnant with
me. There may well be nothing left in my life save that. I was not

born for happiness but for effrontery, and then dedication. That is what I tell Tom too."

"Tom?" I said, with a stifled voice.

"Peacock, the novelist. He was always among us when we were children, I mean tots, and he has been coming to see us again. Shelley is trying to turn him into a vegetarian. He drinks heavily and eats too much meat. No ginger. But he only laughs and says wicked things about the bowels of lettuces and the sexual activities of leeks."

"He of *Headlong Hall*," I said in an arid whisper, thinking I would never be rid of literati who moved in on my private life and made my whole-gait stumble. What was I doing among such people? Did I really wish to belong, or was I merely touring? Peacock was no novelist, but a prestidigitator of ideas. Character and plot had no sway with him; all he did was assemble a group of articulate cranks in a country house and have them talk, at suffocating length, about slavery, paper money, rotten boroughs, the universities. A skeptic or a cynic, perhaps he was both. The faddists of *Headlong Hall,* which I had seen, were really the Shelleys and Peacock himself —and Samuel Taylor Coleridge, who, I suddenly recalled, had read aloud to Claire when she was little. It was clear to me that I had strayed onto the stage of a play whose actors were quite oblivious of me, who ran their lives in accordance with the rules and fetishes of a private, abstruse game. I did not belong, not even as likely raw material for the satirist called Thomas Love Peacock—his very name a laughingstock. Now, here he was, not the wolf stealing up on the fold but luxuriating from within, with Red Riding Hood already on his knee and no doubt double-handed in his trews. She was to be his peahen, I surmised.

"Not a bit of it," she said with worked-at gaiety. "True, he has pretty curls, a lofty brow, a witty way, and Shelley is lanky, pale, with a stoop and a high-pitched voice. But no."

"You mean you have also been considering Shelley?" I asked with a ferocious rush. "All men are meat for you."

"Not a bit of it," she said again, as if this were her second name. "I compare them, that is all. Tom and Shelley used to sail paper boats with us on the pond past Primrose Hill. He is part of our childhood, now grown up, or almost so. Brilliant, but self-indulgent to a fault, as always."

One day (I could see it now), they were all going to form up and make a pantisocracy, in Italy or Albania, leaving Polidori behind to remove intestines from the Guilford family. It would be the natural thing for them to do. They belonged together. They knew one another before they met. They came from the same minting shop in the stars. They did not associate with strangers unless obliged to, and even then only on sufferance. They ran a game that looked inward, and all who attempted to join in bounced away off the circumference. There, in the region you might not enter, there went on a scrimmage, a huddle, and you were born into it. Your mother had to have been buggered with a silver soupspoon or you did not exist. And I did not exist. Oh, they talked to me, insulted me as they would any old friend, but only in the sense that they would ask directions of a perfect stranger. After Byron, Peacock, and who next? Peacock came to tea, then left, but his presence remained among the tribe as one of them, and it would have remained even so had his nickname been Fairy Goldlight instead. Did he want Claire? Did he not exclude her from his list of eligible women? Always he arrived with his bottle, she said, and he stayed until it was empty, prating of how he was going to take her to see the India House Library and the Panorama of Rome. All he had to do was get her to London, and she would be his.

"Do you sing to him?" I said, at last able to compress my frustration and rage into a question not brimming with oil of vitriol. She nodded, but the nod told me she sang to all and sundry, even to Shelley, when he became jocosely horrible, as she put it. And she was going to sing to Keats and Hazlitt when the chance occurred: after the birth. I suddenly saw the instant of birth as the opening of a sluice-gate down which all my expectations would pour; Claire was talking to me only in her capacity of prisoner. She would soon be in the parks with him, and at the Apollonicon, God save us, a chamber organ of immense power, having both keys and barrels. The keyboards were five in number, the central and largest comprising five octaves and the smaller ones (two on either side of the larger) two octaves each. This magnificent contraption would perform Mozart's Overture to the *Zauberflöte, Figaro,* and *Idomeneo.* It would be like sitting in God's lap, even if uninvited, and I could hardly see for rage at the thought of this Peacock ogling her *vallis lucis* while watching her breast surge in time with the organ's mighty bellows. Needless to say, this fop of a cock did not have to earn a living but lived on a slender patrimony. He was self-educated, as one might easily deduce from his paraded learning.

He was indeed the very type that proposed marriage to young women, more as an art-form than as anything firm. He was so attentive to her, in his gathering witty stupour, with his astringent mind flickering even as it succumbed to pollution and rot. "Down with poets," she said he would say, mocking Shelley and Byron and Keats, "all those who vent querulous, egotistical rhapsodies, to express the rhymester's high dissatisfaction with the world and all in it. It is time to devote ourselves to serious thinkers and to the work of science." He came to them to try out the dialogue in his novels and (on Claire) the weird names he had dreamed up to parody his friends with: Byron was Cypress, she told me, Shelley was "Scythrop," Coleridge "Flosky," and Wordsworth "Mr. Paperstamp of Mainchance Villa." I noticed that he had no name for me, even though he did not know me; word of me might just have reached him. In any world of average justice it would have done. I wanted to be ridiculed along with all the others. If this monumental killjoy had been with us at Diodati, we would have behaved ourselves at once: no games, no staying up all night, no ghost stories, and no libertine escapades. He was planning several more novels.

When I first met him I was soaked with rain, but he failed to notice how sodden I was and immediately said to me, "A doctor? Do you think, sir, we can cut the romanticism out of Byron and the

rest? Could we decanker them, using a gimlet and a fretsaw? I tell
you, sir, it is all speed and economics these days. Imagine the stupid-
ity of that man Columbus, an accursed foreigner, discovering a new
world to plague the old with. Poetry, sir, is the mental rattle that
first awakened the human savage, but what need have we of it now?
Well, since you ask, I would dub you Skullpal, sir, how does that
suit you? Doctor Skullpal."

At last he had stopped, but Claire was still giggling. "He calls
me Stella," she said.

"Stella *puella,*" he said, as if none present knew Latin. If this
was my rival, I need have no fears; he was your mere popinjay of
the mouth, so soon drunken that he began to repeat himself, so
incoherently it sounded as if he were speaking backwards. If only he
had been a Guilford, I could have snipped his tripes in a trice and
sent him off to Timbuctoo. Claire, however, took him seriously, as
one of the coming minds: not in Albé's league, of course, any more
than Shelley was, but a man of paralyzing, chirpy wit. Would he
care to have me serve as his physician? I asked him, but he told me
that he was never ill, and that when he would be he would die of it;
the thought of continuity pleased him so. How glib I found his
jocose impromptus: not a man but a jest-monger. I was much more
sentimental than he, and therefore (I thought) a better human soul.

When I next met him, if met were the word, I had Miss Claire
upended before me for purposes of medical examination and was
peering into her *vallis,* half wishing that with scalpel or sword I
might cut out the offending vestige of Lord B. and make her my
own with a new baby. I was engrossed, Claire was half asleep (these
ministrations soothed her, provided my hands were warm), and all I
heard was his reedlike voice, tinged with mockery, but also out of
puff, exclaiming, or asking, "Fishing for trout, sir?"

He had walked into the house, as was his wont, and had come
pottering about upstairs, stick in hand. I did not move, and Claire
heard him not. I waved a hand to usher him away, but he said
something lewd about being interested in purchasing this particular

dry-dock, so I halted the examination, covered Claire, and turned to face him, wiping my hands on a cloth. His face was red as cochineal.

"Why, sir," he brayed, "doctoring has its charms."

"Away with you, Tom," Claire shrieked, "this very minute. Who let him in? Motherhood is private."

It was no use explaining. Besides, my mind was on the interruption, for several times Claire and I had lazily rolled ourselves from the one enterprise to the other, with the inspector turned huffpuff man and my *fille aux mille projects,* as Shelley called her, attentive only to that of her own joy. One occasion had been special.

"Was it ever like this with Albé?" I asked, thrilled still to be where he had been and where he never again would go. "Was it like this with Tom?"

She stopped heaving and crying, asked me never to mention Albé's name in bed, and then, saving her energy for it, scoffed aloud, uttering the name "Tom" with such contempt I half wished he had been standing behind me again. "His member is a bottle," she said.

"An ancient and honoured perversion," I said.

"Honoured in the breech." She could be witty even during congress, and she could be deadly too. On she went, explaining that it would only ever be Albé. "Did you not realize that all the ghost-story talk at Diodati was about loving men who were no longer alive? Men who had served and gone?" Not mine, certainly, and as for Mary—"They were elegies," she said, almost ready to weep, and I knew then that, whatever I did to endear myself, I would never count to her on any level with that same remorseful, basaltlike intensity. Albé had turned her into a pillar of salt, and she was not going to reappear even though she went through motions with the likes of me.

"There is always love," I said, tentative as a newborn bird.

"There is never love, Polly. Love cannot be spoken. Nor can it be written. Love is an inmost privacy, having nothing to do with the beloved. It refers to ourselves. It is what we have to dignify our wanting with."

"Always?" I too felt a peacock, squawking rubbish.

"Your own experience should tell you. Love is not a commodity or an achievement, Polly. It is the ghost of an intrinsic affectation: neither more nor less. Love is a tracing only, where a human being has felt exalted even as his partner has been sick as a dog." Surely she was propounding some higher metaphysics of the lustful part; she was going on, in a wholly different voice, like someone speaking in a trance: *"Farewell then, dearest, I shall love you to the end of my life"*—she paused to gain control— *"and nobody else. Think of me as one whose affection you can count on and never, pray, never forget to mention your health in your letters. May every good and every happiness be yours. Your own affectionate, Claire."*

I gasped, thinking such words addressed to me, but she said no, they had been in her final letter to Lord B. before quitting Geneva. "He had called me *little fiend*," she said, "and he had said to me *Pray go*. I was still able to write to him, and I have written to him from here. I am only writing to the part of me that loved him—not to him as such."

It was then that something appalling drove into my mind and exploded. I realized I could be playful with Claire so long as I had her, mocking Peacock and denigrating Byron in a whole repertoire of facetiae, but it would be miserably different if I lost her, and I could see that I was going to lose her; if nothing ever again happened in my dead-as-dust life, I would lose Claire. *That* would happen, even if I prayed and grovelled. It was like being two men: the sexually successful jester-cum-Lothario, and the washed-up drowned man whose eyes the crabs had taken and whose kit had become morsels as far apart as the Spanish Main and the Sea of Azov. Claire, I found, was merely occupying time. When the day came, she would give me my *congé* as speedily as her lover had, and then I would be twice humiliated, doubly jettisoned, more than ready to settle for some suburban ideal, homely or pretty, so long as it did not have a barb in its tail. And I saw myself trying again and again, and forever failing, then running out of energy and zest,

losing the courage to try, even the heart to confide the sad list of my
defeats to friends, and ultimately lacking even the vim to go after a
Gaby Saxonnex in Piccadilly at whatever price. I was always the
extra man, the reserve who never got to play in the match, brought
back home from life with his bag unopened, his lips unkissed. How
could I be two: the lover and the inevitable runt?

I kept trying to decide what it was about Claire that drew me
on: aloof mind, ready body? Aloof body, ready mind? Neither. She
had learned something from Lord B. about bewildering the opposition without ever thinking of them. Bewilder was not quite the
word; I meant bemuse, perhaps, or confound. Something delectably
self-centred drove her behind that puddingy jowl, those expression-
less eyes brown as my own. For years I would be whisking and
whirring through the rural darkness, the clamour of Reading, on my
way to see her, attired in cape and velour hat, my mind on one thing
only: a new version of highwayman seated in his car as the horse
clip-clopped and the whip wobbled in the breeze of our passage. It
was like being one of the accursed of history, a ghostly rider of dark,
forbidding face and undisclosed intentions, almost in his mobile
fashion a fixture on the roads, coming and going: a ghoul, a reve-
nant, a scoundrel, at full stretch between his home and his need. I
went less and less to Norwich and therefore had no hope of setting
up a practice there; still less of one in Bath, which was overflowing
with doctors and quacks. Rather than have my car become a fixture,
I left it at the hackney stand, and then the Shelleys had no idea if I
was on the premises or not. I began to dote on privacy. I crept about
the house like a burglar, on several occasions managing to find and
sample her diaries, the letters she was engaged in writing. I got to
know the underside of my Claire, the rhythms of her busy little
mind, the daily mental tour she took. For instance:

> Sunday, November 6th. *Rise at nine. Talk all the morning. Read* Prince
> Alexy Haimatoff *and* King Richard III. *Shelley writes many letters. Dine at
> four. Mary and Shelley and I sleep all the Evening. S. goes at ten. Very
> philosophical way of spending the day—to sleep and talk—why, this is mere*

vegetating. I am beginning to become very bored and wretched. It will be worse in the New Year. They want to be rid of me and will soon seek out for me a position as governess. I cannot go back to Skinner Street as Fanny's school-marm Aunts are over from Dublin and it is feared that I would contaminate the niece who is to succeed them in the school. Hum. The Shelleys will soon be saying how sullen I have turned. Already they creep upstairs to talk about evicting me, but I will not go. They find it hard to bear, but I need to stay.

That was 1815. In April she won a lottery and went off to Lynmouth in May. She too was accustomed to being pushed hither and yonder like a parcel. In Lynmouth she lived close to nature and wrote to Fanny Imlay that she was utterly happy living alone:

Wrote to Fanny telling her how much at liberty I am among a few cottages, little rosy-faced children, scolding wives, and drunken husbands. I live in a little cottage, with jasmine and honey-suckle twining over the window; a little downhill garden, full of roses, with a sweet arbour. It is in solitude that the powers concentre round the soul. A sober temperature of mind is truly more delightful than the gayest ebullitions of mirth.

Was I dreaming when I thought that behind all this there flowed a lovely, keen, commodious mind? Love is blind, but is it dense? Less than a year later she was writing to Lord B. as E. Trefusis of 21, Noley Place, Mary le Bonne. And now she was bored again, waiting to give birth, and merely putting up with Polidori, Peacock, and the rest.

I marvelled at how words enabled us to go to the heart of someone, most of all words intended for no eye other than the writer's, and it seemed to me that truth made pilferers, spies, of us all. I looked, prowling about the house on tiptoe in the dead of night, for any letter she might be writing to Lord B., but found none. I was not always there, she was not always writing to him (or so I hoped), and my techniques of search were lame. Not only that: she had a habit of secreting beneath the pillow her effusion of the moment, and fishing that out was beyond me. I had had no practice as a pillow-pocket and never would. My hands could snip the descending colon from the diaphragm by severing the phreno-colic ligament, in the dead such as Lord Guilford, and even in the living, just perhaps, were there need, but not burrow with stealth beneath my Claire's pillow. That would have to wait, except that, on waking, she removed all paper that had lain under her head. We had made love above such a crackle and rustle (a letter to whom I knew not), but that never hindered her; she saw no incongruity in the infidelity, nor did I draw attention to it, eager for my own comfort at all speed.

But prowling I improved at, spurning the Shelleys, who left letters and notebooks wide open all over the house, until one night, drunker than Peacock ever, and primed with laudanum for good measure, I found myself with fist raised above Claire's belly, ready to pound the infant-to-be into pulp, either against Lord B. or against Nature herself. In my other hand I held a scalpel, to cut the whole thing out with, as if carving a cloud, and I hovered there, breathing hard, my head full of racing images from Geneva and Italy, telling myself that, one way or another, things had to change or I would lose all and thus be sent packing to a humdrum life in Norwich. Bath was Eden and Gomorrah, but Norwich was a field of lettuces. Claire did not stir, being a heavy, babbling sleeper, and I stood there for as long as it takes to quaff a cup of tea (polite consumption), not so much debating as marvelling. There she lay, as full of secrets as a pirate's cave—open, penetrable, shameless—and yet an enigma, a woman Byron must have longed to consign, sewn up in a sack, to the Bosphorus. This story haunted Claire, although not as much as the one he told about the Thyrza of his poem, whom he had seduced and had a brace of children by; when he refused to marry her, since she was of mean birth, she killed herself and was buried at a crossroad. He fretted about her ever after but could never erect a stone to her memory. Lies, Shelley had said, but the story had affected more of us than Claire, fabrication or not.

There in the moonlight I described ellipses and arcs above
Claire's sleeping bulk, over her face, her trunk, her feet. Did I wish
to go down in history as the rawhead who killed Byron's pregnant
mistress, merely to deny Peacock and Lord B.? Light caught the
blade and scattered to my hand. There were other women in my life,
of course, yet none so sensual, puzzling, or easy as she. A quiet
smothering would do just as well. I half scared myself as I stood, and
I began to shiver at the merest intimation of the role I leaned towards. Would this be the way to go, better than an undistinguished
medical career, *if* I were lucky? She smelled milky and musky, her
breath sour from wine, her nose rather blocked, her brow speckled
with moisture. It was a classic pose: the assassin in the bedroom,
weapon held aloft, murmuring to himself before he struck, just to
prolong the delicious intactness of the last few moments. I could see
the lure of such a stance, of pausing, savouring, knowing the irrevocable was at hand but revocable in any instant until. . . . Then to
change the world in one swift blow, followed by a quick rummage
in the belly, a surgeon's slash at the cord, the run with the muffled
tiny bundle to the car and its impatient horse. There was not even a
scream. That, I saw, was the very way to have a baby for one's self:
the Byronic way, to be sure, best done by a hired butcher.

Yet how could I adore her and wish to disembowel her, even in
the merest mental drama? What was the source of such contrary
feelings in one so young, so well brought up as I, who posted
through the night to be near his beloved, not to cut her up? Was I
truly infected with the Byronic plague? Or did I feel thus for not
being infected at all, but eager to be rid of him, his power over yet
another of the rejected? I would only be killing Byron by proxy, I
decided, by killing his doxy, his babe. Better to post to Italy and run
him through in the public street with the longest sabre I could find.
Would such a feat merit the journey, the ensuing execution? I
doubted it. Surely some outraged woman would stab him soon, and
then Claire would be as much delivered of him as a newborn child.
Or was the babe Shelley's? Perhaps she never knew. It was certainly
not Polidori's, but it might well be if I stayed around her. Did I

wish to be thought the complaisant custodian of one of Lord Byron's bastards? Biographer turned wet-nurse? Never to doctor again? Much simpler, I told myself as a dog barked and Claire heaved her body through a half turn, gasping and snorting as she did so, much simpler to clatter off to London now and not be there when Claire awoke, not in the least wondering why her stomach had not been sliced wide open and the baby plucked from its nest of clotted cream.

As I stood there, both trembling and shivering, I had the first of those fantasies that came and stayed with me: dreadful images of myself committing abominations on her sleeping form in the tedium of rage. I bit into her nose, pulp and bone, then her ear, tried to bite through her lips, snap her fingers and toes, all to no avail. She was invulnerable. She had no blood. My teeth met without having bitten through anything at all. Nor did she convulse or scream, but went on sleeping with stertorous grace as if there were no one present over her. My shod heel trod on her face, my shod foot forced its way into her, but not a murmur came forth; the dead would have been more responsive, and it was clear that I had discovered the least effective way of getting through to her. Poor Claire, to be thus savaged in sleep by one she trusted and often entrusted her body to, for both health and pleasure. Polidori had grown helpless fangs.

Several times more I looked upon her thus, although never again imagining a savage assault; my fist melted, my scalpel blunted itself and fell to my side like a curl of paper. It was another defeat. I had none of the qualities that made a murderer of gentle, introverted lovers; I was too much the physician, perhaps, as accustomed to blood as to books. Blood was no novelty to me as it was to others. The mysterious new life that bulged within her had nothing to do with any living being save herself—lodged, housed, fortified. My mind had a sudden tremor and gave up, seizing like an engine. It was no use waking her. I crept downstairs and walked to my horse and car, intent upon London and its din.

She wrote to Byron often, she said, but he never wrote back, having severed the bond, so she wrote to his ghost, to the sentimental image of him she watered and tended, pruning him of this or that sin until he stood there a paragon, self-absorbed and absentminded. At this rate she would soon be back with him, fawning on him, fetching and carrying and copying things out for him, picking his rotten teeth and wiping his incontinent backside. In a way we were both doctors to him, tenants of the prize fungus he had become, and there was no way out for us. For the rest of our days we would be his leavings, ever convinced of something within him he had denied us even though he revealed it to Shelley, Mary, Monk Lewis, Hobhouse, and others. It amounted to more than his continuing interest in us, much more than that; it was close to having had a view of God in a supposedly godless universe. He had made us both feel not just useful and precious; he had wafted us high, to his own disgraceful plateau. We wanted to be used again, even if it killed us. We would not be caught dead, as the saying went, in his company again, but oh, we would, we would give anything. Two more grovelling, addicted persons there were not on the rind of the planet, and here I was, riding a hundred miles to and fro in a simulacrum of that infatuation, antagonistic as it had been, from London to Staines and Windsor, thence to Reading and Devizes, Trowbridge, thence to Bath, and back again, past the sleeping citizenry, the cropped hedges, the sundials, the inns, the hovels, all of those people going about serious business while Polidori, phantom of the night, galloped by, dreaming of a less hectic life, yearning for something more sedate, less an imitation of an old folly. It was the beginning of my losing self-respect while the finical quietudes of Norwich beckoned and my father said merely, but with operatic Italian hyperbole, "Bath *again?*" He had worried less about me when I was in Italy itself. Surely some vital piece of the brain was lacking in me, some piece that steered the human lover to something like a stable relationship. I passed thousands of examples of this daily as I rode by. I had never felt more medieval, a Crusader or a jongleur: fine fancies, these, but ultimately ruinous, and yet I made love to my obsession, not knowing how to remedy it or make it taper off. It was not an addiction to Claire, but an addiction to hers because we were both camp-followers, so to speak. Thinking of the lovers I passed, whether they plighted their troths in barn, boudoir, or hovel, I thought of Dante's Paolo and Francesca, the lovers who read together about Lancelot, whom love constrained. But this time, although tempted to look into each other's eyes and to blush with longing, they had other problems, Paolo being short-sighted and Francesca long-sighted, so that each wanted the book to be in a different position, he wanting it up close, she wanting it far away, so much so that they never actually read the text simultaneously, which spoiled the whole episode. Oh, they each read it, of course, and Paolo, never to be divided from her, except by lenses, kissed her mouth all trembling. I occupied my long rides with such revisionary puzzles, knowing that, up close for the kiss, Paolo and Francesca fumbled a bit and had to go by feel. Yet how much wiser they than I, wishing *se fosse amico il re dell' universo*—if the king of the universe were our friend—while making a long, pained streak in the air between London and Bath, no sooner going westward than hating the journey back, no sooner returning than yearning to do the hundred miles again in the other direction.

I almost heard myself, as in Dante, introducing myself with a wry twist of the mouth and an odd sideways motion of my body as if to shield it from view: "I am Polidori, most infernal of lovers; I was of London and Norwich, then of Edinburgh; neither Albé nor Claire has care of my soul, but into La Svizzera I came, and left it jabbed in the heart, fleeing on foot, dripping blood all over the deck of the boat from Livorno. I ended speech (crying on) the name of Byron, then of Claire. Other lovers have sustained my life, but I have no brains left. Edinburgh made me, Geneva unmade me." How ridiculous: a grown man galloping with a head full of Dante, mentally adrift between Geneva and Bath. It was even sillier than what Claire had said long ago about living where she did. "Why, Polly, having as I do a room in Bath is akin to having a Bathroom, and who would wish to live in that?" It was as if my temperature kept on going up, my muscles grew tighter, my eyes went further and further out of focus, my breath became shorter, my heart went faster and faster, and my whole being began to spin until I was dizzy as a goat atop an Alp. I had even tried prayer, that lost conduit, but had felt I was asking favours of myself only; the king of the universe was never looking, or listening, my way.

Long ago I had lost my self-respect, having put in its place a mad chance of ecstasy; but ecstasy, that being thrown out of one's self, had not come about, and all I had been able to find to sustain me was memory: so long as I remembered the few good times at Diodati, all was well. I had been born for that, nothing else; I had walked and dined and jested with the high and the mighty; I had let them wipe themselves on me and use me for target practice. One would usually get over such treatment, deciding that it was all only a preliminary to a full life lived well, but I had no belief in that life to come, with Claire or Eliza Arrow or with any of my Norwich flames. The dreadful thought had long ago arrived and taken root in my much-thumbed copy of *The Sorrows of Young Werther* that life had already happened, was already over. A few months of crucial experience had been my portion, my muddled paradiso, and all the rest was hell. I had even thought of travelling to see Lady Byron, to introduce myself and offer my services, to anger him and extort a response; but the awful news would take so long to reach him, it was no doubt hardly worth doing, at least until he was back in England, if ever. I had thought of opening a suit to Mary Shelley, but the more I had seen of Mary in Bath the less I found her congenial, not when compared to the almost barbaric allure of Claire, the gipsy of Diodati.

Having been able to identify the trouble, and to reason it through in words, a practical mind would have despatched it and moved on to other indignities (and that was to see things at their worst: *deinosis*). I, however, had fixed on Diodati, the style of life and love there. The longer I was there, the less I was able to think of living in any other way, wolfing the sandwich in which humiliation sat between layers of splendour. As in certain modes of witchcraft, my head faced the wrong way, looking forever behind to the source of my enchantment, forgetting the incidental wonders of Geneva (my countess, for instance) for its cynosure. My only link with it, sure enough an underground one, was Claire, who, I had to admit, was superb in the conduct of her own humiliations—she never stopped adoring him, she never stopped writing him, and she had his child attached to him, as to her, by an Ariadne's thread hundreds of miles long. How adroit, how primitive.

"I will catch him," she had said, "even if only for a few years, until he loses interest in the toy." I had never heard a baby referred to as a toy before.

"And then?" I had said.

"Some other stratagem," she had told me, "will reel him in. He is as much a professional evader as I am a fisher of men, but I am more of it than he is of that. You will see."

Would I? Did I even wish to? She frightened me.

Weary and twitching from travel, I arrived at the door in October one brisk day and let myself in to a veritable storm of weeping. What had happened? Instead of telling me, Claire took me into the drawing room and showed me a letter she was writing to Lord B., the first time she had ever done such a thing. "What on earth has happened?" I said. "Is it Shelley? *Mary?*"

"Read," she commanded with choked nose and bloodshot eyes, and read I did, almost feeling the breath and skin of Albé as he would be when he got this missive.

> *Add to this the unhappy state of that poor girl. I passed the first fourteen years of my life with her, and though I cannot say I had so great an affection for her as might be expected, yet she is the first person of my acquaintance who has died and her death so horrible too. This phenomonon will keep us in poor spirits till we are old.*

Saying nothing about the error in spelling, I again asked my blunt and brutish question: "Who? What?"

"Can't you tell?" she said. "My half-sister Fanny Imlay has

committed suicide by taking poison in a hotel in Swansea, and Shelley has had to go and identify her body. Love for Shelley drove her to it, my mother says, but I doubt that. It is more likely that she died of being told all the time that she was not Godwin's daughter. She was illegitimate too. She felt these things acutely. Fanny is gone, and William Godwin is determined that the news shall not be made public. What a thing to care about at such a time!"

There was no consoling her. She seemed to take the blame upon herself, although she took pains to send the news to Lord B., in a perverse way glad to have *something* to relate to him, to get his attention with. I could not reach her beyond the customary hug and the banal, formulaic words of consolation; she was beside herself and very young about it. Something vile and slimy had erupted from the depths of the universe and had struck down an innocent being she was fond of, and Claire was not ready for such horrors. She was too young, and the bairn beneath her heart seemed all the more vulnerable for what Fanny had done to herself. Well, I thought, at least Fanny will never rot with disease, but I said nothing. The reaper was among the young, having already claimed Mary's first baby, who was prematurely born. I doubted my usefulness in such a grieving household and took my leave unnoticed, almost knocking Peacock over as I left, mentally noting that he was too drunk to express any emotion not maudlin and banal.

Worse followed in December, hardly before the other wound had healed, or even been accepted (William Godwin made such a good job of suppressing the news that, one year afterward, Charles Clairmont would write home to Fanny ignorant of her fate, knowing only what Godwin had had bruited abroad—that she had gone to Wales to stay with friends). On the thirteenth Shelley heard from the bookseller Hookham (I was there; I saw him age and falter) that his wife Harriet had drowned herself in the Serpentine, in an advanced state of pregnancy. Off he went to London to claim his children, but thunderstruck and reduced by the event. If the angel of death were abroad, it was having a harvest of the young and suicidal. This, perhaps, was the wages of all the sins we had entertained and toyed with. We were all, in our turn, going to be stalked and struck down for having been too prodigal, too presumptuous, too imaginative, thinking our way into cosmic arcana we should have left alone. Then I regained my wits and told Claire that these two unhappy souls had been marginal to our main enterprises. "It is not, dearest Claire, as if we had lost one of our *selves*—a Shelley, a Mary, a Byron, a *you.*" Little did I realize then that, as in some unspeakable feast of hell's bloodletting, five years hence Shelley would be drowned and gone, as dead as Claire's new baby girl in the same year as he, little Willmouse having preceded them in 1819. And, only two years after Shelley, Byron would be gone too, and he not alone in that. I sensed some drear great black sausage churning up from the sludge at the heart of things. It reared up at us and sucked us down, a force with a terrible maw, lusting after children and innocents, rakes and prodigals, alike. Mary would live on into middle age, and Claire would endure until she was ninety-one, the agonized, incredulous witness of all that reaping, going out like a candle in 1879, buried, as she had asked, with Shelley's little shawl. Alive in 1817, however, she was grief-stricken about Fanny and shocked about Harriet, but also dismayed that Lord B. had written to Shelley without even referring to her: no message, no enclosure. That, she thought, was her finale; yet, with the importunate fortitude she always showed, she at once wrote him a tactful letter, spinning him further into her maternal web, and that perhaps is the trait that helped her to live so long, never taking anything save death as final, never believing words for what they said, always thinking she could go anyone one better once she put her mind to it. Inextinguishable Claire: What were such poor, doomed infidels as we doing scuttling in her presence with our hotheaded lusts and our seething, obtuse manias? What saved her? All the others did her dying for her. Foppish and bizarre as it may be to say so, she deceived Death by shuffling her name from Jane to Clare to Clara to Clary before settling on Claire. Perhaps, too, I fancied, she had written to Death as she had written to Lord Byron, as E. Trefusis of Mary le Bonne, and with him too had arranged an assignation so that he might savor her well-oiled body as eagerly as Lord B. had. Thus she reprieved herself to be our lady of the watch, hugely and inhumanly loved. The clearing of the stage had now begun.

In the event, it was not I but the local doctor who delivered Claire's baby; or, rather, Claire, who was always apprehensive about her physical strength, delivered it herself, saying, "I must be a horse after all." This morsel of new life was a miracle to us, a shaft of light in the funereal parade of the past few months. Shelley, who always liked children (in his bizarre way) was overjoyed, almost as if he were the father. It had been Shelley, after all, who on Magdalen Bridge in Oxford had once challenged a baby and had shaken his long hair in juvenile disappointment when the mother protested that the infant could not talk. "He may fancy, perhaps," pronounced Shelley the atheist undergraduate, "that he cannot, but it is only a silly whim; he cannot have forgotten entirely the use of speech in so short a time; the thing is absolutely impossible." Claire must have told me the story a dozen times in the past month, laughing helplessly at the notion that the child had been talking its mouth off in some anterior state designed, no doubt, by William Wordsworth, for whom all infants came trailing clouds of glory straight from God. Shelley was not pretending: he longed to have "Miss Alba" (Albé's dawn) at home with William, or Willmouse, and his other children, Ianthe and Charles, if he could gain custody of them. It was not to be, however, and little Allegra had only Willmouse for company: the doomed invigilating the doomed. It was not long before Shelley gave up his dream of a colony of adopted children and returned to sailing paper boats with Peacock, sometimes making them fly through the air, hand-held, as if conquering the feebler element first while Peacock brandished his bottle. I thought they would soon perform the mysterious rite of putting the paper boat into the empty bottle, for the sake of the child and the baby, but they never went that far. "Ah," said Shelley, "imagine a boat that flies."

"A Leonardo," I said, nothing daunted. "It is bound to come, and then we will never need ships again."

"We will all be winds," he said, and at once began to talk of moving to a house in Wales or the Thames Valley, "to be our home for ever. *Byron* will come and join us," he said with effusive finality, and at that moment I for the first time wanted no more of Lord B., wishing him far enough away. I liked my harum-scarum itinerant life in England, I wanted him nowhere near it, or near Claire and her baby, of whom I fancied I could become amateurishly protective in no time at all. The idea of a community that included Byron and Peacock and Hogg and who knew who else no longer appealed to me; this was my post-Diodati phase. The past was what I had lived through; the future must not be like it.

It was, though. The Shelleys moved to Marlow and took Claire with them, into a miserable place called Albion House (named for England), whose rooms let in no light, whose books were mildewed and smelled of old rope. Once again Peacock kept on inviting himself in, much to Mary's disgust ("He comes to drink, not to see us"). The Leigh Hunts came from London and overstayed. Godwin brought Claire's younger brother, William, to see us in our new quarters, but Claire found him hard to deal with, quite tiresome, in fact. He made fun of her all day, made her take him for walks in the woods, whence they returned with sheaves of wet bluebells, and in the evening pleaded with her to play chess with him. In between exacting intellectual debates and bouts of writing *Frankenstein,* Mary found time to have her baby, to be named Clara, sanguine about the delivery because she and Shelley were now married, all impediment having been swept away by the Serpentine. When in doubt, I fixed my gaze on little Allegra, her black hair and intense blue eyes, her elaborate curlicue of a mouth, and tried to cheer up, knowing that sooner or later Claire was going to leave again for Italy, to show the baby to the father. Would I be invited, as family doctor to her and the Shelleys? It was certain that they needed such care, but would I be wanted? That old, seedy question came up and up in my mind, never to be answered. It was not a matter of my not being useful, of my having nothing to offer (I was an *habitué* of the whole untidy tribe by now); it was that they sometimes just did not think of me at all, especially Claire and Mary, who, each with a new baby to fondle, created a closed relationship that no one else might even guess at: not of mutual liking but of kindred labour, for Mary was weary and anaemic, having borne three children in three years, and she longed to be rid of Claire *(absentia Claria* she called it). They understood each other too well to be able to stand each other for long, even though they exchanged wet-nurse talk like two seasoned campaigners. Claire was bored, suffering from the same disease as medieval monks ("accidie," or spiritual inanition), and had begun to neglect her appearance and sulk through meals. The entire household seemed to be festering towards some kind of collapse presaged by the damp and the mould, by Claire's tear-laden eyes that only Shelley could appreciate, constantly trying to stir her into better spirits by having her sing to him, read him some Italian, copy out a new poem. She overattended upon Allegra, as if the child had no natal ability to grow aright, as if she had constantly to be reminded of her obligation to grow up into an exactly copied Byron. The love or intimacy between the two of us began to give way to an avalanche of cossetting and dandling, in which I had no role. In vain to pretend, as she had in the beginning, in front of neighbours and servants, that Allegra was a friend's child, sent to the countryside for her health. One could see that this was mother with child, *tout court.* Some even began to suspect that Shelley was the father, as they well might, impressed by his sheer proximity, or even Polidori, which gave me an odd inadvertent thrill. The truth, of course, was that I was already on my way out, every bit as much as when banished from Milan after my adventure with the Austrian officer. Polidori was like a season of the year: he always came, he always went.

What he had to offer did not compare with what Byron had: all those things the Shelleys deemed worthless, such as wealth, fame, title, leisure, and pomp. Claire despised the same things too, but she was resolved that Allegra should have them even if it killed Lord B.

to confer them. "Father's rank: Peer," said the baptismal certificate
eventually executed in March 1818, naming the Right Honourable
George Gordon Lord Byron "ye reputed Father," of "no fixed resi-
dence travelling on the Continent." Claire had always intended
locking him in tight on this, certain that he would be only too glad
to do his best for his child, little thinking what it might cost her to
secure his attention and interest all over again. When Allegra came
into the world, Claire's memories of Albé's vicious side vanished and
she began to enshrine him all over again, at the expense of Polidori,
whose suit had been almost prospering until then. She wrote, but
never sent (averse to casting lyrics into a vacuum), letters of almost
culpable tenderness which she showed to Polidori, working his mind
even while spurning his advances. One of them, unforgettable in its
directness, went as follows, more or less:

> My dearest Friend,
> I do not say that she is a pretty child, though she is certainly very far
> from ugly, but she has good points—pretty eyes of a deep, daytime blue, rosy
> projecting lips, and a little square chin divided in the middle like your own.

On she went, saying how much she envied him, his having a little
darling to crawl up to his knees and drag at him until he picked her
up, when she would roost in the crook of his arm and he would give
her "a raisin" off his own plate and a tiny spot of wine "and she will
think herself a little Queen of Creation." I remembered her phrase
with unlenient clarity, as perhaps the last intimate contact I was
going to have with Claire, who in the past had written to Lord B.
with such abandon and so little care for her English. Now, wishing
all perfect, she showed me draft upon draft, never quite achieving
the right text until months or even years later, when no doubt she
did send the thing, full of creamy idolatry and grovelling cant. She
always had trouble with the paragraph that told him how lucky he
was to have this tiny creature to fondle, as he thought (as she wished
it) This Was the Work of His Own Hands. I almost puked for
embarrassment, but rebuff her I could not, wishing that she would

only address such ravishing importunities to me instead of seeing me, now, as some kind of English master. Bath I used to love to drive to, all that way, but Marlow was a dreary destination, and their being in Albion House only made them all the drearier. Only Shelley had any brio to him. Mary groaned with fatigue and prose. Claire slutted about in her oldest clothes, sighing and slouching, almost as if beginning pregnancy all over again, and lived on in that girlish delirium of unsent epistles, as if Lord B. were Shakespeare himself and Byronically unforgiving of the merest solecism in the style. Here was this woman who had let his nail drive through her countless times, spraying her with his rampant cordial, and she was being finical about the couching of maternal sentiments in deathless periods. All he ever wrote about, I heard, and never direct to her, was red tooth-powder, soda-powders, magnesia (still), toothbrushes, diachylon plaster, and the latest novels, into the midst of which he eventually said that they might pack his *"child* by Clare—pack it carefully." He would try out on Shelley what he later wrote to Hobhouse in more peremptory form, God knew why, and I smiled wanly at the epistolary feinting that went on between Marlow and Italy as the two principals held back and Polly and Shelley stood in. If this was my only remaining way to her, then so be it. Better than nothing. I would counsel her on grammar for ever, knowing that Claire's arsenal of phrases was limited at best; all she ever wished to do, truly, was write the perfect version of the one letter she was equipped to write to Lord B. on behalf of Allegra. In the end she wrote scores of them, but they never went, they never survived, and I think they all drowned in Gooseberry Pond, Marlow, sailed to their doom by Captain Shelley. Always excepting the final one, the last recension, of course. At this time Claire had been reading Plutarch's *Lives,* as if hunting a clue to the aberrations of the great, but her prose remained unaltered by classical example, although her daily blather became more volatile as she talked, again and again, of her *volage* and her lack of a Hobhouse by her side to sap her "with his easy, impudent declarations of all mankind's villainy." Her mind seemed to be always churning, whereas what she set down went round and round on the same ditty to her lord and lover. It was clear that Polly's days were coming to an end; I was a mere companion now, not even a physician to her, and I would have to ply my heart in other places soon, in other ways: become the writer I had always yearned to be, the swain of the lovely girls of Norwich.

Some kaleidoscopes go wrong, creating images so foul that each is worse than its predecessor; the bits jumble themselves and then, out of mere light, arrange patterns from hell. I seemed, after my return to London, to be looking down such a tube, ever willing to believe in the beauty of the shards, but gradually giving up hope that I would see anything pretty ever again. Literary squabbles apart, I put my best energy into being a doctor, but it appeared that, for me at least, there were no treatable illnesses in London. My connection with the Guilford family had vanished into air; the transported entrails had arrived and been found wanting, which was to say not bad enough to have killed off the third earl, and that was that. I had not expected to arrive in triumph, or to be fêted for doing so, but I had expected to earn a living, and I had discovered, alas, while abroad, that one certain way of doubling a hundred pounds was to gamble it. On a lucky day, of course. Such doubling remained in the mind, of course, skulking among the other vagaries and delusions that a doctor-poet-gambler might harbour. My method for living was to take what I did not have and imagine what I would do with it if I had twice that much.

I still wanted to be A Writer; I was publishing, but I was going nowhere, and my *Vampyre* still seemed to most people a fugitive piece of Byron's which I had somehow purloined and was trying to exploit. It was almost too late to retrieve it and call it my own; even with my own name upon it, it still seemed his, who hardly needed it. Worse, however, was the doggerel he had penned in response to a request from Murray, asking him to create some cheerful way of declining my play. Murray was no friend of mine; his remark on reading my diary having been, "You did go with Lord Byron, did you not? I do not find him here." Everyone else had been taking exhaustive notes, for later profit, whereas I had been self-engrossed, thinking that what they wanted was Lord Byron's influence on a young man travelling with him. The doggerel ran thus:

> Dear Doctor, —I have read your play,
> Which is a good one in its way,
> Purges the eyes, and moves the bowels,
> And drenches handkerchiefs like towels. . . .
> But—and I grieve to speak it—plays
> Are drugs—mere drugs, Sir, nowadays. . . .
> There's Byron too, who once did better. . . .
> So altered since last year his pen is,
> I think he's lost his wits at Venice,
> Or drained his grains away as stallion
> To some dark-eyed and warm Italian. . . .

The hit about moving the bowels was clearly aimed at my services to the Guilford family, and I took it amiss; besides, this ostensible letter of rejection was about Byron himself, not about me. When I saw such things, or once again sat in my sparely furnished surgery waiting for patients to fall out of the sky (one only, a child knocked down by a bolting horse—arm fractured), I began to feel hemmed in. Or, rather, to have the hemmed-in feeling that comes from having too much space about you, *incontinent* space, with nothing in it having any reference to you. I felt forgotten or, even if remembered, unprized: done-for, with all my lifetime's potential unused within me. I had no niche in the vast untidy operation called life, and shifting my practice to Norwich, a more amenable town I would have thought, had had no visible effect on my finances. I would return to London to gamble, which is to say that, when I had nothing left, I returned to London to game with it, and ended up throwing myself on my father's charity. I soon became almost a caricature, a doctor living in the country in order to write poesy, escorting his lady-love to tea here and there. Was I besieged with admirers, wishing me to sign their autograph albums as if I were

Byron himself? Not a bit of it. I went without food to keep myself
in opium, and, because I ate so little, I needed the opium more and
more.

Norwich was not without the bigotry of small towns, but the
circles I moved in were Catholic. I had hoped that certain old
families of distinction would bring their ailments to me, but instead
they invited me to their aliments, as it were, especially Dr. Rigby
and Sir George and Lady Jerningham, at whose seat, Cossey, one
dark night in September, clumsy I had perhaps the worst accident of
all. Returning to my lodgings from dinner at Cossey, I drove my
gig into a tree not far from the Hall, almost at the entrance, and
broke my leg. Insensible, I was carried into the Hall, where Dr.
Rigby and another physician tended me *(I making business for
them)*. I seemed lifeless at the time, they said, and I had left my hosts
only five minutes earlier. In the event, I remained there for several
weeks, thriving in that greenhouse of hospitality and affection, and
falling in love with ———, to no purpose; it was one thing to have
one's tenderest emotions heeded and perhaps treasured, quite another
to have them reciprocated. The sonnet my father wrote in the Hall
album, in Italian, and the two that I wrote in English, evinced our
gratitude, but not the drama of the heart that unfolded there. Why, I
wondered, do we survive only to know a fate worse than death?
Several times my hand crept towards my medicine chest and then
drew back, impelled by strictures of my own in *Oneirodynia* that it is
not allowable to take into our own hands our own dismissal.

My exotic days were over and done with. The tide had gone
out, as had the light of life, and all I had from Claire was a short
letter thanking me for taking care of Allegra's indigestion. "We are
eight: the Shelleys with William, now two, and Clara, who is five
months; the Swiss nurse, Elise, of course; and Milly, a girl from
Marlow, in addition to yours devotedly and Allegra, just over a year
old." As if I did not know who and how old. My head was better,
but in no condition to assimilate their already being away in the

Alpine spring— "sky of profound, Persian azure and soft lover's winds," as she said, to torture me a little more. Now I would know, rather like Byron with his damned Augusta, what it was like to live with ghosts, even though, again like him, I might be in love with ———— or with ————, marooned in Norwich as they had been marooned in Bath and Marlow, helplessly breeding and craving to be gone. We were not a group destined to be happy or, for long, free of the reaper's clutch. The furies had seen us at our nonsensical cavorting and had been mocked; now they were paying us back, one after another, and it were simplest, I thought, to let them have their way. Claire would send Allegra to live with Byron, relinquishing all claim on her and him, and never more to see her child's eyes turn violet as sleep lulled them. Little Clara, the Shelleys' latest joy, would survive only a few months more, and then the curse would engulf her too.

Lord B. had seen me, of course, in the very act of sniffing poison, pondering its uses, and had emboldened me to hold back. He had even once found me in the very throes of *felo de se,* at Diodati, when, for once, he was very tender. All I could think of him now, though, was that someone as regularly inured as he was bound to miss the irony in a man's hitting a tree on the way home from a sumptuous dinner, snapping a leg and severely banging his head, only to fall in love with the hosts' daughter during his enforced stay there while convalescing. Experience with Italian sluts and Harrow bum-boys did not attune him to the finer discernments. In the same predicament he would have assaulted the lady like a chambermaid and mocked the good Jerninghams. Had he never been thrown from his gig, or gondola, on a dark night? I could only hope for some mishap when he was in Venice whoremastering and carousing, making fun of those no longer present. All he had ever had to do was heed me, and he would have had my utmost devotion for ever. It was not I, I had mused while recovering and fuming, who needed lessons in morality; it was he, who upon hearing that Claire's child was a girl, had vowed that he would have to be the one to deflower her when the time came, if come it had not already. *Droit de seigneur* required no less.

As I had indicated in an asterisked note to my so-called "accident" sonnet, I had been particularly happy before it happened, but I thought I would never be happy again. My prose was better than my poetry; that was easy to see; but was my doctoring, virtually uncalled-for, better than my prose? I had earned from medicine, since returning from Italy, enough to keep a rabbit in lettuce for a year and was fast becoming a wraith. Back to London I went, convinced that, where there was no healing and no sickness, there might be a need for justice, since there could not possibly be any crime. Ironic. I took to studies of the law, a lost soul in Lincoln's Inn, as unlikely to argue a case as to saw off a limb (except the one I had been sitting on for years). My hands began to shake, my brain failed to retain the dry formulas I was supposed to cram it with (I had used up my talent for study at Edinburgh, doing so well there I no longer had any bearing on success). What next, Polidori? The clergy? Become a sailor? A translator, like my father? Or a leech like Hobhouse?

I realized that the only direction open to me was inwards, failing a rescue by royal commission; Polidori would make a profession of having none. It was almost as if I had been called upon to demonstrate something that can happen only to a person of twenty, and that was long over. Before it there had been a modicum; after it there would be nothing. As by some giant eagle, I had been wafted to the heights of Helicon or Parnassus, living there on nectar and ambrosia, having what we used to call the time of my life, and then down, tumbling awry to the level of *The Morning Chronicle,* in due time to be known as "A person whose name finds mention": no more than that. My dog was lost, a victim of the Alps; no longer would he fetch my cricket ball with that winning mixture of caution and zeal I had loved him for. No more Ambulance; no more dogs. Now I knew what it must have been like to live in the vicinity of Waterloo, which I had seen, when the battle was at its height. Torn out of routine into a whirligig of horror, I reminded myself that I had been torn out of another routine and transported to Europe on the magic carpet of Lord Byron. I did not mind being uprooted, oh, no; I minded being left for dead. Again and again, as I brooded on recent events, my mind deliciously clouded by a dozen grains (and by the legacy of that severe bump on the cranium when I had my accident), I began to see myself acting out a part, an heir of Flicflac, in some trivial play, always the same, always to no applause, always in the wrong place onstage, always muddling my lines and therefore reduced to mere dumb-show by those who cared. I was their jackanapes, their joker, their fool, their clown, their butt. If only I had been a vampyre, a Ruthven, but I was not; I was Polly, former travelling physician to one of the greatest personalities of our time, but also to the Guilford family of the fat bride and the travelling tripes, whose fifth earl L.B. had adjudged the most illustrious humbug of his age. I would always be quoting Lord B., I could see that, or answering trivial questions about his way of brushing his hair, eating his vegetables, wiping his rear. I would get the clap but never the pox, never like him wake up famous after publishing *Childe Harold's Pilgrimage,* never be able to sit in a deep chair and count up the laurel wreaths:

> *Childe:* eleven editions by 1819
> *The Giaour:* twelve editions in 18 months
> *The Bride of Abydos:* 6,000 copies the first month
> *The Corsair:* 10,000 copies on publication day; 25,000 in the
> first month.

Where were *his* readers when *my* books came out? How should such a notorious and sellable person need my poor, brief *Vampyre* on top of all the rest? This was the turd of God I was forced to eat, day after day, supposed to relish it like a toffee-apple, even while trying not to forget my medical lore, not trouble my father, become a barrister—all that.

I had as soon turn my face towards the wall and never rise again, longing never to have to think of Claire's face or of all the journeys by horse and car to Bath and Marlow, knowing all the time that I was again on sufferance, *de trop*, in yet another act of the same play with the same cast. How could people be polite, nay, affectionate, to one's face, yet utterly oblivious within seconds? I had learned nothing from Lord B., that great numb-er of the human heart, that pawnbroker of honest affection. My only crime had been that I kept on hoping, not even to pass muster but just to be dealt with honourably—the young with the young. I was not dealing with bloodthirsty old men, or with the twisted minds of murderers, but with those whose love was pox, whose pox was in the mind as well as the loins. I heard my own mind uncontainedly screaming at no longer being of them, even though I lacked not for fair amicality, goodwill, and tolerant affection. What I wanted was what, without quite realizing it, I had already had, twice, like a beggar picked up by angels and taught to fly the empyrean. The only thing for it was to push myself to the sticking-place and live on, doing what I could, no longer crying out for the impossible, the lost, the dead; but it made a mechanical man of me, a formula-spouting waxwork, a former mystic who, having had celestial vision, tried ever after to express its value in terms of wagers, coins, loans, debts, and IOUs. I had been sentenced to become prosaic: gondoliers and cabriolets, villas and lakes, were no longer for me, nor Alps nor nights at the opera, soirées in Geneva and romantic meetings in august piazzas. I, who could have remedied Allegra's perpetual cold hands, cold feet, red as blood in any weather, had been sent packing, or even left for dead, Lord B. having written to Murray in mid-November, ridiculing me and my misadventure, my extended stay at Norwich, my attempts to launch my career as a physician there. *I am as sorry,* he wrote, *to hear of Dr. Polidori's accident as one can be for a person for whom one has a dislike, and something of contempt.* You should pause there to savor that double blackguardry of the soul, so characteristic of him at his most diabolical. *When he gets well,* the letter went on,

*tell me, and how he gets on in the sick line. Poor fellow! how came he to
fix there?*

> *I fear the Doctor's skill at Norwich*
> *Will hardly salt the Doctor's porridge.*

Five minutes alone with him, my scalpel in hand, and I would
have made a Jew of him, and then a blind man to lead the blind, a
headless aristocratic whore to lead the masses on Bastille Day. Oh,
for a guillotine with which to have shaved him while impaling him
from beneath on a hot stake carved from his withered leg!

Lord B. had discovered dislike and contempt, and Polly had
discovered hate and its dentate privileges. If he and I were ever to
meet again—*no*. If, instead of becoming a pettifogger in London,
meaning a legal practitioner of inferior status, I had gone off to Italy
to lay hands on him—*no*. All I had to do was *kill Augusta*, leaving
Lady Byron to her fate. The key to it all was the mad lord's half-
sister; and, afterwards, either escape or surrender, it mattered not, so
long as the demon took my javelin right where it would hurt him
most. He had called Claire to him, and she had gone; he might have
left well alone. *No*, it had all been Claire's idea; he was not to blame;
but for the jibes in that letter, echoed to me by Peacock, mainly out
of spite, there would be blood to pay.

How to plan it then?

Footpads would be best: parts of her remains sent to him to
play with in his menagerie, along with monkey and crow, would
achieve the best, most penetrating effect, akin to that brought about
by a whole forest of withered trees in the high Alps.

Fate was winnowing the rest of the tribe, so someone would
have to see to the winnowing of him, before it were too late. In his
surprised hands, her naked dried-up heart, rich with an aroma of the
byre, would sit neatly in her emptied head. All very well, but for
hatred and murder you still have to have vigor of heart, and I had
none, limp and sapped.

Would it always be true of human affairs that Claire-hungry

Polidori, smitten with a certain Elizabeth and forever calling at the house in Magdalen Street, Norwich, should go as unrequited as the Harriet (Martineau) who drew my profile on the backs of letters and listened Desdemona-like to my hastily made-up stories? Already Harriet had lost her sense of taste and smell and was going deaf; it was hard to tell the difference between pity and love, and I wondered if my Elizabeth did not feel a certain politic pity for me in her turn, she the adroit goddess knowing that the clumsy, undomestic, literary Harriet was always dreaming about me and living in the romances I spun. I was Harriet's little Byron.

But that had been before I went away with Lord B. Those were my salad days. Even so, on my return, partly unhinged as I was by Byronic snub and London hauteur, I suffered my concussion and, lo and behold, found myself in love with ————. There was Harriet still, as if nothing had happened, deprived of three senses yet beginning already (she said) to pray for my soul, as if she were some Norn appointed to personify for me the brutal bumps of life; she was there to reveal to me what a human being might be reduced to, even as the rest of the world went about its infatuations with the Elizabeths, the ————s, the Byrons. I did not have to be with her to feel I lived in some kind of farcical dumb-show there was no escaping. I could never have what I wanted. I could always have what I wanted never. With Elizabeth, before I really knew what I was up to in affairs of the heart, I felt all the time pumped full of cream and vitriol. With Harriet I would go as hoarse as a raven for shouting. With ————, I would stay coiled up in an agony of the doomed, always treated politely, affectionately, but ever on the level of ideas, never with my mouth against that naked bosom, my pale forehead against her heart spoon, my ruddy cheeks awash with white and tender pulp. As for Albé, well, I would have been closer had I learned from him, as I was no doubt supposed to do in those few crucial months, to see other people as eye baths, receptacles, towels, blotting-paper, chamber pots, jakeses, finger-bowls, thimbles. He used so many in so many different ways, always in the role of one who managed and manoeuvred the raw material of existence, as if it were both his and not his: his toy but not his charge, his mind forever on his poems—his main mind, that is to say. All else he subjugated to them, but those about him did not realize how expendable they were to him, or that their affections came at him only as so many will-o'-the-wisps. Little wrinkles in his nature, that is what we were to him, except that most of us left no trace: only those who left him with a disease made themselves remembered. I felt from the core of him the same indifference I had shown towards Elizabeth's younger sisters when they fawned all over me; the assumption had always been mine, and mine alone, that fate had chosen me to accompany him to Europe to endear myself to him.

That there were limits to the amount of pain a man might endure, I knew: even a man as young as I (but also one wrinkled by the grim suetudes of my growing up). I knew too that I was close to those limits, without being able to touch them and say, This one is barbed, or that one is hot, or another one, the one over here, next to the lips, burns like an acid. Perhaps I needed a Fletcher to see to me, a Maurice to row me, a Rushton to fetch and carry; I was habituated to too many servants to be able to fend for myself with any degree of dignified efficiency. Most of my books had never come back from Italy; or, rather, had never come home from Italy, since I had bought most of them there. I still had my medicine chest, my minor jar of addict leeches, my box of instruments, my collection of organs in their jars, as well as the few books I had brought to the light of day; and my love, ———, to whom I became a devil of a nuisance, until she told me that, if I felt so dismally about the whole matter, I should go back to Italy and seek to serve the man in Rome. Or wherever he was. That I could not bear to do—he would reject me, I knew, having already asked Murray to use his influence to get me a physician's berth in the Admiralty. He wanted to be rid of me, that was clear; I was no longer of use even for the carrying of miniatures from Italy to London.

In his presence—indeed, in spite of it—I had learned some-

thing about my own unseasoned view of love and women, something inherited, perhaps, or schooled into me at home. To me, in my
romantic and no doubt deluded way, a woman (certainly the one
you adored) was like a fold in the land; she had erupted from the
faceless continuum of geology and plants to be the piece of the
universe you worshipped most, and most acutely—only for a brief
time, however, after which she folded back into the contour of
nature. Her flesh was land, her juices were rivers, her hair was a
harvest, her voice was an aviary, her most secret places were awe-
some in their power. You dealt with her as if, even in the most
refined setting, she were the initiating force of Creation: a mystery, a
demiurge, a mare, a herd, a flock, a shoal, onions, treacle, saxifrage,
panthers, and butterflies—a sample of the All, made seizable and
enterable, ripe and unwarlike, and she dealt with you exactly in
response to how you dealt with her. Treated with reverence, she was
a miracle and could perform miracles; treated with hatred, she still
was and could, but much of her was going to waste as well. All you
knew was that your life would not have been bearable had she not
loomed out of the conjoint atomies burgeoning about you. Such had
been my exalted theory; but who at one-and-twenty knew his mind?
    Ironically, how I felt was best expressed not by me, but by his
poem "Darkness," which I had always admired, even in its conception. It began hopelessly enough:

>   I had a dream, which was not all a dream.
>   The bright sun was extinguish'd, and the stars
>   Did wander darkling in the eternal space,
>   Rayless, and pathless, and the icy earth
>   Swung blind and blackening in the moonless air;
>   Morn came and went—and came, and brought no day,
>   And men forgot their passions in the dread
>   Of this their desolation; and all hearts
>   Were chill'd into a selfish prayer for light.

This was the soul-wounding backdrop, but the part that set me
weeping was this:

Even dogs assail'd their masters, all save one,
And he was faithful to a corse, and kept
The birds and beasts and famish'd men at bay,
Till hunger clung them, or the dropping dead
Lured their lank jaws. Himself sought out no food,
But with a piteous and perpetual moan,
And a quick desolate cry, licking the hand
Which answer'd not with a caress—he died.

It upset because it did not rhyme, it did not jingle or rattle, as almost always. I was the dog, not yet dead, and my former master was as good as dead to me. All that remained was to join him, so to speak. Again I saw the stage of that play, with Polidori being the butt, proposing to whores, being much too familiar and brash with women of high station, taking great minds as your equals and playmates, instead of—what? Being sage. Bending the knee. Grovelling. Biting the lip. Being a good boy, so as not to spoil my prospects. I was doomed, I saw, to watch that scene again and again, until each minute variation stood out like a hue in some ever mutable rainbow —what I had once called "the Iris wound/ About the storm's dread boundary"—and I knew what was coming every time, happening in the perpetual present of eternal habit, would it were not so: *Always I walk gently,* with peaceful mien (word I once misspelled as "mein"), to a vast bonfire in the centre of which a Guy Fawkes figure, he of the Gunpowder Plot, seems to be burning merrily, all crackle and exploding smut. Instead of watching from a suitable distance, I cast into the flames armloads of books and papers, toys and clothes, jars of floating meat, jars of leeches, a microscope, a watch and a medal, a dead dog and a walking-stick, a box of scalpels and probes, a bandage-winding machine and a Ramsden generator. None of it burns but remains there, beautifully ordered according to size, reposing like a halo around Guy Fawkes, but at a certain distance above the highest part of the fire. My things are floating above it, not only unscorched but improved, gleaming with unnatural light, more themselves than ever before, tempting me to call them back, to have them circle, swoop, and come back to my hands, as indestructible as light. I say nothing, though; I do nothing. Then I walk into the heart of the fire, my head by Guy Fawkes's feet.

Already I am walking away from the fire, flame streaming from me like guidons, and I walk to my father's house in Great Pulteney Street, Golden Square. *Good evening,* says Charlotte, the servant. *Are you back from Brighton? Yes, I am back from Brighton,* I say. She cannot see the flames but obviously finds me rather strange. I must look singed. It is Monday. I order my dinner with what seems a speech impediment, making Charlotte stare all the harder. I eat it left-handed, as never, but explain that I am not myself. It is Thursday now, and I am going out with John Deagostini to dine; he resides here too with us, so he and I do not have to part when we have finished. *Yes, I am all right,* I tell him whenever he asks. *If dine we must.* He repeats what I have said. *Yes,* I say, *if we must. If I must, at any rate.* Having been thrown out of my gig onto my head, I know that I do not seem quite normal to people, but I go my way, talking in half-sentences, if I have to talk at all, as I do, since he brings up politics and the future of the country. *Oh, you will see much more than I,* I tell him. *I know it.* He stares, thunderstruck, but goes on spooning his Windsor soup, in the end consuming the full meal, whereas I eat little, having no need. I come down for tea but drink only half a cup: no toast, no scones, no cakes. I then occupy myself with some works of Lord Byron until retiring at nine. I ask Charlotte to set a glass of water by my bed (a tumbler), and she does. Please, I tell her, if I am not up by noon, just leave me be; I am not feeling too well. I will try to sleep it off. Safe in my room, I begin to mix the magic potion in half the open cricket ball: one half, the deadly, in a tripod frame, lest it spill; the other, lying empty, near me on the eiderdown. Oil of amber and powdered charcoal give me a dirty, scummy honey of sorts that does not quite dissolve into the brandy, but it does not need to. Opium, my *Doppelgänger,* follows, and *bitters* for the cramps. Then I flavor the whole with garlic, for which you need white arsenic. I have 50 grains. I put in 15, then add the rest. What a mixture is building now, and not a sign of froth. There remains only the Prussian beauty, colour of naught, bouquet of bitter almonds. Then I stop. I have forgotten the incantations. The alchemist has ousted the artist, briefly. Now I do it, keeping a level head, assigning according to temper and temperament, how they dealt with me:

Oil of amber: Mary (for electricity, for hair)
Charcoal: Claire *(her* hair this black)
Bitters: Gaby Saxonnex (a stomachache)
Opium: for me (forsooth a soother, be ye) & Italy
Arsenic: for the clap, from Lord B.
Prussic acid: Switzerland

There is enough here to kill every Austrian born. I stir it gently, aware of some potent volatility rising; stir it with a rod, but a spoon would be homelier, a fork more efficient, a whisk positively divine. It has no bottom, no width; it is nation-wide; a volcano of a drink for them that has the leaning. Now I stir it the other way. In go the leeches. One or two of them should do. They do not put up much of a fight; they must be Austrian leeches, trained by a M. Stendhal. I pluck them out, having tested. Back they go among the others who, after a brief writhe, give up the ghost. Now the volcano is on my hands; I could do my entire self some grievous damage now by sucking my thumb. What else could I add? Fire. That would do it. The prussic would explode, taking my head off, which would be very hard on Charlotte Reed, devoted servant. Now I say the first line of the incantation, memorializing a short life devoted to aping my Maker. (Must above all reunite halves of the ball.)

'Tis to create, and in creating live.

No terrors in that. The first sip could follow. No, wait. Poli in a hurry now. Uttering the line has freed the wild part of me. I say the second, perhaps with a smile that forgives and regrets, or regrets forgiving.

A being more intense that we endow.

I end-stop every line, killing it before my ears. It is all beginning to make sense, sundered as I make it. Now the third, to be said in a tone of almost mystical incredulity, whereas the first I said with —how did I say the first? With juvenile bombast. And the second? With a humble, almost prayerful intonation, Lord. And so to line three to be pronounced thus, as said:

With form our fancy, gaining as we give.

It is not the black mass, it is the insipid mass. The mind has not come to a stop yet. How could it? Would it cower at the sight of the tumbler, a brew dark enough to paint a jakes with? One needs no occasion, simply enough cause. One does it without arranging to please anyone. It comes out of the blue, out of the dark brown, homemade varnish. Easier for a doctor than for anyone else. So to line four, to be uttered with—the same tone as one of the other three? With clerical fervour, yea:

The life we image, even as I do now.

This is what it has been to be shut out, from Ostend to Rome. Verse is logical. I have just proved it. Now is the time, then. Not before I drape him on the table, however, strap him down, and have my assistants brace themselves. The ether flows, turns into the air he breathes. I trepan him easily, removing a rondelle or button of bone for ritual purposes, but the demon has flown out of him, I can tell that. I pass an egg and a black hen over the hole in his skull to cleanse him. He looks like a goblet. According to the clay model of a sheep's liver, which I always consult, he is going to sustain the operation well. Some of his blood goes into a dark green soapstone beaker whereon snakes intertwine. No clysters, no viper flesh (or theriac), but, before proceeding, I insist on Hood's sarsaparilla, ginger brandy, and *fer bravais* (against anaemia), and only then insert my hand into the cavity in his skull and massage the brain, squeezing the blood away from where it is, blotting it with a natural sponge. Now we open up the offending leg, pull the muscles straight, nicking one of them because it is too tight. We are tempted to amputate the foot and install in its place a shining golden orb on which he could glide, but we do not. We blot the blood with pith. I look again. We are not going to need Ambroise Paré's device for raising skull bones depressed by a blow. We have done enough to make him walk well. Does he need the blinding draught of Dr. Polidori? Not if he wakes. Lovely: it is morning, almost noon. I have slept. Have I died already?

If so, it would be none too soon. Without milord, without his friends and hangers-on, without my recently departed Claire, without patients to doctor, without love or hope or literary fame, knowing I will never, like him, wake up famous—in a word, living in absolute unrequitedness, I had as well sink into the ooze in which newts are born. When there is nowhere else to go but down, you leap thither with zest, do you not?

Ah, blackness, to enter which is to complete a vexing puzzle at long last, no longer trapped between the nobles and the newts. To go away for ever is merely the next thing to do, is it not, as in any ritual? *Milord* would not hesitate in such circumstances. He would know how, not give a fig. On then, Polly, do the man's part. After saluting with sword, sheathe it unused, with not a further thought.

What have we here? Breakfast? Only such a repast as would send you skidding aloft to bite the gods. Yet regal in its way: splendid, milord, a little liquid pageant. Consider, even though it will make you cough, our *arsenic* here is really an *orpiment,* meaning a golden pigment, or a *realgar,* meaning powder from a cave or mine; it is a male yellow gold. Surely that would appeal to you. Our blue happens to be the work of a Berlin colour-maker who, pulling a dye from this acid, the *Prussian* one, pulls a rainbow out of hell. And our lovely *amber* is the most mythic, the most spell-binding of all; and perhaps that is why I choose it—the tears of exotic birds, weeping for Polly, or the daughters of the sun also weeping for him. Or is it the solidified urine of a certain lynx species? I know which one Albé will prefer. A sloppy mixture, yes. I did not want it to be all horrors: only two, the rest are to blunt the tooth a bit, make a drink of it, as if I were sitting in the salon of a Genevan brothel. Oh yes, Albé, I saw such places, on my own. Care to sip? No? A jeweller took this ball and halved it with a silver screw. For play or dog, it's one. For friends, having a noggin, it can be two. For Polidori, one half will do. Gurgle-gurgle, then he shall twist it back together, at the speed of the damned while Harriet Martineau goes on praying for his soul, and to hangment with theological decorum. She is going to go on to become a famous, even notorious woman of letters, her burly, rugged face a shrine of well-tempered resignation. Pushed ever further into herself by fate, she prays like someone reaching with her lips for an elusive filmy flower but finds only the husk called Italo-Anglus: the man who was a nightmare to himself.

My duties done, I hold the filled half-ball to my lips, inhaling an aroma that almost sears the moist membranes in my nose. A sheen of molten angels rises from the brim and makes the meniscus vague. I have made a devil of a thing here. Were I an army, a whole army . . . no. It has to be done. Would I mix it and not have the courage to drink it? Or would I have the brains not to do so? I am beyond cavil. A sip should indicate the way things go. Shall it scald or nip? Will the eyes pour? Having swigged the first sip, shall I be able to take the rest or, from contrary coughing, be unable? Then a deep draught would be best, lest commotion in the throat preclude the second. It will have to be quick, then. In and down. Your health, your infernal majesty. Your health, Albé. And this in my parents' house. I will do untold harm to them. Ah, but the good doctor has been off his head since he was thrown on his head into the roadway. They will spare his name. Down, then. Why dally? What is one minute more? An hour? A year? Is there a unit of life not worth having? If you have only five to go, were it not as lucid to throw away all five rather than torment yourself with waiting? I dare not. I must. I shall. With bated breath, then. Breath held. Eyes tight. One last look with open eyes, Poli, before the retching spasm. Coolness of the ball's curve against my lip. It is good to feel *everything*. Up

now. Cant it. Gently. It must not spill. A live coal on my tongue.
Then swallow it. The coal halts. Cautery in throat. Hot blood forming into shapes I have swallowed. No need of a second draught.
What a bolt. A thud. Down the rest. One go. I did. It is a mild
thunder, red-hot. Will there be stages now it is down? I await its
pleasure. Good-bye, all loved ones in the house. I screw the ball
together. Fierce caustic. Oh, for brandy. Ricewater stools. Gas
comes out all over me like veils. I fall. No, I am lying back. I have
befouled everything as if a swamp had plunged from long hiding in
my carcass. Sweat. Vomit. I have no throat. Will it ever be calm
before it ends? My blood will be bright red. Now Charlotte, at ten
to noon, enters to open the shutters and hears me groaning, although
I do not seem to be in any unusual position. Mr. Thomas Copeland,
surgeon from Golden Square, attempts to discharge the contents of
my stomach, without effect. I linger for ten minutes.

Another physician arrives. Three hours later, Polidori's father
reaches London by train, having no inkling of events. An easy-going
and good-natured coroner's jury, keeping the honor of the medical
profession intact, pronounce that he died "by the visitation of God.
A cricket ball lay by him, from his old school."

No one says died "of absence of the beloved," though they
might have done. Lord B., in his superstitious way, has been expecting bad news from some quarter. "I was convinced," he says, "something very unpleasant hung over me last night. So it turns out—
poor Polidori is gone. When he was my physician he was always
talking of prussic acid, oil of amber, blowing into veins, suffocating
by charcoal, and compounding poisons; but for a different purpose
to what the Pontic monarch did, for he has prescribed a dose for
himself that would have killed fifty Mithridates—a dose whose effect, Murray says, was so instantaneous that he went off without a
spasm or a struggle. It seems that disappointment was the cause of
this rash act."

Paul West's many books include the novels *Rat Man of Paris*, *The Very Rich Hours of Count von Stauffenberg*, and *Gala*, as well as his nonfiction books *Words For A Deaf Daughter*, *Out of my Depths*, and *Sheer Fiction*. A Guggenheim Fellow, he has won two Fellowships in Fiction from the National Endowment for the Arts, the Hazlett Award for Excellence in the Arts, the Aga Khan Prize for Fiction, and most recently the Arts and Letters Award from the American Academy and Institute of Arts and Letters. In 1988 he was made a Literary Lion of the New York Public Library.